M000081735

SNOWGLOBE
스노볼

SNOW GLOBE

스노볼

SOYOUNG PARK

Translated by Joungmin Lee Comfort

DELACORTE PRESS

Text copyright © 2020 by Soyoung Park
English translation copyright © 2024 by Joungmin Lee Comfort
Jacket art copyright © 2024 by Sasha Vinogradova

All rights reserved. Published in the United States by Delacorte Press, an imprint of Random House Children's Books, a division of Penguin Random House LLC, New York.

Delacorte Press is a registered trademark and the colophon is a trademark of Penguin Random House LLC.

This book is published with the support of the Literature Translation Institute of Korea (LTI Korea).

Visit us on the Web! GetUnderlined.com

Educators and librarians, for a variety of teaching tools, visit us at RHTeachersLibrarians.com

Library of Congress Cataloging-in-Publication Data is available upon request.
ISBN 978-0-593-48497-5 (hardcover) — ISBN 978-0-593-48498-2 (lib. bdg.) —
ISBN 978-0-593-48499-9 (ebook) — ISBN 978-0-593-80927-3 (int'l. ed.)

The text of this book is set in 11.5 Bembo MT Pro.
Interior design by Michelle Crowe

Printed in the United States of America
10 9 8 7 6 5 4 3 2 1
First Edition

CAST OF CHARACTERS

ACTORS
Jo Miryu

Goh Haeri

Goh Maeryung

Goh Sanghui

Goh Rhim

Goh Shihwang

Goh Wooyo

Kim Jenho

Bae Serin

Hwang Sannah

Jo Yeosu

DIRECTORS
Cha Seol

Cha Guibahng

Cha Hyang

PRODUCERS
Yibonn Media group:

Yi Bonyung

Yi Bonshim

Yi Bonwhe

Part 1
ME

THE AGE OF SNOWGLOBE

In the living room, Grandma is sunk in her chair in front of her favorite TV show, a heavy quilt draped over her lap. I look down at the weather ticker scrolling away along the bottom of the screen.

-50°F

That's a three-degree drop from yesterday. A snow-cloud icon trails the temperature, suggesting flurries throughout the day, and Grandma pushes herself out of the chair, shuffling to the electric space heater with the kettle in hand. My brother, Ongi, appears in the living room, wearing his standard morning look: a toothbrush in his mouth and a scowl on his face.

"I wish I were still in school!" he whines, because schools close in temperatures below -50°F.

"Just brush your teeth, please," I respond flatly, which comes out garbled as I'm still brushing mine, and turn back to the TV. As usual, Grandma has it on Channel 60, the station that airs *Goh Around* round the clock.

"No! Hear me out," Ongi persists, stepping in front of me

and ratcheting up the grievance in his voice. "I was sixteen ten months ago when I was in school. I'm still sixteen today, but just because I graduated, I'm now expected to endure this brutal temperature?"

His face is blocking my view of the TV. What does he want me to do about the weather? "Stop spraying toothpaste all over the floor, would you?" I snap, suddenly irritated.

Ongi is my twin brother born exactly ten minutes before me. He likes to pretend to be older and wiser, which is no end of laughable. He should know well by now that I only came second to make sure he got out safely—kind of like a captain being the last one off the ship. I've been taking care of him since we shared a womb.

Grandma, back in her sagging chair, swivels her head in our direction. "Ongi, my sweet," she calls. "Don't act like a baby in front of your girlfriend."

Ongi's eyes bug out, and he races to the kitchen sink, where he spits out the mouthful of foaming toothpaste with extra force.

"Grandma!" he cries. "Jeon Chobahm is *not* my girlfriend!"

Grandma has dementia, and she's been confusing me with my brother's nonexistent girlfriend for some time now.

I leave Ongi to stew and head back into the bathroom, where I turn on the wall-mounted faucet and fill the tin basin under it. When I scoop up the frigid water and rinse my mouth, the cold sends a shocking jolt through my teeth down to my jawbone, which immediately begins to ache. My hair is next. I'm staring into the basin, steeling myself against the brain-chilling assault to come, when Grandma appears at the door with the kettle in her hand, a plume of steam escaping its spout.

"Watch out, dear," she says, and stoops to carefully tip the kettle over the basin. "I made this hot water for Ongi, but he wants you to have it instead."

I watch as she sticks her hand in the basin and swishes the water around to even out the temperature. Over the rising steam, her face is aglow with pride and joy that her grandson grew up to be such a considerate young person—a true gentleman who knows how to care for his girlfriend. Meanwhile, said young man is washing his hair at the kitchen sink, howling as he dips his head under the frigid stream. I can't help but laugh at his antics as Grandma shuffles back toward the door with the empty kettle.

"Thank you, Grandma," I say.

She stops in her tracks. Turning around slowly, she searches my face for a long moment with her watery eyes.

"You sound just like my granddaughter," she says in a voice full of longing. Then she turns back around and heads out the door for her worn chair.

In the mudroom, Ongi and I struggle to pull on our heavy snow boots. It's made all the more difficult by the layers of insulated clothes—tops, pants, and tights—we have on under our thick snow bibs. Next come out parkas, expedition-weight mittens, and ski masks. Then, finally, the hoods go up, and we're ready.

"We're off, Granny! See you later!" Ongi calls toward the living room in his usual upbeat tone.

But as he turns the doorknob, Grandma's urgent voice stops us short.

"Wait! My goodness, Ongi! Chobahm is on TV!" she cries.

Ongi and I exchange a look as she coos at the TV. "Aww . . . Chobahm! My sweet baby girl."

I don't have to look to know that it's Goh Haeri on the screen. Ongi refuses to acknowledge it, but the beloved actress and I look very much alike. We even share the same birthday, and for what it's worth, it so happens that we're both lefties. But no one, except for Grandma, would ever mistake me for her, what with my rough cheeks perpetually inflamed from daily exposure to bone-dry, subzero air, and my coarse hair cropped short for quick washing in frigid water. In contrast, Haeri's porcelain skin, rosy cheeks, and trademark long, shiny hair radiate her Snowglobe pedigree.

About Snowglobe. With the world now at an average annual temperature of -50°F, Snowglobe is the only place with a temperate climate—the only location with warmth and color—in the whole world. It's a special settlement that was built atop a geothermal vent and is enclosed in a gigantic weatherproof glass dome. But not just anyone can live there. Its lucky residents are actors, whose unscripted lives are recorded in real time and edited into shows, which are then broadcast to the open world for entertainment. Goh Haeri isn't just an actress, she's a megastar, and she's just been named the new weathercaster—one of the most coveted jobs in Snowglobe. She'll set the record as the youngest weathercaster in the history of the settlement.

I turn a flat gaze to the TV screen. Dressed in a stylish suit, Haeri looks like she was born to fill the position.

"Hi, it's Goh Haeri," she greets the viewers in a buoyant tone. "I'm so excited and honored to be serving our community as the new weathercaster. Make sure to tune in to *News at Nine* on New Year's Day!"

She treats us to her perfect smile, and then the camera cuts away.

I wonder, not for the first time, if I'll ever be able to meet her in real life. If my hair grew in proportion to my desire for a life in Snowglobe, I could shave my head bare every night and I'd wake up the next day with it sweeping the floor. Sometimes I wonder if my intense longing for the place might be responsible for Grandma confusing me with Haeri—as though she can see my soul yearning to flee this godforsaken icebox in favor of Haeri's life in Snowglobe.

Ongi turns back to the door, clucking his tongue in distaste.

"What?" I hiss, glowering back at him.

"If only you hadn't talked so much nonsense about how you might be Goh Haeri's lost twin and—"

"Stop." I cut him off with a cuff to the ribs. I can feel the color rising to my face at the memory. "Unless you want to dig your way out of a snowbank!"

But he's wearing too many layers to be warned off, and he boldly resumes running his mouth. I shove him and he shoves me back, and then we're snatching at each other and ducking and banging into walls—until we finally end up laughing too hard to keep fighting and we pull ourselves together, then open the door and step outside.

Fifty degrees below zero. The frozen world welcomes us by snatching the breath from our lungs. My nose instantly freezes and stings, and within a few blinks, ice crystals form on my eyelashes and cloud my view.

"It's so damn cold," Ongi says with a full-body shudder.

From age six, my twin brother and I accompanied each other to school every day for ten years. Since graduation in February, though, our daily commute has been to the power plant.

I look up at the marbled sky, its gunmetal gray promising a second squall in three days. In the bleak world below, squat log cabins dot the white expanses between tall pines, their branches heavy with snow.

Ongi and I start for the bus stop. Our commute to the power plant could be made on foot, but with a brooding sky like this, the bus is safer. We trudge through the knee-deep snow, and before long, my breath turns my ski mask into an icy mess over my mouth and nose—though better the mask than my face. A few feet ahead, Ongi pauses under a tree and waits for me to catch up. *He can be so sweet,* I think. But no sooner do I arrive than he jumps up to a branch to send an avalanche of snow down on my head and shoulders, laughing hysterically.

Seething, I scoop up a handful of snow and pack it into a tight ball. He bolts, shouting, "Race you to the bus stop!"

"Wait!" I shout, already on the move. "Jeon Ongi, you cheater!"

Snow grabs at our boots with each sinking step, rendering our best effort at a dash into more of a lurching shuffle.

"Loser does laundry for a month!" Ongi yells.

"Oh . . . You're so done, Jeon Ongi!"

I struggle through the clinging trap of snow with everything I have. And when we dive for the bus stop, it's my hand that touches its bent pole first.

"Ha! Who's laughing now—" I say victoriously, gasping for breath. Sure, I won by a hair, but a win is a win. I'm bent over with my hands on my knees, catching my breath, when Ongi snatches my arm and jerks me behind him.

Annoyed, I straighten to see him narrowing a hard gaze at a figure ahead. *Just another commuter waiting for the bus, so what about it?* is my first thought, but then the person turns in our direction, and when she acknowledges us with an awkward dip of her head, neither Ongi nor I return it.

The woman is Jo Miryu, a former Snowglobe star. Discovered at nineteen, she lived in the settlement for seven years, starring in a hit noir series. She returned home a few years ago when the network abruptly canceled the series, and yet, at twenty-nine years old, she still has the face of a wood sprite and a frame that is five foot seven inches of pure grace. Her youthful innocence makes it all the more difficult to believe that the success of her series was due to the multiple homicides she committed throughout its run. By the time it was canceled, she had brutally murdered nine men, and her director had snatched the National Medal of Arts for outstanding directorial achievement. Like millions of her fans, I can recite a long list of other trivia about the starlet. I even know her blood type, which is A.

When Miryu returned home, however, she was shunned for the brutality she had dealt in Snowglobe. Even her own family fled to another town upon news of her homecoming, unable to swallow the idea of welcoming a killer into their midst. Ongi and I were thirteen back then. I remember the whole town twitching with hysteria. Kids were being warned against her—we weren't to speak to, or even make eye contact with, the woman if we happened upon her on the street.

I don't know what it says about me, but I've always been more intrigued by her than terrified. There's so much I'd like to ask her about Snowglobe. Ongi, who knows me like no other, digs his heels into the snow and shoots me a warning glance: *Don't even think about it.*

Suddenly, the roar of gears rips through the air, and the dark green, rusted-out double-decker pulls to a stop. Buses—being the only means of transportation in our town—regularly pack in about a hundred commuters during rush hour. The door hisses open and the line begins to move, only to stop.

"Get off my bus!" Mr. Jaeri, the bus driver, erupts in an angry shout, and I look up to see that a few feet ahead, Miryu has just mounted the steps.

"Please . . . I just need to go to the post office," she pleads in a small voice, but Mr. Jaeri throws out his arm and blocks her.

"I said, Get. Off. Now," he rumbles.

All essential businesses and services—the post office, grocery stores, laundromats, clinics, and so on—are located inside the power plant. It's convenient for most of us who already work at the plant, but not for an outcast like Miryu. They are left to sustain themselves with whatever game they can snare or fish they can catch in the wild and only go to the plant when they have no other choice.

"Please." Miryu tries again. "My ankle's hurt, I can barely walk. Can I please get a ride, just this once?"

Mr. Jaeri barks out a laugh.

"Oh, poor little cupcake," he says in a mocking tone, then in a booming voice yells out, "No!"

"Why do you even engage with her?" someone shouts from inside the bus. "Let the others in, and let's go already!"

A handful of children join in, "Yes, Mr. Jaeri, let's go! Or we're all going to be late for school!"

Miryu drops her gaze and, without another word, turns around and steps off the bus. People shuffle forward and we move ahead. I'm about to climb aboard behind Ongi when I hear a small "Excuse me."

I turn to see Miryu staring at me pleadingly.

"Yes?" I manage to get out.

"Can you please stop by the post office and see if there's any mail for me?" she asks, then adds apologetically, "The name is Jo Miryu."

It takes me a moment, but I find myself nodding in agreement, too stunned to speak.

"Thank you. Thank you so much," she says, her features softening with relief. "Can I meet you back here at the end of your day, then?"

I murmur a *yes* just as the line surges forward and pushes me up into the bus. Then the door is hissing shut, and Ongi shouts through the closing gap, "Don't you wait for her!" He turns to me and in an angry whisper says, "Are you nuts? Don't you know what she could do to you? Don't you know what she's capable of?"

I shrug, avoiding his gaze. He's still furious when I murmur to no one in particular, "Sure, she killed nine men. But *I'm* not a man."

"What?" Ongi breathes, staring at me with exasperation.

Meanwhile, Mr. Jaeri shifts into gear and pulls away, chewing tensely on his bottom lip. He's likely cursing his luck this morning. How could he not be worried about upsetting Miryu?

THE GREAT UNWASHED

"Hi, sweeties!" Mom calls, waving at us from a corner of the power plant's central hall, where she's chatting with some friends.

The sight of her makes me feel lighter. We don't get to see a lot of each other—there are a total of four shifts at the plant, assigned by lottery, and as a first-shift worker, she's here from six a.m. to four p.m. every day.

I wave back and make a beeline for the stack of free *TV Guides* on the nearby newsstand. *TV Guide* is a weekly magazine that provides the upcoming program schedules for the hundreds of Snowglobe channels available for viewing every day, and thus is essential for daily life. Honestly, depending on the week, the slim volume can be even more entertaining than the shows themselves. Reading about which new programs are about to premiere and which series are ending is always captivating, regardless of whether or not I tune in to them.

"Yes!" I exclaim under my breath as my eyes alight upon this week's special feature—an interview with Cha Seol, director of *Goh Around,* also known as the person I admire the most in the entire universe. I thumb the corner of the magazine, weighing my options. It's tempting to just devour the whole article right now, but another part of me wants to wait and savor the pages in the comfort of my room at the end of a hard day's work. I tuck the magazine away in my parka's internal chest pocket, choosing the latter. A few moments later, though, I find myself reaching for it again.

"I'll just check out the Tips," I say to myself, taking out the guide. The Tips section, with its weekly career advice for aspiring actors and directors, is my favorite section of the magazine.

"Hey, Jeon Chobahm, are you even listening to me?" Ongi's voice interrupts my focus, instantly annoying me. I lift my eyes to his scowling face. "I said, don't you ever speak to that woman again, do you understand?" he says, reaching toward the stack of *TV Guides* for his own copy. As much as I want to throw a retort back at him, it isn't worth it to make a bigger deal of the incident, so I just brush him off.

"God, you need to relax, Jeon Ongi," I say, looking back to the Tips.

A minute later, I'm pulled away again by the plant supervisor's shout. "Hey, Jeon Ongi, you lazy lump!"

The man is standing by the loading dock across the hall, looking constipated, as usual. "What are you doing?" he yells more loudly. "Get over here and start unloading!"

Ongi takes off like a rocket. "On my way, sir!" he shouts in reply.

The two of them go through this routine daily. I'm

snickering when someone slaps me on the back, chirping, "Jeon Cho!"

I turn to see my friend Jaeyun flashing her toothy smile at me.

"Jaeyun! You're back!" I cry, delighted. "How was your tour?"

"Good! I made it back in one piece," she says, then continues wearily, "The storm raged for three days straight."

Jaeyun is a train engineer on the Ja-line, one of the fourteen railways that comprise the freight network that extends, like arteries from a heart, from Snowglobe to the outer settlements. It's via the railway that food and other essential supplies are distributed throughout the open world, as well as occasional nonessential items mail-ordered by those able to pay a stiff premium. Deliveries are dropped off at the power plant of each settlement along the routes. From the Gah-line to the Ha-line, train engineers are selected from towns situated at the line's terminus—settlements on the fringes of civilization, like my hometown settlement. Jaeyun, who is only a few years older than me, has held the position for six years now.

"Did you know that the TV in the engineer's cab turns off in bad weather?" she says, rolling her eyes. "So here I am, staring at nothing but the infinite tracks ahead, all alone in my cab without anything to distract myself with. The wind is screaming. Snow's blowing everywhere. And as if that's not enough, thunder is sounding right above my head. The next thing I know, I'm on my knees, praying for the first time in my life."

She pauses to shudder for emphasis, but I know her

dramatics are mostly for my entertainment. In truth, she's one of the bravest people I know. She wouldn't be doing what she does, otherwise. But I play along.

"Oh, man. You have to tell Ongi about it when you see him," I say. "The wimp thinks he wants to be a train engineer."

In fact, the only reason Ongi is volunteering as a warehouse hand is to keep a close eye on all things rail-related. With Jo Woong, the other engineer of the Ja-line, nearing retirement, the supervisor is said to be scouting about for his replacement.

"Ongi?" Jaeyun says, surprised. "I thought he wanted to stay close to home."

I give her a blank look. If he does, it's news to me. When I'm silent, she continues, "Considering your grandmother's health? Who'd take care of her when you go off to film school, if Ongi has to spend half a year away from home on a train? He should stick around, for her sake."

Oh, film school . . . I shrink into myself, the stock line in the stock rejection letter I received a week ago all too fresh: *While your skill set and potential are impressive, we regret to inform you that we are not offering you admission . . .*

Snowglobe's Film Academy is the most prestigious educational institution in the world, producing top-ranking directors year after year. The rejection letter is the second of its kind I've received, the same as the one I got last year.

I squirm on my feet as Jaeyun, clueless, flips through *TV Guide* and finds this week's special feature. The boxed copy containing Director Cha's quick bio, which I already know by heart, jumps out at me. She was one of those brilliant people who was accepted into the academy on her first try, and graduated with the highest distinction to boot.

"You're not going to treat me like a stranger when you become this famous, are you?" Jaeyun teases, jabbing me lightly with her elbow.

Fighting back the shame rising up inside me, I deadpan, "Of course I am. What do you think?" and the two of us burst into laughter.

I try to enjoy the moment, pushing the rejection letter from my mind. After all, what matters is that I *will* create the most amazing show of all time, the kind no director has ever produced before. As long as I know that, I can't beat myself up over the *when* of it. What's a few years' delay in the great scheme of things? Nothing. At least, that's what I have to tell myself. Because if I stop believing in my future, I'm afraid I won't be able to endure the punishing monotony and hopelessness of my so-called life. Not for another minute.

"Second shift! Get moving!" the supervisor shouts, and the two hundred or so workers scattered around the hall begin shuffling toward the gigantic motor in the center.

"Come on!" he urges. "Hustle!" He starts his obnoxious marching clap, the rhythm of which we follow to position ourselves at the workstations: human-sized hamster wheels connected to the central motor. Those of us with odd ID numbers begin the shift by walking inside the wheels, while those with even ID numbers begin the shift sitting just outside the wheels, working the hand cranks attached to the wheels' stub axles. As the wheels turn, their kinetic energy is harnessed through a mechanical amplifier coupled to an electromagnetic energy harvester, whose output subsequently turns the central motor to generate electricity. Simply put, power production depends entirely on human physical labor, without which our world would screech to a halt. There wouldn't be freight trains or commuter buses, not to mention electric kettles that can heat up ice-cold water in minutes for a hot cup of cocoa. Forget hot cocoa. The stench of all the sweaty, unbathed laborers alone would pose a serious public health hazard.

I start my shift inside the wheel, doing a kind of speed walk to sustain the minimum speed of four miles per hour required to power the wheel's built-in TV screen. My need for entertainment aside, a sleeping screen is sure to draw the supervisor to my wheel like a paper clip to a magnet, and then I'd have to suffer his insults up close.

—*Where's your sense of community?*

—*If you're not willing to contribute to society, why don't you just walk out there and freeze to death?*

. . . and so on and so forth.

I put on the headphones corded to the TV and click the remote to Channel 60—*Goh Around*. It's my go-to choice for when I want to turn my mind off. Having seen all the available episodes aside from a few, I can let my attention drift in and out and still keep up with the show's general narrative.

"Those who work at a pace of exactly four miles per hour"—the supervisor's voice pierces through my head-phones, jarring me—"are the type of losers with no ambition, no drive, and no future prospects. The dregs of society."

Turning my head, I'm jolted to see him right next to my wheel, a megaphone raised to his mouth.

"How can one be so content with doing the bare minimum? Would it kill you to be of use to society?" he thunders. Leaning sideways against the handlebar, he stares at me with open contempt.

Would it kill him to be just a little bit less obnoxious? I think. Suddenly, Miryu's face rises before my eyes. I wonder if the supervisor would have the guts to talk to her this way. Fat chance. Trying to ignore his glare, I replay the exchange with Miryu this morning in my head. Whose mail is she waiting for? Her estranged family's? Or something from the ex still alive in Snowglobe?

"Turn up the heat, all of you!" barks the supervisor, finally pivoting on his heels and marching away from me. "At this rate, we won't even be able to pay for the streaming service!"

A collective groan goes up at that particular threat. Still, it delivers the desired effect. Everyone picks up the pace, moving a bit more vigorously.

Most of the electricity produced by laborers like us in the open world is sent to Snowglobe, where it powers the lives of the actors who dwell within the domed superstructure. In exchange, they share their lives with us in the form of reality shows.

The whir and vibration of the central motor intensify. It isn't long before my sweat-soaked thermals begin clinging to my skin.

"Folks, it was only a couple of generations ago that the pit toilet was the norm." The supervisor's amplified voice descends from the second floor this time. *Here he goes again.* I fasten my eyes back on the TV screen and crank up the head-phones' volume.

Christmas being only two days away, Channel 60 is marathon-showing every Christmas-themed episode of *Goh Around*. Presently, four-year-old Haeri is playing quietly with her doll, a diamond bracelet adorning her tiny wrist. Her mom, sitting by her side and watching her play, wants to know if Haeri likes the bracelet, her Christmas gift. Haeri says nothing. In fact, she doesn't even appear to hear her mother.

I've seen this episode before. At this point in the show, Haeri has been mute since the Halloween party a few months prior, where she had a terror-induced seizure following an encounter with someone dressed as a ghost. Though I know that Haeri regains her speech and her smile by spring, these episodes always break my heart.

The camera zooms in on little Haeri's angelic face.

"The pit toilet was every little kid's nightmare." The supervisor's voice works itself through my headphones once again, overlaying the scene on my TV screen like some sort of absurd voice-over. "And for a good reason! Do you know how many people fell into those pits of waste during their midnight visits?"

Though I'm not especially squeamish, it's disorienting to be so rudely jerked back into the world of the pit toilet while my eyes are resting on Haeri's dreamy life. Without my per-mission, the image of the closed-off pit toilet at our own house flashes through my mind. In the background, the supervisor rambles on. He never stops.

"How would you have liked it if you'd had to peel down

your pants and squat over the steaming pit in fifty below? Would you have frozen your ass off or what?"

Before the advent of the electromagnetic energy-harvesting technology, electricity was an incredibly rare commodity. No access to it meant there was no way to prevent frozen or burst pipes, making indoor plumbing a dream for common people.

"What a time to be alive!" the supervisor intones. Producing an apple from his vest pocket and raising it to his mouth, he adds, "Do you know how lucky we are?" Without waiting for an answer, he crunches into the fruit.

Every day, each worker gets a ration of fresh fruit and vegetables, which are grown in the greenhouse inside the power plant. The cost of maintaining such a greenhouse is deducted from our paychecks, of course. Today's lunch included exactly one-eighth of an apple. But not for the supervisor, apparently.

"Lucky? Ha! He must have gotten all our shares of luck, then. Gobbling up a whole apple just for himself," Mom grumbles inside her wheel, adjacent to mine. Darting a quick glance around us, she leans toward my wheel. "Is what Ongi told me true?" she whispers. "You spoke to that woman?"

She is referring to Miryu, of course. That woman. That monster. That bitch. Just a few of the monikers people have adopted so as to avoid speaking her true, vile name.

"Yup," I say, trying to sound casual. "It was really nothing, though. Mr. Jaeri wouldn't let her on the bus, so she asked me to stop by the post office to see if she has any mail."

Mom gasps, her eyes wide with alarm.

"Sweetie," she exhales. "Do you have any idea how dangerous that woman is?"

She looks ready to lunge for my remote and switch my screen to *The Killer Next Door* as proof. At home, the show is banned for its scandalous, violent content, which my mother has deemed inappropriate for developing minds. She doesn't know that Ongi and I already binged the entire series—seasons one through seven—in secret, over ninth-grade winter break while she was at work and Grandma was napping.

"I know, Mom," I assure her, thinking back to the emotionless look on Miryu's face in one episode, when she'd leveled her gun at the man she'd fallen head over heels for in spite of herself. How does a person do that? What went through her mind? I know Mom would kill me if she could hear my thoughts right now, but I can't help myself—the questions bubble up on their own.

And it isn't just Miryu I consider. What would I have done, had I been her director? How would I have handled an actor like Miryu? What kind of decisions would I have found myself making—not just as a director, but also as a human being? Would I, too, have continued to work on a show filled with savage acts of betrayal and murder? Say what you will, but the show's ratings record is yet to be broken years after its final episode aired.

The image in my mind switches to one of Miryu's acclaimed directors, Cha Guibahng, receiving his National Medal of Arts for her show. But in the next moment, his solemn face morphs into my own, and suddenly it's me standing before the sea of flashing cameras, the same gold medal glimmering on my chest. My pulse quickens at the vision, and I feel a surge of energy through my legs turning the wheel. Before I know it, I'm running. Sprinting.

One day, I'll break out of this icebox, this tomb of deprivation and bleak uniformity. I'll get to Snowglobe, where I'm certain my story is waiting for me—a story that I, and I alone, can bring to life. Inside my wheel spinning to nowhere, I can already see myself there.

MYSTERIOUS VISITORS

After my shift, I head for the post office, sailing down the long, narrow plaza that connects the central motor hall with the plant's main entrance. Essential businesses line the sides of the plaza, all a drab gray that makes them blur into each other. Even the post office is just another hole in the wall—nothing like the shiny, candy-apple-red buildings in Snowglobe. But what does it matter; we're lucky to *have* a post office. Without it, we'd lose touch with friends and family who aren't nearby, and mail-ordering anything from Snowglobe would just be a dream. High postage rates mean the place is rarely busy, though, and ordering anything from Snowglobe is a rare luxury.

Still, every year, Mom splurges on our birthday cake, which she orders from a special bakery in Snowglobe. The gorgeous cake, made to order by the pâtissier—an actor, of course—travels all the way to our post office by train. Thinking about it makes my heart swell; me and my brother will be lighting candles and hearing our family sing "Happy Birthday" in just a few days.

"Hi, Chobahm!" Suji says from behind the counter, the grin on her face so giddy it makes it seem like she's been waiting for me all day long.

Suji uses a wheelchair because she was born without the use of her legs. Since she can't work the hamster wheels, she fulfills her civic duty at the post office instead.

I return her greeting and begin to say, "Do you have mail for—" I don't even get to utter Miryu's name before Suji thrusts a shiny gold envelope at me across the counter.

"Check out the front," she says, barely able to contain her excitement.

Puzzled, I turn it over and reveal a red wax seal embossed with the most recognizable logo of them all, that of the Yibonn Media Group. The Yibonn Media Group, which everyone calls the Yibonn, owns, controls, and operates the Snowglobe broadcasting system. In turn, the distinguished Yi family descending from the eponymous founder of the company, Yi Bonn, is commonly called the Yibonns, as opposed to the too-ordinary *Yis,* which is a reflection of society's esteem for the family's role in establishing the institutional framework that has sustained the Snowglobe order all these years.

"It's from Yujin!" Suji cries out.

My eyes round with surprise and I tilt the card-sized envelope this way and that under the light, taking in its elegant gold shimmer.

"Don't get choked up yet," Suji says, rolling her wheelchair back a few feet to a small pile on the floor covered in gray cloth. With a magician's flourish, she pulls back the fabric, and my jaw drops.

It's a washtub-sized box *full* of brownies. I've seen brownies countless times on TV, with them being Haeri's favorite treat and all, but never in real life. And these brownies are adorable—decorated with Christmas trees made out of red and green frosting. A pen in one hand, Suji begins checking off the items on the shipment list.

"Ten bottles of orange juice: check. A box of fresh strawberries: check."

My nose begins to burn like it does when tears come. Yujin, my best friend, is the first Snowglobe actor to come from our town since Miryu ten years ago. The thought makes my heart swell all over again, and I'm touched that she found the time to send me a note—and all these amazing gifts—only two months after moving to Snowglobe.

Snowglobe.

"Oh, right," I murmur, suddenly remembering my mission. "Do you have any mail for Jo Miryu?"

Suji lifts her gaze and gives me a quizzical look. When I don't correct myself, she makes a sour face. "Who would send anything to her?"

I shrug. She returns to the shipment list, and I tuck Yujin's card in my chest pocket like the rare treasure that it is.

"Shin Yujin sent you fresh strawberries? A whole box?" Ongi cries in amazement, helping me stow the full sled in the bus's luggage compartment. Suji insisted that I borrow it to haul the bounty home.

I gesture for him to quiet down, conscious of everyone about to board the bus with us, many of whom have never tasted fresh strawberries.

"How many bottles of orange juice, did you say?" Ongi asks, hushing his voice.

"Nine," I mouth, leaving out the fact that I gave a bottle to Suji. Fresh strawberries, orange juice, brownies . . . saliva pools in my mouth at the thought of sharing the treats with Mom and Grandma when we get home.

Approaching our stop, I'm surprised not to see Miryu waiting for me. She seemed so desperate. Overhead, the gloomy sky is closing up for the evening, so Ongi and I don our headlamps.

I feel a pang of disappointment and turn up my headlight, sweeping the area with its beam again.

"Would you please listen to your older brother?" Ongi warns. "You *will* stay far away from that woman. You will!"

He steps into his skis and I grab the sled's pull rope and attach it to his harness. Ongi has volunteered to be the beast of burden in appreciation of his good luck, and being the *big* brother of a sister with connections in Snowglobe.

I carefully scan the area one last time for Miryu, ignoring Ongi's impatient look, and a faint, shadowy form begins to take shape in the murk at the base of a nearby tree. Before I know it, I'm already moving toward it.

"Hey! Where are you going?" Ongi yells. "Come back!"

He rushes after me, but the loaded sled he's tethered to hampers him and I make it to the tree alone. To my amazement, the dark pile reveals itself to be a person crumpled on the ground. My heart slams. I quickly drop to one knee beside the figure and turn them over onto their side, peeling the ski mask down under their chin so I can listen and feel for breath. And that's when my heart slams for the second time. It's Miryu, blood leaching out of her scalp and crusting on her forehead. Fighting down the dread surging inside me, I bring my ear close to her mouth and nose. She's breathing.

"Jeon Chobahm! Step away, right now!" Ongi shouts furiously, wrestling with the rope he's managed to get tangled in.

Turning back to Miryu, I try to rouse her.

"Miss, are you okay? Open your eyes, please!"

No response. I give her shoulder a hard shake. "Miryu! Wake up!"

Her eyelids flutter ever so slightly.

"Please! You can't sleep here!" I shout, and slide my hands under her arms so I can drag her through the snow toward the sled. But the two layers of thick mittens I have on keep slipping and sliding around and I can't keep a grip on her, so I peel them off and hold them in my teeth.

"What the hell are you doing?!" Ongi demands. He's right in my face now, finally having freed himself. But this is no time to argue.

"Unload the sled, please," I tell him, breathing heavily. "Quick. We need to get her to the plant." Without waiting for his response, I continue on toward the main road with Miryu, heart pounding. She's surprisingly heavy. Deadweight. I think I can finally appreciate the full meaning of the word. And thank goodness for the boost of adrenaline coursing through my veins right now.

The plant houses the clinic, but the next outbound shuttle isn't until daybreak, and Miryu needs immediate medical attention.

"We'll have to use the sled to take her there ourselves," I tell Ongi.

"Are you insane?" he erupts, snatching my wrist. "To save a murderer?"

"What other choice do we have? Just leave her to die out here?" I shout back, letting my eyes cut into him. My vehemence seems to throw him off for a moment, but then he strengthens his grip around my wrist.

"Come on. It's nearly sixty below," he says, pleading now. "It's not safe to be outside for more than half an hour!"

He's right. Truth be told, I'm not all that confident that I could make it to the clinic within thirty minutes, not while towing a full-grown woman behind me on a sled. Still, I'll have to try. I'm good on skis.

"That's why *I* am going," I respond, wrenching myself free and snatching the ski poles from his other hand.

Ongi stamps his feet in frustration. "You'll *freeze* to death in the middle of nowhere!"

"If Dad had been a chicken like you, we wouldn't even be here!" I shout back. "Do you know that, Jeon Ongi?"

His face goes blank. That may have been harsh, but I'm too worked up for calm deliberation.

"I'm not going to die today," I tell him. "There's too much I want to do; I won't let it happen. I promise."

He stares at me. Then, squeezing his eyes shut, he pulls the thick wool hat over his face and screams into it for a long breath. After he's done, he empties the sled and helps me load Miryu onto it.

"I'll go home and gear up," he says. "Catch up with you as soon as I can." And then he's off, kicking up snow.

My twin brother is going to save me in case I keel over on the way. I don't argue with him, not that I have the time.

Thirty minutes is all I need. I'll be fine. I pick up the sled's tether, then draw a big breath, plant my poles in the snow, and push off with my left foot. The heavy sled makes it rough going at first; but it isn't long before I get into a steady rhythm.

Whoosh, whoosh—

My skis glide smoothly over the snow as I set off down the road, following in the tracks laid by the shuttle. A thousand thoughts swirl in my mind, but I keep focused on the path ahead. You never know when the odd elk or wild horse might surprise you by jumping into the road.

Every so often, I find myself glancing over my shoulder to look at Miryu on the sled. After all, it's just me and the ruthless killer out here in the dark, and the thought sends a fresh chill down my spine every time it occurs to me. *"Focus, focus . . . ,"* I chant aloud to drive away the creeping unease, fastening my eyes on the path before me.

I'm not sure how long it's been, but the sparsely illuminated road ahead seems to stretch on endlessly. In the beam of my headlamp, trees cast dark shadows on the snowy ground before closing in on me like falling dominoes. Doubt rears up inside me, quickening my breath; and the heavy-duty ski mask I'm wearing doesn't help. I want so badly to yank it off, but doing that in this temperature would be beyond foolish.

Pulling a full sled on skis is vigorous exercise, no doubt, and I'm damp with sweat. Still, my body is losing heat faster than it can generate more. My legs seem to be slowing down, and maybe my mind is, too, when the sky—without preliminary flurries or spitting flakes—decides to unleash a genuine squall. Just my luck. I hunch into the wind.

Stuffing back the feeling of doom rising within me, I replay the story Mom likes to tell us.

It was in the early days of Mr. Jaeri's shuttle-driving career. One morning after a storm, the wheel got away from him and the bus spun across the slick road into a ditch. In his inexperience, Mr. Jaeri kept revving the engine, which only drove the wheels deeper into the glaze of ice hidden under the snow, further canting the bus at an unnerving angle. Needless to say, the bus couldn't simply be picked up and put back on the road by Mr. Jaeri and the unlucky riders. To make matters worse, there was only an hour or so's fuel left to keep the engine alive for heat. After that, the temperature inside the bus would plunge to match the frozen tundra's, turning it into a walk-in freezer. The chance of another motorist coming by and seeing the stranded bus was close to nil, as the only other vehicle in town was a quasi-ambulance used by the plant's physician for house calls.

Thankfully, Dad and his heavily pregnant wife, Mom, were among the passengers on that fateful day. Seeing no other way to save his wife and unborn twins, Dad set off for the plant on skis, a trip that would normally take forty minutes by bus.

It was about two hours later that the stiff, frost-rimed passengers, now huddled together for warmth inside the dead bus, heard the approaching sirens. Minutes later, they were evacuated to the clinic for emergency care. It was there that Mom finally saw Dad again, lying in the ICU, his skin gangrened black and blue from frostbite.

Dad had always dreamed of seeing the ocean, so three days later, she hired the ambulance service—at a dreadful fee—to spread his ashes on the beach. That December, Ongi and I were born. Weighing in at 5.7 and 5.5 pounds, we were pretty robust for preterm twins.

Mom never tells us the story without reminding us that Dad would have done the same thing even if she hadn't been on the bus with him; that he was the kind of person who would spring to action no matter what the odds, rather than sitting back and waiting for fate to claim him.

The storm rages on. I can't feel my feet or hands, or anything else for that matter, but I pull myself along, sustained by the story.

Snow keeps whipping furiously around me in bitter, blinding drafts like a monstrous white presence bent on erasing me. Numb with cold, I can't begin to fathom how many more miles it is to the plant, or if we'll be able to reach it. I glance down, amazed to see my skis still slogging through the snow under me. And it is in this foggy state of mind that I finally see the light of the power plant glowing dreamily in the distance.

I stagger into the clinic. The doctor gasps and her eyes go wide with shock as they sweep over me, then Miryu. A wave of relief, then exhaustion, hits me. While there's nothing I want more than to collapse in a heap, that will have to wait. I scrape up the last of my strength and help the doctor move Miryu onto the examining table.

The doctor swiftly goes to work, removing Miryu's

snow-encrusted outerwear. I try to help with Miryu's thick, fur-lined boots, but my frozen fingers just fumble. In fact, I'm feeling so incredibly drowsy that I might as well be in a waking dream.

"It's worse than I thought." The doctor's voice drifts to me as if from a great distance, distorted.

Glancing over, I see massive bruises on Miryu's shoulder and leg. An animal attack? Unlikely. Miryu is an expert hunter. On the other hand, there's no shortage of people with undying hatred for her. Did they finally go ahead and do what they'd been threatening? That, too, is unlikely, considering how scared people are of Miryu. I can't imagine the average townsperson having the guts to get close enough to inflict this kind of damage.

A grim look on her face, the doctor turns up the heating pad under Miryu. I pull the elk-hide blanket up to her chin. We have to bring her core temperature back to normal.

Later on, swabbing Miryu's bloodied face with antiseptic-soaked cotton balls, the doctor turns her attention to me.

"If you don't mind my asking, Chobahm," she begins, addressing me by my name. Being the only twins in town, Ongi and I have been accorded a level of celebrity since birth. "Why did you decide to help Miryu?"

Did I really just hear her say Miryu's name? I've never heard another adult do that. Registering my shock, she gives me a soft smile. "We'd been pretty close as kids. We even connected a few times in Snowglobe while I was in medical school."

All institutions of higher education, including medical

schools, are in Snowglobe. Therefore, throughout their years of training, medical students are obligated to appear in medical dramas, though not as official actors. In exchange, they receive free tuition. An added benefit of this practice is that viewers at home get to preview their future physicians' and surgeons' professional aptitudes and bedside manner.

But why *did* I help Miryu? I couldn't say. As I bend down to pick up Miryu's clothes, which are strewn on the floor, the doctor resumes, "I had no idea back then that the girl was going around slaughtering people left and right," and there is a tinge of sadness in her voice.

Here it's important to note that actors don't get to watch any shows, not while they actively live and work in Snowglobe. This keeps them away from spoilers that might change their behavior and dampen the viewer's pleasure. For instance, a husband might be actively cuckolded, but lacking access to his own show, he wouldn't find out about it before the rest of the world. Brutal, yes. But such is the nature of entertainment TV.

The doctor suggests I warm up with a cup of tea. I peel off my parka and shuffle to the kitchen on my thawing legs, suddenly famished. The cupboard shelves are disappointing, to say the least, with the cocoa powder container sitting empty by a near-empty container of coffee beans. I'm halfheartedly contemplating the tea options—green and olive leaf—when a sharp cry rips through the silent air. It's Miryu. I race back.

"Shhhh . . . I know, I know," the doctor says softly. "You're doing great. Just a couple more stitches."

I've never been sewn or even poked by a needle, but just imagining the pain makes me wince.

Too expensive for use in minor procedures, pain medications are reserved for those in excruciating pain, such as women in active labor. Major treatments and nonroutine procedures are handled at the real hospital in Snowglobe. In other words, common people have to grit their teeth and bear the pain until their luck turns or death releases them.

"B-black . . . The black . . . ," Miryu mumbles, her eyes darting wildly under her eyelids. Her cracked, cold-bleached lips struggle to issue more sounds. I have to look away to suppress the sympathy rising within me. The woman is shunned by everyone for a good reason. I head back into the kitchen and drop a green tea bag in the mug.

The doctor looks up from Miryu. "You have to take care of that frost damage," she tells me. "Get the salve in the small blue tub and cover your face with it. Then take it home and apply more every hour. We don't want scars on that pretty face. I'll bill Miryu for it."

It is only then that I wonder what my face looks like. I set down my mug to locate the salve.

"And *never* pull another stunt like this," the doctor says. "Have you thought of what losing you would do to your mother?"

What would it do? It would kill her, of course. Mom's only wish is for us to be safe and happy. I can't believe I needed someone else to remind me. *How could I have been so stupid?*

"I'm sorry," I murmur, my voice dwindling in my throat.

In front of the mirror, I'm stunned to see that my cheeks and nose have taken on various shades, textures, and finishes. I dip a finger in the thick salve and carefully spread it on the damaged skin, tensing at the initial sting. But the sting quickly dulls, giving way to a cooling sensation. And that's when the thought of my twin brother hits me with the force of a sledgehammer.

"Ongi!" I cry out.

The doctor pivots from the examining table.

"Ongi still isn't here!" I shriek. "He was supposed to catch up to me!"

With that, I snatch up my parka and rush to the door. I'm halfway out of the clinic when the doctor lunges for me and takes me by the arm.

"You don't think you're going back outside, do you?"

"I have to find Ongi! He must be in trouble!"

"Slow down!" she demands, clutching me with both hands now. "You were damn lucky not to have died out there. You're crazy if you think you'll be that lucky again."

I try wrenching free, but the petite doctor is surprisingly tough.

"Let me go!" I scream, hysterical. "I can't save *her* and let my own brother die! Please!"

But the doctor responds by tightening her grip, and I have no choice but to tussle with her.

Then there's a knock at the door. Both our heads snap toward it.

"Ongi?" I gasp.

But the person walking in isn't Ongi. Not even close.

"Hello," the man says, a smile revealing straight white teeth. The rich shine of his full-length fur cloak jumps out at me, along with the fine, ink-black suit underneath. No one from this town wears anything but dull, thickly insulated boots, but the leather wing tips capping his long legs have a

brilliant shine. And his face under the lush fox-fur hat . . .
There's something familiar about him. I've seen him before,
I'm sure of it.

"You must be Ms. Jeon Chobahm," the man begins. "I'm
coming from your mother's house. Your brother told me
where to find you."

My brother? This man saw him at home? All the fear and
tension drain out of me, and I turn to the doctor. She shoots
me a relieved smile, then narrows her eyes at the man, as if
she, too, is trying to place him.

"Do you have a minute, Ms. Chobahm?" the man asks,
his eyes fixed on me like I'm the only one in the room. He
hasn't so much as given the doctor an acknowledging glance,
let alone noticed Miryu on the bed in the corner.

"Do I know you?"

He smiles. "The director of the film school is waiting for
you outside, Ms. Chobahm."

A long moment ticks by; then I hear myself echo him,
"Director of the film school?"

A thrill shoots through me.

THE DEATH OF ONE

Exiting the clinic, I follow the man down the darkened plaza toward the plant's front entrance.

"She's waiting around the corner," he says.

"Out in the cold?"

The man smiles and opens the heavy door for me. The supple shine of the leather glove hugging his hand screams Snowglobe. Then I know.

"Cooper Raffaeli?" I gasp.

It's him: the leading man of a hit show that ended two years ago!

"Bingo," he chimes. And with a self-deprecating laugh, he adds, "The biathlon champ who's as tough as tofu."

All jokes aside, he looks pleased to have been recognized. In fact, he appears genuinely content, far more at ease than he was on-screen.

In Snowglobe, Cooper was a professional biathlete who competed in races that combined cross-country skiing and rifle marksmanship. In the final round of each race, death row inmates were brought in as targets, a practice that Cooper could never make peace with. Each victory came with enough guilt to crush any sense of triumph, but he persevered. Episode after episode, fans everywhere tuned in to witness the almighty athlete's psychological unraveling, while empathizing, crying, and torturing themselves right alongside him.

I can't believe it's him standing before me in the flesh, *the* Cooper Raffaeli.

"We used to watch your show every Wednesday and Thursday during supper!" I say, my voice jumping with excitement.

Those of us toiling away in the open world live through our favorite TV shows, riding the rise and fall of the characters' fortunes as if they were our own. That's how we escape the burden of our own bleak existence, if only for a while: by immersing ourselves in the lives of those who get to live where the sun shines. And their failures, in particular, be they financial troubles, ugly divorces, or the most wrenching heartbreak, can inspire in us an odd kind of peace, a sense that the world may be an equitable place after all.

"Didn't you move out of Snowglobe when the show ended?"

"That's correct," Cooper says. "But I got lucky. It turns out Snowglobe needs lots of people—not just actors."

I release a squeak of awe. Then, floating on the thought, I trip over my own ankle like a fool, but Cooper, he of the catlike reflexes, catches me by the elbow and forestalls my face-plant. I cut my eyes away from him, trying to hide the grin spreading across my face.

Two more sets of double doors and then we're outside. The storm seems to have slackened. Through the lingering flurries, I see a black limousine gleaming at the curb. As with the brownies, I've never seen one in real life until this moment. On TV, though, I see limos all the time, mainly depositing actors at the Yibonn estate for events.

With a gloved hand on the limousine's glinting door handle, Cooper leans close and whispers, "Just don't act *too* surprised." A wink.

Is this a dream? Or did Cooper Raffaeli really just wink at me? Ongi's not going to believe me when I tell him.

Cooper finally swings the door open, and I stoop to peer inside. I'm a bit surprised to see that the interior is only half the size of its elongated exterior, if that. But more importantly, there is no director of film school waiting for me. Puzzled, I climb in anyway, sinking into a plush seat behind the darkly tinted privacy window that separates the driver's compartment from the passenger's. A few moments later, the driver's-side door opens, and I twist around in my seat to see Cooper settling behind the wheel. Just as I'm wondering if we're driving to another location to meet the director, there's a soft whir, and I turn back around to see the wall in front of me slowly rolling up, revealing a set of shapely legs belonging to someone sitting opposite me. Through the clear material of long boots, I can see slim, fine-boned feet pedicured with emerald polish and intricate, hand-painted designs. The big toe on each foot is further adorned with a cubic zirconia of a deeper emerald shade, taking the splendid nail art to yet another level. The clear knee-high boots, the elaborate nail art, the emerald color scheme . . . everything is straight out of this year's Snowglobe spring fashion look book.

"How do people live here?" wonders the disembodied voice of my fellow passenger.

She has yet to be fully revealed, but I can now see a sleeveless cream-colored bouclé dress that brings to mind a little lamb. She hugs her bare arms against the frigid air that I must have ushered in with me. After a few more seconds, the wall has lifted completely, and with a soft smile, she introduces herself. Unnecessarily.

"But you already know who I am, don't you?" she says, shaking her signature fiery bob.

Do I know her? Well, yes, I do, as a matter of fact. She is Director Cha, who single-handedly molded Haeri into the superstar she is now. The woman is only my idol, my North Star, that's all.

"Hi! Hello!" I say, my voice shrill.

She lets out a soft laugh. "It's nice to meet you, Ms. Cho-bahm."

My heart beats frantically at the sound of her voice pronouncing my name. A thousand winks from Cooper wouldn't even come close to having the same effect.

"I'm sorry about film school this year," she continues. "I can imagine your disappointment."

I don't believe it. She knows things about me! My mind goes blank with reverence and gratitude.

"I . . . yes. A-a little bit," I stammer. And before I can stop myself, I'm babbling. "But not a lot! I mean, I'm okay because I'll—I'll just apply again next year, and the next year. And the next year?"

Ugh! What a dork! How about a cool, mature *That's okay,* followed by *I've been working on a show idea that will have viewers glued to their screens,* or *You are the inspiration for my lifelong dream of becoming a show director.*

But perhaps those truths don't need to be spelled out. Director Cha gazes at me warmly, as if she already understands all that I can't articulate.

"That's great," she says, pausing to refocus her eyes on me. "But what if you could use your talent to help me out *now*?"

Help her? Me? I just stare at her, uncomprehending.

"It's not really a personal favor," she continues, her voice taking on a more serious tone. "It's for Snowglobe, or rather, its viewers."

In all the wild fantasies I've entertained about attending film school or sitting in on Director Cha's special lecture, my being of specific use to her never even occurred to me. It takes me a moment, but I give her the only correct response I know.

"Of course, Director Cha," I say. "I'd love to help. Whatever you say."

A rich smile of satisfaction settles on her face. Then she pitches the next question. "How much do you think you look like Goh Haeri?"

I give her a blank stare.

"A lot," she answers for me. "Obviously, it'd take some work—but not *too* much. A little upgrade here and there, and everyone will take you for Haeri, is what I think."

What is she trying to say?

"In other words," she resumes, dragging out the final consonant as she fixes me with her eyes, "I'd love for you to be our new Haeri."

I'm still trying to register what I've just heard when her smile vanishes. "Haeri took her own life yesterday."

The words go off like a bomb in my ears. I look at her, shell-shocked.

Is this a joke? If it is, she has a sick sense of humor. No. Director Cha had to have misspoken. I need for her to correct herself, and immediately. But she doesn't. She simply waits for me to register and process the horror.

Goh Haeri, the world's sweetheart, wrapped in silk and protected from all of life's hardship and sorrow in sunstruck Snowglobe? Killed herself? Why? Wasn't she going to be our new weatherperson shortly? Her favorite holiday, Christmas, is only a few days away. It makes no sense! "But I just saw her this morning!" I protest. "On TV?"

Director Cha stares at me wordlessly, compressing her quivering lips into a thin line. I can barely breathe. Haeri—my birthday twin who grew up with me on the other side of the screen—*gone?* The first of many tears breaks free and falls into my lap.

A JOB MEANT FOR ME

I t was back in the fifth grade. Yujin said to me, "But seriously. You do realize how much you look like Haeri, don't you? You even sound alike."

"I guess I look like her," I allowed, feeling strangely sheepish. "But do I really sound like her, too? I don't hear it."

That night, after everyone went to sleep, I tiptoed out into the empty living room and clicked on the TV, pouncing on the mute button as soon as the screen came to life. With the space heater turned off for the night, my teeth began to chatter almost immediately, but I stayed glued to Channel 60, poring over Haeri's features. Her brows, eyes, nose . . . the arch of her upper teeth when she laughs. I admit it. We could be carbon copies. What if Haeri, not Ongi, was my twin? What if the two of us had been switched at birth somehow?

Once I let the idea into my conscious mind, it was all I could think of. I wanted so badly to probe Mom for proof, but I could never dredge up the words; and by the end of the year, my suspicion had hardened into conviction. Then one night, Mom caught me choking back the sobs in bed, and it all blew up.

"It's not fair to Haeri . . . ," I blubbered. "Why should she have to live apart from us?"

The incident became an instant family classic that gets retold to this day. Grandma, who had helped deliver Ongi and me at the plant's clinic, was a living witness whose testimony quelled the last of my suspicions. As if to further mock the fallen theory, Ongi's features began morphing after Mom's, right down to the shapes of his hands and feet. It's too bad he didn't inherit her personality.

The embarrassing memory notwithstanding, my sense of connection to Haeri only grew stronger over the years. Seeing her twirl in a new summer dress, I would feel my own mood lift, me picturing myself in her clothes. Sure, there have been times I felt envious, but I don't really long for an actor's life, not even Haeri's. I want a *director's* life.

Every September, school gyms across the open world bustle with students auditioning for Snowglobe. Participation is mandatory; so every single year of my school career, I had to do a half hour in front of the cameras.

The first half of an audition is spent with a panel of teachers who probe the auditionee with all kinds of questions. The second half is for the auditionee to showcase whatever they have that might contribute to Snowglobe.

In seventh grade, when it was my turn to shine before the distinguished panel, I launched straight into a stiff presentation of show ideas I'd thought up. Sadly, I was cut short by an agitated, interrupting teacher with no power of imagination.

But that was then. Since graduation freed me from the mandatory spectacle, I haven't even thought to register for one. Directors are banned from acting, and actors are banned from directing; it's been that way since the founding of the film school. The idea is that it would be inequitable to double-dip.

"With all due respect, Director Cha," I say, my voice so small that it's barely above a whisper, "I'd really like to direct one day."

She lifts a brow. I drop my eyes to the floor. There's no one in the world I want to impress more than her, but I screw up my courage and continue. "If I become an actor, I can't apply for the film school."

I feel her gaze on me, but I can barely meet it. A long moment passes; then she finally lets out a laugh.

"I think you've misunderstood my proposal, Ms. Chobahm," she says, leaving her seat to cross over to my side. "Your name would not appear in the Snowglobe database, so you'll still be able to apply for film school—if that's what you want, of course. Imagine that. A director unlike any other; who can truly see from an actor's point of view."

She dips her face to catch my eyes. *A director unlike any other.* I gulp. "If you help me now, I will help you become a director later. That's a promise."

She's smiling, but her intense amber gaze is as hard and intimidating as a tiger's.

"That doesn't mean I can get you into film school at will. I'm a working director, completely unaffiliated with the school. But this is a start." Crossing her legs, she briefly looks away before turning her eyes back on me. "Just imagine how much a year in Snowglobe will broaden your perspective, let alone boost your application. And the interview . . ." She lets out a two-note laugh. "I already feel bad for the rest of the applicants."

She looks at me expectantly, her face radiant with victory and self-satisfaction, and I hear myself say, "I would hate to benefit from Haeri's death."

Director Cha draws herself up, all traces of her smile wiped off her face. My mouth goes dry. Am I insane? What have I done? But her smile returns. A smirk, really. She leans back. "I didn't travel all the way here to do you an act of charity, if that's what you're thinking." She pauses to fix me with her predator's eyes. "Haeri *needs* to stay alive. She can't just give up on her life like that."

Just past midnight, the snow has finally stopped, but the wind picks up again and rattles the windows. I sling my backpack on one shoulder and walk out into the living room. Despite my concern that the backpack I've carried since fourth grade would be too small for my trip, it isn't even half full. It turns out there's little to pack when you're leaving for a destination that doesn't require the donning of full arctic gear every time you step outside. Extra parkas, clunky boots, insulated underwear, ski masks, and the like . . . all of it can stay home. In fact, Director Cha told me that if it were her, she wouldn't pack a single thing, since anything I want will be provided for me in Snowglobe.

"Did you pack a change of underwear and socks, at least?"

Mom asks, unzipping the backpack and slipping in a bottle of orange juice.

"Mom, I've already told you—I'm not taking any of this. Keep it for Ongi and Grandma. Please." I pluck out the juice, only to discover containers of strawberries and brownies she had already snuck in.

"Mom—I can get these whenever I want," I sigh, moving to take out the containers, too, but she stays my hand.

"What do you know about the diet of film school students?" she says, giving me a look.

As far as Mom knows, I'm going off to film school, thanks to an applicant dropping out and opening up a spot for me. That was the story Director Cha and Cooper had given her while I was pulling Miryu through the storm. I can't tell anyone, not even my family, that I'm moving to Snowglobe to replace Haeri; because the whole point of all this is to keep her death a secret.

The twice-weekly show has been running for sixteen years now, throughout which fans have watched Haeri grow from an infant to a teenager. Who didn't hold their breath while watching the three-year-old Haeri toddle precariously across the floor with a glass jar in her hands? And who didn't melt for the shy, adorably squirming seven-year-old Haeri when she was introduced to a new playmate, Yi Bonwhe, the then-eight-year-old heir to the Yibonn Media Group? Whose heart didn't flutter along with Haeri's when her crush surprised her with the gift of a headband? And whose heart didn't break with hers when she discovered that he'd been going out with another girl?

Throughout her sixteen years of life, Haeri was a special

friend and family member to devoted fans everywhere. To show the sweet girl hanging herself from a chandelier? Unthinkable. Even announcing her death in *TV Guide* without providing the footage would be in clear violation of the law that dictates that no part of an active actor's life shall be intentionally withheld from public view. Complete surrender of one's privacy is the price they have agreed to pay for the warmth and comfort of Snowglobe.

Then there is the Werther Effect, the phenomenon of copycat suicide, as explained to me by Director Cha. I wasn't familiar with the concept, but it's infused me with terror; especially for Grandma, who sees me in Haeri. News of Haeri's death would destroy her. Keeping Haeri's death a secret might just be the best thing for everyone.

And that is how I find myself committing to Director Cha's vision, in which the show would conclude with Haeri waving goodbye to Snowglobe on her eighteenth birthday, when a youth born into an actor family is given a once-in-a-lifetime chance to choose between privacy and a life on display. Haeri's decision to pursue her life outside Snowglobe will be sure to shock everyone, but nothing could be more traumatizing than the truth of Haeri's sad, unattended end.

Time will pass as it does. Snowglobe will continue to churn out one entertaining show after another. Stars will come and go. And though hard-core fans will occasionally wonder what became of their sweetheart, eventually she'll fade from their memory, too.

"This is a job you alone can do, Ms. Chobahm," Director Cha told me, dissolving all my complicated feelings. This is my chance to break out of a life that could be lived by anyone, break out of a life defined by a hamster wheel spinning to nowhere. Only I can correct Haeri's final exit. What more is there to fret about?

"Don't you want to say goodbye to Grandma?" Ongi says, nodding at her door.

"I want to let her sleep," I say.

Ongi shrugs.

"She thinks I'm your girlfriend, anyway."

"Remember. You're her favorite grandkid," he says.

I nod. As students, Ongi and I received a meager serving of fruit at the school cafeteria, and Grandma always insisted on feeding us the daily ration she got at the plant, too.

I remember the look of concentration on her face as she cut the already bite-sized portions in two. Without fail, she would hand me the slightly bigger half. It was her way of caring for the runty twin born with arrhythmia, whose early years were marked by frequent trips to the doctor's.

As quietly as I can, I crack open her bedroom door. Gazing in at Grandma's sleeping face, I bid a quiet farewell. "Bye, Grandma. I'm going to be on TV for real! Cheer for me, please? I love you. See you soon."

CURE FOR PAIN

I give Mom one last hug. As she turns to hide her tears, my eyes fall on the small glass cube on the table, inside which sits a miniature camera crafted of pure gold, a tiny diamond sparkling at the center of its lens. Cooper presented it to Mom, saying the souvenir was given to all families of film school students. I hadn't realized such a custom existed, but the shiny article certainly added credibility to our story.

"I'm holding down the fort, so you don't need to worry about a thing. Just focus on your studies," Ongi says, reaching for the deep register he employs when he wants to sound like the mature and reliable older brother. He chews his lip to fight the tears pooling in his eyes. I just nod my head, trying to match his tough front.

I turn back to Mom, who is also holding back tears.

"Oh, Mom, you'd think I was going off to a death camp or something," I say, trying for some humor.

"I know, sweetie, I know," she says, wiping her eyes with the back of her hand. "Mom's being so silly, aren't I? We'll come visit you soon."

She smiles, and I smile back the best I can. Unlike other college and university students in Snowglobe, film school students don't get to visit home, for the simple reason that there are no scheduled breaks. The upside of this inconvenience is that families get to visit them in Snowglobe. But I'm not really going to be attending the film school, so I probably won't be able to invite them.

With a final goodbye, I flee to the foyer. Saying goodbye is always hard, but the guilt of lying to my family has made it ten times worse. Swallowing back the tears, I unsling the pink backpack with the brownies and orange juice it contains and set it on the floor against the wall. But then Mom's disappointed face rises before me, and I pick the darned thing back up.

With Cooper behind the wheel, it's almost uncomfortably quiet inside the limousine. Director Cha reaches into the mini-fridge and pulls out a slim glass bottle.

"I believe the occasion calls for a toast," she says, peeling the foil around its neck.

The legal drinking age is twenty-one, both inside and outside Snowglobe. "One celebratory glass of champagne won't kill you," Director Cha assures me with a wink.

Pop!

The sound makes me jump a little in my seat.

She hands me the thin stemware, then tips the bottle and begins filling my glass with golden liquid. As I watch, mesmerized, the tiny bubbles rise from the bottom and pop at the gently sloshing surface. She fills her glass and clinks it against mine. A smile on her lips, she then tips her head back and drains the whole thing in one long gulp. I don't know what else to do, so I try a tentative sip.

Yuck! My face immediately puckers at how sour it is.

Is this how it's supposed to taste? I somehow imagined it would be sweet. I don't realize I've started sliding my tongue in and out of my mouth like a sick animal until I notice Director Cha grinning at me over the rim of her glass.

It is in this moment that the astonishing surreality of my circumstance hits me for the first time. When I woke up this morning, I was just another dispirited teenage worker headed to the power plant. And look at me now. I'm riding in a limousine with one of the world's most acclaimed directors, headed to Snowglobe on a special mission. I am replacing the dead Haeri in order to spare the world the devastation of her suicide. In exchange, my family will be financially rewarded and I'm promised a bright future as a director. And Haeri . . . Haeri. What does she get out of this?

The next thing I know, I'm saying, "Director Cha . . . do you know if Haeri left a suicide note?"

Her hand lifting the glass to her mouth pauses in its tracks, and she regards me a moment.

"What makes you think there was a suicide note?" she says finally, her intense tiger eyes boring into mine. "Besides, don't you think that question is a bit intrusive?"

This last remark confuses me. Intrusive? Into Haeri's private life? Since when was Haeri's privacy ever her own? Her whole life was on display for the public's entertainment, no holds barred. Even her first date—turned disastrous by her overactive bowels—was no exception. Cameras kept rolling right up until the flustered girl, her face twisting in pain and embarrassment, abandoned her date and raced to the nearest public restroom to disappear into one of the stalls.

Laying your life bare for public consumption. That's what is asked of a Snowglobe actor, and I'm on my way to answer that call now. The sudden realization takes my breath away. Whipping around in my seat, I call out to Cooper in the driver's compartment.

"Excuse me, Mr. Raffaeli!"

There's no need to panic when the only thing I'm being asked to do is slip into a life, and not just any life, but Haeri's placid life of stupendous comfort. Yet I need to hear it from someone else. Someone who knows.

Cooper doesn't seem to hear me behind the privacy window separating us, so I raise my voice and try again. "Mr. Raffaeli! Can we please make a quick stop at the plant?"

Still no response. The limousine keeps on cruising.

"I forgot my things! Please!" I shout, but the result is the same.

My blood quickening, I'm lifting myself awkwardly from my seat and raising my knuckles to the glass, about to give a few knocks to get his attention, when Director Cha grabs my wrist.

"Buy them new in Snowglobe," she says. And something about her tone reminds me of the plant supervisor, triggering an odd sense of defiance.

"I left the frostbite cream at the clinic," I say, turning to look her square in the eyes. It is true, and I couldn't be more thankful for it.

Director Cha's expression falls briefly and she recovers. "Snowglobe will have all the frostbite cream you need and more," she says, trying for a softer tone—one of placating, and it doesn't sit well with me, either.

"Yes," I respond, "but I'm supposed to apply the cream once an hour to prevent permanent scarring." Then, tilting my head to one side and giving my best impression of Haeri, I add, "I couldn't imagine Haeri with scars on her face."

A few moments tick by as we stare at each other in silence. Then, finally, she allows a smirk to creep over the corners of her mouth.

"Fine," she says, letting go of my wrist. "And from now on, you will get the okay from me before you do anything." Then she presses the black button on the side of her seat and orders, "To the plant, Cooper."

The limousine takes a sharp left, and the cant of the moon-light spilling in through the glass roof shifts, drawing my eyes to the shards of glass glinting on the carpeted floor. I glance up at the stemware rack mounted over the bar. It can hold four glasses. Three are gone, but Director Cha and I each have only one in hand. *So what?* I'm about to chalk it up to rough roads when the limousine hits another bump. I shoot my eyes back to the rack. The lone glass barely rattles around in its spot before recovering complete stillness.

The doctor must have stepped out for a minute. Miryu is sleep-ing in the corner bed behind privacy curtains. Through the gap, I can see her lying under the elk-skin blanket, her pale face slick with frostbite cream.

I tiptoe over to her bed and try shaking her gently. "Excuse me," I whisper, leaning closer to her face. "Miryu, I need to talk to you."

Maybe it's the rare sound of her name being spoken aloud

that gets her attention. Her eyelids begin to flutter; then, all at once, her eyes flash open and she's on me, clutching my arms. My heart jumps to my throat.

"Help!" she cries in a ragged voice.

"Y-you're okay," I manage to get out. "You're at the clinic. Being treated?"

Her terror-stricken eyes stare right through me.

"The black . . . the black limo," she mumbles, her quaking hands desperately clinging to my parka.

The black limo? A knot of dread forms in my stomach.

"The black limo?" I repeat. "Did you meet the people from Snowglobe, too?"

She lets out a savage scream, pressing her eyes shut and clasping her head with both hands. A large, ugly bruise covers the top of her right hand.

"What's wrong? Is it your head?" I say, trying my best to keep panic at bay.

"Stop! Stop it!" she shrieks. I watch her helplessly as she rocks herself back and forth, her head still clutched in her hands.

The image of broken glass on the limousine's floor returns to my mind's eye. Can a limo's state-of-the-art suspension soak up the impact of colliding with a large animal, such as a full-grown human?

"Did you get hit by the black limousine?" I ask.

Miryu freezes. The air seems to still around us, too. I picture the black limousine driven by Cooper running her over in the dark. But why would they just drive away, leaving her there to die? It doesn't make any sense.

"Stay away from those people," Miryu murmurs. "And that place, too. It's not—"

She doubles over and begins dry-heaving.

It's not *what*?

"What do you mean by those people, or that place?"

"Sno—"

As soon as the syllable comes out, green bile erupts from her mouth and runs down the elk-skin blanket.

Then, suddenly, the doctor slams out of the bathroom, calling out Miryu's name, water dripping from her wet hair. Behind her, the clinic's double doors swing open and Cooper walks in.

"Miryu?" he echoes, looking around the clinic. "That name sounds familiar."

I get the odd feeling that nothing good will come of Cooper seeing Miryu behind the curtains, so I hurry to usher him out of the clinic.

"I'm sorry it took so long," I chirp, steering him by the elbow back toward the doors. "But I'm all set now. Let's go." I snatch up the blue tub from the table as I pass it and call out to the doctor, "I've got the cream! Thank you, Doctor! Bye!"

Cooper keeps looking back toward the sound of Miryu's awful retching.

"That's tough," he says as we finally exit the clinic.

"Gastric cancer," I say, wincing for effect. "It's awful. It's even worse out here, since we don't have enough pain medication to go around."

Cooper nods his head in grim acknowledgment. "That's what drove my mother to kill herself. Pain."

I murmur an awkward acknowledgment of my own, somehow feeling like I've been caught. He continues, a bitter smile on his face, "I thought about it every day while I was in

Snowglobe. What if she'd held on for two more days until my acceptance letter came? I could have finally gotten her something to stop the pain."

He lets out a resigned sigh, turning to me with a smile that seems to apologize for unloading his grief on me, which only makes me feel guiltier.

We're silent for a moment as we continue toward the power plant exit. At the door leading outside, I finally ask him the question I'd have asked Miryu in different circumstances. "Life truly is wonderful in Snowglobe, isn't it?"

A hand on the door, Cooper turns to consider me for a long moment. "Absolutely," he says at last, and flashes a big smile. "I won't say that it's pain-free. But there are all kinds of cures for pain in Snowglobe, and in abundance."

"Do they have pain medications you steep in hot water, too? Like tea bags?" I ask.

This draws a chuckle from him. "All your questions will be answered once you get to Snowglobe," he says, and raises the flap of his cloak over his mouth before pushing open the door.

Back inside the limousine, Cooper's remark about painkillers keeps swirling in my head. Did Haeri take anything before doing the unthinkable? Would the absence of pain have made her end a little less dreadful? And . . . *why* did she kill herself? In Snowglobe, no less? And what about Miryu? Why was she so terrified of Snowglobe?

MINUS A CHARACTER

"Here we are," Cooper's voice says through the limousine's speaker.

Director Cha flips open her armrest and a telephone surfaces—a vintage corded rotary phone with ten holes marked with numbers zero through nine. There's one exactly like it at the plant's office, the one and only phone in the whole of our village, in fact, a hotline for direct communication with the central office.

She lifts the receiver from its cradle and puts a forefinger in the hole for zero, turning the circular plate all the way to the right. When she releases her finger, the plate returns to its start position with a series of clicks.

"Prepare for takeoff," she says into the receiver. In a few moments, light pours into the limousine, halfway blinding me. When my eyes adjust, I'm astonished to see an airplane hulking beside the window. I've never seen one in real life. And this isn't just a plane people use for business trips or vacations. Rather, it's a military transport used during the Warring

Age, when civilizations around the globe clashed brutally as the climate shift became more and more dramatic.

"Open up the cargo hold," Director Cha commands.

A moment later, the rear of the plane opens and a ramp drops down. Then the limousine is on the move again, slowly rolling up the ramp into the plane's cavernous hold. When we come to a stop, the rear closes with a heavy clang.

Suddenly, there's a heavy jerk forward, and the plane begins taxiing across the empty plain. I want so badly to get out and look at the view as the plane takes off. But Director Cha explains that, for safety, we have to remain where we are until the plane reaches cruising altitude. Or it may just be that she's reluctant to step out into the cargo hold, where it must be freezing. If so, I don't blame her. As a native of Snowglobe, she could be morbidly afraid of the cold.

The engine of the plane grows louder and louder as we pick up speed, and I'm pushed back in my seat as the plane lifts off the ground. I'm weightless for a moment, and then we're soaring. My ears still feel like they're underwater when the speaker crackles to life and tells us that the plane is at cruising altitude. Cooper gets out of the driver's seat and opens the door for us, and I step out into the huge, wheeling arc of the cargo hold and look around in amazement. At the front, a floor-to-ceiling glass wall separates the cargo hold from the plane's cabin. And the cabin? It might as well be someone's living quarters, lavishly furnished ones at that, complete with what looks like a luxury dining room.

As I stand there with my mouth agape, Director Cha puts her arm around my shoulder and guides me toward the cabin.

At the glass wall, an overhead sensor blinks red once, twice, and the glass slides open, just enough to let us in.

Director Cha nudges me forward and then turns to Cooper, who's trailing a few feet behind.

"What are you doing?" she says sharply. "Go take care of the floor."

Cooper tenses.

"Really?" he says with an incredulous laugh. "I'm supposed to take on custodial duties now, too?"

Director Cha regards him coldly. "You have to prove your worth. If you want to remain in Snowglobe, that is."

Cooper's face flushes. "Forgive me, Director Cha. I'll see to it now," he says, and heads back to the limousine.

Director Cha ushers me into the cabin, and as the glass wall closes behind us, she shows me to a cream-colored sofa facing the glass wall.

"This is the best seat," she says, gesturing for me to sit. The best seat? *For an unimpaired view of the cargo hold, maybe,* I think. Why sit here when we could be looking out the windows at the sky? But I do as I'm told, and Director Cha kindly clamps the seat belt across my lap and walks over to the intercom. Pressing a button, she says, "Open the cargo hold."

I look at her, puzzled. She just told Cooper to stay in there to take care of the floor. A heavy, muffled clang rings out from the far end of the airplane, and to my astonishment, the door behind the parked limousine lifts and a slice of light cuts through the dark space. I look to Director Cha at the intercom, alarmed, and her placid stare chills me to the core.

On the other side of the glass wall, Cooper sticks his head out of the passenger window to investigate the noise.

"Cooper!" I yell to him, but he doesn't seem to hear me. With a rush of panic, I try pushing up to my feet, to pound on the glass wall and get his attention, but the seat belt keeps me trapped. I yell his name again and again, grappling to open the seat belt, but I can't. I wave my arms wildly, trying to catch the motion sensor, but the glass wall remains closed.

"Cooper!" I scream, feeling sick. "You need to come inside! Please!"

The outside air whips violently as the rear of the airplane continues to open and the cargo hold becomes brighter and brighter, the limo rocking from side to side. I can see the moment Cooper realizes what's happening. His face blanches with shock and he looks toward the cabin. Then he jumps into action. He flings open the limo door and staggers to the glass wall, hunched forward against the draft at his back.

"Director Cha!" he shouts, slapping the glass with both hands. "Open the door!"

But she just looks on dispassionately. Cooper's face goes slack with understanding. The limousine behind him begins rolling back toward the widening mouth of the cargo hold and I watch as it drops off the back of the plane, twirling madly and disappearing from sight. The draft inside the cargo hold pulls at Cooper and he struggles to keep his footing, his bloodless palms trying to maintain purchase on the flat, unyielding surface of the glass.

"Falling to your death is supposed to be a gentler way to go than hypothermia," Director Cha offers into the intercom.

I can't pull my gaze from Cooper. His face twisting with rage, he slams his body against the glass, shouting and cursing. But his efforts achieve nothing, not even a hairline crack in the glass. At last, Director Cha strides over to the glass and stops inches from Cooper, still desperately clawing at the glass between them.

"Thank you for your service," she says, and lifts a hand, waving him a final goodbye.

There's no more time for rage or hate or disgust. Vessels bloom red in Cooper's eyes, and just as a single tear rolls back toward his temple, he's snatched clean out of the plane, mouth open in a mute cry.

With a click, the seat belt across my lap releases on its own. I stagger to my feet, but my knees buckle and I crumple to the floor. Unable to move, I lie there on the carpet, staring numbly at the spot Cooper occupied just moments ago, pleading for his life. On the far side of the cargo hold, the door begins to close, shutting out the light outside. In a few moments, there's another heavy clang, and the roar and hiss of the air give way to a dizzying silence.

Trembling, I look to Director Cha. "What did you do?"

She doesn't seem all that joyful. I remember Ongi wearing a similar expression when I carelessly sat on the paper mobile he had worked so hard to craft in art class. Letting out a weary sigh, Director Cha moves to an upholstered chair by a white marble coffee table with an electric kettle on top.

"You can sit wherever you want now," she says.

"Wh-why did you kill him?" I choke out, in a ragged voice. My cheeks are a mess of tears and frostbite cream caked upon raw flesh. If I lived a thousand years, I could never forget the look on Cooper's face. How did Miryu do it—kill a person—not just once, but nine times?

"This is where his part ends," Director Cha says matter-of-factly. "That was the script from the beginning."

My heart sinks with doom. Who *is* this person?

She switches on the kettle. "Cooper talked too much," she says. "And he was weak. Not a good fit for such a meaty role."

"So you *killed* him?"

She regards me for a moment.

"It's too bad," she says. Then, leaving her seat, she comes to stoop beside me. "If Haeri hadn't killed herself, Cooper wouldn't have had to die like that."

I bite my lip, running her words through my mind, trying to see if I heard them right, but I just feel more disoriented. She's crazy, and this is so messed up.

"Come. Have a cup of coffee with me," she says. And with a pat on my shoulder, she returns to the table, where she begins grinding coffee beans with a small handheld grinder, as if nothing is amiss.

"Does the same fate wait for me at the end of all this?" I say, trying my best to steady my voice.

She laughs and then turns to look at me. "I thought you wanted to be a director. Remember? The deal is, you help me, then I help you."

I return her gaze the best I can, trying not to give in to the cold sense of dread and powerlessness descending on me. But I can't help it. I can't stop the tears from coming.

"Oh, sweetie." She sighs and pauses with her hand on the crank, shooting me a look of exasperation. "Why are you so upset?"

Why am I so *upset*? All I can think of is how much I hate her. She ruined it for me, ruined it for all of us. "I'll never forget the look on Cooper's face," I choke out between sobs. "It will haunt me until the day I die."

I never could have imagined I'd ever feel this way about the director who's been my idol for as long as I can remember.

She leaves the table to kneel beside me on the floor. Pulling me into her arms, she says, "I was worried you'd say you want to go home." The relief in her voice is distinct. And that's when I realize with shock that the thought hadn't even crossed my mind.

"People die every day in Snowglobe," she goes on, stroking my back as I continue to cry, shuddering in her embrace. "Of murder, accident, illness, old age. But we can't mourn them all." She pauses and lifts my chin with a gentle hand, looking into my eyes. "And Cooper? When's the last time you saw him on TV? Life's too short to mourn a has-been like him." Another pause. "Don't feel guilty for putting yourself first. That's how it should be."

Her words soothe me, in spite of everything I know. When I finally stop crying, I ask her, "Did you see Haeri's last moment?"

"Not yet," Director Cha answers.

And I realize, of course she hasn't—I'd forgotten that even directors don't have access to footage recorded within the week.

"Will you?" I ask.

She's silent a moment. But then something hard settles in her face. "Yes. I have to. I'm the director."

Yes. As with any other act of the last sixteen years, Director

Cha will review Haeri's last act, too, captured from all possible camera angles. I can imagine her poring over the footage, dry-eyed. Is it strange of me to think that maybe she can do that, not because she isn't devastated by Haeri's death, but because she's that strong?

Pulling away from Director Cha, I stagger to the nearest window seat and collapse into its plush cushion. By the time the cabin begins to fill with the aroma of freshly brewed coffee, my tears have completely dried.

Director Cha brings me a cup of coffee, but I turn it down with a weak shake of my head.

"Okay, then," she says. "Why don't you get some sleep?" She lowers herself into the seat opposite mine. "It's going to get busy as soon as we arrive."

She produces a newspaper and opens it wide to read, taking leisurely sips of coffee, and I turn my gaze out the window, feeling hollowed out and numb. But it isn't long before my stomach drops at the thought of my family.

"My family thinks I'm headed off to film school," I blurt, my voice shrill with panic. "I swear, Director Cha. I didn't tell them anything!"

"I know," she says, lazily turning the page of her newspaper. "And from now on, your family is the one in Snowglobe."

Part 2

YOU

CHAPTER ONE

THE PROMISED LAND

Every time I start drifting off, Cooper's hemorrhaging eyes pop into my mind, jolting me awake. Eventually, I stop trying to sleep and look out at the vast emptiness of the ink-black sky instead. I don't know how much time has gone by when the stars begin to dim and the dark fades into purple with the seeping light of dawn. When the entire sky turns pink and the far horizon burns a fiery red, the voice in the speaker announces our imminent arrival at Snowglobe. Then the plane veers left, and my searching eyes fall on the glass dome below, glinting in the first light. *Am I still on planet Earth?* I wonder. The sight of it is nothing less than surreal. The gigantic dot is a lone, intensely green circle set inside a vast white plane.

The plane descends and the green dot begins to grow, revealing a miniature display of buildings, skyscrapers, and candy-colored vehicles the size of ants crawling along the highways. My heart beating frantically, I search for the film school whose majestic campus I can paint from memory, having studied it every day in the brochure taped to my bedroom wall.

"What do you think? Do you like it?" Director Cha's voice interrupts.

I nod, my eyes fixed on the view outside. If I'm excited, I don't want her to see it, not just yet.

"Hey, Haeri," she says.

Without meaning to, I turn my head. I'm not sure how to take it.

"That's right. That's you from now on, whether or not others are watching," she says, gazing at me warmly, her eyes swirling with tender sorrow.

Director Cha was fresh out of film school when she was brought on to helm *Goh Around*. I can't imagine how she felt after sixteen years of blood, sweat, and tears dedicated to bringing out the best in the starlet and her family. I'm just a fan, and I can barely breathe when I think about Haeri being gone.

Every single Snowglobe show is a reality show without a script, so no one in Snowglobe is what once would have been regarded as a professional actor. The theory behind this practice is that even the world's best-crafted fiction is just a facsimile of real life, therefore an inferior form of entertainment. But watching an ordinary person going about their everyday life is no one's idea of fun; and therein lies the critical importance of a talented director with an eye for drama and suspense, who can breathe life into the mundane by selecting the right shots and assembling them into a coherent, artistic, and ultimately entertaining sequence. Simply put, a director collects the raw materials that are other people's lives and uses their creative vision to develop them into a living story.

For all the talent and hard work that go into creating a show, however, it's ultimately viewership that determines its longevity and its director's career. A show regularly drawing under ten thousand viewers over a six-month period gets the axe no matter its artistic or sociocultural achievements, and a director who loses five shows in that manner is expelled from Snowglobe and sent to the village of retirees, of which little is known other than the fact that it exists somewhere outside the domed paradise.

To state the obvious, a director and her crew of actors form a symbiotic relationship in the pursuit of their common goal, which, at its most fundamental level, is to remain in Snowglobe. At least, that's what I learned in social studies at school.

"Jeon Chobahm doesn't exist anymore," Director Cha says, searching my face. I understand what she means, not that it makes it feel any less strange to hear her say it. She takes my hands and squeezes them gently. "I promise you, Haeri"—and the sound of her voice calling me by that name begins to erase the girl who is Jeon Chobahm—"there will be a happy ending for you." A pause. "For everyone."

As if on cue, there's a quick jolt, and the plane touches down.

Because the dome is an airtight structure made of tempered glass panels, flying in is impossible. I put on the hat, mask, and dark glasses Director Cha hands me and follow her off the plane and to another shiny black limousine that waits for us on the runway. There she rushes to open the door and practically shoves me in before climbing into the driver's seat herself.

Her hands gripping the wheel, she glances nervously through the limousine's heavily tinted windows.

"Haeri, sweetie, can you duck down?" she says through the speaker. Her tone has softened noticeably since she started calling me by my new name.

I obediently lie sideways and out of sight. With my face to the plush seat, I let the engine hum softly in my ear as Director Cha steers.

It isn't long before the noises of a busy downtown begin to filter into the limo. My heart skips. From where I am, I can't see a thing, but the sounds of cars and people tell me with no uncertainty that I'm in Snowglobe.

A series of familiar chirps sounds each time the limo comes to a full stop. It takes me a minute, but I realize with a flutter that I'm hearing the crossing signals I see on TV. At one such stop, a voice expresses her wish for a white Christmas, which is tomorrow, if you can believe it, according to another. Then there's the excited yelp of a puppy. It's just spotted a fellow leashed canine crossing the street.

"They have to be friends with everyone, don't they?" says one of the humans, a warm smile in her voice.

"Oh, I love your dog's outfit!" sings the other human. "The world's tiniest Santa!"

"Haha. Thanks. He sure is, and he carries candy in his pocket. Here, have a few, and Merry Christmas!"

"Awww, thanks! Merry Christmas to you, too!"

It's another half hour until Director Cha tells me we've arrived at her home. Soon after, the limo makes a slight upward lurch, and then a rotating parking platform is raising us off the ground.

Paved roads without snow or potholes, crosswalks and traffic lights, people walking puppies dressed in Santa costumes, strangers sharing candy, homes with car lifts . . . I can't help but smile. I've arrived.

"Home at last!" Director Cha announces. "Now we can relax."

I sit up and let myself out of the limo, stepping into her peach-colored garage, where two other vehicles sit, gleaming in the low light. The garage alone is big enough to fit our entire family home. Director Cha watches me from a door that must lead inside, a soft smile on her face.

"Start reviewing past episodes in your mind," she says. "It will help you adjust to your new life in Snowglobe."

"Do you think that'll be enough?" I ask in a small voice.

I thought I knew everything about Haeri and her life, but I never imagined she would kill herself. Did I really know anything of the real Haeri?

"Do you think I'll be able to act like her? To *think* like her?"

A belated concern, but it occurs to me now that such a thing might be just as important as my physical appearance. "All I know about Haeri comes from watching her on TV," I say.

"And that's all you need to know," Director Cha answers without missing a beat. "Believe in yourself. I do."

Strangely enough, right now, Director Cha reminds me of

my fifth-grade homeroom teacher—my favorite—who used to tell me how much she believed in my potential as an aspiring director.

"Come on, sweetie. You'll be fine. Let's go in and relax," Director Cha says. "There aren't any cameras in a director's home, but you already know that, don't you?"

Murmuring a yes, I take in a deep breath and follow her inside.

Stepping into her living room, I'm immediately struck by its bird's-eye view of the city, its lake sparkling blue down below. I'm crossing the floor to the giant bay window when someone shrieks, "Haeri!"

Startled, I turn to see an old woman rushing to me from the sofa, her arms outstretched. She looks . . . familiar?

"Oh, my lord! It's really you, my baby!" she cries out, her eyes brimming with tears.

My stunned brain finally catches up to the visual at hand. It's Goh Maeryung, Haeri's grandmother. With her long salt-and-pepper locks twisted in a bun atop her gracefully aging face, she is the picture of effortless elegance and beauty. Her magnetic gaze, even more charismatic in real life, instantly seizes me, and I stare at her in awe and disbelief.

It was thirty-nine years ago when Goh Maeryung, nineteen and pregnant with her first child, made her way into Snowglobe. Now a proud mother of four and a grandmother of one, she is the matriarch of the only biological multigenerational family in Snowglobe.

"How was your trip? You must be exhausted, sweetie. It's such a long way," Maeryung coos, pulling me tight to her chest. I can't help but notice the incredible softness of her pale blue cardigan against my cheek. If she wonders why I'm dressed in a bona fide burlap sack, she doesn't linger over it. Then she holds me at arm's length and examines my face.

"What happened to you?" she asks, a crease of pain appearing between her brows.

I'm utterly dazed by her presence. "It's just some frostbite," I force out.

Maeryung claps a hand to her mouth, eyes wide with shock. Only then do I realize that the common condition might be viewed as rare and dangerous here in Snowglobe.

"Frostbite?" she cries. "On your pretty face?"

I'm not sure how to react. Despite the deep sense of intimacy I've developed toward her and her clan over the screen, I'm starstruck and tongue-tied before the actress in the flesh. Meanwhile, Maeryung, who has never laid eyes on me until now, has no such scruples. She strokes my hair with the kind of tender affection you'd give your real granddaughter, lost and now returned.

I stretch my face into an awkward smile, and Director Cha lets out a laugh.

"Relax," she tells me. "It's natural that a grandmother would fuss over her granddaughter, isn't it?"

"Yes, of course, Director Cha," I say. So everyone's already pretending that I'm Haeri—even down to the grandmother who must be out of her mind with grief? Shouldn't there be some kind of introduction? I feel Maeryung's hand squeezing my shoulder.

"Let's move forward," she says. "Your uncles and aunts have no idea. Thank goodness it was just your mother and me at home that day." She breathes a sigh of relief.

In addition to Haeri and her mom, the household of six headed by Maeryung includes Haeri's two aunts and an uncle, all of whom are Maeryung's children. Her uncle, the youngest of the siblings, was born just two months after Haeri. Back when the bombshell of Maeryung's geriatric pregnancy was dropped, many people, including my mom, clucked their tongues in disapproval, speculating that the aging matriarch was so desperate to stay relevant that she tried to upstage her own daughter, whose pregnancy was generating a great deal of anticipation.

Maeryung continues, "You know how much your aunts and uncle love you, sweetie. Let's never let them find out, okay?"

I stare at her, baffled. Is it even *possible* for me to fool them? The aunts and uncle aren't strangers off the street, or mere fans. They're family who Haeri had been living with. No matter how much I look like Haeri, expecting me not to blow my cover seems hopeless.

"Grandma," I say, and the ease with which the word rolls off my tongue surprises me, though it shouldn't. After all, I've practiced it every day on my own grandma.

"Yes, sweetie," Maeryung coos, pleased to see me falling into the groove. Feeling encouraged, I continue, "Grandma, I don't know if we should keep secrets in our family. I just don't think I can—"

A stinging flash of pain erupts on the side of my face, cutting my sentence short.

"What is *wrong* with this girl?" Maeryung shrills.

It takes a moment for me to realize that Maeryung has just

struck me. Stunned, I blink stupidly, the shock of her open hand scorching the raw flesh on my frostbitten cheek.

Then Director Cha is there, stepping in front of me protectively.

"What are you doing?" she demands, glaring fiercely at Maeryung.

"Didn't you hear, Director?" Maeryung retorts. "She's babbling nonsense before we even get started! What are we going to do with such a fool?"

"So you *hit* the girl? Are you crazy?"

Maeryung doesn't back down.

"Do you have a problem with me disciplining my own granddaughter?"

I feel a jolt go through my heart. *But I'm not your grand-daughter. And even if I were, how is this disciplining?* I'm shaking now, flooded with adrenaline. I want to start arguing with the old lady, but what am I supposed to do if she hits me again? Hit her back?

"Discipline?" Director Cha hisses. Leaning her face close to Maeryung's, she says, "Behave. That is, if you want to stay in Snowglobe. There's no place on my show for a demented grandmother."

Maeryung isn't fazed. "Director Cha," she says with a bark of a laugh. "Let's not forget that you've come this far by riding on the coattails of your grandfather. Me? I had to claw every inch of my way up here on my own, then fight to keep my position. Remember, I've been at it for close to forty years now."

Her voice drips with the conviction that no one could mess with her, not even Director Cha. Truth be told, even if Director Cha delivered on her threat and gave Maeryung the boot, an actor of her stature is likely to get snatched up by some opportunistic director.

Director Cha sneers. "You wouldn't be here without my grandfather's charity." Her amber gaze fixes Maeryung with a warning. *Know your place.*

Maeryung had been cast by the legendary director Cha Guibahng, Director Cha's grandfather. If Maeryung's family is the only multigenerational clan in Snowglobe in front of the cameras, Director Cha's family is its counterpart behind them.

Maeryung, reaching around Director Cha, snatches me by the wrist and pulls me to her.

"Look who's talking charity," she jeers back. "Aren't you the one living off my own flesh and blood?"

Then, turning to me, she cups my still-throbbing cheek in her palm. "Forgive me, sweetie. I should have known better than to lay a finger on my precious baby."

The sudden and complete shift in her tone makes me recoil in disgust. But she just strokes my back and continues. "Your grandma is so shaken up by what happened the other day that she's not herself."

Something hot and sour comes up in me then. And before I can stop myself, I'm shrugging off her hand. "Did you treat Haeri this way, too? Hit her one minute and act all sweet and loving the next?"

Her face goes hard and I steel myself for another blow. But she throws back her head and bursts into a hearty laugh.

"Attagirl!" she says, gazing at me proudly. "Yes! A girl's gotta have mettle to survive in Snowglobe." The corners of her mouth curl up in a faintly sinister smile. "But you won't mouth off to your grandma in front of the cameras, will you, sweetie? Haeri and Grandma are best friends—always have been. But I'm guessing I don't have to tell you that."

Before Haeri was cast as the new weather presenter, she had wanted to become a clothing designer, to follow in the footsteps of her beloved grandma. That's how special the bond is between the two, or so we were led to believe.

Despite everything, Maeryung's remark reminds me of my purpose here in Snowglobe.

"No, I won't," I reply after a long moment, adding a barely audible "Grandma."

"That's my sweetie," she says in a syrupy voice. Taking my hand in hers and squeezing it tenderly, she looks me in the eyes. "Now let's get working."

Director Cha turns to me then. "Yes," she says. "As the incoming weather presenter, you have been invited to the Christmas party hosted by the Yibonn. It is tonight."

THE YIBONN MEDIA GROUP

Director Cha guides me to the guest bathroom and closes the door. I switch on the shower and listen as the sound of rushing water fills the room. When warm steam begins to rise, I step in under the soft spray, glancing up nervously for a regulator that isn't there. Back home, coin-operated showers dribble lukewarm water and stop mercilessly when your time's up. At first, I find myself hurrying through the routine, but it starts to feel like I'm in a magic booth, standing under a soft, soothing cascade with my eyes closed. *So this is what they call a* relaxing *shower,* I realize—*the first one of my life.* Eventually, I turn off the shower and step out and towel off. And this amazingly plush towel . . . I keep my face buried in it for a while, letting it soothe my frayed nerves.

At last, I slip on the underwear and silk robe supplied by Director Cha and let myself out, making my way to her dressing room. The dressing room, a space dedicated to clothes, accessories, and makeup, is a standard feature in every Snowglobe home, though its opulence depends on the popularity of the occupants. What a concept. Back home, we just heap our clothes in a freezing corner of our house.

Director Cha's dressing room is huge—hardly a surprise—and even more spacious than her garage. I'm looking around in amazement when my eyes fall on a still figure watching me from an ornately decorated makeup table. It's Goh Sanghui, Haeri's mother. Unlike Maeryung, however, she doesn't jump to her feet or cry out my name in joy or surprise. Instead, she visibly stiffens in her seat. I was told that Sanghui was the one to discover Haeri. I don't know what to say, let alone how to summon the nerve to call her *Mom*.

"How . . . how do you do?" I say, squirming at the absurdity of my greeting.

Sanghui says nothing, her unreadable gaze firmly fixed on me.

Maeryung's voice flows in then. "Come on, sweetie—"

I turn to see the old woman backing her way in through the door with a tray of little sandwiches and glasses of orange juice.

"What's this 'how do you do' business with your own mother?" she says with a smile.

"I—I'm sorry," I stammer.

Maeryung sets the tray on the counter amid the perfumes and beauty products and crosses the room to me. Her smile holds, but I can see impatience simmering beneath it. She takes me by the shoulders and steers me to the makeup table, where she plops me down by Sanghui.

"Sorry?" she says, leaning down, arching her brows at me through the mirror.

"I'm sorry—" I say. "I mean, that was silly of me, Grandma, wasn't it?"

Her brows relax. "That's my girl."

Sanghui picks up a tube from the table and squeezes its clear, viscous contents onto her palm, then begins massaging it onto her emotionless face.

"Haeri, my sweet, you must be starving. Eat!" Maeryung says, and before I can respond, she's holding one of the bite-sized sandwiches up to my mouth. Reflexively, I'm opening wide to accept the morsel when a perfect arch of saliva shoots out of my mouth. I drop my gaze, burning with embarrassment. Maeryung, however, seems deeply pleased. "Tell me, sweetie," she says with a trill of laughter. "Salmon and dill sandwiches by Grandma. They're the best, aren't they?"

I nod in silent agreement. Smoked salmon wedged between slices of fresh cucumbers and pillowy-soft bread. The exquisite flavor and texture combination is unlike anything I've ever had. Embarrassment be damned, I'm soon reaching for another square, followed by another, and another, stealing glances at Sanghui, who's applying assorted liquids and creams of various shades to her face. In my defense, I haven't eaten anything since lunch yesterday, outside of the two sips of champagne in the limousine. I'm still munching away when Sanghui speaks for the first time.

"You'll have to monitor yourself at the party," she says coldly.

"What?" I mumble with my mouth full.

"You look like you're about to swallow the plate, too," she offers without even glancing at me.

I feel color rising to my face and swallow audibly.

"It's fine, Haeri," Director Cha says. She must have floated into the room at some point. "Everyone likes a girl who eats. Munch away for the camera."

But all I want is to scrub my mouth clean of the smoked salmon, and with it, its humiliation.

"Very well done," Director Cha says to Sanghui. She's gazing contently at my reflection in the full-length mirror. "They don't call you the best makeup artist in Snowglobe for nothing."

Even to my own eyes, I am Haeri incarnate, my face framed by tousled waves from an exquisite wig of rich, chocolate-brown hair. Expertly applied makeup conceals the ugly frost nips on my cheeks and nose, not to mention any blemishes and other imperfections native to my face. And whatever else Sanghui did to my hopelessly chapped and fissured lips, they're now dewy with life. It's magic.

"Do you still think I'm a demented witch, Director Cha?" Maeryung teases.

"I'd never deny our Lady Goh's mad sewing skills," Director Cha concedes playfully.

Standing awkwardly among the women congratulating each other on my stunning transformation, I study my reflection in the mirror. My shoulders are bare in the yellow strapless gown conceived and realized by Maeryung, its floor-length, billowy hem trimmed with hundreds of feathers. In making sure that my skin would look flawless against the playful dress, Sanghui even coated my neck, shoulders, arms, and hands in makeup. Her discomfort with the task was painfully palpable, though, as she flinched each time her skin came in contact with mine.

Maeryung hands me a pair of clear shoes and I take them, marveling at their beauty.

"I custom-ordered these glass shoes for you a whole month ago," she says.

They're not made of glass—not really. They're probably made of that same clear material Director Cha's knee-high boots are made of. Still, I'm reluctant to slip my cracked and callused feet into the fancy shoes. Half an hour ago, Sanghui dismissed Maeryung's suggestion of a full pedicure, saying no one would even notice my feet under the gown, the subtext being that she'd rather not be near me unless it was absolutely necessary. And who could blame her? No matter how much I look like Haeri, I'm a complete stranger shipped in to take the place of her dead child. Sanghui's aversion is natural. What's unnatural is this grandma, who takes my foot into her hand and shimmies it into the shoe, chirping about how proud she is of her granddaughter, the newly crowned weather presenter who's on her way to the Yibonn's Christmas party.

"They fit like gloves!" she cries.

And I have to admit that it's uncanny how the footwear custom-made for Haeri fit me so well. I gaze down at them, feeling sorry for the fine shoes that ended up on my coarse feet, but Maeryung adjusts the gown's feathery hem and it drops down, hiding my feet from view.

"This is it," Director Cha says, taking a big breath and

squeezing my shoulder. She fixes me with a solemn gaze. "It's time to get your head in the game now. Stay sharp."

Stay *sharp*? I haven't slept a wink since I was swept up in this whirlwind of events. Though I suppose it's all kept me on high alert, to say the least.

"No need to work yourself into a froth, though," she continues. "Remember, most people at the party are also new to Snowglobe."

Luckily, the first public event I'm attending as Haeri is the annual Christmas banquet for debut actors. Though Haeri is a veteran actor herself, she's also the incoming weather presenter, so she was invited as a special guest. In other words, I'll mostly be with people who have never met Haeri in person. Plus, the Yibonns' private residence is a camera-free zone, discounting the ones hired specifically for the event; and any footage obtained by those cameras is reviewed by the family before it's released to the public.

To state the obvious, no member of the Yibonn family is required to earn their keep by acting in a show. As the founding family and guardian of Snowglobe, the Yibonns are exempt from the fundamental duties of every man, woman, and child, which is to participate in the production of either electricity or entertainment.

"Basically," Director Cha resumes, "do your best to remember the etiquette we went over, and forget everything else."

If only it were that easy. She looks at me with a pleased smile, as if I've absorbed all the obscure rules she rattled off while I was being made over: food service proceeds to the right, counterclockwise, starting with the guest of honor.

Beverage service progresses to the left, clockwise. Silverware. Always start from the outside and work your way inward for each course, etc., etc. But it's the forms of address that really get me.

"The president and vice-president are addressed as such, meaning by their titles. Their kids and grandkids should be called Young Master or Young Lady. For example, Yi Bonwhe, the heir, is Young Master Bonwhe. Everyone else is sir or madam."

I am used to him being called *Mr.* Yi Bonwhe, as that's how the news media refers to him. But *Young Master* Bonwhe? That's just as laughable as *Bonwhe, my babe,* or *bae, boo,* or any of the other cringe-worthy monikers I've heard my friends squeal back home, including Yujin when she was just one of us.

"I swear I retain most of what I see on TV," I tell Director Cha with a nervous smile. "But rote learning has never been my strong suit."

This draws a hearty laugh from Maeryung.

"That sounds just like my Haeri!" she says, her voice rising with delight. "Don't you worry, sweetie. Everyone knows you're under tremendous pressure to perform as the new weather presenter, and the youngest one in history at that. If you think you've made a gaffe, just flash them your lovely smile and blame it on the nerves."

Flash my lovely smile. And how am I supposed to do that? I can picture the smile she's talking about better than anyone else, but I'm not sure if my facial muscles are capable of replicating it.

"Maeryung's right," Director Cha agrees, looking as if

Maeryung has snatched the words right out of her mouth. "Break some china or spill your champagne, whatever—you'll be fine, as long as you remember who you are," she says, then pitches her voice low for effect and adds, "Haeri."

As I nod back awkwardly, I see Sanghui glaring at me in the mirror, her face twisting with bitter contempt.

ME IN THE MIRROR

The iron gates open and the limousine rolls into the Yibonn estate's magnificent garden. In the backseat, I breathe a quiet *"Wow,"* unable to contain my awe; and it doesn't matter how many times I've seen it on TV. Its scale in real life is simply staggering.

December. Even in temperate Snowglobe, the month marks the dead of winter, and yet, sprays of water arch skyward from fountains across the garden. Forget about the time of year. That water can exist outdoors in its liquid state is a wonder in and of itself.

The car pulls to a stop and the door opens. I pick up my jaw and step out of the limo.

"This way, please," says a security guard with a decorous sweep of a hand. I turn toward the mansion rising up from a massive stairway, and I'm stunned all over again. It's a long way up to the gold-clad front doors.

Teetering in my new shoes, I mount the first step and begin a careful ascent. It's not the easiest thing in the world, walking in these shoes, but I figure them out quickly enough.

All is good until about halfway up, when I step onto the next stair and my ankle gives out. Flailing my arms like a cartoon figure, I pitch over backward and, mercifully, fall into the arms of a fellow partygoer behind me.

"I got you!"

Aflame with embarrassment, I steal a glance at my savior. And the face I see stuns me into a blank state. It's my best friend, Yujin. In some ways, she knows me better than I know myself, which means I'm more likely to be busted by her than anyone else at the party.

"Th-thank you," I manage to get out, struggling back to my feet.

How could I have failed to guess that Yujin would be here at the banquet for new faces?

"No problem!" Yujin says excitedly. "Ms. Haeri, right? I'm a big fan!"

Ugh. I give her a flat smile and turn back to continue my wobble up the steps. But Yujin, always open and friendly, calls out, "Congratulations on your new role!"

I stop and turn slightly to look at her. In an elegant sea-green dress under a yellow pashmina stole, my best friend looks happier than ever. Seeing her poised to make her mark in Snowglobe fills me with pride, but with Cooper's face invading my thoughts, how can I possibly expose her to the dangers of knowing who I really am? I can't let her find out. Not ever.

In an instant, she's back beside me with a smile. "We're going to be late, Ms. Haeri. Let's hurry," she says.

I respond with another tight smile, hoping to communicate that I'm not interested in friendship, but she babbles on.

"We're the same age. Can I just call you Haeri?" she persists, and I have no choice but to shift tactics. Haeri wouldn't blow someone off in the middle of them trying to small talk. I'll have to lose her after some bland chitchat.

"So you saw the promo?" I acquiesce with another forced smile.

"Of course!" Yujin says eagerly. "And every single episode of your show, too. Right up to the day I left home—" She claps a hand to her mouth and shifts her eyes nervously. After a moment, she continues in a hushed tone, "But I won't breathe another word about it, of course. I respect the anti-spoiler rule."

Being appointed the upcoming year's weather presenter means that Haeri achieved the most success in Snowglobe that year, so Yujin openly fangirling Haeri is completely acceptable. Haeri's rise to the position makes her a bona fide celebrity among celebrities. Still, bringing up specific details about her show—for instance, Haeri's new diet regime, or her misplaced wallet kicked into a corner under her bed? That would be a serious violation of the anti-spoiler rule. There is no actor who wouldn't be affected when blatantly reminded that the stuff of their private lives is being enjoyed by millions of strangers, whether it be bankruptcy, addiction, marital strife, or even murder. Such viewer interference would be detrimental to a show's authenticity; so actors, especially newcomers, must be careful not to disclose the specifics of shows they used to follow out in the open world.

"How do you get around so well in those heels?" I ask Yujin, hiking up the hem of my gown to my ankles and paying careful attention to the next step.

"Practice," she says with a proud smile. "Didn't skip a single day over the last two months."

Upon entry to Snowglobe, new actors stay in a dormitory for two months. During that time, they're encouraged to shed habits from the open world and replace them with the ways of Snowglobe, which apparently includes walking in high heels. This period also helps them fall out of touch with any shows they used to watch so they won't be at as much of a risk for leaking spoilers.

"Oh, by the way . . ." Yujin segues seamlessly. "Would you believe it if I told you that my best friend back home looks like your twin?"

My heart rate spikes, and I let out an awkward laugh.

"Nah," I say, dropping my gaze. "There's no way your friend has my flawless skin."

"You're right," she agrees easily. "It's brutally cold and dry where we're from. Still, she resembles you *so* much, right down to the irritated look you have when you're not in the mood for socializing."

Yujin bursts into giggles, and I feel a pang of guilt that I'm not being a better friend to her.

"I used to tell her that if she ever ended up in Snowglobe," she continues, "she should avoid running into Haeri no matter what! One person has to *die* if you run into your clone—did you know that? There can only be one."

"I didn't know," I say, arranging my face to look appropriately entertained. "That's wild." The truth is, that myth is already etched into my brain, thanks to her obsession with the topic.

Yujin looks serious now. "It's true," she says, nodding. "An actor who gets entangled with their doppelganger either goes insane or dies. It's said that there are a total of three clones for each of us, including ourselves."

We finally reach the top of the stairs, and the sight of the grand entrance saves me from responding to her theory. Two doormen stand outside oversized double doors, swinging them open as we approach. We slip into the mansion, where a grand foyer and vaulted ceiling rise before us. A woman in a tuxedo and white bow tie stands under a festive Yibonn banner that spans the width of the hall.

"Welcome to the Yibonns'," she greets us with a courteous smile and a bow. HAHN HUIYUN, her name tag reads. She is the mansion's butler.

Everyone serving at the Yibonn mansion is also a working actor, of course, though their workplace is camera-free most of the time. Some prefer it that way, while others consider it a disadvantage to their career.

"Allow me to show you to the tearoom, Ms. Haeri," Butler Hahn says, and extends a hand toward a sweeping staircase leading up to the second floor.

Yujin takes her cue and chirps, "I'll see you later, then!" She winks and glides off toward the ballroom.

As I watch Yujin disappear, I picture myself directing a show with her as the star, a fantasy she and I have nurtured since fifth grade, doodling storyboards and scribbling script ideas in the margins of our textbooks, or drinking hot cups of cocoa while leafing through *TV Guide* for inspiration.

Director Cha's voice echoes in my head again. *I thought you wanted to be a director. Remember? The deal is, you help me, then I help you.*

I smile to myself, my heart lifted. If I knock it out of the park as Haeri, our fantasy just might come true.

At the top of the staircase, I follow Butler Hahn and stop outside a closed door. She gives the door a couple of soft raps; then she presses a small gold button on the wall and speaks into it: "Ms. Goh Haeri is here, Madam President."

A few moments later, the door eases open and reveals Yi Bonwhe standing on the other side.

"Hi, please come on in," he says, holding the door open.

Butler Hahn bows from the waist. Am I supposed to do the same? Perhaps. But I haven't digested the idea of bowing to someone who's only a year older than me. The same goes with the puffed-up title of Young Master, which I briefly roll around in my mouth before deciding to abandon it.

"It's an honor to finally meet you," I say instead, reaching for a buoyant yet graceful tone. "I'm Goh Haeri."

"Finally?" he says, giving me a quizzical look.

Shoot! Distracted by high society's pompous titles and etiquette, I forgot that Haeri is well acquainted with Bonwhe. Plus, as her grandmother is the personal tailor/stylist of Yi Bonyung, the corporation's president and Bonwhe's grandmother, Haeri has been to various official and unofficial events hosted by the clan over the years.

"I meant to say"—I scramble for a moment—"that it's nice to *finally* introduce myself to you as the new weather presenter."

I consider inserting a pacifying *Young Master,* but the words are caught in my throat. So I coax my facial muscles into

Haeri's lovely smile, but a funny look flits across Bonwhe's eyes, and he searches my face. My heart pounding in my chest, I'm about to look away when his expression goes blank.

"Sure," he says placidly, and takes a step back to usher me in.

I can't help but wonder, did I do something? Or is the young heir just more aloof than I'd imagined? He hasn't smiled once—not even to be polite—nor has he said a word of congratulations regarding my promotion. Still, people can't seem to get enough of him. And I can't say that I'm immune to his charm, either. In a dove-gray suit cut to break your heart, the raven-haired boy is the picture of male beauty. Taken individually, his features are handsome, but on the canvas of his face, they come together as a work of art. Against this level of perfection, the red rose boutonniere on his lapel is a mere afterthought.

"Thank you," I say, stepping into the tearoom cautiously. It's a low-key space meant for casual gatherings over tea and light refreshments. But as I take more of it in, I'm stunned by the opulence. The amount of gold adorning the panels alone is enough to mold a life-sized caribou sculpture. My eyes wander, and as if on cue, a mounted caribou head with a majestic set of antlers appears, staring down at me from the wall.

"It's good to see you, Ms. Haeri," says a figure sitting at the table just below it, and I'm startled. It's the president herself.

Bonwhe's incredible good looks didn't come from nowhere. If his allure is the resplendence of a red rose, his grandmother's is the infinite elegance of a white lily. And her skin? It's hard to fathom that she and my own grandma are the same age. In fact, her face is smoother than those of most people in my town, regardless of age. Just a little perk of not living in a world where the average summer temperature is a balmy 5°F.

What's life like for someone who doesn't have to toil away for ten hours a day at the power plant, or trade in their privacy for comfort and leisure? It's an idea I can't grasp in the moment, and I push it down as I press my hands to my abdomen and tip my torso forward to show my respect.

"It's wonderful to see you, too, Madam President," I return, and as I do, I imagine myself bending to the president to receive my own National Medal of Arts, feeling as though the fantasy has already come true.

With a warm smile, the president gestures for me to join her. When Bonwhe takes the seat on the president's right, I take the seat to her left.

"What kind of tea are you in the mood for today?" the president asks.

I wish I knew. Not that it matters. I doubt I could taste anything in this moment. But I know it would be a huge faux pas to refuse any kind of hospitality offered at the Yibonns', so I tell her, "I'd love some rose tea, please."

To my relief, the tea sommelier appears and begins preparing the order. Rose tea; I wasn't even sure if such a thing existed. Pressed for a response, I made it up, inspired by Bonwhe's rose boutonniere. Lucky for me, there's no request too silly for the Yibonns' tearoom.

The president takes a sip of her own tea and sets it down on the table. "Congratulations on becoming our next weather presenter, the youngest ever," she says.

Then, sliding a blue jewelry box across the table, she sets it in front of me and gestures for me to open it. Curious, I take the box and oblige, to reveal an exquisite brooch. My jaw drops—it's shimmering gold, with a likeness of Snowglobe carved into its center; I've never received such an extravagant gift. I feel terrible admitting it, but all the special birthday cakes Mom indulged us with over the years don't come close to comparing. When she sees this brooch, though, she'll understand.

But no. This gift is for Haeri, so I *won't* be bringing it back home. My heart speeds up and I put the brooch back in its box and close the lid, somehow feeling caught in my lies.

"Thank you, Madam President. I'll cherish it for the rest of my life," I hear myself say. The rest of my life? Haeri only has a year of counterfeit life left.

The president smiles. "It will go well with your shawl," she offers, which I take to mean that I should try it on now. I promptly take out the brooch again and attempt to pin it to my chest, but it's not easy. Watching my fingers fumble repeatedly, the president turns to her grandson.

"Would you, Bonwhe?"

Her grandson shifts his bored gaze to me.

"May I?" he says, and his polite speech barely conceals his annoyance. He looks at me with a gaze that seems to say, *Look at this girl who can't even put on a brooch without help.*

"Yes, please," I answer, trying to contain my embarrassment. "Thank you."

The sommelier appears by my side with the rose tea, perfuming the air around us with its fragrant steam. As the young heir rises from his seat, I scrape my chair back to meet him, but he gestures for me to stay. Then, picking up the brooch with his elegant fingers, he bends to my left shoulder. Without realizing,

I'm gazing off into space while his sweet breath rides on the steam of the rose tea and tickles my face.

The president looks on contentedly, explaining that her go-to gift for a newly inducted weather presenter has always been a tailored suit, but since my grandmother is the world's best suit maker, she decided she needed something different this time.

"That is so thoughtful of you, Madam President," I say, locking my gaze on hers to distract myself from Bonwhe, who's hovering just inches from my chin.

At last, Bonwhe steps back and appraises his work. "That looks pretty good."

Then the doors of the tearoom swing open and everyone's attention is drawn to the parade of guests entering the room. From what I can tell, most of the people are members of the Yi clan, but the face of Yi Bonshim, vice-president of the corporation, jumps out at me.

Though she may *technically* be ready to run the company, the vice-president is frequently mired in controversy, so the current president will likely hang tough until her grandson comes of age.

The most recent gossip about Bonshim is about her and her new boyfriend plotting a lovers' escape to an undisclosed location outside Snowglobe. Today, though, she is waltzing into the tearoom with her husband, a glazed smile on her face, and her arm linked with his in a show of marital harmony.

Her party progresses toward our table, and she directs a cool glance at me before looking away with deliberate disregard. Other people in her company, including her husband, make a point of offering me their congratulations, and despite my hammering heart, no one seems to have the faintest clue that they're talking to a stand-in.

We remain in the tearoom only long enough to greet each other before we're called to the ballroom for the banquet. I take the moment to excuse myself and flee to the restroom for a last-minute checkup and pep talk. This restroom, also glinting with gold, is a Yibonn restroom, all right. But I no longer have the energy to entertain myself with thoughts of life-sized caribou sculptures. Suddenly, I feel warm, heavy, and so incredibly tired. It's as if I'm sinking in quicksand to the core of the earth. Is it the rose tea? Or the lack of sleep? My heart beats not only in my ears, but also in my elbows and knees. Is it my imagination or is my forehead actually getting warmer?

Thankfully, my reflection in the mirror is still picture-perfect Haeri, with Sanghui's artful makeup concealing the creeping fatigue. If anything, my flushed cheeks only seem to emphasize Haeri's youthful exuberance.

Then a funny thought comes to me. What if it were the real Haeri staring back at me from the other side of the glass? Lifting a hand, I slowly extend it to the mirror, expecting its hard, cold surface on my palm. But the glass gives without resistance, swallowing the tip of my index finger.

Gasping, I recoil and stare into the mirror. My own wide eyes stare back at me. I'm not drifting in and out of sleep, am I? This is not good. Not good at all. Then the gilded walls begin to spin dreamily around me. How am I going to keep it together until this party ends at midnight?

THE WEATHERCASTER

till unnaturally warm, I'm able to pull myself together and make my way to the ballroom. As the guest of honor, I'm seated next to Bonwhe at the VIP table on the dais, and I'm helped to my seat just as the president is concluding her celebratory address. She raises her champagne glass, and everyone in the ballroom rises, their glasses in the air for a toast.

I hold my glass up, and the president says, "On the same night when people in the Warring Age celebrated the birth of baby Jesus, we celebrate the rebirth of each one of you as a Snowglobe resident."

Her words slip past me as I skim the tables, and my eyes catch on Yujin at a table below us, her perfect white teeth on display as she smiles with pure delight. I can't help but smile, too, but then she catches me watching her and I reflexively turn my face to one side, only to be confronted by Bonwhe's impassive profile. I glance away, my toes tingling in my shoes.

The president continues, "Now I am happy to introduce today's guest of honor and Snowglobe's new weather presenter—Ms. Goh Haeri."

I rise from my seat to a swelling of applause and curtsy to the sea of new actors below.

"Thank you, Madam President, and congratulations, everyone!" I enthuse to another roll of clapping and hooting. "It's so wonderful to see you all here!"

In Snowglobe, the concept of weather is a bit different. Here, natural meteorological phenomena such as wind, rain, and snow have to be manufactured. This means that the cobalt-blue sky, or sunsets of orange, pink, and purple, are all just a projection onto the glass ceiling above us. It's the weather presenter who draws the weather for everyone, be it a friendly sky or gale-force winds and pelting hail. The daily drawing, which is televised live during the evening news, involves multiple lottery drums, each designated with specific atmospheric conditions, such as temperature, humidity, and wind direction. The role of the weather presenter is to stick their hand into the drums and withdraw one of dozens of tumbling balls from it in order to determine the next day's weather. Needless to say, the process is set up so that the weather generated isn't *too* random. In other words, no snow in July or scorchers in February.

What's truly interesting is that it's the common people living in the open world who are the most eager to see the daily drawing.

Tomorrow's high will be in the low thirties . . .

The allergy season is upon us! Pollen count will remain high tomorrow . . .

It's going to be a great day tomorrow for outdoor enthusiasts . . .

And what do these forecasts have to do with those of us who are locked in the gloom of perpetual winter, one might ask? They inspire hopes and dreams of living in Snowglobe, where we would do all kinds of things and know all kinds of people. And who are we without hope?

Though the weather forecast had always drawn a huge viewership, the status of the weather presenter skyrocketed when Bonyung became president and began implementing changes that would take the enterprise to the next stage of growth.

One such change is the Actor of the Year Award. The winner is announced at the end of each December, then crowned as the upcoming year's weather presenter. This rewards the viewership by letting them see their favorite actor live on TV every day, and also rewards the actor, who is given a permanent Snowglobe residency. Permanent Snowglobe residency is, by far, the best prize any actor could win, as it means their survival no longer depends on ratings. They can stay in Snowglobe for as long as they wish, long after the show reaches its natural end and slips into oblivion.

I realize now just how shrewd the decision was to incorporate the Actor of the Year Award into the annual welcome ceremony. Those actors know that any one of them has the potential to win the jackpot, but seeing Haeri tonight will inspire them not to forget.

I take in the sea of actors below still clapping for me, their faces bright with hope and admiration. And though I know the applause is really for Haeri, I let myself bask in it, smiling from ear to ear.

"Thank you," I respond. "Thank you."

I, Haeri, am the shining symbol of hope in their new lives, and the realization fortifies me. I might be more ready to take on the first act after all.

I survive the formal dinner following the toast without too much trouble, recalling Director Cha's quick course in table manners. What I can't remember, I pick up by furtively copying Bonwhe, at my side. But from the hors d'oeuvres to the desserts, I can't taste a thing. I'm so wiped out that my body feels like it's turning into a lump of molten lead, and as the night continues, I feel more and more sluggish.

When the feast finally concludes, I follow the executive members down from the dais for a casual visit with the new actors. Everyone is anxious to meet the bigwigs, but Bonwhe, in particular, is in high demand. I watch as googly-eyed young women swarm him, jostling for position in the hope of the briefest exchange. The dance party is starting soon, and perhaps one of them will get lucky. Someone taps me on my shoulder and I turn around, only to jump when I see Yujin smiling at me sheepishly.

"Would you mind showing me some steps?" she says. "I learned a few at the training center, but I could totally use a refresher."

I don't know how to turn her away gently. It isn't that Director Cha forgot to prep me for the dance; she tried to teach me some simple steps, in fact, but was defeated by time and my poor skills. Hence, plan B. She told me to make myself scarce during the dance portion of the night by hiding out in one of the bathrooms, but Yujin caught me before I could slip away.

"I'd hate to step on Young Master Bonwhe's feet," Yujin continues. "You know what I mean?" Her eyes grow distant as she gazes at Bonwhe, who's surrounded by hordes of admirers.

Young Master Bonwhe? Who is this girl? Whatever happened to her signature, *Bonwhe, my babe*?

"Of course, I *do* get that comic blunders can spark romance," she goes on, clasping her hands in front of her chest as if in prayer. "But I hate the thought of my own feet scuffing such a perfect piece of art."

I know only too well how she feels about Bonwhe, and I'd help her out if I could, but I'm not the real Haeri. Instead, I grab the first young man I can and press him to her.

"You'll learn faster with a partner," I say, sure that I've found a clever way to get her off my hands. But the guy wraps his arm around the wrong waist—mine. Before I can react, he's pulling me toward him, snatching up my right hand with his left in a dance position, grinning.

"At your service," he says, and begins to lead.

"What? Wait!" I protest lamely. "The music hasn't even started!"

"Perfect time to get in our practice," he counters.

I don't know the first thing about dancing, but I can picture how Haeri would handle herself in my place. Always poised, she would gracefully indulge the bold stranger and begin syncing her steps with his. She might even challenge him by saying something like, "Okay then. Show me what you've got."

So I let him lead me around the floor, my hand clutching his in a death grip. I figure that by maximizing my time in the air between all the sways and glides, I should be able to minimize the chance of stepping on his feet or tripping over my own. Yujin's eyes track my nonsensical steps with intense concentration. When I glance up at my partner, he's wearing a roguish grin.

"Not quite the dancer I thought you were," he remarks. "Trick of the camera?"

My heart jumps, but then I see my chance for escape and seize it. Pressing my lips together in an expression of disapproval, I pause, making sure to plant my heel on top of his left foot. He lets out a sharp cry.

"Please be mindful of the anti-spoiler rule," I say, looking him square in the eyes.

"What?" he breathes, frowning indignantly. "How does that count as a spoiler?" Then he's lifting up the hem of my gown and bending down to inspect my feet. "Do you have gimlets for heels or something?"

My mind flies right out of my body. Before I know it, I'm driving a hard knee up to his chin, forgetting where I am and who I'm supposed to be. There's an audible clack of his teeth snapping together, followed by a keening cry. Yujin looks on, slack-jawed, but thank goodness for the din of the room— everyone else is preoccupied with Bonwhe and Bonshim, who are still making the rounds.

The guy just shoots me a look and hurries off without another word, his ears aflame.

"What the heck?" Yujin says, hurrying to my side. "How did a creep like that even get in here?"

She sticks her tongue out at the guy's disappearing back. Though my heart is pounding, I shrug. "They're just here to cause drama and conflict."

Yujin cocks her head and gives me a long look.

"It's uncanny," she says. "You even *sound* like my friend, the one I was telling you about? Just like her, really."

I give an awkward laugh and follow it with a quip about how smart her friend must be. But the night feels endless, and I'm exhausted; exhausted and hot, too, like I'm burning up.

As more and more people flood out to the dance floor, I pick my way through the well-wishers and admirers and sneak out of the ballroom. I feel like a fire has been stoked inside me, and I'm hurrying down the long, empty hallway toward the bathroom when voices ahead stop me in my tracks.

"Can you believe it?" cries one, and its familiar timbre instantly raises an alarm. "She was so sweet, nuzzling her cheek to my chest—and then *bam!* smashed her spiked heel right into my shoe!"

It's my rude dance partner, who's just turned the corner and is strolling down the hallway toward me with another guy.

"It was purposeful, for sure," he continues. "She probably didn't want to seem easy."

Oh, how I wish I could take my other knee to that chin of his. But I don't need to invite trouble. Not tonight. Clenching my teeth, I dart a quick glance around the hallway. With a wall to my right and a dark hallway blocked with red velvet rope to my left, I have no choice, really. I duck under the rope and flatten my back to the wall, and just as I do, one of my shoes slips off. The darned thing lies on the floor by the brass stanchion. I consider reaching for it, but it's too late. I can't risk being found hiding here like a thief. Holding my breath, I pray that the approaching jerk won't notice it. But of course he does. He stops and picks up the shoe, ponders for a moment, then calls out my name.

I watch his shadow on the floor as it crosses to the rope and suck in a breath, inching sideways along the wall; I'm moving deeper into the unlit hallway when, like a miracle, another hallway opens up. I turn the corner and pick up my pace, jogging down the hall.

"Hey!" I hear behind me. "It's you there, Haeri, isn't it?" The guy's voice recedes as I broaden the distance between us, and the rhythmic clicking of my one shoe rings out like gunshots in the still dark. If I could just lose the guy, these hallways might prove the ideal hideout for the rest of the night. I stop and pry off the other shoe and continue jogging.

A left, a right, then another right. I try to remember all the turns. Despite how tired I am, I'm relieved to note that running on the marble floor is a breeze compared to running in shin-deep snow. My feet bounce off the floor as if on springs. If I were feeling anything like my normal self, I'm sure I could keep running like this for days.

I don't know how long I've been at it when I realize that I can't hear the guy anymore. But better to be safe than sorry. Barely slowing down, I look back over my shoulder. All I see is the murk of the empty hallway stretching into black. I've lost him, I'm pretty sure.

When I face forward again, I'm confronted by a mirror gleaming mere feet away. I stop in my tracks, but not quickly enough. There's not even time to cover my face. Momentum drives me straight into the glass, into my own terror-stricken reflection.

A PIECE OF SECRET

It all happened so quickly. Forget protecting my face, there wasn't even time to close my eyes. I met the mirror head-on, imagining the glass cutting me to ribbons. But the next thing I know, I'm engulfed in absolute darkness, unscathed.

What happened? I wonder. *Did I imagine the mirror?*

My heart still pounding, I reach out into the dark, and the tip of my finger hits what feels like a button. Without thinking, I press it, because that's what buttons are for, right?

There's a sudden jerk, followed by a moment of weightlessness. Then the floor beneath my feet drops, and I'm descending at a terrible speed. Panic shoots through my veins, and I can't even scream. Then, suddenly, it stops, and everything is still again. I'm crouched on the floor, breathless. And when I finally lift my eyes for a slow, terrified glance around, I'm shocked to find that I'm in the same darkened hallway I started in, one shoe clutched in my hand.

Staggering to my feet, I decide to backtrack to the main hallway, only to become aware of a soft, steady vibration traveling across the floor under my feet. I glance down, and I'm mystified all over again to see a hardwood floor. Where is the marble? And why am I freezing all of a sudden? No sooner do I think it than my hair stands on end and my skin prickles with cold. The air has a bite to it, almost as vicious as the open air back home.

I set down the shoe and step into it, lifting my bare foot off the frigid floor to stand on one leg. I know well that in this kind of cold, my feet will stick to the floor in a matter of minutes. And dammit. That jerk has my other shoe.

My mind races. If I managed to blunder my way out of the mansion, where am I now? Wherever I am, I need to find my way out, quick, as I'd be lucky to last five more minutes here in this feathery ball gown.

I can make out the faintest haze of light seeping in at the far end of the hallway, so without hesitating, I spring toward it, furiously rubbing my hands against the flesh of my arms to generate some heat, however insignificant.

"Hello—! Is anyone here?" I call, watching my breath puff out like a cloud into the freezing dark. "Anyone—? Please—?"

I continue toward the light, the cold driving pins into my hands and feet. And when I finally reach the hallway's end, what greets me chills me to the core.

Towering there and ablaze with light is an enormous well of thick glass, inside which a staggering network of wheels—human-powered wheels—whir with motion. It takes me a moment, but I recognize the scene for what it is: power production. It's what I did for ten months after graduating in February.

But while the wheels in my power plant were smooth,

uniform in size, and arranged in concentric rings sprawling from the focal point of the central motor, these wheels, varying in size, have teeth and are fitted together more or less vertically inside a glass well as tall as a five-story building. It's almost like a giant aquarium, if you swapped out the colorful sea creatures in shimmering water with sweaty, bedraggled laborers in grimy uniforms. As I stand there listening to the deep hum of the central motor in disbelief, it hits me. This must be a prison camp.

Snowglobe is populated with fallible humans, after all, so it has a correctional facility where dangerous criminals can be contained and reeducated. Of course, incarceration only happens if the accused is found guilty of an offense punishable by imprisonment.

Miryu had once been caught in the Snowglobe police's dragnet, but was ultimately released because of a lack of evidence. There might be more cameras than people here, but access to unedited footage is strictly limited to directors, so police have to collect witness testimonies and evidence the old-fashioned way.

If this is Snowglobe's correctional facility, though, it looks like it's essentially a power plant—only, the convicted laborers lead an even bleaker existence than free citizens toiling at power plants, if that's even possible.

Another interesting piece of information. Being incarcerated doesn't free an actor from the gaze of cameras. Actually, prison shows are perennially steady performers; so new prison designs are rolled out every once in a while to prevent viewer fatigue. And yet I haven't seen anything like this on television.

"Hello—!" I call out, knocking on the thick glass. It burns my skin on contact, and I pull my hand back. "Help! Let me in, please!"

Never in my life have I wanted to be inside a prison more, but no one even glances my way.

"Help! Please!" I shout, but the collective noise of the gearwheels drowns out my voice. Growing frantic, I try to catch someone's eye, flailing my arms and pounding my fists against the glass. At last, someone looks in my direction. A man with a pink heart-shaped tattoo below his right eye. I try to hold his gaze, but his dull eyes stare straight through me.

"Excuse me!" I cry out to him. "Please—Can you see me?"

He stares off past me. He doesn't even blink. My heart racing, I shuffle along the curved glass wall, trying desperately to edge myself into someone else's line of vision.

"Let me in! I'm freezing to death!"

I'm shivering so hard that my ribs hurt, but my fists have gone numb. I circle the structure, looking for a door, an opening.

"Help—please . . ."

I can feel myself slowing down, my lungs tightening with each intake of the frigid air. Still no one on the other side notices. Then the thought hits me: What happens to Haeri if I die here?

Vanished into thin air: Haeri goes missing at the Yibonn Christmas party!

A headline like that would make the top ten unsolved mysteries of the century. But it would also mean that Director Cha would no longer need to cover up Haeri's tragic end.

Sure, her mysterious disappearance wouldn't make for *closure,* but it just might have to do.

The cold squeezes me. I don't know how much longer I can hold on. The idea of giving in begins to tug at me, just as it did on the night of the storm. It would be so much easier to let go, but I couldn't do it to Mom, Grandma, and Ongi. Their faces rise in my mind, and I have to catch my breath to suppress tears. Frozen tears crusting over eyeballs is a real thing.

Scraping up the last of my strength, I turn around and begin shuffling back down the dark hallway. If I can't join the prisoners, then I need to find my way back to the mansion.

I've taken ten or twenty steps when I notice another mirror propped against a stone wall, glinting in the murk a few feet away.

Normally, I'd have concluded that I was trapped like an animal, and that there was nothing I could do to save myself. But not tonight. Drawing closer, I lift a trembling hand to the mirror, and just like before, my fingertips dip right into its surface. Then I'm stepping into it with my whole body, my eyes clenched shut this time. Where will I end up? Back in the marble hallway inside the mansion? Or somewhere even more hostile than here?

Ahhh . . . Glorious heat envelops me. I open my eyes and find myself in the Yibonn tearoom's gilded bathroom. A cosmic *thank you* on my lips, I lock the door and lie down on the heated marble floor. Spreading my limbs, I roll around on it, turning from my back to my stomach to soak up the warmth, giggling with the simple joy of being alive, giggling like I do when Mom massages my tired calves after a long day at work.

Then the door handle scrapes, and I bolt up. My pulse jumps when another scrape comes. Harder, more impatient this time.

"It's occupied!" I call out, feeling a surge of annoyance.

Did they even knock? I roll my eyes and quickly check myself in the mirror. Not bad. Not bad at all. My disguise is holding up, except for the tiny fissures that have appeared on my lips since their most recent freeze-thaw cycle. I'm reaching for the neat stack of hand towels on the counter when, to my astonishment, the person outside begins pounding at the door.

What in the *world*? Just how badly do they have to go?

"Just a minute, please!" I say sharply, and dab at my forehead and nose with a hand towel.

Then, putting on the most gracious smile I can muster, I unlock the door and swing it open. My heart leaps to my throat. It's Bonwhe standing there, tall, suave, handsome, and looking as stunned as I feel. We stare at each other, speechless.

"What are you doing here?" he says after a moment, his eyes jumping past me to scan the inside of the bathroom.

"I'm—I'm so sorry," I apologize for no clear reason. "I had an urgent need, and all the others had lines and . . ."

He brushes past me and leans in through the doorway as if to inspect everything. Then he turns back to me. "What are you up to here all by yourself?"

He looks and sounds unsettled, and the situation reminds me of Mom standing with her ear pressed to the bathroom door, calling to Grandma, who can't be trusted alone anymore. "What do you mean?" I snap, a sudden outrage rising within me. "What *could* I be doing in a bathroom?"

He draws himself up and stares at me, surprised, and I do my best to hold his gaze, fighting off the image of myself rolling around on this bathroom floor just a minute ago. "And how about you, dude? What are you doing here? The men's room is over that way—"

I raise my chin in the other direction, and that's when my eyes just about pop out of their sockets. This is no tearoom. Behind Bonwhe is a bedroom, complete with a bed fit for an entire royal family, and a leather recliner parked across from it.

"Dude?" Bonwhe echoes, arching his brow.

"What?"

"You just called me *dude*."

"Dude?" I repeat vacantly. Then I realize, I actually did. "I couldn't have, Young Master," I say, laughing. That sounds silly even to my own ears.

Bonwhe draws back, the arch in his brow growing sharper. I let my laugh fade and dip my head to him, then say seriously, "You must please excuse me, Young Master, so you may see to your business in peace."

With that, I step out of the bathroom and cross the room, heading straight for the door, but Bonwhe's brilliant black loafers appear before me, stopping my progress.

"*Please excuse me? See to your business in peace?*" he repeats. "Is that all you have to say after breaking into my bedroom?"

Brows squeezed together in distaste, he peers down at me, and my head begins to throb.

"And what's with the limp?" he asks, shifting his eyes to my feet.

"Oh, that . . ."

Where do I begin and end the tale of the lost shoe?

"To tell you the truth, Young Master, I haven't been feeling so great," I answer instead.

And it's true. I've never felt so out of sorts. Even as I speak, I'm not sure if I'm really *saying* these things or if I'm just *thinking* them. My breath comes increasingly quick and hot. I hurt everywhere, like I've been hit by a truck. And this headache? Sorry not sorry. I can't really care about violating the sanctity of your bedroom. Not the way I'm feeling right now. I need rest. Just a moment's shut-eye, that's all.

I look past him, and my eye catches on that white bed. It's as fluffy as whipped cream. It wants me to lie on it. Now I'm dragging my feet toward the bed like a nail drawn to a magnet.

I only manage a few steps before Bonwhe grabs my arm.

"Whoa. You're burning up!" he says, releasing me a second later. "Are you okay?"

"See? That's what I mean," I murmur. It's all I can manage before pitching forward into the sea of whipped cream. I hear the remaining shoe slip from my foot and drop to the floor with a thud. Then everything goes black.

LOVE AND GRACE

nock, knock—

K My eyes flutter open, but I'm so weak that I can't seem to move.

The two-note knock comes again. I want to call out an answer, but all I can manage is a low rasp.

"I'm coming in, Ms. Haeri," a voice says.

A second later, the door opens and a woman walks in, dressed in an ink-black suit, her hair in a slicked-back bob. She leans over the bed and peers at me.

"Can you tell me who I am, Ms. Haeri?"

Her face does look familiar, though I can't place it.

"I'm Yu Junguhn, Young Master Bonwhe's personal assistant," she says. "Do you remember me?"

It comes to me then. Assistant Yu. She appears in the press rather often, always one step behind the young master, following him like a shadow.

I smile in recognition and nod.

"How do you feel?" she says. "The dance is over and people

are looking for you, Ms. Haeri. Do you think you might be able to try to sit up?"

I nod, and she slides a hand behind my back to prop me up against the headboard with some pillows. I'm feeling depleted, but no longer like I'm about to drop dead.

"How long have I been sleeping?" I say, my voice coming out in a squeak.

"About an hour. Your fever still hasn't broken, though." She places a bed tray on my lap. "Young Master asked me to check on you. He thinks you might have the flu."

She puts a bottle of mineral water and a clear pill container on the tray, then uncaps the bottle herself and hands it to me. "Or maybe you put too much pressure on yourself over tonight's event."

Tell me about it.

"Please take these," she says, unscrewing the pill container and pressing it into my hands. "Young Master himself relies on them when he's under the weather."

I do as I'm told, swallowing all three pills inside the container with a gulp of the fancy water. Assistant Yu removes the tray, and I take a big breath before swinging my legs out to the side of the bed.

"Take your time, Ms. Haeri," she says while consulting her wristwatch. "We still have ten minutes."

Supporting myself on her shoulder, I get to my feet. I'm feeling better, for sure.

"Let me fix your gown," she offers, and begins patting it down here and fluffing it there. When she bends over to fuss with the hem, I do a quick check of the wig on my head. It seems to be holding firm.

In a meek voice, I venture, "I hope Young Master Bonwhe wasn't too troubled by my surprise appearance."

Honestly, I never imagined that the scion would be sending his personal assistant to care for me. Considering the look on his face while confronting me about my trespass, it would have been less surprising if he'd ordered me to be thrown off the Yibonn property, like some kind of plague victim.

"You took him by surprise, for sure," Assistant Yu allows. "No guest has ever presented themselves in Young Master Bonwhe's room, after all."

It amazes me that she keeps referring to him as Young Master Bonwhe. Would it be such an egregious breach of conduct if she called her boss simply by his name, given that she's been caring for him like family since toddlerhood?

"*Presented,*" I say. "Is that the word he used?"

"No," she answers. "What he actually said was that a lunatic, possibly sick with flu, had wandered into his room, and I should see if she needed medical attention."

"A lunatic?" I repeat, my pulse quickening.

Assistant Yu makes a face, perhaps regretting the overly frank divulgence, and ignores my questioning. "I think it's time for us to head down," she says instead, then she produces a pair of glass shoes—my shoes, to be exact—and places them neatly at my feet. I can only blink at them.

"Is everything okay, Ms. Haeri?" she asks.

"Yes, of course," I say before standing up and stepping into them.

As Assistant Yu ushers me out of the room, she says, "If you don't mind my asking . . . How *did* you enter Young Master Bonwhe's room?"

I suck in a breath. I know I can't be totally honest, though I also still don't actually know what happened. "I don't know," I reply. "I was running through a hallway, and then, all of a sudden, I found myself in the bathroom."

"Running through a hallway?" she echoes, her eyes growing sharp. "Why?"

"I had a disagreement with a male guest in the ballroom," I say vaguely. "He wouldn't leave me alone, and I definitely wasn't in the mood to continue engaging with him, so . . ." I let my sentence drift off as Assistant Yu opens a door and leads me down a set of concrete stairs.

"On days like today with lots of guests," she explains, "we close off certain sections of the house. Keeping the hallways dark sends a clear message that they're off-limits, you know?"

I remain quiet, unsure what to say.

"How dare he drive you out of the ballroom and into the hallways," she continues, her voice harder; then, suddenly, she stops her descent and whirls around toward me, her jaw set. "What was his name?"

Despite my high heels and that I'm standing two steps above her, her eyes are level with mine.

"A mere first-year actor prowling around the Yibonn mansion like it's his own?" she presses. "Is he fearless or just stupid?" She's cracking her knuckles as if she's limbering up for a fight.

"I didn't get his name," I say, feeling like a tattletale all of a sudden. "He only followed me into those hallways."

"Regardless," she says firmly, and turns around to resume her descent of the stairwell. "As an ordinary guest, he's certainly not you, Ms. Haeri, though you should refrain from wandering into Young Master Bonwhe's personal quarters again."

I murmur an apology and teeter after her. But I can't help but wonder about this stairwell. At no point in the journey that ended in Bonwhe's room did I encounter stairs. Are the mirrors some kind of cutting-edge elevator? Secret portal? Is the labor prison I discovered connected to the mansion somehow?

"Forgive me." Assistant Yu's voice interrupts my thoughts. She turns back to me, offering her hand for support. "Formal wear can be inconvenient, especially if you're unwell," she says, mistaking my slow pace for trouble walking in my spindly shoes. Her kind gesture warms my heart, and I thank her and take her hand.

I owe Haeri, big-time. Assistant Yu wouldn't treat me with the same level of courtesy if I were just another actor invited to the party. Bonwhe wouldn't think twice about throwing me out if I were just an average person who broke into his room. Haeri has cultivated all this grace and goodwill over years of work. It makes me wonder once more, *Didn't you know, Haeri, that you were adored by everyone? Why did you do it? Why?*

The thought of her saddens me again, but it also strengthens my commitment to giving her a happy ending.

Back in the ballroom, I return to socializing with the other guests and find that I'm almost enjoying myself.

"Hey!" Yujin says, appearing at my side. "Where have you been? I've been looking for you everywhere."

I deliver the line prescribed by Assistant Yu: "Oh, I just needed to check on something for the new job."

Assistant Yu swore me to secrecy regarding my surprise visit to the young master's room. The Yibonns detest gossip.

As the night wears on, I'm inundated by well-wishers. It feels as though every time I turn around, someone new swoops in, delivering congratulations, and I respond to them with a slight variation on my feelings of shock and delight.

After a while, though, I find myself questioning the truth of my words. Was Haeri really shocked or delighted by her new job?

"Tell us more, please!" the people demand, and I feel like a fraud, standing here speaking for Haeri as if I knew anything about how she felt. I know it's what I've come here to do, though, so I reapply the smile and channel the sweetheart.

"Well, I was flooded with gratitude—and love—for all the fans who've been rooting for me." I think that's how *I* would have felt, at least.

Between these exchanges, I catch a glimpse of Bonwhe, who is surrounded by a crowd even thicker than mine. There's the shoe thief, too, staring at me with a puzzled look on his face. Ignoring him, I look to Yujin's table. My best friend is laughing away with her fellow actors. I wish I could hang out with her. I wonder if she got the chance to dance with Bonwhe.

"It's lovely to meet you, Ms. Haeri!" cries a woman, leaning toward me, too close. "Are you ready for the live forecast? How have you been preparing for the new role?"

I glance around at all the people milling about for their turn with Haeri. A clutch of them suddenly double over and dissolve in laughter. People are giddy, enjoying themselves, and if a few edge toward silly, who could blame them? Most of the people have just arrived in Snowglobe, so this is probably the first real party they've ever attended. It's the first party *I've* attended.

"Ms. Haeri?" The woman's voice brings me back. "How are you preparing for the livecast?"

I mumble a quick apology for my drifting thoughts and force my attention back to her. Yeah, the livecast. A new knot forms in my stomach. Up until now, I've only thought about it in the abstract. The truth is, I'm not sure how I'll get through any of this.

The party stretches on for several hours before Director Cha rescues me and escorts me back down the staircase and to the waiting limo. The ride to her house is a blur, and when we finally arrive, I step in through the front door and tumble to the floor.

"Haeri!" Director Cha cries, rushing to my side.

The pressure to perform kept me on my feet, but without the crowds of people, I can no longer stand. The pills Assistant Yu gave me helped, but their effects have gradually worn off, and once again I'm cycling between fever and chills, and my whole body is throbbing in pain. What kind of wretched flu *is* this?

"I'm sorry. I should have given you the shots first," Director Cha says, draping my arm across the back of her neck and picking me up. She carries me to the sofa and lays me down, then throws a blanket over me and disappears into another room. When she finally returns, she has a small tray of syringes and vials.

"Is it the flu?" I croak, watching her stick the needle into a vial's rubber top and drawing its clear liquid into the syringe.

"Yes. Flu and cold," she says flatly, tapping the syringe and making the air inside bubble to the top. There's a tickle in my throat, and I sneeze violently. Flu and cold. My experience with both has been limited to what I've seen on TV.

In science, we learned that flu and cold had been some of the most common viral diseases of the Warring Age. When the climate changed and Earth turned into an unyielding ball of ice, however, the viruses died off—alongside billions of other life-forms on the planet. But inside Snowglobe, the climate-controlled enclosure preserved those viruses, and I, of course, have no immunity.

"I dropped the ball in all the chaos," Director Cha says. "Immunization is a requirement for everyone entering Snowglobe. I'd actually secured your shots before you came, but completely forgot about them."

I nod sympathetically. As far as I know, this is her first time bringing in a stand-in from the open world. It's easy to see how a few details might escape her.

She takes an alcohol pad and wipes a patch of my shoulder. The cold against my skin makes me shiver again. Back home, I used to watch with morbid fascination when a doctor or nurse administered shots to actors on TV. Now it's my turn.

"Have you done this before, Director Cha?" I ask, feeling uneasy all of a sudden.

She jabs me with the needle. The initial prick is startling, but the real pain comes when she pushes down on the plunger, forcing the medicine into my flesh, and I let out a small cry.

"Hold still for one more," she says. And, stabbing me with the second needle, she adds, "Come hell or high water, you need to be better by tomorrow morning. It's the championship."

I realize that she's right. I hadn't thought about it, but tomorrow is Christmas, and the day of the annual biathlon championship game. The championship is, by far, the most anticipated sporting event of the year, both inside and outside Snowglobe, and therefore, competition for tickets is almost as intense as the event itself. But Haeri, as the newly crowned weather presenter, has been invited by the Yibonns to attend the game with her family.

"There are people whose lifetime dream is to attend the game in person," Director Cha says.

I myself have hoped to be a spectator, at least once before I die.

"Of course, Director Cha," I say, eager to please. "I'll do my best to recover."

She lets go of my arm as a wave of relief washes over me and my eyelids grow so heavy that I can barely hold them up. The feathery ball gown I'm wearing begins to feel like the warm, soft underside of a mother bird's wing. Director Cha pulls the blanket up over me.

"Good night, Haeri," she whispers. Then the light goes off.

Haeri. I wish she would stop calling me by that name when there are no cameras around. It makes my heart clench with sadness every time I'm reminded why I'm here. But I'll push that away for now. Right now, I need to rest, so I let myself drift into the only realm where I can still exist just as I am.

A HAPPY ENDING?

"Haeri." A voice breaks into my consciousness. Then, a few moments later, "Ms. Goh Haeri." It's the same voice, louder now. "Rise and shine."

I twitch my eyes open to see Director Cha leaning over me. Is it morning already? It feels like I just drifted off a minute ago.

"How did you sleep?" she says, opening the shades and letting light flood into the room. I shield my eyes with my hand, blinking as I gaze out the windows at the brilliant blue sky. In an upset for everyone who wanted a white Christmas, Fran Crown, the outgoing weather presenter, ended up drawing an incredible bluebird day. To *me,* this weather is the real Christmas miracle.

In the open world, the year-round pewter sky alternates between spitting and dumping snow. I've never once woken up to a sky so crisp and blue—just looking at it feels therapeutic.

It's true that a snowy day would be the most appropriate backdrop for the championship game, but a sunny day means more clarity on all the drama playing out across the athletes' faces as they labor toward the finish line.

"Did they overdo the brilliance or what?" Director Cha says, frowning up at the sky.

Whether a heartbreaking azure or flaming ruby, the sky in Snowglobe is just an image displayed on a screen on the glass dome, after all.

No matter. I prop myself up on an elbow and allow myself to enjoy the simulated blue sky. What's the value of reality, anyway, if it's always gloomy?

My nose is stuffy, but the headache, fever, and body aches are basically gone, and I feel human again. I'm reclining on the sofa, stretching out my arms and legs and marveling at the efficacy of Snowglobe medicine, when Director Cha holds out a familiar gold envelope. My pulse jumps.

"I opened it by mistake. I'm sorry," she says, without even trying to affect the sentiment. Her tone is rather cool. "Why didn't you tell me that your friend made this year's crop of actors?"

I push up from the sofa, suddenly hearing the blood coursing in my ears. I don't want to show her how shaken up I am, but my fingers quiver as I take the envelope.

"So you saw her at the party?" she says with a tight smile. "Shin Yujin, right? Did she recognize you?"

"Not at all," I deny, perhaps too fiercely. "We didn't even get to talk much. There were too many people waiting to meet me."

She regards me for a moment.

"I must have been in a real hurry to overlook that kind

of detail," she says finally, easing herself onto a stool by the coffee table. "With your home settlement being such a desert for talent, it didn't occur to me to check whether anyone you knew was here. My mistake."

And leaving Yujin's letter in my backpack was *my* mistake. A big mistake. "I didn't think you'd be going through my stuff." I toss the envelope carelessly on the coffee table as if it's nothing of importance to me. "Yujin probably wrote to all her classmates. She's the sort of girl who wants to be friends with everyone, you know?"

"Maybe," Director Cha allows. "But the standard gold envelope is something of a precious commodity. Newcomers at the training center only get two each."

The knot in my stomach tightens. "Yujin didn't recognize me," I say.

Director Cha doesn't bother to acknowledge this. Tossing me a change of clothes instead, she says, "Jeon Chobahm's luggage will remain under my care."

Outside the bay window of the sunstruck dining room, a panoptic view of the city unfurls, its lake sparkling cerulean under the bluest Christmas sky. All is bright, all is quiet, as if in cruel contrast to the black storm whirling inside me. The ten-seater table is set for one with a bowl of breakfast porridge and a tiny saucer of pills. I also see Yujin's brownies, roughed up during their journey, sitting battered on a plate off on one end of the table, alongside the orange juice.

"Get some food in your stomach so you can take the pills," Director Cha says.

I slide into the seat set with the bowl of porridge, but I need to say something before I can eat.

"Leave Yujin alone. Please," I say, surprising myself with the grim authority of my own voice.

"*What?*" says Director Cha.

"If Yujin ended up like Cooper, I wouldn't be able to keep smiling like Haeri," I say, looking at her fully in the face.

Director Cha's amber eyes flash with irritation, and she laughs unpleasantly. "Oh, this is rich," she says. "Are you threatening me? I'm impressed!"

I don't answer, holding her gaze with mine. She needs me. That's the bottom line. And if that's all I have over her, I'm going to leverage it, threat or not.

"I respect that you refuse to act like a weepy little puppy," she continues, her tone changing. "And you know what else?" A pause. "Your attitude makes me think we'll get along even better than I imagined."

She sounds genuinely happy now. I just stare at her, unsure of how to take it.

"We'll let Yujin be," she says, raising her coffee mug to her mouth. "For now."

For now?

"I need you to promise me," I say, even though I know I'm pushing it.

She fixes me with her tiger eyes over the brim of her mug. I want to look away, but I dig my nails into my skin and hold her gaze instead.

"If you keep on acting like Jeon Chobahm, I have no choice but to eliminate what makes you Jeon Chobahm. Do I make myself clear?"

"I'm doing my best," I tell her. "And I did yesterday, too, even while I was deathly ill."

"I know you did," she allows. "Do you regret it?"

Do I regret it?

"No," I say after a moment. "It's just—" I begin, helplessness washing over me. Director Cha leans forward, staring at me expectantly, but I don't know where to go from here.

It was reckless of me to rush headlong into this. That much is clear to me now. But even if I could go back in time knowing what I know now, would I make a different choice? Turn down the chance of a lifetime? I'm not sure.

You help me, then I help you.

There are two sides to everything, and I can choose to focus on the bright side of this, too. It is for the best, after all, to give Haeri the happy ending she deserves while sparing the world the trauma of her death.

"For crying out loud." Director Cha mutters bitterly. She lifts her face to the ceiling and squeezes her eyes shut for a moment before opening them again.

"Why can't these girls just be grateful for the cushy life that's been handed to them?" she says, her voice tight with frustration. Dropping her eyes to me, she continues, "Did you notice the way people looked at you at the party? And don't tell me you didn't like it; you have what everybody *wishes* they had. Superior genes, fame and fortune, the power to determine the weather, and let's not forget—the privilege of being able to live out your life in Snowglobe!" She pauses to gather her breath. "Think about it. No, really. Think about it. You are one of the luckiest humans on the planet."

I think of the thunderous applause swelling in the ballroom

for me last night, and of all the faces watching me on the dais, lit up with hope and admiration. A sudden shiver runs up my spine and I slump forward with a whimper.

"What now?" Director Cha sighs. "Are you still feeling sick?"

"No," I murmur.

Her speech has activated something far more potent than a cold or flu. It's activated a craving. A powerful craving for the best year of my life, which, as she reminds me, is here for the taking.

"Is it really okay for me to seize this luck," I ask, "when it came to me because Haeri died?"

Using the word *luck* in the same sentence as Haeri's death feels wrong, which is probably why I'm reaching out for further affirmation, exoneration. Director Cha rubs her temples with a pained look on her face, as if I'd just toppled a tower she'd painstakingly erected.

"Tell me," she sighs. "Why on earth do you insist on attaching guilt to her death? Is it because you're not dead yourself? I'm asking because I really don't get it."

Does she have a point? I didn't cause Haeri's death, that's for sure.

"It feels like I'm taking advantage of everything she earned," I say. "Her fame, popularity, the dream job. She achieved it all, not me—"

"Who achieved what, did you say?" She cuts me off, her voice shrill with incredulity. A sudden rage glints across her eyes, scorching me, and she shouts, "It's *me* who achieved all that! Without me, she wouldn't exist! And without my grandfather, Goh Maeryung wouldn't have existed, either, which means we wouldn't need to discuss her dead granddaughter! No actor makes it big without a brilliant director behind them!"

Shaking her head in bitter disgust, she pushes out of her chair and begins pacing the room. Her frustration is profound, like an early scientist trying to convince an ignorant audience that the earth is round, not flat. I can't say she's wrong, either. Take the book report assignment at school. Everyone is assigned the same book, yet reports vary, depending on what element of the plot or character each student decides to focus on.

Suddenly, she spins around and faces me.

"I gave my all—my *all*—to nurture her into someone who deserves the permanent residency. How do you think I felt when my life's work disappeared overnight?" she demands, her voice shot through with fury.

I feel bad for her, but I don't know what to say.

"That *foolish* girl," she goes on. "Pluck a star out of the sky and put it in her hand, and she'd whine about how the sharp points hurt her. Unrestrained self-pity. Ungratefulness to the extreme. Unbearable happiness. That's what she died of. She drowned herself in it. Don't you make the same mistake."

Her flaming eyes stare right into the depths of me, and I feel very, very small. But I have to know. My voice shrunk to nothing, I ask, "Do people really choose death over too much happiness?"

In all my years of TV watching, I've never seen anyone kill themselves because they were too happy. Director Cha lets out a nasty laugh. "Do you know why Cooper's show was such a hit?"

I shake my head, not because I don't have a theory, but because I'd hate for it to be the wrong one.

"It's because people recognized their own weaknesses in him. Cooper was an indomitable biathlete with five consecutive world championships, but he couldn't stop crying over the blood on his hands. Humans are very good at that—finding something to be miserable about, even in absolute happiness." She pauses to let that hang in the air for a moment. "Spoiled as she was, the girl sought out misery. It didn't matter what I told her. And you—you're acting just like her. *Foolish!*" She is shouting again, shooting me another blistering look of disgust. "Wringing your hands over imagined guilt when you have the opportunity to turn your whole life around?"

I hang my head, unsure of how to feel anymore. With a withering sigh, Director Cha plops back down in her seat and sits in silence.

"Sorry, that was long-winded," she finally says, her voice softer. "Your porridge must be cold."

"That's okay," I murmur.

"Then eat up, so you can take the medicine. Let's get that flu out of your way."

I take a spoonful of the glutinous porridge and bring it to my mouth.

"Sanghui will see to your makeup herself, at least until the frostbite heals. Be careful not to run into your other relatives without your face on."

"But aren't there cameras all over the house?"

"I'll edit out anything that's problematic."

"So it's true that no one else has access to the raw footage—"

"Since when did our sweet Haeri become so interested

in the ins and outs of directing?" she says, shutting me up. Becoming a director is Jeon Chobahm's dream, not Haeri's.

With a pleased smile, she slides a small pink tub to me across the table. "Frostbite cream. This one's prescription-strength. Apply it twice a day to a clean face," she says. Then, as if it's an incantation, she adds, "You'll be as good as new in three days' time."

SEEKER OF MISERY

poiled as she was, the girl sought out misery. I turn over the remark in my head, gazing at the scenery gliding past the limousine window. The streets of downtown Snowglobe are all decked out for Christmas. As hard to fathom as it is, could Haeri have grown sick of this town, like I have of my own? Yes, she had the option of leaving at eighteen, but for what alternative? For a life shackled to a human hamster wheel? I can see how she might have succumbed to despair. Still, is it reason enough to end your life?

Soon the car slows to a stop in front of a house I know well. We've arrived at Haeri's home. I pay the driver, who is still dizzy with the fact that the next weather presenter is in her cab, and open the door to get out.

"Have a lovely Christmas, Ms. Haeri," she says, stars in her eyes.

I wish her the same, and she gives me a melancholy smile and says, "Thanks. But it's just another day for me."

I recognize the actor. She's had a lot of bit roles, but despite a seven-year career, she has yet to land even a minor repeat role in a single program. How does one survive in Snowglobe for that long with so little to show for it? Her appearances are always brief, but they're also memorable, and even significant at times. When people see someone like Haeri or Cooper riding in her cab, they notice it.

Creditable bit-role actors such as her and thousands of others are called the *licorice,* as in sweet essentials. Be they taxi drivers, baristas, or janitors, these actors provide necessary context and texture to their show's backdrop while also moving the story forward, however tiny their parts. I once read in *TV Guide* that the licorice are cast at the director's conference. Once their names make it onto the cast list of a show that will air in the upcoming season, their stay in Snowglobe is guaranteed for its length. All things considered, it might be these actors who are the truly lucky ones.

The cabdriver glances into the rearview mirror and says, "I thought I was finally getting the day off this year, but then I got called in at the last minute. You're already my fourth rider today, Ms. Haeri."

It's precisely this kind of relatability that endears her to the viewers.

"That must have been a bummer," I sympathize. "What were your plans today before the call?"

"Oh, nothing special," she says with a shy laugh, but a twinkle comes to her eyes. "I was just going to relax with the biathlon championship on TV. Eat a few tangerines, maybe."

But for the part about the tangerines, her holiday plan sounds familiar. I guess the lifestyle of the working class is the same whether you live inside or outside Snowglobe.

"I hope you'll get off work before the championship starts!" I say in a brighter tone.

"I hope so, too, Ms. Haeri," she says, smiling again, then adds, "Enjoy your special day! Happy"—her smile falters and she quickly corrects herself—"*Merry* Christmas!"

Taking a deep breath, I climb out of the cab and shut the door; then I turn to face Haeri's home—a two-story redbrick structure encircled by a fenced-in lawn. There's a donut-shaped ornament of evergreen branches and belled ribbons hanging on its front door. *A wreath,* memory supplies. I open the gate and cross the lawn still patched with last night's snow, and climb the front steps. Another deep breath, and I finally push open the door.

"Hi! I'm home!"

Goh Rhim, who was crossing the living room, sashays over and gives my arm a friendly jab. "Where have *you* been all night?"

Rhim, the younger of the aunts, is the second-most-popular member of the Goh clan. She spends her life clubbing and is twice divorced at just twenty-four. It's past midmorning, but Rhim still has bedhead and wears an oversized sleep shirt that comes down to her thighs. What really impresses me, though, is that she can hang out comfortably in a T-shirt even though it's the dead of winter.

"The cab took me to Director Cha's after the party, so I just spent the night there."

"What about the afterparty? You didn't go out with the newbies?" Rhim says, sounding disappointed.

"Do I hear my puppy?" Maeryung sings as she walks out

of the kitchen, wearing oven mitts. "Director Cha called me last night. She told me you'd already passed out on her sofa."

The two must have coordinated their stories already. "Are you ready to eat?" she asks with a smile. "You must be hungry."

"Not really, Grandma," I say, surprising myself again. "I had brunch at Director Cha's."

"Oh, good. Why don't you go upstairs and take a shower, then? Grandma's baking her signature brownies for you."

Brownies. In my resolve to remove all traces of Jeon Cho-bahm in me, I pretended not to see Yujin's brownies at Director Cha's. Ultimately, Director Cha swept the treats into the trash in front of me, with a rich smile on her face.

"Yes! I love brownies!" I say enthusiastically, heading for the stairs. I put on a big smile for the camera over the banister. I'm well aware that they're everywhere, these cameras, hiding in our clock, fish tank, piano, family portrait. They're in the fences, picnic tables, trees, and in thousands of other places. I climb the stairs with my smile plastered on, and just as I get to the second floor, I hear Maeryung call out, "Sanghui! Your daughter's home!"

Sanghui walks into the bathroom, where I'm waiting, and glances up at the camera on the far wall. For obvious reasons, the bathrooms in Snowglobe are designed with privacy features, such as chest-high walls around the toilet and opaque glass panels in the shower.

Why not have camera-free bathrooms? Because actors

who have had enough might hide in them to ugly-cry, or otherwise vent their outrage, despair, and misery in private; and there's no fun in that. And though many still curl up in a ball and sob behind these privacy features, viewers still retain some access to the actors' internal turmoil, and that's all that really matters.

"Director Cha says not to worry about the cameras during makeup," I say to Sanghui. "She says she'll edit it out."

Sanghui doesn't acknowledge this.

"Remove your own makeup," she says coldly, and gestures toward the bottles and tubes of cleansing products on the vanity.

I begin working on my face, consulting the instructions on the back of each product. After a few minutes, my bare, blotchy skin begins to emerge.

"I'll be back in ten minutes," she says. "Be done showering by then." Then she walks out of the bathroom, slamming the door behind her.

It's a long while after I finish showering when she returns, her face as hard and cold as when she left.

"What's the greasy stuff on your face?" she spits, looking me over with distaste.

"It's the frostbite cream that Director Cha gave me," I say, but she ignores this, too, roughly setting her makeup box down on the counter.

She grabs a purple jar and scoops out its contents with a finger. But when she brings the finger to my face, something seems to overtake her, and she begins to wheeze.

"Would you like me to do it?" I offer hesitantly.

Her eyes snap to me with the strength of five hundred daggers.

"I—I just want to make it easier for you," I add in an even smaller voice.

"What?" she wheezes.

Maybe I should have kept my mouth shut and just let her work through her feelings. But it's too late now. So I try again: "I understand how painful it must be for you to see me here—"

A loud clatter cuts off my words. The purple jar hits the floor and rolls away, pitching half of its creamy contents on the tiles. The next thing I know, Sanghui is crouched over her feet, head clasped in her hands, shaking and wheezing.

"Are you okay?" I gasp, crouching down on my knees beside her. I don't even realize that my hand is on her shoulder when she shrieks, "Don't touch me!"

I pull back immediately, murmuring an apology, and she hisses, "Get away from me. You make my skin crawl."

You make my skin crawl. The words cut through me. No one's ever spoken to me like that before. But I understand how she feels, I do.

She's rubbing her chest, struggling to draw a full breath as I stand there awkwardly. I could be cleaning up the mess on the floor, but I'm afraid anything I do now would only provoke her further.

"Why?" she chokes out between ragged breaths. "Why can't you just die when you're dead?"

She gives me a look that chills me, her face contorted with hatred and resentment. I don't know what to say, or what is even happening.

The door swings open and Maeryung walks in, immediately sucking in a sharp breath at what she sees. Hurriedly, she closes the door and swings back around to take in the scene, her eyes jumping from me, to Sanghui, to the purple jar on the floor. In the next moment, she's on me, jerking me around by the shoulder. Her long, fussed-over fingernails dig into my skin.

"What is it now? What did you do this time?" she shouts in an angry whisper. "What awful thing did you do to break your mother's heart?"

Sanghui bursts into tears and howls, "Mother, why did you have me? Why did you have me only to give me this miserable life?"

Maeryung releases me and goes to her daughter.

"Shhh. Sanghui, sweetie," she whispers, gathering her daughter in her arms. "You can't do this now. Rhim's downstairs."

My shoulder throbs from Maeryung's taloned raking. But it's nothing next to the chilling drama playing before my eyes.

"Be strong, sweetie," Maeryung says, gently rocking Sanghui in her arms. "Show your daughter how strong you are. That's what a mother does."

But this only seems to enrage Sanghui.

"*Her!* How is she my daughter?" she wails, pushing her mother away. "There was no such thing as my daughter to begin with, and you—"

Maeryung seizes Sanghui's head and shoves it back into her bosom, stifling the rest of her sentence. Then she glances at me sharply. "Go to your room and Grandma will do your makeup there. Close the door and wait for me. *Sweetie.*"

Thoroughly shaken, I stagger to my room, wondering what Director Cha will make of all this. The sound of someone humming floats up the stairs. I glance over the railing to see Rhim sitting on the sofa with headphones on, painting her nails without a care in the world.

Inside my room, golden rays spill in through the window slats and stripe the lime-green walls. A lovely April day. That's what Haeri's room is even on Christmas, even as black gloom churns inside me. I feel hollowed out. Did Maeryung shake out my soul when she thrashed me like a doll?

Never have I witnessed a grown-up crying out loud, and with such abandon. Not in real life. On Dad's memorial day every year, I see Mom dry silent tears with the back of her hand, but completely letting go like Sanghui did just now? Never. I didn't know adults *could* cry like that, and the discovery is terrifying. And how about the things she said?

Why can't you just die when you're dead?

There was no such thing as my daughter to begin with.

Her chilling words ringing in my ears, I have a terrible thought. Is Sanghui grieving her daughter, or is she upset about something else? For some reason, my mind throws up a show I caught on TV once, about moms who'd been driven mad by postpartum depression and loathed their own babies.

A ROOM OF MY OWN

With a cautious click, the door eases open and I look up. Maeryung walks in, a scowl on her face and Sanghui's makeup box in one hand.

"Didn't I tell you to lock the door?" she says. "What if your aunt walked in?"

Her voice is hushed, but it might as well be a thunder roll for the scare it puts into me. Who knows when she'll erupt again?

"Don't be caught without makeup until your face heals. Not even at home," she says, echoing Director Cha.

She sits me down before the vanity and grabs a stool for herself, then goes to work on my face with a practiced hand. I'm dying to know what's going on between Haeri and her mom, but I know better than to ask.

After a little while, she steps back to evaluate her work and tells me as if in passing, "Forget everything your mom said when she was upset." Then she affectionately tousles the long, silky hair of my wig and says, "Your hair's going to be in a cute bob, starting tomorrow."

Nothing else for it, I murmur my acquiescence, and she gives a rueful sigh.

"You know, sweetie—" she begins, looking at me in the mirror. "You can't assume that no one is watching just because there's no one watching."

The forced smile on her face makes me look away, and I almost stare directly into the side camera. "I'll be careful, Grandma," I say, darting my eyes back to the mirror and trying for a smile myself. I realize then that I'm no longer startled by Haeri's face staring back at me.

"The brownies!" Maeryung cries all of a sudden, startling me. She kisses the crown of my head and rushes off, leaving my scalp to prickle unpleasantly under the wig where her lips touched.

Off to one side of the white vanity is a matching white-framed bed with a bookcase headboard, on which five stuffed animals rest in a neat row. Being a loyal fan and a student of the show, I'm familiar with its various camera angles. And if memory serves, the menagerie conceals a camera or two.

"How was your Christmas Eve?" I find myself saying as I pet the stuffed animals one by one, just like Haeri used to. It isn't long before I notice a pinhole camera hiding in the white tiger's left eye, and another in the right eye of its moon bear friend. I try picking up the tiger, but it's glued to the shelf, probably concealing the port on its butt snaking with cables.

Here it's worth noting that the electricity feeding all these cameras doesn't come from the power produced by those outside Snowglobe. Any power used for the production and transmission of programming comes from Snowglobe's Central

Power Plant, the sole surviving nuclear reactor from the Warring Age. The only reason this relic, despite toxic waste and potentially devastating accidents, is kept alive today—under stringent and rigorous management of the Yibonns, of course—is its irrefutable reliability, which ensures uninterrupted services.

Every once in a while the opinion gets resurrected in the fringes, that nuclear energy should be readopted to free up the masses from the oppression of the hamster wheels. But humanity is not taking that risk. Not again. And why should we when the world teems with people capable of producing safe and clean energy just by the sweat of their brows? And how else would all these people make a living in this frozen world if we got rid of the power plants?

I glance around the room, becoming conscious again of the cameras hiding everywhere: in the vanity mirror, the wardrobe, the wall clock, and the list goes on. I let out a long breath, suddenly feeling like I'm in jail.

With my face all made up, though, I'm expected to jump back into the role, so I get up and go to the walk-in closet and open the door. Haeri's enormous collection of clothes and accessories greets me, lifting my mood, at least for the moment.

"What should I wear today?" I hear myself say, channeling Haeri again. I might as well do it up.

Jeon Chobahm wears the same drab parka and boots every day of the year. But Haeri? She never wears the same outfit twice. I begin browsing the massive collection, feeling increasingly overwhelmed by the options. In the end, I settle on a safe, everyday turtleneck-and-jeans combo—more my taste than Haeri's, really—and head to the changing room.

The changing room, an L-shaped space in which privacy

walls come up to the neck, is where child actors get dressed. Adult actors can change anywhere they please.

The tension in my body begins to release as soon as I step around the partition with the outfit. Can I just sit here and zone out for five minutes? For all its outward comfort and abundance, Haeri's life is no picnic, and the thought pins me inside the changing room.

"Sweetie!" Maeryung's voice travels from the bottom of the stairs, jolting me back to awareness. "The brownies are nice and warm! Come and get 'em!"

"On my way, Grandma!" I call back.

A brownie is something I can find the energy for.

Jeans and sweater on, I head downstairs and follow the scent of chocolate to the kitchen. Maeryung gestures toward the platter stacked with brownies sitting on the table, and I select a perfect warm square and bite into it, making my eyes huge in a show of delight, à la Haeri.

"Oh my god, Grandma," I gush. "These are so good!" I give Maeryung a thumbs-up as she gazes at me with a loving smile painted on her face. Indeed, the treat of all treats that I finally, finally get to taste *is* to die for. But then the image of Sanghui sobbing on the bathroom floor pops into my mind again, and my throat tightens.

As though Maeryung senses my loss of appetite, she places her hand on mine and says, "Just have a little taste for now, sweetie. We're going to have lunch when your aunt and uncle come home."

I smile back, thankful for the out, and just as I'm placing the brownie back on the platter, the front door opens. I hear it close, and Shihwang, the older of the aunts, strides into the kitchen with a bag of kelp. She puts it down on the counter with great ceremony. "I had to go to five different stores to get it. No one's open on Christmas, you know." She playfully flicks her eyes to Sanghui sitting at the far side of the table and turns to me. "Your mother spaced out on the key ingredient."

At thirty-two years old, Shihwang is the polar opposite of Rhim in every way. While Rhim would come home drunk at some ungodly hour, belting out a tune for the whole of the neighborhood to hear, Shihwang won't hesitate to shut her up with a swift kick to the rear.

"Hey, what are you eating?" Rhim asks as Wooyo, the youngest of the clan, wanders into the kitchen, sucking on what remains of an ice pop.

"Melon pop," Wooyo replies, finishing it off and tossing the flat wooden stick into the trash. "It's a new flavor," he adds, then turns to me with a grin. "Sorry, niece. I didn't get you one—it would have turned into a puddle by the time we got home."

I smile back at him the best I can. These people are Haeri's family, and the terror of being discovered paralyzes me.

"How about me?" Rhim protests.

"I've got news for you, Rhim," Wooyo replies. "The river of love only flows downward." Then he snatches the half-eaten brownie from her hand, popping it into his mouth.

Sanghui turns to me with a faint smile on her face. "I'm going to get started on your miyeok soup."

And though I know she's just acting, it's chilling that she can fake our relationship just an hour after what went down in the bathroom.

"Wait a minute." Rhim starts again. "If the river of love

143

flows downward, shouldn't Haeri be looking after Wooyo?" Then she giggles at her own dig, glancing gleefully back and forth between Wooyo and me.

Uncle Wooyo is two months younger than Haeri, after all.

"Haeri is already busy enough looking after her immature aunt," Wooyo returns.

"What?" Rhim yelps, moving to poke him in the head with her knuckles. "You little brat! Have you ever been married? Gotten a divorce? Talk to me again when you have some life experience!"

Wooyo swiftly ducks behind me, and Rhim swings her leg around to give him a kick, which he deflects with his human shield, me. The two of them continue going at each other with escalating excitement: Rhim snatching at Wooyo and Wooyo dodging her attacks by steering me this way and that in front of him. Then Wooyo accidentally swings me by the hair, hard enough to make my head snap back, wig and all, and the image of my shorn head flashes before me.

"Stop!" I scream, clutching at the wig with both hands. "Jesus! Not my hair!"

Wooyo immediately steps back, holding his palms in the air in a gesture of apology.

"I'm sorry—are you okay?" he says, concerned, but stunned, too. It's not like Haeri to react this way. Rhim and Shihwang also stare at me wide-eyed.

Maeryung tut-tuts loudly from the sink where she's helping Sanghui with lunch prep.

"What kind of aunt and uncle are you?" she chides. "Do you need to be getting into monkey business today? Of all days?"

Rhim and Wooyo glance at me apologetically. Christmas is an extra-special day for Haeri.

Maeryung sets a bowl of miyeok soup before me.

"Happy birthday, Puppy," she says, and kisses my cheek, once again setting off an unpleasant prickle all the way up the side of my face to the top of my head. I thank her with the sweetest smile I can muster.

Today is Christmas, which is Haeri's birthday. Her family is gathered around the table for a special lunch, trading stories and jabs.

"What? You're still only seventeen?" Rhim says in mock frustration. "When will we get to go clubbing together?"

"What do you mean, *still*?" Shihwang says. "*Already* is more like it. It feels like yesterday when I carried her around on my back."

Wooyo pounces. "Rhim never carried us around on her back, so she can't have those nostalgic feelings."

"You're cruising for it, little bro," Rhim says with a sour laugh. "I'll carry you around on my back now, if that's what you want. Just so I can slam you on the ground, judo style."

Lunch continues with Haeri's aunts and uncle hamming it up for the cameras, and soon enough, it's over. Though I'm careful to stay in character, it feels odd to be celebrating my birthday without the special cake my mother always orders for me. Of course, I would be eating it in my freezing house. Here, it's warm, but Haeri gets no cake or presents, which is what she prefers.

Today is not only Christmas and Haeri's birthday, but it's also her dad's memorial day. He was killed in a car accident on his way to meet baby Haeri at the hospital where Sanghui had just given birth. Needless to say, this tragedy, being a Snowglobe affair, was broadcast to the world.

Haeri was ten when she finally learned the details of her father's death. On her thirteenth birthday, she announced that she wanted to celebrate the day quietly, without cake or gifts or any other fuss. Because it's Christmas, people still show up with gifts, but Haeri's birthday celebration with her family stays low-key.

Come to think of it, no one at the Christmas banquet last night wished me happy birthday. The cabdriver almost slipped, but she caught herself in time.

Sanghui strokes my back affectionately. "I'm sure your dad is celebrating your birthday somewhere, too," she says with a sad smile, and I snatch a look at her.

By the time Haeri was born, Sanghui and Haeri's father had already gone their separate ways. Sadly, Sanghui was far from over him, and his tragic death plunged her into a grief so impenetrable that it kept her from bonding with her baby for a long time. And each passing year, the baby looked more and more like her dad, the only man Sanghui had ever loved. I can't help but wonder, why can't she love her, too?

I close my eyes and steeple my hands in front of my face. I think of the birthday girl who, in just a year's time, will turn eighteen, then make the staggering announcement that she's planning to leave Snowglobe. Though she might have prayed for her dad today, I pray for her. I pray that she's found peace.

And before I open my eyes, I say a prayer for the ones I love: *Happy birthday to you, too, Jeon Ongi and Chobahm.*

I picture my twin brother in front of our fancy birthday cake, just like any other year. Mom and Grandma are smiling beside him, their faces aglow in the dancing light of the candles, which Ongi is about to blow out alone, without me, for the first time in our lives. Feeling a smile bloom on my face, I finally open my eyes and look around the table, at each of the faces beaming at me.

"Thank you for the birthday wishes, everyone!"

"Here we go, on our way to witness Priya's two consecutive wins!" Rhim declares, her voice high with merriment. Everyone's getting ready for the championship.

Priya Maravan, Rhim's favorite biathlete, is the defending champion whose victory is assumed.

"I don't know, Aunt Rhim. I think Chun Sahyun will win," I assert, trotting out the name of Haeri's favorite, who happens to be mine as well.

Wooyo is pondering the gift-wrapped boxes piled high under the Christmas tree.

"I guess we're opening presents when we get back, then," he says after a moment.

Christmas wouldn't be Christmas without presents heaped under the tree. Rhim claps her hands like a schoolgirl. "Yes! Nothing like opening presents while watching championship reruns!"

It's then that the light dims, and then all at once, dozens of vividly bright beams of light slice the air and begin sweeping the living room. The beams are shooting out of various objects in the house from the cameras concealed in them, crisscrossing everything and everyone in their paths. A few more seconds pass, and there's a loud *clap!* and the beams vanish. This is the *slate* Director Cha described to me at breakfast.

"Two or three times a day and without notice, filming pauses for about ten minutes," she said. "This is when we check sound and video and dump accumulated footage into central storage."

This is not the kind of information you'd learn from *TV Guide.* Excited, I told her I didn't realize filming ever stopped, and she told me that technically, it didn't, since the three sections of Snowglobe took turns breaking; but that the important thing was for everyone to return to the scene and be ready to pick up where they left off. Essentially, this means that a few times a day, actors get to take a ten-minute break.

Immediately, everyone scatters to wherever they'd rather be. I race to my room and fling myself on the bed. With no cameras watching me for a change, I'm tempted to yank off the wig and let my scalp breathe, but I can easily imagine Wooyo or Rhim barging in without knocking, so I resist the urge and lie there. Just then, the phone rings, almost startling the wig off me. I take a couple of deep breaths to steady my heart and reach for the receiver.

"Hello?" I speak into the perforated mouthpiece, mimicking the people I've seen do it on TV. This is my first-ever phone conversation, and I can't help but feel slightly giddy about it.

"Did you get the lockbox, yet?" The voice of a breathless woman bursts out of the receiver.

"Pardon me?" I say, confused.

"If you did, put it away somewhere no one can find it," the voice, notably raspy, instructs.

"I'm sorry, but I think you have the wrong—" I begin, but the line goes dead.

So much for my first phone conversation. Deflated, I fiddle with the dead receiver before returning it to the cradle.

The real Haeri would have given her number to Yujin yesterday, and Yujin, who likes to talk, would have gone out and bought herself a telephone first thing today. Picking up the receiver again, I wedge it between my ear and shoulder. Then I stretch my arms before me and admire my painted nails, just like I've seen Haeri do.

"Hello? Hey, it's me!" I chirp into the silence, simulating a phone call with Yujin. "Did you get to dance with your Bonwhe yesterday?"

I shift the receiver to the other ear, but it drops to my lap on the way. Picking it back up and repositioning it, I chirp again, "Sorry, what were you saying?"

Then I'm pretending to paint my toenails, issuing *uh-huh*s and *no way*s into the mute receiver at appropriate intervals. Next, I'm saying, "Where are you staying, by the way? Do you want to grab lunch tomorrow?"

Then I add a little tee-hee at my own monologue.

I think of the times when Ongi and I were little, how we used to imitate people on TV while holding paper cups over our ears.

"Hey, Jeon Ongi! It's me," I'm saying now. "Did you manage to get to work on time today? How was your birthday?"

The presence of a real receiver in my hand, with its sleek and ergonomic design, enhances my playacting. I lie back on the bed and roll around with it, stretching out the cord like Haeri used to.

Then the softness of her bed becomes irresistible, so I set down the receiver, roll myself up in the feathery comforter, and gaze at the ceiling. Its lime-green color is warmer in the golden wash of the sun. A room of my own. I've dreamed of it my whole life.

Spoiled as she was, the girl sought out misery. Haeri should have pinched off any unhappiness that tried to sprout, whether it was a narcissistic grandmother or a mother whose skin crawled at the sight of her. That's what I would have done. I would have chosen to live. I would have found a way.

WITHOUT A SCRIPT

When we arrive at the Jaeum Mountain Resort, I'm instantly spellbound by the magnificent view. The Jaeum mountain range, known for its craggy mountains full of snow-capped peaks, rises abruptly above the lush alpine forest sprawling toward the border, providing a perfect backdrop for today's championship.

Maeryung spots Bonyung at the gondola lift, smiles wide, and makes a beeline for her, leaving the rest of us to trail behind.

"I heard about your incredible party yesterday, Madam President," Maeryung says, her voice so high that she might as well be singing.

Bonyung smiles back. "Thanks to *you,* I got at least a dozen compliments on my outfit."

"Oh, I don't know, Madam President," Maeryung purrs. "A model like you can make anything I put on her look good!"

The two ladies peep and chirp at each other for a while longer; then Bonyung closes the loop by wishing us a good time at the championship.

"Aren't you going to watch the championship with us, Madam President?" Maeryung asks, clearly disappointed. She'd assumed, as I had, that we'd be sharing a box with Bonyung as guests of the Yibonn Corporation.

Bonyung always watches in one of the VIP boxes reserved for her clan and a dozen or so special guests, so I'm surprised when Bonyung explains, with a smile, "Since this year's special guests are a big, blessed family of three generations, I decided to watch from the finish line." She gestures to our group with another soft smile, and I can't help but notice how tired she looks today. "But I'll leave my son-in-law and grandson with you, if that's okay," she adds.

Maeryung accepts this easily and lets Bonyung wander off, and as we wait for further direction, the six of us sort ourselves into pairs based on which player we're rooting for: Wooyo and me for Chun Sahyun, Rhim and Shihwang for Priya, and finally, Maeryung and Sanghui for whoever Bonyung's son-in-law's preferred athlete might be, their only goal being further ingratiating themselves with the husband of the Yibonn Corporation's president-to-be.

Then Assistant Yu is there, escorting us to the VIP boxes, which are glass gondolas programmed to track our favorite athletes. In my gondola, it's me and Wooyo, but then Bonwhe steps in behind us, apparently also rooting for Chun Sahyun.

Doing my best impression of a lady of poise and elegance, I ease myself down onto the plush bench that hugs the inner contour of the gondola. Bonwhe, settling in on my right, hands me the seat belt without saying a word. Today, he's dressed in a black velvet blazer and a white turtleneck, a sartorial choice that's perfectly aligned with his family's understated elegance.

And with a face and frame like his, who needs the bells and whistles?

A cheer rises from the crowd, and I face forward to look out, only to see myself on the Jumbotrons. Giant versions of me sitting beside Bonwhe look back at us. Then Wooyo inserts himself into the frame, leaning into me with a stupid grin.

I stifle a laugh at his antics. Today's event is my uncle's first official Yibonn invitation in a long time, and he's decided to go for major glam. In addition to his regular nose piercings, he's also borrowed Rhim's favorite pearl necklace and earrings, as well as Haeri's diamond bracelet, which I happily loaned him when he asked earlier.

"Ladies and gentlemen," booms the announcer's voice. "Let us now cap the year with the annual biathlon championship!"

The Jumbotron shifts to the announcer and I lean back in my seat, eager for the competition to begin. The men's event opens first, since Priya Maravan's popularity soars above that of any male contender this season. The twenty-one finalists in the men's event—each wearing a race bib indicating his preliminary ranking—are introduced one by one as they take their positions at the starting line. They wave and pump their fists in the air as the crowd roars and claps for them; I realize that any of these finalists could fill in as a military sniper at a moment's notice, and my heart swells with pride to be in the presence of such collective talent.

The starter's gun blasts in the air, and I suck in a breath.

"Ladies and gentlemen! The athletes have left the starting line!" the sportscaster shouts over the erupting crowd.

Wooyo leans across me to ask Bonwhe which male contestant he's rooting for.

Bonwhe squints in contemplation. "I don't know," he says after a moment. "I haven't found anyone really exciting since Cooper."

"I feel exactly the same way!" Wooyo exclaims, half standing up off the seat in excitement.

Bonwhe responds with a polite smile, though he still doesn't give me so much as a glance. Just yesterday, he mobilized his personal assistant to make sure I was taken care of. Now he's the ice king himself, cold and unapproachable.

"I almost cried when Cooper announced his retirement," Wooyo laments. "He used to train at the park in my neighborhood every day, then he just stopped showing up. Not long after that, I heard he'd gone home."

As he begins to sing Cooper's praises, I fix my gaze on the racecourse below, fighting off the image of Cooper's red-flecked eyes wild with terror, but it's hard to focus. All around us, gondolas glide up and down on their cables, tracking the athletes charging to the front of the pack, and Cooper slips out of the plane in my mind.

"What an upset," the sportscaster cries out. "Ladies and gentlemen! Kim Jehno edges forward to take the lead!"

A roar of excitement surges through the crowd, and I refocus my gaze on the arena below. The athlete with bib number twelve is pushing his way out of the first shooting range on skis.

The biathlon was spawned by ski warfare during the Warring Age. It's gone through a few alterations since its adoption as a sport. Now there are a total of three rounds of shooting. In the first round, athletes are required to be in a prone position as they shoot at stationary targets one hundred and fifty feet away. In the second round, they fire from a standing position, at machine-pitched targets the size of a baseball. The airborne targets are color-coded, and the athletes have to hit the ones matching the colors of their uniforms, which requires tremendous reaction speed and accuracy. Athletes who miss their targets do not advance to the next round. In the third and final round, athletes can shoot from any position, but they must kill a death row inmate within thirty seconds of entering the shooting stalls, which are also color coded. For added excitement, the human target is given a small shield with which to deflect the bullets. In fact, the human target is free to do whatever it takes to defend themselves, including dodging behind or climbing up one of the trees lining the range.

What are the chances of surviving the onslaught? Not zero. During a championship game several years ago, an inmate evaded each of the eighteen bullets headed her way. And, as per the rules of the game, she was freed immediately. Afterward, she went on riding off the fame—or the infamy—of her survival, even getting to star in her own TV show, *The Survivor*. But the plug was pulled after two seasons, and she had to give up her Snowglobe residency and return home. Needless to say, no female champion was crowned that year, a rare event indeed.

The sportscaster's amplified voice rises feverishly. "Ladies and gentlemen, Kim Jehno's fourth shot takes down Pierre Verdain! Do we finally have a champion?"

In the next instant, Pierre Verdain's heart monitor lets out a long, drawn-out beep, confirming Kim Jehno's victory. The Jumbotrons light up, showing the victor, who clenches his fists in the air and releases a triumphant cry.

Seventeen years old. A second-year resident. The youngest biathlon champion in history!

The upset of all upsets. As indicated by his race bib, Jehno was a mere twelfth in the preliminary, and only a first-time championship competitor. He really had no business taking the trophy today, if those numbers meant anything.

Reactions among the crowd are split. There's wild celebration for those who feel that they witnessed history being made, and crushing disappointment turning into rage for others.

Myself, I feel absolutely miserable. Watching Pierre Verdain scramble desperately from tree to tree in a doomed attempt to save his own life, all I could think of was Cooper. Of course, Pierre was a death row inmate who may have deserved the ending he got. Apparently, he attacked his director upon learning that his show wasn't getting renewed. The court, finding him guilty of attempted murder, sentenced him to death, a harsh sentence in ordinary circumstances, but in this case, the target of violence had been a director, and an actor harming a director in any way is the most serious kind of crime.

The people below begin to stand from their seats, and the gondola carries us back down the mountains. As we approach the landing, we can see the new champion returning his rifle to the officials. Kim stands waiting for us, and Wooyo is going berserk, yelling, "Oh my god. I'm so excited!" again and again.

A chance to personally congratulate the champion fresh off the win is another perk of being a VIP, and one Wooyoo has never had before. The door slides open and he bolts out, thrusting his hand to Kim for a handshake.

"Congratulations, Champ!" he cries. "I'm your new biggest fan!"

"Thank you so much," Jehno replies kindly, taking his hand.

Bonwhe offers his hand and a few courteous words of congratulations, and Jehno stares at Bonwhe, awestruck, for a second, before gathering himself to say thank you. The heir's presence is having an effect on the mighty champion.

I move to congratulate him next. But just as I open my mouth, Jehno draws an exaggerated breath and wipes his hand across the chest of his race suit.

"I've always wanted to meet you," he says, locking eyes with me and extending his hand. His greeting throws me for a loop, and all I can respond with is "Me?"

"Yes," he says, holding my eyes. "I'd promised myself I'd ask you out if I won today."

Camerapeople from various news outlets jerk forward, closing in on us in the half circle they've formed around the landing, and as I take Jehno's hand, I notice a small action camera perched on his shoulder, my face framed in its viewfinder, reflecting my dazed expression.

Suddenly, the stadium erupts in another thunderous cheer, even more deafening than when the champion snatched his victory, and I turn to the Jumbotrons to see the two gigantic faces they display: mine and Jehno's. Our exchange is being livecast across the stadium.

The pounding in my heart jumps to my ears. I look to the thousands of bobbing faces waiting for my next move and realize that, for the moment, all of these actors are viewers, watching the show within the show.

Haeri's life was punctuated with moments like this one, but as far as the romantic grandeur of these moments go, this one takes the cake.

Thankfully, I happen to know exactly how Haeri would respond in this situation. Coming back fully to myself, to Haeri, I respond with a cool "Go for it, then."

This seems to catch him by surprise. His confident grin wavers.

"You said you'd promised yourself to ask me out," I say. "So do it—like you mean it." I cross my arms in front of my chest and look him dead in the eye.

His grin returns, even brighter this time. Bringing his palm to his chest, he makes a show of steadying his wildly beating heart. In the crowd, someone begins chanting my name, and gradually, more and more people pick it up until the whole stadium is pulsing with it.

"Goh Haeri! Goh Haeri! Goh Haeri!"

I sweep my eyes around the stadium, both terrified and exhilarated. I have these people wrapped around my finger, and the realization electrifies every cell in my body. I feel . . . untouchable.

Jehno holds up a hand, and the chant trails off. Into the silence that descends, he says, "Haeri, would you like to come see the New Year's fireworks with me?"

The crowd holds their breath; you could hear a pin drop. I'm stalling, drawing out the moment for effect, when an impatient shout goes up in the crowd—"Say yes!"—which provokes a brief period of shouts that rise in protest of the disturbance.

I wait. There's no hurry. I'm the one holding the key,

after all. And when everything is still again but for the breeze swaying the treetops, I let a smile flower on my face. "Sure," I say. "That sounds fun."

The stadium erupts once again. Jehno punches the air with a clenched fist, engulfed in triumph for the second time today.

THE SECOND PROPOSAL

"—This year's biathlon championship buzzed with a few surprises both in and out of the arena," the news anchor says in her news anchor voice as the screen cuts to the scene where I'm accepting Jehno's proposal.

"You go, girl!" Rhim squeals, slapping me on the back.

Snippets of audience interview follow.

—I camped outside the box office for three days straight for the event. It was totally worth it!

—The only downside of living in Snowglobe is missing out on my favorite shows, but what we were treated to today made up for it!

Wooyo, who's reaching for yet another gift to tear into, looks up at Maeryung. "Mom, were you nuts about Snowglobe shows, too, when you lived in the open world?"

Maeryung looks up from the crumpled wrapping paper and ribbon she's gathering into a pile.

"Who *cares* what kind of lives other people are living?" she says. "It's our own lives that we need to pay attention to."

Rhim admires herself in the folding mirror she's propped

up on the coffee table, a new sapphire necklace glittering around her throat. "I'd just go ahead and die if I had to live my life chained to a hamster wheel."

Her comment stirs a deep sense of gloom inside me. I can't imagine going back to slaving at the wheel ten hours a day.

You help me, then I help you.

The exhilaration I felt at the stadium altered me. I don't *ever* want to go back to being who I used to be, and I never want to set foot in another power plant. Can I really bet on getting called to film school someday? How can I bring up the subject with Director Cha without sounding like Jeon Cho-bahm?

"Are you okay, niece?" Wooyo's voice brings me back. Brows knitted, he looks at me with mild concern. I brush him off with a "What? I'm fine," and move on to the next round of presents that were left for me outside the front door. With Haeri's birthday falling on Christmas, people who wish to befriend her tend to go wild on this day.

I'm working on a small box wrapped in Rudolph the Red-Nosed Reindeer gift paper when the phone rings.

"Here come the calls for you again, niece," Rhim says with mock envy, elbowing me.

Across the room, Sanghui flips idly through the pages of a new cookbook, refusing to even glance toward the TV screen, which is currently showing me standing next to the champion.

No one makes a move to pick up the phone, so I hurry upstairs to my room, the half-opened gift still in my hands. When I pick up the phone, I'm relieved to hear it's Director Cha on the other end.

"I saw the news," she says, sounding delighted. "And the championship broadcast, too, of course. I'm itching to work on the footage."

Which is great, but I can't help second-guessing how the day ended. Lowering myself to the edge of the bed, I ask, "The date . . . Saying yes was right?"

"Absolutely," she assures me with a merry laugh. "Why are you even asking?"

I have to think for a second to decide how to phrase it; then I just blurt it out: "Because I'm not sure how to proceed from here on."

"What do you mean?" she says, sounding genuinely mystified. "Have you never been on a date?"

I never have, in fact. Not because there's something wrong with me, but because no one *dates* out in the snowbound, wind-thrashed world where people are limited to crammed family homes and the power plant. But that's beside the point. I clear my throat and begin, "What I meant is . . . when does Haeri begin hinting that she wants to leave Snowglobe? If we want viewers to believe her shocking decision, we need to take them along on the journey of her heart. Right?"

The line goes silent for a moment. Ugh. I've definitely slipped out of character, and probably overstepped my boundaries, too. I'm steeling myself when a deep, satisfied laugh swells out of the receiver.

"So it wasn't all talk!" she says, sounding both amused and impressed. "You really have been paying attention to how these things work."

I can't decide how to take her remark; then she breaks the

silence. "Relax," she says reassuringly. "It's a compliment." She laughs again and adds, "I wasn't wrong. You and I will get along beautifully."

She said something similar this morning, before or after praising me for refusing to act like a weepy little puppy.

"Tomorrow's your studio visit," she reminds me, changing the subject.

The visit is part of my training as the new weather presenter, a kind of informal orientation.

"I want you to stop by and see me before you head out," Director Cha says. "We need to discuss an important matter."

My heart kicks up. An important matter?

"Sure, Director Cha," I say, fidgeting with the Rudolph paper still hugging the half-opened gift on my lap. I'm distracted by a thought.

"There's one thing I want you to be thinking about between now and then," she continues.

And that's when I finally blurt out, "I have something I'd like to discuss with you tomorrow, too, Director Cha."

A moment of silence. "You do?" she says. "What is it?"

Yes, I never want to go back to the graveyard of hamster wheels!

I want to tell her right here and now that I'm already fearing the day when the curtains will come down. "It's kind of too complicated to discuss on the phone," I hedge.

A long silence.

"Okay then," she says. "What's wrong? I thought you'd still be riding high on the championship."

"I am," I say, feeling the pulse of the rapturous crowd in my chest.

"Then why do you sound so sad?"

It must be the tone of her voice, I don't know, but it gets me talking. "I *feel* sad. Sad and anxious."

"What? Why?" she demands, irritation edging into her voice.

I tear off a big strip of the Rudolph gift wrap then. And it feels good, like giving in to something.

"It was incredible to see the whole stadium going crazy over me. I've never felt that kind of rush," I admit. After that, words just start pouring out of my mouth. "It really is magical here. This phone? The blanket I'm sitting on right now? It's all amazing. And did I tell you I've just gotten a new cassette player for Christmas? I can't wait to bring it with me on my walks around the lake, and—"

"I get it, sweetie," Director Cha says with a contented sigh. "Like I said, admitting you into film school is not within my immediate power as a working director, but don't you worry—I have a plan. You just focus on your part."

It's scary how quickly she intuits what I can't say, as if she's known me, Jeon Chobahm, for seventeen years.

"Yes, of course, Director Cha," I murmur. Her response, though somewhat reassuring, is still not what I wanted to hear. In containing my disappointment, I squeeze the gift I've finally extricated from its excessive packaging. A palm-sized, four-digit combination lockbox.

How curious, I'm thinking, when it hits me. The misplaced phone call.

Put it away somewhere no one can find it.

Is this the thing that the hurried caller was talking about? Not that I can make heads or tails of anything.

"If you really want to know," Director Cha's voice pulls

me back, "there's one thing I can do." She pauses here for a long moment, taking her sweet time. My heart picks up again, and I clamp my mouth shut lest she hears it. "I may not be able to make you a film school student myself," she goes on, finally. "But I *can* turn you into Goh Haeri. Forever."

The receiver feels suddenly heavy in my hand, and I revise my grip around it, stifling a whimper.

"I'll ask you again tomorrow," she continues. "Officially. But now that the cat's out of the bag, what is your first thought? About living the rest of your life as Goh Haeri?"

The knuckles of my hand clutching the lockbox have turned white. Then an image invades my mind, of my heart dropping to the cold, hard floor, where it flaps about like a struggling fish.

"Watching you at the stadium today, I realized that you're more than just a temp. You've got what it takes to become Haeri. New and improved."

Glancing up, I catch my face in the vanity mirror. *What are you doing? Why aren't you saying no?*

"What happens to Jeon Chobahm, then?" I say. "Would she disappear?"

"No! Of course not," Director Cha says. "I'd tell people she got her start as a director right out of film school. Her family would be handsomely provided for, for as long as she works here in Snowglobe—it's the same deal all the working actors and directors get, but you already know that. And if she wanted, I could even arrange for them to get together regularly at a third location."

I stare at the girl in the mirror. *What is there to think about?* she seems to be saying.

The broadcasting station is on the top floor of SnowTower, the same building that houses Director Cha's home. Producer Yi Dahm, a folding chair on her arm, leads me down the hallway. "Please excuse our cramped space," she says. "It's not designed for live audiences."

I smile and chirp that it's no problem, my mind festering with anxiety. The talk with Director Cha that was supposed to happen this morning didn't—urgent business brought her to the hospital.

Producer Yi sets up the folding chair by the main camera, using her foot to nudge away the cables snaking around the floor.

"This should be a good spot. No coughing or chair scraping, please," she says with a playful grin.

I thank her and settle into the chair, glancing up at the soaring glass walls all around me.

"Up there is the newsroom," Producer Yi says, pointing it out for me.

The broadcasting station is a glass-tube structure with a square atrium in the middle, on the top floor of which sits the newsroom. And two floors down from the newsroom, in the atrium, is the studio where I'm currently sitting. A reporter crossing the newsroom glances down and gives a wave. Waving back, I shift my gaze to the news desk in front of me.

The two anchors of *News at 9* sit at the desk, reading over their stacks of paper and getting ready for their nightly reporting. I catch myself thinking that I'm watching them on TV at home, where a complicated love triangle involving the two anchors and Producer Yi unfolded. Mom and I used to say that the three of them should just give up sorting out their feelings and live happily ever after as a fabulous throuple.

I glance around for Fran, my soon-to-be predecessor, but he's nowhere in sight. When I ask Producer Yi, she tells me that Fran usually gets to the set five minutes before the start of the weather segment, at around a quarter to ten.

"I'll introduce you to the anchors later on. They both tend to be a bit tense before the show," Producer Yi says, her gaze on Anchor Park, who is frowning in concentration at the desk.

He's cheating on you! I'm itching to say. *With Anchor Chung, your so-called best friend!*

But this is an itch I'm not allowed to scratch. Squirming in my seat and trying to focus elsewhere, I spot an unlikely telephone booth standing in a corner.

"Is that a prop?" I ask Producer Yi.

"No," she says. "It's a hotline between the newsroom and the studio. For urgent communication only. We can't have the phone ringing in the middle of a live broadcast, so it stays on mute."

On mute? Then how do they know if someone's calling?

As if she read my mind, she adds, "The booth flashes white when there's an incoming call."

"That sounds pretty," I say, hoping to see it in action today while I'm here.

Producer Yi twists around for a quick look at the other booth perched a floor up behind us.

"Okay then," she says. "It's time for me to head up."

Up in the booth, her team sits behind a console, overlooking the news desk below.

"The Control Room. It's where we compose, monitor, and transmit the livecast," Producer Yi says, her voice bright with pride. According to what I learned in school, there's the

Control Room, and then there's the *Master* Control Room. The former, which is located here inside the news studio, assumes exclusive control of Channel 9 between the hours of nine and ten p.m. while *News at 9* is on the air. During this hour, the Control Room's authority overrides that of the Master Control Room. In other words, the Master Control Room cannot, for any reason, interrupt the news hour without the Control Room's permission. This is a rule designed to ensure media independence, and it is one of the few surviving legacies of the Warring Age. Come what may, the mic stays hot until the anchor's sign-off phrase.

Still, all this is in theory. *News at 9* has never had to invoke media independence, as the fair and just Snowglobe order safeguards it anyway. And the Yibonns are a family of *spotless* integrity—far above the kind of corruption and scandals that would undermine the people's trust and destabilize the institution. Well, there *is* Vice-President Bonshim, but her scandals are strictly personal.

The show ends with a summary of the day's trending news.

"Here's today's news bites." Anchor Chung reads the transcript rolling off the teleprompter as images of flames, wreckage, and stunned onlookers play across the giant screen behind her. "A house fire broke out yesterday in District Two when a candle flame spread from a family's Christmas cake. The blaze was put out an hour later by the fire department, but not before causing millions in damage . . ."

The screen then cuts to the next story. The mug shots of three men. "Three inmates convicted of murder and breaking broadcasting regulations . . ."

My eyes grow wide when I recognize a familiar face. It's

the prisoner with the heart tattoo under his eye, the one who was sweating at the wheel at the Yibonns' secret prison during the Christmas party.

"Authorities revealed that the death penalty was administered just before Christmas, on the twenty-third of this month."

On the twenty-third? How could that be?

"In other news . . ." Anchor Chung's voice brightens. "Quality Bakery reports that this year's Christmas cake sale . . ."

Didn't I see him alive on Christmas Eve? I'm chewing over the report, confused, when someone taps me on the shoulder. I look up to see Fran, smiling and giving me a quick wave as he hurries to the weather set. The sight of his face, which I saw nightly on TV at 9:50 sharp over the past year, instantly distracts me.

"Let's turn to Fran for tomorrow's weather, shall we?" Anchor Park announces, and the rotating platform they're on begins to swivel counterclockwise, tucking away the news desk and presenting the weather set. Fran, resplendent in a tiger-striped suit, stands smiling by a row of seven glass drums in which dozens of clear weather balls spin and tumble in a chaotic dance. When the platform comes to a stop, Fran smiles more widely, revealing two rows of white teeth that sparkle brilliantly under the studio's overhead lights. The lights are positively blinding; and I simultaneously wonder how he tolerates them, while also acknowledging it's the lights that make Fran, Fran.

"All my fellow Snowglobe residents out there, please take a moment to check out the curtain of northern lights rippling across the sky," Fran says.

Fran had once been a quiz show host, and then a survival

show host, and he runs his piece with exceptional flair. He continues, "Now, I'd love to pick a nice gift for those out there working over the holidays." A wink and a cheeky smile. "Not unlike the news team right here . . ."

He sticks a hand inside the first glass drum and draws a ball, which he holds up for the camera. At first, all you can see through the clear sphere are the lines on Fran's palm. But a yellow sun gradually materializes within, the heat of Fran's palm activating the ball's thermotropic material.

"It looks like tomorrow's going to be another beautiful day with oodles of sunshine!" he announces cheerfully.

He turns the sphere around in his hand to get the night-time weather forecast, and the camera zooms back in, focusing on the twinkling star and its pale halo materializing inside the ball. Fran's voice continues, "And tomorrow night, a clear sky will allow us to see the *amazing* Milky Way."

I watch in awe as Fran glides through the rest of the segment, from tomorrow's highs and lows, to humidity, sunrise, and sunset. His energy is infectious, and I find myself smiling with him.

When the show ends, a staff member with spiky green hair appears on the set and feeds the loose weather balls back into the drums.

"Would you like to come up and hold one for yourself, Ms. Haeri?" Fran suggests, holding out a ball.

I'm there in the next instant, more than eager. "Handle it with care, please," the green-haired staff member cautions me as I take it.

I cradle it with both hands, marveling at its weight. "It's lighter than I expected," I say, my voice full of wonder.

I have a toy weather ball back home, a common gift for children. The toy displays weather icons and changes in response to the temperature of the hands that hold it. Ongi and I found out later that Mom chose to gift us the weather ball instead of buying herself new slippers. She ended up squeezing one more season out of her raggedy slippers with holes in the back so we could play weather forecaster.

"This one seems to want to stay blank," I say to Fran, spreading my fingers around the ball for better heat transfer. "Is it because the weather segment is over?"

"Not a bad guess," Fran grins, and, pitching his voice low in mock self-importance, he says, "No one but me can awaken these weather balls."

The green-haired guy lets out a puff of laughter at this. He explains, "On January first, when you come in for your first day of work, we'll take your fingerprints and register them in the system. And then you'll be able to activate the weather balls." Turning to Fran, he repeats in a ribbing tone, "Awaken the weather balls . . . What? Are you a magician or something now?"

Fran deadpans, "Not a magician. Just a weather god."

I like his response.

THE OFF-LIMITS ZONE

ackstage, in the dressing room, Fran has traded the tiger-print suit for cozy sweatpants and a matching hoodie. He's working a cotton pad soaked with makeup remover over his eyelids, explaining that without heavy makeup, stage lights would make a death mask of his face—of anyone's face, for that matter.

"How'd you like the livecast?" he asks.

"I liked it a lot," I say. "And it's amazing how at home you are on set."

I turn my gaze to the sky outside the wraparound window. Various shades of purple and green shimmer over the city and the sprawling woods beyond.

"Isn't this room marvelous?" Fran says. "You can come here and relax anytime, even on days you're off. And ring the concierge on the second floor for anything you want. They'll stuff you." He takes a long gulp of the beet juice that said concierge sent up. "I considered making this my bedroom. Seriously—no one has it better than the weather presenter, not even President Yi."

I cross the floor to the giant window. With my face an inch from the glass, I look down at the knee-buckling view you get at 204 stories above street level. It's a long way down, that's for sure.

This dressing room was once reserved for VIP entertainment, and the weather presenter did their nightly makeup and script reading at a corner of the news desk they shared with the anchors. When Fran took the position, however, letters from fans began inundating the station, saying that the new weather presenter needed to be properly accommodated if he was going to battle cancer successfully. In four months, the fans' advocacy paid off, and Fran was given access to the underutilized VIP space. Two months after that, the station announced its official redesignation as a dressing room.

"You may find it hard to believe, Haeri, but out in the open world, even things like stationery and postage are a luxury. People struggle to get by every day." Fran pauses a moment, as if to let me process the information. "And yet, they all came together and supported me. I still get choked up when I think about it."

Stripped of the stage makeup, his face bares the ravages of cancer, a disease that, despite all the advances in medical technology, continues to evade us. In a way, it's not unlike the human species, which continues to exist despite an environment that wants it gone.

"Because I lack formal training, I don't have much career advice to give you," he resumes. As I sit, listening to him, I realize how thin and bony he looks without the benefit of a suit or shoulder pads. "But I can say that I hope you'll always show up as your blessed self for all the viewers out there who'll be rooting for you. I know that we come from very different backgrounds, and as someone who moved to Snowglobe when I was nearly forty, I can tell you that giving back to fans is the least we can do."

Nodding wordlessly, I'm visited by a scene from the past. Ironically, it involves the grating supervisor from the power plant back home. He had said something similar to Yujin on her last day at the plant.

Don't go around mindlessly wasting electricity when you get there. Those so-called actors with their dull, barely watchable lives squandering what we break our backs to give them? They're parasites, if you ask me.

Viewers demand that actors lead intense lives, that their highs be high and lows be low in exchange for the free electricity we produce to sustain their lifestyle.

A wan smile comes over Fran's face. There's almost no trace of the energy he had for the cameras just half an hour ago.

"The cancer came back around the same time I landed the position," Fran says, pulling my attention back to him. "My first thought was that I was finally done. Who would want to see a dying person presenting the weather? And all the treatment just seemed to be prolonging my pain and misery, rather than prolonging my life. It was the most hopeless I'd ever felt. There were times I even wished for a pink slip, so I could go ahead and end this life in peace."

His eyes go remote with the memory; then he snaps back to focus on me. "Healthwise, I'm no better," he says with a weary sigh. "As a matter of fact, the cancer's worse than ever. But you know what? I vowed to keep fighting for my life until the last doctor throws in the towel."

"Where did you find the strength to go on?" I ask him.

"The fans," he says simply. "One day, I walked into the newsroom and saw their letters of support heaped up on the chief's desk, cascading to the floor. I vowed to live the rest of my life for them, whatever I have left. And to the fullest. I won't quit until they decide it's time."

Hunched in his chair, he looks nothing like the Fran I saw on set—tall, charismatic, exuding energy, exuding life. I think of my dead grandfather, of how cancer multiplied relentlessly inside him, devouring the once robust and gregarious man in both body and mind. In the face of such devastation, Fran has decided to not merely exist but to *live,* for it's his duty as an actor. And what did Director Cha say when we first met? *Haeri can't just give up on her life like that.* But Haeri *did* just give up on her life like that, and I am here to pick up the responsibility she shirked. If anyone should feel burdened by guilt, it's Haeri, not me. With that conclusion, I feel some of the anxiety and doubt over Director Cha's proposition fall away.

"Thank you for sharing your insight," I tell Fran, and the words come from the bottom of my heart. "I'll never forget it."

Fran smiles weakly at me, and there's a knock on the door. I turn to see Anchor Park peeping in, and Fran gets up. "I'll only be a moment," he says apologetically, and moves to follow Anchor Park out the door. Of course, I know what Anchor Park wants—he wants to vent about his complicated relationship with Anchor Chung.

Left alone in the dressing room, I turn to the full-length mirror. Fran told me he practices his lines, which he writes himself, in front of it. In a few days, I'll be doing the same.

My answer to Director Cha's proposal solidified and out of the way, I can finally focus my attention on the details of the work facing me. What should my opening line be? I try on Fran's opener for size: "Good evening from the studio—"

Then the room grows dark and all the cameras hiding in the dressing room announce their whereabouts by projecting their light beams. In a few moments, they all fall to black, and there's the loud clack of the slate. I turn my attention back to the mirror and begin again: "Hello, and good evening. I'm Goh Haeri, your new weatherperson."

I try for Fran's easy smile, and my reflection is marred by—*What?*—a smudge of mascara or something on the mirror. It's blacking out my two front teeth. I blow on the glass and take a finger to the offending smear, and my finger dips into the silvered surface, as if into a pool of mercury.

This again? Stupefied, I try the toes of my left foot, feeling faintly ridiculous. But the glass yields. My heart begins to pound. I slide the foot in a bit farther, and before I know it, I'm sucked back into the mirror and plunged into darkness. This time, though, I manage to keep blind panic at bay. I take a deep breath, prepared to remain calm and investigate this time, but my groping hand happens on the stupid button. A scream caught in my throat, I begin to free-fall again, my internal organs cartwheeling inside me. Then everything comes to a halt. When I recover myself and crawl out into the light, I'm struck silent to find myself outside, on the edge of a forest.

Up above, crows fly, silhouetted against a sky rippling with northern lights. Then my eyes catch the glint of another full-length mirror propped against a huge tree a few feet off. For a long moment, I just stand there frozen, my eyes fixed on my own dazed reflection. And in the silence of the woods, I hear the faint hiss and pop of a fire.

Is there someone out here? I trudge deeper into the forest, following the sound, and it isn't long before a warm glow begins seeping into the darkness between the trees. Then, finally, a bonfire comes into view, burning peacefully in a small clearing. Next to it sit a lantern and an empty rocking chair. I'm thinking how cozy—and random—the scene is, when a cold metal object is thrust against the back of my head.

"Raise your hands and turn around slowly," a voice commands.

My heart seizes and I do as I'm told, turning to come face to face with Bonwhe, who's leveling a rifle at my forehead. For his part, Bonwhe looks just as stunned as I am, if not more. He immediately lowers the rifle.

"What in god's name are you doing here?" he says, letting out an incredulous laugh.

"Where *am* I?" I ask, feeling my forehead buzzing.

"Off-limits zone," he says.

Off-limits zones are camera-free areas closed to actors. Entering without authorization is against the broadcasting laws.

"What?" I protest. "I had no idea!" *What happens if he reports me?* "I swear, I never meant to wander in here," I say, the image of the new prison I stumbled upon flashing before me.

Tilting his head to one side, Bonwhe eyes me quizzically. Then his features soften and he lets out another laugh. Apparently, this is funny for him.

"Relax," he says. "I believe you. But what are you going to tell Cha?"

I give him a blank look. What am I going to tell Director

Cha? What am I going to tell *myself*? Can someone tell me what's happening?

"Whatever access point you used, it must have taken you a couple of hours to get all the way out here. Do you have an explanation for Cha? About your break away from the cameras?"

There's a sharp edge in his voice when he says Director Cha's name. I shift uneasily on my feet, confused by everything that's happening.

Bonwhe hands me a blanket, and I take it, finally realizing how cold I am. Our fingers brush in the exchange, and his fingers feel just as cold as mine. And I don't know if it's the faint look of apology he gives, as if he should have remembered it sooner or something, but I suddenly feel put-upon and frustrated. Before I can stop myself, I'm saying, "Hey, I didn't get here on foot, you know. There's a mirror over there that whooshed me here against my will."

Stiffening visibly, he echoes, "A mirror?" and the distress in his voice is stark.

"Yes," I say. "Right over there." I point a finger back in the direction I came from. In the distance, the 204-story SnowTower I was just sitting inside glitters like a Christmas tree. "And can you please explain to me why the mirrors in Snowglobe are—"

"Sit, please." He cuts me off and half forces me down into the rocking chair. He takes a quick glance at his wristwatch. "You have eight minutes before the slate goes off. Tell me what you've learned. From the moment of the mirror till now. Be concise."

"What?" I breathe, astounded all over again.

"Right now," he demands. "We don't have long."

If I couldn't imagine him ever worked up or unsettled before, I can now.

"It was at the Christmas party," I begin, trying to be concise. "I'd wandered into a dark hallway trying to get away from this guest and literally ran into one of the mirrors. And then today, I was just trying to wipe a smudge off the mirror in Fran's dressing room—"

"A guest at the party? Did they see you use the mirror?" he presses, agitated.

"No. I'd lost him before that."

"And how about just now?"

"I was alone in the dressing room. The slate had just gone off."

Bonwhe seems to relax a little.

"And you'd never encountered one before the party, correct?"

"Correct."

"Did you run into anyone else on your travels? Did anyone see you?"

I hesitate, thinking of the dozens of inmates I saw working the wheels inside that glass tower. In the end, though, I shake my head, and not simply because I think the answer would please him. None of the inmates noticed me, and though there was that one guy with the face tattoo, I'm sure he didn't see me.

Possibly the prison has the same two-way mirror construction as the dome enclosing Snowglobe. You can look in from the outside, but not the other way around . . . ?

Bonwhe scrutinizes me for another long beat; then a funny look comes over his face, and he suddenly calls out. "Jo Yeosu!"

Confused, I twist around in my chair, expecting to see this person called Jo Yeosu approaching, but all I see is trees surrounding us, bathed in the soft orange light of the bonfire. When I swivel back around, further confused, Bonwhe's eyes are dead set on me.

"What? Did that scare you?" he says, still watching me carefully.

What is he talking about? I wasn't looking around because I was scared.

"Don't worry. There're no cameras or trespassers here," he says. "There shouldn't be." He flicks his wrist for another look at his watch. "It's important that you don't use the portals again."

I've never seen anyone on TV using one of these mirrors. But why isn't this amazing means of transportation more widespread? Because the ride is too terrifying? Too rough?

"Are the special mirrors only for the Yibonns or something?" I ask.

Bonwhe glances away, looking caught. It's a few moments before he nods in silent affirmation.

This somehow reminds me of the break room at the power plant, of the supervisor. Again. Despite it belonging to everyone, the obnoxious man shamelessly monopolizes it, going so far as to dock a day's pay for anyone caught lounging there when he's not around. And what does he do in the break room? He paints, apparently. And dances.

The Yibonns' secret mirrors reek of a similar kind of

entitlement. They want to enjoy the northern lights in peace, in the woods where they can have a bonfire going and maybe even roast some marshmallows. And they want to do it without having to trek through the wilderness like common folks.

Does Bonwhe perfect his brushstrokes or shake his butt in the privacy of these woods? Who knows? He can do or be whatever he wants here, free from all the cameras, and free from the eyes and ears of all his helpers, who might turn what he says and does to juicy gossip in the staff room, or worse yet, in the settlements they come from.

"The mirrors are a family secret per the president," Bonwhe says, and his voice lacks its usual cold indifference.

We are silent, listening to the fire snap and crackle. Then, out of nowhere, he says, *"The Yibonn family does not pursue power or seek special privileges."* It's a line from his grandmother's New Year's speech. "Absurd, right? That someone sitting in a gilded study inside a palatial home would give lip service to equity." He flashes a sour smile.

Is he really poking fun at his own family's hypocrisy? I feel an odd sympathy for him. "I doubt anyone considers the mansion an unearned privilege," I say. "And the president's support of Fran was really something, too. You know, turning the VIP room into his private dressing room? Everyone praised her generosity and sacrifice, putting actors' well-being before the Yibonns' convenience."

"Really?" he says. "Who's everyone?"

Mom and Grandma, of course, and maybe a handful of other people I know back home.

"Everyone in the world?" he repeats, and waits.

"I won't use the portals again," I say in place of an answer. "It's not like I even wanted to use them to begin with."

"You haven't told anyone about them, have you?" he says, finally looking at me again.

"No. And I won't."

He studies me for a moment, then seems at last to accept my answer. "Thanks," he says. "I appreciate it."

He treats me to a smile then, for the first time. And am I imagining the look in his eyes?

"You're very welcome," I respond carefully. "I think your family deserves everything they have. Had the Yibonns not conceived and implemented the Snowglobe order, we'd still be killing each other over the territory like those people in the old days."

And then I'm on a roll. I recite the evils of war and the Yibonns' tremendous contribution to world peace, all of which was drilled into me over a decade of public education. Bonwhe plops down on the ground by the rocking chair, his eyes glazing over as I go on. When I finally pause for a breath, he quips, "I had no idea you were such a fan of the Yibonns."

"Who would think ill of them?" I ask.

He shrugs and takes another look at his watch. Then he leans back against the tree behind him.

"You've been talking funny lately," he says, glancing at me. "And did you really call me Young Master in my room that day?" He snorts. And the small, complicitous smile he gives me then transforms his face. There's softness in his voice now, almost sweetness, and I catch my heart quivering in spite of myself.

Then it strikes me. Is there something going on between

these two? Was the cool indifference he maintained toward Haeri at the party and at the championship just for show? No, it can't be. These thoughts are pushing my brain into over-drive when, all of a sudden, the rocking chair swings back and I'm almost supine in it.

"You know what?" Bonwhe says, holding the chair in position and looking straight at me, his face inches from mine. "You act like a different person."

I clutch the armrests, barely even able to breathe.

THE SECRET CORRESPONDENTS

"You're right. I don't feel like myself," I say, fighting to maintain composure. Haeri didn't know of the mirrors. That much is certain. Bonwhe slowly releases the chair back into its upright position. I continue, "When I first saw my fingers disappearing into the mirror . . ." Here I trail off, gazing at my hand in a show of horror and disbelief.

Wait a minute, though. Why the *dressing room* mirror? None of the mirrors outside the Yibonn mansion were magical. I remember wiping steam off the bathroom mirror at Director Cha's.

So many questions. If I weren't on the verge of being exposed right now, I would absolutely press for details.

"I've been feeling awful lately," I say, sighing wearily. "First there was the killer flu, and then these mirrors—" I pause to shoot him a tragic look. "And finally, being held at gunpoint today."

Bonwhe glances away. "I'm sorry," he says, clearing his throat. "I was scared, I guess. I'd never run into anyone out here."

I let a moment tick by before accepting his apology. "It's all good," I say, silently cheering myself.

He's quiet. Did it do the trick? I steal a quick glance at Bonwhe's face as he gazes into the fire. There's a concerned crease between his brows.

"I'll look into what happened in the dressing room," he says. "But please—"

"Not a word," I finish for him. "And I'll stay off the mirror."

"Thanks," he says, his face opening up again with a soft smile.

Crisis averted.

In full possession of myself now, I say, "I should get going," and look toward the mirror. Bonwhe offers his hand in exaggerated gallantry.

"How have you been feeling since the flu?" he says. That tender attentiveness is back in his eyes.

"Good. Thanks," I say, and taking his hand, let him pull me to my feet. His fingers don't feel like icicles anymore, either. Have we synced to each other's temperature? Feeling my pulse accelerate, I let go of his hand before he can let go of mine.

"You scared the hell out of me, locking yourself in the bathroom like that," he accuses out of the blue. "I thought you were doing something terrible in there. Your last letter read a lot like a farewell, and I was pretty worried."

A letter? Your last letter? Since when were Bonwhe and Haeri on writing terms?

He continues, "Don't ever write like that again. There's no reason for you to thank me anyway, and it's just scary," but I barely hear it because of the word *letter* still buzzing in my head.

A farewell letter between these two? Bonwhe knows something about Haeri that I don't, that even Director Cha doesn't. My heart begins a slow pounding.

"I promise," I say, "that I won't thank you again."

I give him a half smile and then hurry off toward the mirror. Nothing good will come of my remaining here with him. I'll just give myself away. Plus, I need time to process all this information. But Bonwhe catches up to me in a few long strides.

"Let me take you back," he says. "You don't want to end up somewhere unexpected."

He has a good point, so I acquiesce, and we head for the mirror together.

"So, you had only been rocketed into my room that day. I wish I had known it all this time," he says, the last of the tension in his face finally lifting.

"Right?" I say, matching his light mood. "A trick of the mirror. I swear I didn't plan it."

This closeness between Bonwhe and Haeri is so strange. Dying to know more, I let my mouth run ahead of me.

"This might feel like a random time to ask, but . . . *why* do you care about me?"

He gives me a slow, long look. "Because you're you?"

I don't know what I expected, but his response tickles my heart. Feeling bold all of a sudden, I press, "What do you mean?"

"I decline to comment further."

"Why?"

He sighs. "I just want to help you get through the year. So you don't dwell on the past when you leave."

What now? How does *he* know? Had Haeri been truly planning on leaving at the end of the year? And what past?

"I want you to leave it all behind," he continues. "Memories of Director Cha and the way she abused you all these years. You go and be free. I'll remember everything for you."

The crackling of the fire travels through the still air. I stare at him vacantly, half-formed thoughts jamming my neural circuits.

"Cha will pay for what she did. It's a promise," he says, looking into my eyes. "I'll make her life hell on earth."

Such a chilling statement. But how about the way he's gazing at me right now? What did he say about Director Cha? I can't think straight. I can't think.

Then we're standing side by side before the mirror. He takes my hand. "Don't let go, and don't touch anything." Then I follow him into the mirror.

The lift, the vessel, or whatever it is that contains us, immediately begins speeding through the darkness. After three rides, I finally see that I'm not being sucked into a black void. There is a path, after all, though it's only visible when dim yellow lights flash above, alerting us to an upcoming curve or split. The low light lends a cinematic cast to Bonwhe's features, and I feel my heart skipping all over again. His free hand, I notice, is grasping a steering wheel of some sort.

All of a sudden, all my weight is being pushed toward my legs; and before I can react to the sensation, *whoosh*—the vessel rockets up at a terrifying speed. My head snapping back, I look to Bonwhe.

"Stop staring at me. You're going to wear out my face," he says, grinning, and it reassures me.

"Can it take you outside Snowglobe, too?" I hear myself ask. What if I could whoosh back home and say a quick hello to my family?

"This thing? No," he says. "You're limited to a handful of locations."

Bummer. I make a face. "So it's not as amazing as I thought." Bonwhe just laughs.

A few moments later, we arrive in Fran's dressing room. The view from inside the mirror is smoky, reminding me of a limousine's tinted windows. Carefully scanning the room, Bonwhe makes sure no one's there to be surprised. He's still holding my hand.

"Was it you who found my shoe at the party?" I ask.

"Yup. Why?"

"No reason. I've got to go," I say, and let go of his hand.

"Happy birthday," he says. "I left you a present last night."

"Oh?"

"At the place," he adds. "With the letter."

Okay. At the place. With the letter. But where is the place?

I murmur my thanks and step out of the mirror. A faint whir signals his departure, and only then do I turn around to face the mirror again, where I see my reflection undulating on its rolling surface.

Leave it all behind . . . Memories of Director Cha . . . Go and be free. Little had I imagined that Haeri's lovely smile concealed Maeryung's vicious assaults or Sanghui's bitter resentment.

Her life was the picture of love and happiness. But I guess it was only that—a picture.

I can see how she would have resented Director Cha, who left all her pain and suffering on the cutting room floor as if they were nothing.

Cha will pay for what she did. It's a promise. But would that constitute a crime? It's a director's responsibility to control every scene of a show; no one would say otherwise. Also— is it right for the future head of Yibonn Media to harbor animosity toward a director who is merely doing her job?

"Just what is up with these two?" I mutter in frustration. And how am I going to locate Bonwhe's gift and letter, which Haeri would have run to fetch, her heart aflutter? Bonwhe seems to prove the futility of trying to replace Goh Haeri with Jeon Chobahm.

I wait in the dressing room until Fran returns, and we head out to the elevator. He wants to know how I'm getting home, and I tell him that I'm actually stopping by Director Cha's on the 162nd floor.

Populated by the rich and the famous, SnowTower is an exclusive community within the exclusive community. Fran's director, another megasuccess, also lives here. Naturally.

"I live in SnowTower, too," Fran explains. "For a while now. In-patient treatment," he adds.

It only makes sense. The hospital in SnowTower is the world's finest, with top-tier medical staff and state-of-the-art facilities. It also costs an astronomical amount.

"I didn't realize you'd been admitted again," I say.

Fran makes a face.

He sighs. "Do people know about my hospitalization last summer?"

Shoot!

No, they don't. Of course not. I only know because I watched his show. A resigned smile spreads over his face as I try to deny it.

"I guess I shouldn't be surprised," he says, pressing the call button.

The elevator arrives with a merry ding and we step in. I press the button for the 162nd floor, and Fran presses *73* for the hospital.

"Once you start commuting in, stop by the seventy-third from time to time and say hi?"

"Of course," I chirp. "But I think you'll be packing up and heading back home soon."

This isn't just wishful thinking. Fran is *decades* younger than my grandfather was, and he can afford any treatment recommended by the best medical team there is.

"I know you'll beat it, and for good," I add, reaching for my brightest tone.

Fran smiles. "If I don't see you on the seventy-third, I'll see you at my place," he says. "I'm going to have you over for some of my famous pasta. Did you know that it used to be my retirement plan? To open a pasta restaurant? I'm that good."

"That sounds amazing," I enthuse. "And if you end up going with the restaurant, please consider me for your team when *I* retire?"

"Ooh, I like that idea," Fran says with a wink.

Another ding, and I step out on to the 162nd floor. Watching the doors close on Fran, I fight back the tears by stretching my face into a wide smile.

I cross the spacious lobby of the 162nd, a green space made to look like a small indoor park, and make my way to Director Cha's door. I press the buzzer and wait. I can make out muffled voices inside, and it's a good minute before Director Cha opens the door for me, her buttoned overcoat implying that she just returned home herself.

"How'd you get here so early?" she says, straining to smile.

Then a woman emerges from behind her and streaks past me to the elevator. Her head tilted away from me, she jabs the call button several times impatiently.

I turn to Director Cha and mouth, "Who is sh—" but she's already on it.

"Housekeeper," she says quickly.

Turning back to the woman, I offer a friendly "Hello," to which she responds with a quick, awkward half bow, eyes snapping to me for a split second before immediately swinging back to the call button, which she gives another stab. Why does she look so familiar?

"What are you doing? Come in." Director Cha ushers me inside, an edge of agitation in her voice.

The elevator arrives as I step into the foyer, and I quickly glance over my shoulder to catch the woman staring at me. Our eyes meet for an instant, and then she's gone.

THE SHOW OF ALL SHOWS

"I'm surprised you got here so early!" Director Cha says again, swinging the door shut and consulting the wall clock. It's 10:48, and she told me to stop by at 11:00.

"I didn't want to wear Fran out. He looked exhausted," I say, my eyes falling on a lone medical glove lying on the otherwise pristine hardwood floor. Noticing me noticing it, Director Cha snatches it up and nudges me toward the dining room.

"Let's go," she says.

In the dining room, she wants to know what I'd like to drink. I tell her water's fine, but she insists I choose something more exciting, since she's about to have red wine. "It has been a day," she says.

I settle on a tall glass of iced plum tea for its purported digestive benefits. The back-to-back rides in the mirror have me feeling a bit woozy. Between sips of tea, I tell Director Cha about my visit with Fran, whose quiet strength and commitment make me feel emotional all over again.

"You don't grow old in Snowglobe for nothing," sighs

Director Cha, twirling the wineglass in her hand and watching its contents swirl. "If young actors these days were only half as dedicated as Fran . . ."

If that remark was a dig at Haeri, it didn't escape me. I tip the glass back and let an ice cube slide out into my mouth. Rolling it around against the inside of my cheek, I notice for the first time how tired the director looks.

Cha will pay for what she did. It's a promise.

Am I obligated to let her know that Bonwhe is watching her? That Haeri's secret friend might throw a wrench into her plan—*our* plan? But then Bonwhe's face comes to mind again, his eyes full of warm affection for me, for Haeri, and I can't imagine saying a word.

Don't use the portals again.

Had it been someone other than Bonwhe on the other side of the mirror, I would have found myself in some serious trouble. So I need to keep my promise not to tell anyone anything about the secret elevator or encountering Bonwhe tonight.

"Haeri." Director Cha's voice brings me back. "Enough about Fran. I want to hear about you now. Have you thought about my proposal?"

Bonwhe's voice echoes in my ear again: *Leave it all behind . . . The way she abused you all these years . . .*

What does that mean to me? And no one's put more loving care and effort into the construction of Haeri's life than Director Cha. Should she be punished for that? I know what I've decided.

"I'd like to become Haeri," I say.

A smile of gratification blooms across her face.

"Then Haeri you will be," she says, gazing at me proudly.

"Your life will be the life against which everyone measures theirs. I'll make sure of it." A pause. "You just have to keep doing what you've been doing. Smile, laugh, be lovely, be confident. Keep being yourself. Keep being the girl who can't be intimidated even in a packed stadium, and whose response had the biathlon champ *and* spectators teetering on the brink, you know what I mean?" Then, pitching her voice low as if sharing a secret, she adds, "You do that, and before you know it, we'll have entered the castle."

Castle? What castle? Puzzled, I ask what she means and, a sly grin forming on her lips, she asks me instead, "Bonwhe . . . what was he like in person? Be honest. Have you seen anyone better looking?"

I don't know what to say. What is she after? Still, her question has me imagining us holding hands, and my heart starts to skip.

Because you're you.

"Tall, handsome, smart, rich, and with impeccable manners to boot. What girl your age wouldn't melt at the sight of him?"

She's watching me carefully, trying to get a read. I drop my eyes to the cold glass in my hand and wipe at the beads of condensation with my thumb.

"How would you like him to be your man?"

I lift my face and give her a blank look, not understanding. She smiles and continues, holding me with her eyes. "The heir of the world's finest family, poised to inherit power and money? I happen to think he satisfies all the qualifications for being Goh Haeri's partner. What do you think?"

"I—I thought the Yibonns tend to marry their children to equals."

This is true. It's unthinkable for a Yibonn heir to marry a common actor instead of someone of a fine lineage, like a director or something.

"They tend to," she says, stressing the *tend*. "But I'm sure you can recall an exception, what with your encyclopedic knowledge of Snowglobe."

There has been an exception, yes, and it involves none other than Bonshim, Bonwhe's mother and the vice-president of the Yibonn group. She married an actor, Bonwhe's father. The thing is, this exception had only been allowed because Bonil, the eldest son, had been next in the line of succession, not Bonshim. And when he shocked the world by formally opting out of the title in his midtwenties, it pushed Bonshim up in the bracket, making her the dynasty's new heiress. By that time, she'd already married the commoner and given birth to Bonwhe.

Some years later, news broke that Bonil had ended his engagement to his longtime fiancée. And that tragic fiancée happens to be Director Cha.

"I want to make a show where a common actor marries into the fine family. No director has ever dared something like it over the past hundred and twenty years," she says. "Yibonn weddings are the most-watched TV broadcasts there are! Isn't it too bad that viewers don't even get a *glimpse* into these celebrated couples' lives, outside of a handful of publicity appearances?" Here she retrains her tiger gaze on me. "I want to pull the family into the show. And *you're* going to help me. You have excellent intuition for show production. Most importantly, though, you have guts. Heck, *I* can barely intimidate you." She chuckles.

At her words, something inside me loosens again.

A job calling for me and me alone . . .

"What about Vice-President Bonshim, though? She didn't join the cast when she married her husband."

Not only that, her husband quit the show, or was made to quit the show, though which one, we'll never know.

"That's because she married a lowlife nobody who wasn't even a licorice," Director Cha spits. "You're nothing like that! People have watched you for seventeen sweet years. You're their family. They're attached. Invested. I'm going to leverage the fandom to bring cameras into that mansion. You were only just reminding me of how fans' relentless demands turned the VIP room into Fran's own dressing room. Imagine what they would do for you.

"Doesn't it sound so much better than churning out one limp episode after another until retiring to some godforsaken village full of bored has-beens?" she says. "You and me—let's make a show that will go down in history."

Am I crazy to think she's speaking to me as an equal partner? But then Bonwhe's words invade my mind again.

Leave it all behind. . . . The way she abused you all these years.

I push them away. I'm not Bonwhe's Haeri. I'm the Haeri who shares a dream, a vision, with Director Cha.

Cha will pay for what she did. It's a promise.

Without realizing, I'm shaking my head. I cannot, and will not, let him do that.

"Yes, of course, Director Cha," I say. "What do you need me to do?"

With a winner's smile, she sinks back in her seat.

"Nothing," she says flatly.

I blink at her, and she lets out a laugh.

"We don't need to choreograph everything," she explains. "Once you start frequenting the Yibonns' with Shihwang, opportunities will present themselves. You know, to be alone with Bonwhe?"

Yes, now I remember, Haeri was supposed to work with Shihwang—a senior tailor at Maeryung's shop, which supplies the Yibonns.

"You becoming the weathercaster has put the plan off schedule by a year, but so what?" Director Cha says. "I think it works out even better, if anything. And the new champ asking you out hot off the podium? We couldn't have asked for better promotion!"

Wait. The plan has been pushed back a year?

"So Haeri knew about the plan?"

"Of course she did," Director Cha says. "She was appalled, if you can imagine." An incredulous laugh. "She thought me coming up with a plan for who she should marry was crazy."

Appalled? Even though the proposed spouse is Bonwhe? Bonwhe, who cares so much about her? Then again, that might have been the problem for Haeri. That the director would want to use Bonwhe to infiltrate the Yibonns.

"Her attitude was unfortunate," Director Cha goes on, drawing her mouth down. "All I ever wanted was to give her the best of everything."

It strikes me then that Haeri might have disclosed the director's plot to Bonwhe. Could this explain his animosity toward Director Cha?

I'll make her life hell on earth.

My stomach clenches.

"Enough about her," Director Cha declares with a wave of her hand. "What's on your mind? You look like you have a thousand thoughts."

For a moment, I debate whether or not to come clean and ask what I should do regarding Bonwhe's puzzling resentment toward her. But the moment passes. I'll deal with it myself later if it comes to that. It's only right for me to take some agency. I mean, I couldn't expect Director Cha to figure everything out for me and not consider myself a mere puppet of hers, could I?

I return my focus to her vision, and the question comes to me.

"How can you know that Bonwhe will fall for me? We can't control someone's heart."

"Of course we can," she replies without missing a beat. "It's easier than you think. Once two people share a secret, it creates a bond between them. It's almost a law. Just look at the two of us." She pauses to gaze into my eyes, smiling. "I guarantee you that the Yibonn heir has a soft spot he wants to protect. Don't we all? All you need is to make him open up to you."

"But how?" I push back. "Why would he let me in on something he couldn't tell anyone else?"

"Because first you will let him in on something *you* can't tell anyone else," she says, grinning at me expectantly.

"Do you mean I should tell him who I really am?"

Her grin vanishes and she draws back in her seat, staring

at me with a look of bewilderment, and I shrink, hating myself.

"Listen to me very carefully now, sweetie," she says calmly, setting her wineglass down on the table. "You have a grand-mother who, for all appearances, adores you to pieces, but who savagely berates and abuses you behind closed doors. And how about your stunted mother, who's incapable of having a relationship with you because you remind her of her dead, unrequited love? No one imagines the truth, including your own uncle and aunts, who live under the same roof as you. How's that for a secret?"

I see her point, but it's possible that Haeri had already told Bonwhe about her family.

"You be open with him about these rough spots in your seemingly perfect life. At the very least, he'll feel sorry for Haeri. Perhaps even identify with her? Who's to say? And if you time this right, stripping down to your raw, real self at the perfect moment . . . he'll be helpless—because we are talking about Haeri, the lovely, after all."

Her eyes lit, she pronounces these words with ironclad conviction. I take a big sip of my drink, flushing as if caught out doing something. We're silent for a moment.

"Did you *create* Haeri's secret?" I flinch as soon as I ask, brac-ing for the worst. But Director Cha doesn't burst into flames.

"No," she replies evenly. "I'd never hurt her on purpose."

I don't know why, but her response comforts me more than it should, and the next thing I know, I'm saying, "Thank you for finding me, Director Cha. I'm going to prove you right," in a voice that I barely recognize as my own.

She treats me to the warmest smile I've seen on her face. "The idea that you're a replacement is history now," she says. "From here on, you're the only Haeri."

I'm feeling light-headed as desire and purpose swell up inside me again, crushing the doubts that have hobbled me all this time once and for all.

I am Haeri.

Part 2

YOU

CHAPTER 2

THE SURPRISE GUEST

The door opens halfway, and Producer Yi pops her head into the dressing room.

"Knock, knock," she says, already stepping in. "I'm here to check out the garden. The world's highest?"

She pivots on her heel to admire the hundred vases placed around the room, each holding a hundred roses of every pastel hue imaginable.

"A hundred times a hundred is . . . ten thousand roses?" she says, her gaze falling on the card sitting on the makeup counter. Snatching it up, she shoots me a sly glance and begins reading it aloud. *"Happy one hundredth day! Keep up the good work. My weather is in your hands! Your friend, Jehno."*

With an exaggerated squeal, she teases, "Goh Haeri! Please accept the champion's heart already?"

"Oh, come on," I protest, smiling awkwardly. "You just read it yourself! *Your friend?*"

As promised, there was the famous first date to the New Year's fireworks, which was followed by another date on Valentine's Day. It was on this date that Jehno surprised me with an exquisite pendant in the shape of a shamrock. I declined the gift as politely as I could, telling him that it was too expensive for me to accept. But Jehno, who is not a fool, understood the subtext and strategically retreated a step while appointing himself my new best friend. A week later, from the editing room, Director Cha called to praise me for the move.

"A friend?" Producer Yi snorts. "What kind of friend keeps feeding you slices of his heart and soul?"

She'd never stop.

I watch her gaze dreamily at the garden, inhaling deeply through her nose and exhaling through her mouth, a serene smile on her face.

Out the wraparound window, a perfect rainbow arches across the night sky. The meteorological event is a surreal one even by Snowglobe's standards, and I can't help but feel unduly responsible for the stunning view I created.

A minute later, we're joined by the two anchors of *News at 9,* who want to check out the reported garden for themselves.

"Oh my," one breathes.

The other looks around in wonder. "What's going on today? Is this the apocalypse? A rose field inside and a nocturnal rainbow outside?"

I tug at the elbow of Producer Yi, who's looking nearly intoxicated by the fragrance in the air.

"Aren't you going to tell me who the guest is today?" I say.

Today is the one day of the month when a guest is invited to the studio for the live weather drawing. Normally, I'd meet them backstage for small talk and a quick rehearsal before we go on, but the producer wants today's guest to be a surprise.

"No need to fret, girl. I know you'd do more than just fine—even if the guest were a cat," she says.

"Just tell me one thing," I plead. "It's not Jehno, is it?"

I pray that it isn't. She just laughs coyly.

Ten minutes later, the revolving platform does a one-eighty, parking the weather set in front of the live-feed camera, signaling the start of my favorite time of day, the ten minutes during which viewers' delight or disappointment hinges on the weather balls I draw.

Standing in the studio lights more brilliant than the April rays, I sing out my opening line.

"Hi, everyone. It's Goh Haeri, reporting live from the weather studio."

Even to my own ears, I sound good. I sound pleasant, confident, and professional—as seasoned as one can be after the first hundred days on the job; and it fortifies me.

"According to legend, if you wish upon a rainbow, the resident fairy will make that wish come true . . . ," I begin, sliding right into the groove.

While Fran imbued the segment with his own dynamic brand of energy and flair, I try to engage the viewers with a style that plays on my own natural strengths. Therefore, the hour tends to feel composed, conversational, and even therapeutic, if I do say so myself.

"If you can, look out the window right now and wish on tonight's rainbow," I say. "*My* wish is that all *your* wishes come true."

Then I close my eyes and bring my hands together. Without a live audience, it's a little hard to believe that so many people tune in to the segment, though I myself was one of them. But then the morning news roundup has dispelled any doubt.

—*We have something to celebrate today. Yes, the first weather segment hosted by our new weathercaster, Goh Haeri, set a new single-day ratings record for the network.*

—*Do you know who I'm wearing today? Yes, it's a Wang. By Wang Dohyoung, of course, a fashion designer and a first-year Snowglobe resident, who finds herself suddenly inundated with orders since our weathercaster appeared on the show wearing her dress.*

—*The hairstyle predicted to trend this spring among women of all ages is the chestnut-brown bob, already going viral in some circles since our popular weathercaster began rocking it a few weeks ago. She really has breathed new life into a style that can be considered kinda blah, didn't she?*

I straighten my back and stand taller. Putting on a perfect smile, I begin, "Today we have a surprise special guest! *I* have no idea who it is, so, ladies and gentlemen, let's find out together. Please welcome today's guest with me!"

Turning to the walkway on my left, I'm jolted to see Bonwhe striding toward the set. My eyes grow wide. Wider than they did a month ago when the guests, a soon-to-be-married couple, took a dramatic tumble after tripping over each other's feet.

Bonwhe steps up onto the set and acknowledges my reaction with a casual smile and a slight dip of his head.

"Should I face the camera over there?" he asks.

I murmur an affirmation, and after that, he's right at home

on our stage. The usual preshow warm-up designed to help guests shake off nerves and familiarize themselves with the flow of things would have been a waste of everyone's time. Bonwhe's eyeline management for the camera, in particular, is impeccable. I could have taken notes from him during my first couple of weeks on the job, in fact. He even picks up the slack for me, graciously, when I forget to introduce him in my current state of discombobulation.

"Hello. My name is Yi Bonwhe. I'm a Snowglobe resident of nearly twenty years," he says, serving up a smile that's perfectly in tune with the tone of the show.

His ease and comfort on the set are comparable to that of the two anchors of *News at 9,* who've been at it for two years.

I want to pull the family into the show. And you're *going to help me. You have excellent intuition for show production.*

"Thank you for joining us today in the studio, Mr. Yi," I say. "We're so happy to have you."

I notice a private look of bemusement flit across his face when I say "Mr. Yi."

"Thank you, Ms. Goh Haeri," he responds. And steadying his gaze on me, he adds, "It's been a while."

"Yes, it has," I say brightly. "The last time I saw you was at the biathlon championship."

This isn't true, of course, but I'm not about to bring up our secret encounter involving the mirrors. I move on to the usual question. "So who are you drawing the weather for this evening?"

"My nephew. He's in kindergarten," he says, flashing the smile of an adoring uncle. "He's going on his first school trip tomorrow, and I'm hoping for a beautiful day for him and his classmates."

"How sweet," I coo, which isn't an act. I'm thoroughly charmed. "I'll be sure to send good vibes his way!"

Then we're moving down the row of drums, with Bonwhe drawing the blank weather balls and me activating them in my hands.

"Tomorrow's weather will feature bright sunshine with a few fair-weather clouds building up to isolated evening showers in some neighborhoods. Total accumulation, one inch. Lows around fifty-five with highs topping out at seventy-five. Humidity at fifty-four percent, with a light breeze blowing out of the southwest at two and a half miles per hour. Visibility, two and a half miles."

—*Cut.*

Producer Yi's cue comes through my earpiece, concluding today's livecast.

I'm just pulling out the piece and thanking the crew when the studio door flies open and a gaggle of employees who have been pressed against the other side, waiting for their chance to meet with Bonwhe, crowd into the room. I watch as he shakes everyone's hand and exchanges greetings, all without his polite smile wavering once. His human shadow, Assistant Yu, is right there, of course, gently but firmly discouraging anyone who holds up a Polaroid or handcam to document their personal sighting of the shining heir. When I finally catch her eyes, I gesture toward the dressing room to remind her of the postshow tea.

Ordinarily, guests are invited in for light refreshments and a warm-up *before* the show, but the routine was altered to fit today's extraordinary guest.

"I'll be right back," says Assistant Yu, standing in the hallway. "Please leave the door locked in the meantime. You never know who's going to barge in with a camera."

With that advice, she turns around and heads for the elevator, leaving me and Bonwhe alone in the dressing room.

Bonwhe quietly takes in the scene, letting his eyes sweep over the indoor rose garden. He rubs his brow absently and I feel an odd tick of regret. He has to guess that it's Jehno's work.

"Are you feeling okay, Young Master?" I say, maintaining a high level of formality for the hidden cameras around us.

He flicks his wrist and checks the time on his watch.

"Yes, of course. Thank you," he replies. "But Assistant Yu will be disappointed when she gets back from the florist."

So that's why she left.

"She insisted it was bad manners for us to show up empty-handed," he explains, taking in the roses again. Then his gaze pauses on the makeup table, on Jehno's card. I don't quite understand my behavior then, but I snatch it up and shove it in the drawer. The look he gives me says he already knows, and he consults his watch again.

"Do you have a tight schedule today, Young Master?" I ask.

"Oh, no," he answers lightly.

A second later, beams of light checker the room, and then comes the clack of the slate.

Bonwhe grins.

"Been waiting for this," he says, focusing his eyes on me. I open my mouth to ask him how he knows when they call the break, but then I clamp it shut, realizing that Haeri might have asked that question already.

Bonwhe eases down on the vanity chair, giving a quick, absent glance at the counter crowded with various products.

"How have you been?" he says, shifting his eyes to me and smiling softly.

My brain launches into a montage of recent events. As with most actors, I, too, quickly adjusted to life in Snowglobe. Though the fear that I'm not measuring up to a Haeri worthy of everyone's love and worship prickles inside me 24-7, the pressure has put me on an accelerated learning curve, forcing me to perfect all of Haeri's habits and tics. The cost of this high performance? Chronic exhaustion and anxiety that simmers just beneath the surface. And in my weak moments, Cooper's voice echoes in my ears: *I won't say that it's pain-free. But there are all kinds of cures for pain in Snowglobe, and in abundance.*

Nuzzling my cheek against Maeryung's and walking hand in hand with Sanghui are still torture, but I'm getting used to it. You can get used to anything, really. And I do reward myself with the kinds of cures only Snowglobe can offer: daily runs in the park through fresh morning mist, followed by decadent chocolate parfaits. Sadly, the latter means a few excess pounds, inspiring Maeryung's and Sanghui's backhanded compliments behind the scenes. On the days when their ridicule cuts deep, I skip dinner and turn to my own cure for pain—the monthly letters my family sends me, courtesy of Director Cha, which I read and reread in a camera blind spot. The financial support, also arranged by Director Cha, has allowed Mom to quit the plant and spend time at home with Grandma. In addition to laughing and crying together at their favorite TV shows, they can now treat themselves to occasional fresh fruit from Snowglobe, and Mom even took up knitting. Life is good, she says, and the news delivered in her familiar handwriting never fails to recharge me.

So that's how I've been. And as for how I am today? Jehno's ten thousand roses perfuming the air of my dressing room should be enough of a boost to sustain me for another week without chocolate parfaits.

"I've been great, thanks," I say, unable to disclose any of the truth. Then, dialing up the brightness in my voice, I add, "It's like the job has breathed new life into me."

It's no lie. The ten minutes on set have become the most relaxing time of day for me, during which I'm free to perform a role without feeling like an imposter. Even Haeri has to act the part of Haeri, the weathercaster, doesn't she? And no one is above impersonating a superior, more attractive version of themselves when they come to draw the weather with me, and I'm talking about people who already act for a living. Remembering this helps me feel less like a fraud, which I still do sometimes, despite my best efforts.

I arrange my face into a blissful expression and look into Bonwhe's eyes.

"You know," I begin, "I've been thinking about how lucky I am to be loved by so many people. And the fact that they tune in to my channel every day is such a blessing." Then I shift my gaze out the window, to the rainbow that's just started to fade. "It's sort of made me rethink my decision to leave."

Boom.

"Really?" is Bonwhe's response, which is underwhelming. And what was I expecting? A little more enthusiasm, I guess. Maybe even joy.

He stays quiet for a minute, then smiles a little. "Are you ever going to collect the gift I left you?"

My heart slams. It feels like he's seeing right through me.

THE PHONE CALL

"Too busy" is the lamest of all excuses. But what else can I say? *I ran into a wall the other day and damaged my brain, so can you please remind me where to find it?*

It isn't that I haven't tried to find the dead drop. In fact, every time I hear the first slate go off, which usually happens before dawn, I drag myself out of bed and use the ten precious minutes to poke around. Cornered now, I finally blurt out, "It was because of Jehno."

"Jehno?" he echoes, clearly unsettled.

"Yes, Jehno," I repeat. "It's not like I could ever tell him about it, and it feels kind of weird for us to be secretly writing each other."

My ability to lie on the spot appalls me. I've never given two hoots about Jehno, nor have I led him to believe otherwise.

Bonwhe swivels in his chair, taking another slow look at the ten thousand roses filling the room.

"Is that why you're reconsidering your decision? Kim Jehno?"

"Maybe," I say, which may come back to bite me later, but it will have to do for now.

"Then what about Cha Seol?"

I just stare at my feet. What do I say?

"Do you forgive her?" he presses.

A long moment goes by and I finally look up at him, weary. "I don't know," I finally say. "I guess I just want to focus on all the good things in my life right now. And on taking care of myself, you know?"

Bonwhe casts his eyes back to the roses, pondering my response. Then, pushing up from the chair, he says, "I didn't think anyone could make you stay in Snowglobe."

Ugh.

He reaches a hand into his jacket and produces a silver brooch from an inner pocket.

"Take it. It's yours, after all," he says, holding it out to me.

I give him a blank look.

"It's a sperm whale," he explains.

I'm about to ask him what this is about when someone knocks at the door. Acting on pure instinct, I snatch the brooch and slip it into my pocket. A moment later, Assistant Yu is walking in, carrying a bouquet of one hundred roses— exactly one-hundredth of Jehno's contribution. I watch her expression shift to defeat at the sight of the roses that have transformed the dressing room.

Bonwhe's already wearing his official face. He doles out a few stock compliments about the show in his official tone, and I match them all with equally stock replies. A few minutes later, our teatime concludes without a drop of tea having been consumed, and me even more confused about him than I was before.

It's almost eleven when I finally make it to Fran's private rooms on the hospital floor and he greets me with a tired smile.

"I wish I were home, treating you to some pasta like I promised," he says wistfully.

The private rooms he occupies might as well be a home—there are a big bathroom, an extra bed for visitors, and an over-sized leather sectional parked before an entertainment center complete with a giant TV and an elaborate stereo system.

Sadly, Fran doesn't look any more robust than he did when I last saw him a few months ago in the dressing room.

"Don't worry, Fran. I'll hold you to that promise," I say, turning up the cheer in my voice. "But how about the skyline from here? It's spectacular!"

On the top floor—the 204th—you're so far above every-thing that the world below might as well be a toy city locked in a photo. Here on the 73rd floor, though, the magnified view twitches with life.

"You weren't going to hog this for yourself, were you?" I say jokingly. "Please invite me more often?"

Strictly speaking, Fran didn't invite me today. In fact, he kept thwarting my threat to visit, holding out for the day when he'd be allowed to move back to his flat and resume a normal life. But weeks and months fell away, until I finally said I was coming to see him in celebration of my hundredth day on the job—whether he liked it or not.

"Great show today, my friend," Fran says, treating me to the brightest smile. "You were extra radiant next to this month's special guest."

He's been calling me friend for some time now, though I'm not sure if I deserve the designation. Then again, I don't know if anyone else checks in on him to say hi with any regularity.

I thank him and return the compliment, telling him how good he looks, which is patently false.

"I'd better be, with all the Botox I've been getting!" he replies.

I make a show of laughing at his joke, and he deadpans, "Come on, you haven't noticed? Look. The bunny lines above my nose? They're gone."

He lifts his face up for my inspection, and he's right. His skin is as smooth as a baby's. But Botox treatments while battling cancer? I never would have thought someone would do that.

"I figured I should spruce up once in a while for all the die-hard fans out there. It has to be depressing to see someone looking so bedraggled and sickly all the time."

I feel a stab of shame then, for all my self-pity over the struggles that come with being the world's most beloved girl. So what if all I do is tell one lie to cover another? It's nothing next to what Fran is going through.

"You're an inspiration, Fran," I tell him honestly.

He gives a smile tinged with sorrow, then quickly changes the subject.

"Come check out the deck with me," he says, climbing out of the bed with some effort. He gestures for me to follow, and the glass door slides open automatically as he approaches.

I follow him out into the crisp night air, the city glittering below like so many gems.

"Access to this deck is limited to people in private rooms, so it's usually just me and a few others out here," Fran explains, then adds, "Living the life, aren't I?"—flashing a playful grin.

A patient-doctor pair appears from another sliding glass door, and they settle by the far railing, talking softly.

"Hi, Dr. Cha!" Fran calls out, already heading for them.

The patient swiftly heads back inside, but the doctor turns in our direction. She looks almost startled. Large-eyed, and with her hair up in a sleek bun, she reminds me of someone.

"Hi, Fran!" she says, her voice notably raspy. "What brings you out so late?"

Have I seen her before? I wonder.

Then it hits me. The cleaning lady at Director Cha's. And now she's here on the VIP hospital floor, a name tag announcing her as Dr. Cha Sohm pinned to her lab coat.

Fran introduces us as the doctor shifts uncomfortably on her feet, straining to smile.

"Haeri, meet Dr. Cha Sohm," Fran says, adding with a wink. "*Dr.* Cha is Director Cha's little sister."

I remember an article in *TV Guide* saying that Director Cha has neither the time nor the inclination for new friendships because she has the best of friends in her two little sisters. I didn't know that one was a doctor, though.

"Such an honorable family," Fran gushes as the doctor's forced smile morphs into a sort of grimace.

I stand there awkwardly, not sure what to say, and the

doctor makes to depart. "It was great seeing you, Fran, and a pleasure meeting you, Ms. Haeri," she says, edging backward toward the doors. "You both have a good night."

She gives us a quick smile and turns, and I realize that the patient never went inside. She's waiting for Dr. Cha just outside. All that's visible is her eyes, the rest obscured by her long, dark hair and a blue surgical mask. Sensing my gaze, she turns to look, and our eyes meet for a moment. For one thunderous and paralyzing moment.

It can't be.

I must have imagined it in the low light of the deck. Because . . . Because Haeri is *dead,* period. But those eyes? I know them better than my own.

Back home, in my room, I phone Director Cha, my heart beating frantically in my chest. The answering machine picks up on the third ring.

—*Hi. You've reached Cha Seol's home. I'm unable to come to the phone right now. Please leave a message after the beep and I'll get back to you as soon as I can. If this is an emergency, please call my editing office."*

She doesn't give the number for her editing office.

I hang up and throw myself on the bed. The clock on the nightstand reads 11:52. Almost midnight. But what am I so anxious about, calling her this late? I'm going to tell her I saw someone whose eyes reminded me of Haeri's?

Realizing how ridiculous it is, I change into my pajamas and get into bed and try to fall asleep. But I can't stop thinking about the girl's eyes.

—Clack!

The sound of the slate rouses me. Blinking open my eyes, I check the time on the wall clock. Three a.m. The phone explodes with a ring. Reflexively, I snatch up the receiver and hiss into it, "Hello?"

Silence. Pressing the receiver to my ear, I strain to listen. Then finally comes a delicate "Hi," in a familiar voice, and my heart freezes.

"We saw each other on the deck," the voice says. "Did you recognize me?"

I cover my mouth, stifling a whimper.

"Hello? Can you hear me?"

I want to respond, but I can barely even breathe, my throat seizing with shock.

"I saw photos of you attending the banquet for me in the newspaper," the voice says, then gives a small laugh. "I couldn't believe it."

"Haeri?" I squeak. "Is it really you?" This is wrong. So deeply wrong.

"The lockbox. Do you still have it?"

The lockbox? Then it comes to me. The slight nasal voice rasping through the phone line demanding that I put the lockbox away in a safe place. Now I can put it together—that raspy voice. It was Dr. Cha Sohm's.

"Can you take it out for me?" the voice says, but I'm too stunned to move, or even fully register her words. I'm sitting there paralyzed, clutching the receiver and shaking, when the voice comes at me again, jolting me.

"Quick! You have to open it and put it back before the slate goes off."

"Haeri," I repeat, choking with confusion. "Is it really you?"

A slow moment ticks by. Then she says, "Open the lock-box. You'll see."

I reach into the desk drawer and retrieve the lock box I had halfheartedly stashed away. Its dials are set at 0000.

"What's the combination?" I croak.

"Nine, one, one, two."

I line up the dials. There's a click, and the lock is undone.

THE TRUTH

What the box contains is a single Polaroid photo, lying facedown.

"The photo will show you why you had to step in for me," Haeri says.

My heart in my throat, I flip over the picture. Haeri's face stares out of the Polaroid, all too familiar but for the shock of third-degree burns covering her nose and mouth area. With a gasp, I drop the photo.

"I'm alive," she says into my ear. "Been alive all this time. Just not camera-ready. Thanks for filling in for me, by the way, going to the banquet, the championship, the fireworks and everything. And of course, the forecast," she says. A rueful sigh. "Director Cha was vehement about holding me back until my face heals."

"Director Cha?" I echo vacantly.

"Yes, of course. She is absolutely convinced that no one would want to see ugly Haeri."

"That's ridiculous," I say, my eyes on the photo going out of focus and my stomach clenching. I can believe it now. That

Director Cha would have exploited Haeri, manipulating her like a puppet. And when the puppet got scratched up, she stashed it away for a shiny new one. A tear falls from my face onto the photo.

But what about me? How could she propose that I live the rest of my life as Haeri when she knew Haeri was living and breathing?

"I . . . I'm so sorry," I get out, feeling sick to my stomach. "I didn't know."

"That's okay. I'm all healed now. Well. Almost." Her voice returns brightly. "A little bit of makeup and no one will notice."

"That's great," I say, meaning it.

She's silent a moment.

"Do you really think so?" she says finally. "What do you think will happen to you when I come back?"

A whole new kind of doom settles over me then, instantly parching my tongue and throat. All my fears have been about getting outed as a fraud, never about being faced with the return of a dead Haeri.

Sighing heavily, Haeri continues, "Knowing what you know—you're aware that Director Cha wouldn't just let you go home."

Cooper's face, his mouth open in terror, rises before my eyes, and my voice gets away from me.

"My family!" I shriek.

"Shh—yes." Haeri drops her own voice to a whisper. "That lady's always a step ahead of us."

Us. It takes me a moment to register the word. How comforting the sound, even as the tears rush to sting my eyes again.

"And that's why we have to connect as soon as possible. I can help you," she says.

"You want to help me?"

"That's a given."

But why? Shouldn't she be resentful of me, an impersonator poised to displace her for good?

"You only got dragged into this mess because I'd burned myself. Stupidly," she says. "If I hadn't been so careless, you'd still be at home. I'm sorry. I'm the one who should apologize."

I want to deny it so badly. *No! You've done nothing wrong! You didn't do this to me!* But the words are caught in my throat. *I did it to myself. I hated my life, so I stole yours.*

My chest begins to heave, and suddenly I'm sobbing, shuddering and gasping through tears. But I know I have to pull myself together. Finally, I steady my voice enough to say, "Wouldn't you get in trouble? What if Director Cha catches us on camera?"

I glance at the clock again. Five minutes until cameras resume. It's a half-hour drive from here to SnowTower. I spring to my feet and move to the mirror, the phone's long, curly cord stretching behind me. Holding my breath, I bring my hand up slowly, but when my fingertips touch the glass, its cold, hard surface presses back. Of course. The Yibonns wouldn't bother with a regular home. And what if it *were* one of their mirrors? I don't know the first thing about navigating it.

"Come visit Fran again tonight," Haeri says. "I'll meet you on the deck."

Is she crazy? "But what about the cameras? Director Cha will see us!"

"Don't worry," she assures me. "Dr. Cha is with us. I'm calling from her office right now."

Dr. Cha. Did she supply her sister with the vaccines and frostbite cream, too? Even more confused, I push back: "Why would she help us instead of her sister?"

In a stark voice, Haeri replies, "Someone has to stop the director. People can't even grasp what she has done."

I think of Bonwhe, and how much he hates her. Before I can stop myself, I'm blurting out, "I know another person who might help—"

But Haeri cuts me off. "We don't have much time. I have to be back in my room before the slate."

Okay. I'll talk to her about Bonwhe when I see her later.

"Meet you out on the deck," she says. "Make sure Fran's with you so Director Cha doesn't get suspicious. Dr. Cha will take care of Fran after that."

I feel my heart drop, just thinking about the cameras capturing me and Haeri side by side. Director Cha would be furious. Does Haeri know what kind of danger this exposes us to? And what about my family?

"We'll get caught," I insist, my voice a pathetic bleat in my ears.

"We won't," Haeri counters calmly. "There's a blind spot, the only one on the seventy-third floor. I'll see you tonight."

I gaze numbly at my dark silhouette in the mirror as Haeri gives me a quick set of instructions about the blind spot, then breaks the connection. I hurry back to bed and close my eyes. A few seconds later, the slate goes off and everything resumes.

I want to thank her. I want to tell her that I'm sorry, again and again. I want to summon the strength to admit that I'm no victim here, that I was all too happy to steal what's hers. But the truth is, I can't.

I spend the day trying my best to pretend that everything is fine and go about Haeri's life as though nothing has changed. When night falls, I return to the 73rd floor and greet Fran with a hug and hand him the kale juice I brought—a little surprise from his favorite juice bar and the perfect excuse to stop by. He takes a sip of the juice and smiles widely. His buoyant mood makes me feel extra guilty about dragging him into today's mission as a prop, but there was no other option.

After some time chatting, I suggest going outside to enjoy the night air, and he happily agrees. When we walk out onto the deck, the doctor is sitting on the bench, and Fran heads straight for her, singing out warmly, "Hello, Dr. Cha!"

The doctor looks up and returns the greeting and Fran continues, "Isn't that your patient over there?"

He's referring to Haeri, sitting in a wheelchair at the far end of the deck. She's partially obscured by a protruding column, which I can only guess is on purpose for the cameras.

"Yes," Dr. Cha replies with a sigh. "She needs to stay inside during the day. She's being treated for facial burns, but thankfully, she's nearly all healed." Then, in a darker tone, she adds, "It's depression she's fighting now."

Fran nods, a knowing expression on his face. The doctor makes as though she's going to head back in, but then she turns to Fran. "You haven't had your vitals checked this evening, have you? How about we do it now before I clock out?"

Fran looks to me, and I nod enthusiastically. A few

moments later, Fran and Dr. Cha disappear into the building, and as if on cue, wet drops begin to splatter on my head and shoulders. It's the rain Bonwhe and I drew together yesterday.

Whirrrr—

I look up at the sound and see that the automatic awning is sliding out, activated by the precipitation. By the time it extends over the whole of the deck, the erratic tapping of the raindrops has turned into a steady pitter-patter.

"Rain *was* in the forecast," I chirp for the cameras. Then, stretching my arms over my head, I sneak a concerned look at the depressed burn patient—also for the cameras—before heading to the blind spot on the opposite end of the deck, as if in deference to the patient's need for privacy and quiet.

By the rules of architectural symmetry, the other end of the deck is also half obscured by a protruding column. The blind spot is tiny, and anyone bigger than us would have a hard time disappearing behind it.

Sucking in my stomach, I wedge myself into the narrow space behind the column and begin edging sideways, my hair standing on end at the thought of the rain stopping, and the awning retracting to expose me to the cameras above in my crab walk.

When I emerge from the other end, Haeri greets me from her wheelchair, her eyes soft and smiling above the blue surgical mask. Met with those eyes again, all I want to do is pour my heart out, tell her how happy I am to find out that her suicide was just a nasty lie—the worst story anyone could ever come up with.

But all I'm able to manage is a stupid grimace before she lifts a hand and pulls the mask down to her chin, showing me her flawless face. Is it makeup? There's no trace of the burn I saw on the Polaroid. Slowly, she pushes herself out of the wheelchair and stands before me.

We stare at each other, transfixed. Is this what it feels like to have an out-of-body experience? A raindrop splashes on my nose, waking me from my trance.

"Haeri—" I begin, but she puts a finger to her lips and I'm reminded that we're in a blind spot, not a deaf spot. If we can't talk, though, what are we to do? It's then that Haeri lunges for me and seizes my arm. Then a sharp sting in my neck flashes me back to the flu shot Director Cha gave me. The next thing I know, Haeri is taking a small step back, her eyes hard and mouth clamped tight, a strange-looking syringe clutched in her pale, trembling hand. I find myself slumping limply into her, my eyes falling shut. I feel as heavy as a lead brick sinking to the bottom of the sea.

Part 3

US

BANISHED

My eyes fly open and I bolt upright, but something jerks me back. Feeling woozy, feeling drunk, I look around and discover that I'm in a strange bed, wearing a hospital gown, an IV line snaking out of the top of my left hand. And is that my right ankle handcuffed to the bed frame? I try sitting up again, bewildered, but there's a metallic clank and I'm yanked back again, and my eyes jump to a handcuff shackling my wrist to the bed.

What the hell? Alarm stirring deep in my core, I prop myself up on my free arm and look around at my surroundings. I seem to be trapped in a bed parked inside a giant birdcage. Through the metal wire grid, I see a single naked bulb dangling from the ceiling beam, bathing the drab interior in dull yellow light. I can hear running water from what sounds like a sink. A bathroom? This is no hospital. This is someone's home.

Terror sizzles through me and I thrash, jerking wildly against the shackles, trying to free myself. The IV comes loose, but the effort is doomed. Still, I don't stop until I realize that the thrashing is making the bed inch back and forth on its rolling casters. I look around the room, frantic for an escape, and a woman wrapped in a cheap bathrobe slams out of the bathroom, one eye squinting against the soapsuds dripping from the wet pile of hair on her head. We both freeze for a moment, staring at each other, and then she's padding over to me. Before I know it, I'm letting loose a scream, a savage, heart-stopping scream that tears through my chest. It's the only thing I can do.

Stopping in her tracks, she plugs her ears and cries out, "Hey! Chill out! Stop the screaming!"

I refill my lungs with air and unleash another scream, and another. Eventually, she unplugs her ears. She holds her hands in the air and approaches me slowly, repeating, *"Whoa! Shhhh . . . whoa, whoa,"* as if trying to soothe a large, angry animal. *"It's okay. Shhh . . . Calm down now! Who's a good girl?"*

Not me. I continue to scream my lungs out.

"Hey!" she shouts over my piercing howls. "You can scream all you want, but no one can hear you. This is the only house within a mile radius!"

I respond with a fresh scream, and she digs a remote control from a raggedy couch and turns on the TV. With a few rapid clicks, the volume is raised high enough to drown me out, but I don't stop. I scream until my throat seizes up and she finally mutes the TV. All I can do is warn her off with the most hateful look I can manage.

"You're pretty robust for someone who's been out cold for three days."

Out cold for three days? And was I shackled to this bed the whole time?

"Watch some TV and chill out," she says. "I'll go rinse my hair, then I'll get you some food."

Before I can ask her any questions, she's turned the volume up again and is shuffling back into the bathroom, where she leaves the door open to keep an eye on me. As if I could do anything, shackled to a bed inside a cage.

With no way out, I take in my surroundings as best as I can. There are a couch, a recliner, a coffee table, a TV, and this bed-cage crowding the claustrophobic room. But where's the telephone?

That's when the image of Haeri comes back to me, a syringe in her hand and a grim look on her face.

—*Let's turn to our favorite weathercaster for tomorrow's forecast.*

It's Anchor Chung! I snap my head to the TV, and the camera pans to Haeri on the weather set. She's dressed in a lemon-colored pantsuit I don't recognize, gazing into the camera and giving everyone the full effect of her smile.

"Do you know the ideal air temperature for living?" she chirps.

The sperm whale brooch from Bonwhe is pinned to her breast pocket.

"According to scientists, that temperature is seventy degrees Fahrenheit."

She opens her smile. Sweet, lovely, and self-assured. This Haeri is definitely not the vulnerable, downcast, and somewhat tense person I met on the deck. But why should she be, now that she's reclaimed her rightful place in the world?

Still, something doesn't sit right with me. I can't help seeing a third person, as if the girl on the screen is neither Jeon Chobahm *nor* Goh Haeri. There's some vague difference that I can't put a finger on, and it troubles me.

"Today's high was exactly seventy degrees, accompanied by a cloudless blue sky," she continues. "I hope I can deliver another set of perfect conditions for tomorrow, which is Saturday!"

She smiles even bigger then, and sticks her hand into the first drum.

How can she smile now? It's as if she doesn't know I'm locked away in this strange house. Or does she know? Are there cameras here? Does Director Cha know I've been missing for three days?

Suddenly, I realize how cold I am. Air is nipping at my nose, and the only heat is radiating from a lukewarm electric pad topping the mattress under me. *What on earth?* The dark, drab home, the antiquated TV, the threadbare furniture, the frost in the air . . . It hits me with the force of a blow. This isn't Snowglobe.

A sick feeling is rising up in me when my captor shuffles out of the bathroom, her hair wrapped in a towel.

"What the heck?" she yelps. "Who's watching this crap?" She snatches up the remote and clicks off the TV, then turns to me and says, "You hungry? I'll fix you some gruel."

Gruel? Is this a joke?

"Who are you?" I snarl. "And where am I?"

"Where?" she echoes, moving into the kitchen space off in a corner of the room. She opens a container and scoops some rice into a pot and says, "Have you heard of the retirees' village? The place where the also-rans spend the rest of their lives until they drop dead of boredom?"

"The retirees' village?" I repeat vacantly.

The strange woman holds the pot under the faucet and turns the water on; then she reaches for the bottle of soju sitting on the counter, a bendy straw sticking out of its narrow mouth. She takes a long sip from it as if it's soda, and my stomach turns.

The retirees' village. Other than its general location—that it's outside Snowglobe—so little is known about the place that it has taken on an almost mythic status.

"Then why am *I* here?" I hiss.

She ignores my question and sashays over to my cage with a bowl, then thrusts it in through the metal grid. "Eat up. I'll upgrade you to porridge tomorrow."

Outrage surges through me. *"Why am I here?"* I shout. *"And who are you?"*

"Who am I?" the woman repeats, gazing out at nothing for a moment, as if pondering the question herself. "Just call me Big Sis," she finally says, and laughs. "No need for formality."

I will never, ever call this woman Big Sis, not if she were the last person on earth.

"What? Am I too old to be Big Sis or something?" she says. "I'm just a little over thirty, you know." She waits, and when I don't answer, offers, "How about Coz?"

I keep glaring at her, feeling my lip curl.

"Fine," she says with a shrug. "Call me whatever you want. *Ajumma*—is that it?" Then she mutters sourly to herself. "Kids these days. . . . They think anyone over twenty has already gone to seed."

"Identify yourself," I demand, my voice shaky with mounting dread. "Your name and why you're doing this to me."

She snorts. "Identify myself? No problem. Name, Cha Hyang. Occupation, power plant worker."

"Cha Hyang?" I repeat, the name landing in my ears with a thud. Trying to steady my voice, I say, "Are you related to Director Cha?"

"Yes," she replies bitterly. "Related by blood dirtier than anything."

Director Cha's sister is a resident of the retirees' village? This is news to me.

"Did . . . Director Cha send me here?" I ask hesitantly.

She gives a casual "Mmm-hmm" of affirmation and gestures toward the gruel.

"Get it while it's hot. You're left-handed, aren't you?"

She grins as if expecting me to thank her for having shackled my right hand to the bed instead of my dominant left. When I keep glaring at her, she sighs and makes her way over to the sagging couch parked against the cage.

"Eat," she urges. "You can resume hating me after. Oh, and the IV you just pulled out? That was the last one I had, so you have no choice but to shove things down your gullet from now on, like it or not."

Undoing the towel on her head, she flings it across the room and sinks back into the couch, fanning her long, dark, wet hair across the headrest like seaweed washed up in the tide. Judging by the way she dries her hair, electricity must be a precious commodity here in the retirees' village.

I stare at her, seething and wanting to cry at the same time.

"What's the matter?" she says, shifting her gaze back to

me. "You couldn't shut your trap a minute ago, and now you can't open it to dribble down some gruel?" A sigh. Then she reaches a hand under the couch, groping for something. "Well, I'd be pissed, too, I guess, if someone promised me a life of silver and gold only to change their mind and banish me."

Her words freeze my heart all over again. Is she serious about Director Cha doing this to me?

Then the woman cries out a triumphant *"Yes!"* pulling out a bottle of soju and holding it aloft like a trophy. Her eyes shining with joy, she pops the top and inserts the spent straw from the coffee table, then starts sucking out the contents as if it were iced coffee or something. Turning to me, she says without irony, "You want a sip?"

This woman operates on a whole different plane. "What do you *mean,* change their mind and banish me?"

"What do you mean, what do you mean?" she says, blinking at me. "Seol thought the other girl—what's her name? Chobahm? Bambi?—was a better fit for the role. Amazing, isn't it? The replacement that was supposed to cover for just a few months turned out to be dynamite. You've been fired."

"What?" I murmur, uncomprehending.

She darts her eyes away. Stealing a glance at me, she says, "It's not something to starve yourself to death over. Who knows? Maybe the Bambi girl won't work out and Seol will call you back? But until then, I'm your guardian—and warden—whether you like it or not. By the way, you're about to burst a blood vessel, glaring at me like that. Take a break."

This woman. This drunk. She doesn't make any sense.

"But I *am* Jeon Chobahm!" I shout angrily.

She chokes, spraying soju out of her nostrils.

"What?" she squeaks, coughing.

"I *said,* I am Jeon Chobahm!"

"No, you're not," she manages between choked breaths. "Seol sent me Serin. Bae Serin."

What a fool. She keeps hacking away, and for a minute, I feel more pity than anger. When the cough subsides, she makes a face and holds up the bottle for an assessment.

"Did I drink too much?" she wonders aloud. Then she goes on asking me how many fingers she's holding up. Watching me steam wordlessly, she demands that I count backward from twenty.

"Stop your nonsense and let me out. Now!" I'm shouting again.

"You know what? You sure can act. I mean, you rage like a real victim of mistaken identity. Ha! I'd have fallen for it, if I didn't know any better—I'll tell you that," she says. A moment later, she gives a nervous laugh, refocusing her eyes on me. "Are you serious?" A pause. "That you're Jeon Chobahm, and not Bae Serin?"

"How many times do I have to say it?" I hiss. Clutching at the cage with my free hand, I shake it. "Let me out!"

She mutters under her breath what a good idea it was to tie me down, then looks up at me, a sober expression transforming her face. "So you're Chobahm?" she says. "The stand-in that Seol rushed into Snowglobe for the Christmas party? You're the Bambi?"

Watching the answer settle into her eyes, I feel my heart fall. A sudden sense of powerlessness and futility comes over me. I want to reach for that bowl of watery gruel to fill the growing hollow inside me with something, anything, but I know better than to eat anything touched by this degenerate.

Sluuurrrp—

Hyang's straw hunts down the last drops of soju in her third bottle. Scraping up the last ounce of strength left in me, I lash out at her again.

"If you're done getting shitfaced, let me out, you idiot!"

She heaves a long sigh, her breath reeking of alcohol, and says, "You just wait for me here."

As if I have a choice.

Wobbling to her feet, she fishes a key out of her pocket and goes to a closed door. She unlocks it; then, cracking it open with exaggerated care, she slips inside and eases the door shut behind her.

There's the sound of drawers opening and closing, then murmured cursing, followed by the sound of stuff being dumped on the floor and the rustling of paper. When she finally reemerges, she's carrying a VHS tape and a few letter-sized envelopes.

"It'll be faster to see it for yourself," she says, pushing the tape into the VHS player by the TV.

The TV screen turns on and displays a buzzing school auditorium. The camera swoops down to the blackboard on the stage, and a banner of white letters comes into focus. THE 115TH ANNUAL ACTOR AUDITION: STUDENTS, it reads, and just beneath it is another set of letters scribbled in yellow chalk: AH-D-3.

The 115th? That's when I was still in school.

A girl in two pigtails appears on the screen, and I go numb.

"Hi," she says. She looks and sounds just like Haeri, like me.

Only, the patch of skin running from under her nose to her chin is a taut, shiny pink like a burn scar. The Haeri in the Polaroid had the same scar.

"My name is Bae Serin. I'm a first-year student," she says.

That voice. My eyes rove to the student ID sewn into the breast pocket of her uniform, 9112, and the phone call comes back to me like a thunderclap.

What's the combination?

Nine, one, one, two.

Staring into the camera, she offers her brightest smile. Apart from the scar and the general grubbiness and air of deprivation about her, the girl's resemblance to Haeri is uncanny.

Yujin's voice echoes in my head.

It's said that there are a total of three clones for each of us, including ourselves.

A SUBSTITUTE FOR THE SUBSTITUTE

Hyang pauses the tape, suspending the girl named Serin in motion, her mouth open like a baby bird squawking for food.

"That's Serin. The Haeri you met in Snowglobe," Hyang says.

"Why?" I breathe, my pulse racing. "Why is she in Snowglobe pretending to be Haeri?"

"Months before Haeri died, Seol sneaked her into Snowglobe for a series of facial surgeries."

I look back to the screen, gripped by the scar on Serin's face.

"She wanted a new Haeri," Hyang continues. "A Haeri whose ambitions matched her own, a Haeri as hard as herself."

You've got what it takes to become Haeri. New and improved.

What if Yujin's outlandish doppelganger theory, which I've dismissed for years—that everyone has two doppelgangers—turns out to be true? Then Cha Seol has found them all—Goh Haeri, Bae Serin, and me, Jeon Chobahm. I suppose it can't have been too difficult, since participation in the annual audition is mandatory for all students, and a working director, as a member of the scouting committee, has access to every audition tape.

"According to Seol," Hyang continues, "Serin was a perfect fit, driven by an obsessive desire to live like Haeri someday."

It doesn't take a director to recognize that drive in Serin. She broadcasts her fandom by inhabiting her idol completely. Her pigtails, her smile, her inflections and pauses: she's all Haeri.

Hyang presses play and Serin resumes: *The first thing I want to do when I get to Snowglobe? Make friends with Haeri, of course! My mom says when I was a little girl, I would run to the TV and kiss the screen whenever Haeri came on, talking to her on TV as if she could hear me. Call me crazy, but I think she might love me, too. I could be her long-lost twin!*

Serin lets out a trill of a laugh, which she then reins in with a lovable smile, Haeri's smile, her eyes squinting to produce two soft arches. And though no one would mistake her for Haeri yet, the sparkle in her eyes commands attention.

"There was a small problem," Hyang explains, fidgeting restlessly with the envelope she brought out from the room. "Serin got that scar on her face when she was three, so Seol recruited help from Sohm, a gifted plastic surgeon and her little sister, who thought the world of her big sis, and began fixing Serin's face to get her camera-ready. Everything was going according to plan. Until Haeri killed herself." Hyang's face clouds over. "I had been worried that she might be too nice, too soft to continue her life as Haeri . . ." She trails off, her voice wavering.

The true Haeri's tragic end knifes at my heart anew. She had borne it all—the unloving mother jealous of her success, the vicious, narcissistic grandmother, and a director who used her mercilessly. Who would have thought that behind the smile that nurtured the public's dream of Snowglobe, she was quietly dealing with so much sadness?

"I was going to take Haeri in," Hyang resumes, her voice thick with emotion. "When Seol first told me of her plan with Serin, I wrote back to tell her to send the other girl. I guess I was already worried that Seol was thinking of complete disposal."

"Complete disposal?" I murmur in disbelief.

Hyang drops her gaze.

"And then the poor girl's sudden exit created a void that Seol was hard-pressed to fill, since Serin's face was still months from being ready. And that's where you entered—as a cover for the cover."

I didn't travel all the way here to do you an act of charity, if that's what you're thinking.

Not only am I not the original, but I'm not even her relief. I'm a relief for the relief, a disposable placeholder.

"Months passed and Serin's treatment finally ended. Seol's original plan was to"—Hyang hesitates a moment before pressing on—"to discard you here. But then you turned out to have all the qualities she'd wanted for Haeri. She was torn, because she'd already invested so much in Serin. So she wrote back to tell me that I'd be taking Serin, since Haeri was gone. She wanted a backup, in case anything else came up." She gives me a pained look. "How did I end up with you instead of Serin?"

So I give her my account, up to where Serin jabbed me in

the neck. I guess she swapped her outfit for mine in the blind spot before ducking around to the other side. And that's how Bae Serin became the new Goh Haeri.

Hyang is silent for some time, and then she begins feeding the letters through the metal bars of my cage. The pages are dense with Cha Seol's script.

> *I've been watching the audition tapes on repeat. Serin would make a perfect Haeri, if it weren't for the hideous scar. Sohm should be able to fix it for me, though.*

> *Thoughts. Lots of thoughts. I wish we could talk about it all over a drink or two, though I can already hear your objection. Haha. But I know I can tell my sisters anything. Right? I shouldn't have let you leave us, leave Snowglobe. It's my greatest regret.*

> *Long time no write! I've been busy, if you can believe it, wink wink. Long story short, I brought Serin here to Snowglobe. When I first broke the news about Haeri's incurable illness, there was a little gleam in her eye that told me I didn't need to dance around the subject. Not for her. She has been 100% on board ever since. A bigger challenge was getting rid of the cameras inside her hospital room, but Sohm took care of it for me.*

Rage boils up in me all over again and I crumple the letter in my hand.

"Why are you showing me these?" I snap. "Aren't you on *her* side?"

"I hoped the letters would come in handy one day," Hyang says. "I was going to tell the girl everything once she got here. But she went ahead and killed herself before I got the chance. The girl died without knowing anything. No, she died *because* she didn't know anything. I don't want you to fall into the same trap."

"So you're telling me what you couldn't tell her? Why? Do you think this is some kind of confessional? Why couldn't you have talked some sense into your sister and saved Haeri before it was too late?"

Hyang hangs her head, but I'm so worked up that I can't stop laying into her, whether she deserves it or not.

"There's only one Haeri, and that doesn't change no matter how many other people look like her. How can you and your sister think you can replace someone who's still alive?"

I'd never hurt her on purpose.

My heart clenches, remembering the grim look in Cha Seol's eyes as she said it.

Then I remember my own role in all this, how willing I was to participate in the scheme, and how breezily I've slipped into Haeri's life. Who am I to judge anyone else's actions? Tears start streaming down my cheeks, guilt and shame flooding me. I want to crawl into a hole and never come out.

"Come on," Hyang says. "You'll have plenty of time to cry. Get something in your stomach before you pass out."

Wiping the tears dripping from my chin, I choke out, "I should have told her I wouldn't do it. I should have refused. That day in the limousine . . ."

"You had no choice once Seol came to you," Hyang counters matter-of-factly. "The Christmas party was an emergency.

She'd have extracted your cooperation any way she could. Snowglobe directors are half mad, every one of them. And Seol? She is completely mad." Hyang's face turns hard. "But she's not the only one. There are two of those sociopaths. The other is our grandfather, Cha Guibahng."

Hyang's face is blurry through the tears that won't stop pooling in my eyes. Cha Guibahng? Their grandfather, who got a National Medal of Honor for the show he directed?

"It's in the whole goddammed lot of us," Hyang goes on. "And I'm not excusing myself, either—I've coasted through life on the Cha name."

Reaching under the couch again, she pulls out a bottle of wine this time and unscrews its top. Then she produces an extra-long drinking straw she's somehow fashioned out of two regular straws and slips it inside and begins to drink. I'm watching her siphoning the red liquid up to her mouth when I suddenly become aware of how thirsty I am. Finally, I snatch up the bowl of rice gruel and gulp it down as if it's cold water.

"I want to go for a walk," I say.

It's been days since I woke up in the strange room. Hyang is reclining on the couch, her legs up on the armrest, a fantasy novel from the Warring Age balanced on her stomach.

"What?" she says, glancing up from the pages.

"I said I want to go for a walk," I repeat, sitting up. I finally convinced Hyang to let me out of the bed-cage and onto the couch, but she handcuffed my right wrist to it behind me, and shackled each of my ankles to a twenty-pound ball and chain. She's convinced that if I weren't restrained, I'd race to the kitchen and take a knife to my own jugular or somehow blow myself up like a firecracker. Happening on a forgotten pair of scissors kicked under the couch one day, she shrieked as if they were a snake before picking them up and throwing them out the window.

Since then, the woman has had to make do with her own incisors whenever the need for the instrument arose. I'm no psychologist, but her reaction must be some kind of trauma response related to Haeri's suicide.

"I'd kill you before I even dreamed of killing myself," I assured her, but it hasn't inspired her to grant me more physical freedom.

"I'm headed out," I call over my shoulder, hefting the balls on my ankles to get a head start as Hyang fusses over something in the kitchen. It took me two weeks to convince her that I wasn't capable of dashing at sixty miles per hour while dragging forty pounds behind me, or that I had any interest in telling people in the village that I'd been a stand-in for Haeri.

In the end, what persuaded her wasn't my words, but the staggering total of 227 games of Omok, 101 games of poker, and 359 games of Go-Stop I indulged her with. Talk about the price of freedom.

Meanwhile, the woman seems to have no life outside of watching me. And though she claims to have a local friend, exactly *one,* I haven't seen her go out to visit said friend, nor have they come to see her.

"How about when you were in Snowglobe? Did you have any friends or were you a total loser there, too?" I asked her once, the venom rising up in me again.

"I told you I have a friend!" she snapped. "I had a friend in Snowglobe, too. She went home when her show got canceled, that's all."

This friend of hers makes it into Hyang's speech quite often, though, which makes me think she might actually exist. When we got on the subject of hot cocoa one day, Hyang got all sentimental and weird, remembering how the friend had gotten her hooked on it when they used to be joined at the hip in Snowglobe. Soon after, she told me that witnessing this friend being brutalized by the system was what made her leave Snowglobe for good.

This revelation caught me by surprise and made me look at her in a slightly different light. I wonder if she's the only director who voluntarily withdrew herself from Snowglobe. And does that make her a conscientious objector? Or just a quitter?

Standing on a patch of frozen mud outside the front door, I check the thermometer. A pleasant 17°F, as forecast. I inhale a deep breath and take the fresh air into my lungs, feeling my whole body awaken, then heft each ball attached to my ankles and hurl them in front of me, and begin to trudge ahead.

Beyond the glass dome, the sky is a familiar gray. Like Snowglobe, the retirees' village is enclosed in glass. But without the screen lining the inside of the dome, residents have an unrestricted view of the frozen world outside: the postapocalyptic sky and featureless plains that stretch to the mountains rising on the far horizon. Thanks to the glass dome's superior R-value, though, the average daytime high stays around 14°F. Nighttime lows, however, regularly plunge to -4°F.

"Hot damn, it's cold!" Hyang cries as she catches up to me. It's only 17°F, far from disagreeable by my standards, but she's bundled up in four layers, paying for the three decades of soft living in Snowglobe, where the mercury never dips below the freezing point.

I heft the balls at my feet again and take a few measly steps forward. This is my way of locomotion these days. By the time we reach the town's thick glass border, I've worked up a good sweat.

"Hey, Bambi, it's snowing," Hyang says, her breath escaping in a white puff.

Outside the dome, large snowflakes have begun falling softly.

"I told you, Ajumma, the name's Chobahm," I snap, the name *Bambi* setting me off again. "It means early summer night. *Cho* is short for early summer, and *Bahm* for night. How do you beat me in Go-Stop all the time when you can't even manage the two syllables?"

"Relax. *Bambi* is one of my all-time favorite movies."

I roll my eyes.

"Do you have early summer out in the open world, too?" she says, changing the subject. "What's it like?" She sounds genuinely curious.

"No," I tell her curtly, and sit down on my ball, shifting my gaze to the falling snow outside.

I don't bother offering the other ball to Hyang. She wouldn't take it anyway, preferring to keep a safe distance from me. In her words, she doesn't aspire to die of strangulation by chain.

In truth, however, we both guard against taking too much comfort in each other's company.

"Then how come your parents named you that?" she asks.

I let out a sigh. "The year they married, it was the hundredth anniversary of the Yibonn," I tell her. "They were one of the lucky couples invited to Snowglobe for the ceremony."

I continue with the story Mom told us on countless occasions, her eyes shining with delight at the memory. It was May in Snowglobe. The air was gentle and infused with the sweet smell of spring. She and Dad, holding each other's bare hands without worry of losing digits to frostbite, took a long, leisurely stroll along the promenade lined with streetlights.

"That memory inspired my name," I explain as Hyang listens quietly. "I have a twin brother named Ongi. My dad had already named him before he knew my mom was having twins. I was kind of a surprise."

Her eyes open wide, but she doesn't say anything and we sit silently for a while.

"Here," Hyang says finally, tossing me something wrapped in a handkerchief she fished out of the inside pocket of her coat. When I undo the knot on top, there's a steamed bun nestled in it, still warm. This must be why she was dallying in the kitchen.

I take a big bite and start chewing.

"Good, huh? I slaved over it," she jokes.

"I might even say it's delicious, if you unshackle me," I answer.

"Spoiled," she mutters, pulling out a bottle of soju from her coat pocket and fitting it with a drinking straw. "Do you realize what an expensive treat that is?"

"What's it to you? I'm sure Seol paid for it anyway."

She shoots me a warning glare.

"Does she know her money's supporting your drinking habit, too?" I add for good measure. I can't help it.

"She sends me living expenses, so what?" Hyang snaps back, clearly offended. "Normally, I'd never ask that woman for help with anything, not even for soju money. But how am I supposed to make a living now that I'm saddled with your care? I can't work at the plant and leave you alone all day. I wouldn't have come here if I'd thought I'd need her money."

Okay, fair enough, but I don't back down. "If you hate her, then why are you helping her?"

"Help?" Hyang breathes, incredulous. "What are you talking about?"

"Keeping me locked up here. What do you call that, if it's not helping her?"

"You've got that all wrong. I'm not helping her. I'm keeping you alive!" She gives me a look of pity. "*You* are not allowed to exist. Not in Snowglobe. Not in your hometown. Not anywhere."

"So don't just stand there and pretend you're helpless! Get these things off me!"

"I can't do that," she says flatly. "Once you start skipping around town, people will begin to gossip. And nothing good will come of it."

"Who said I'd be skipping around town?"

But she doesn't answer. Instead she just sits, silently, watching the wind picking up outside, whipping clouds of fallen snow into the air.

"I have to get back to Snowglobe," I say. "But I need your help, Ajumma."

She snorts, looking at me as if I've just made a bad joke. When I don't react, she sighs and gazes off into the distance.

"You want to live as Haeri, is that it?" she asks, disgust in her tone.

"No," I say. Then I stand up and I look her in the eyes. "I want to *eliminate* Haeri. I want to end her existence so Cha Seol can't exploit her anymore."

TAKING THE LEAP

Back home, Hyang is beside herself with agitation.

"It's not an idea I came up with five minutes ago," I say. "I've thought hard about it over the past three weeks."

"When did you have the time to think hard about anything?" she shoots back. "I busted my butt shuffling cards and dealing Baduk stones to keep you occupied and away from any cute thoughts. Now this?"

She brings her fist down on the coffee table, rattling a half-empty bottle of soju, which tips over and rolls to the floor. Ordinarily, she'd leap for the spilled liquid like a wild animal at a desert oasis, but she doesn't even give it a fleeting glance. Fear and frustration churn in her eyes, the same amber as her big sister's.

"Why do you think I've been losing all these games to you?" I say, trying for levity. "My mind has been busy elsewhere." But Hyang isn't entertained.

"Eliminate Haeri? I don't think you want to kill Serin, so

what exactly do you mean? *No*—what do you think you'll be able to do? In Snowglobe?" she demands, her voice rising again. "Do you really think, even for a second, that Seol wouldn't sniff you out the moment you set foot on her turf? And she wouldn't bat an eye *snuffing* you out. Other people's lives mean nothing to her!"

I gather my thoughts as best I can and begin calmly, "Please, Ajumma, let me just explain. I could bide my time here, watching the days fall away while playing card games and chess matches with you. The handcuffs and ball and chain will eventually come off, but I'll never be free. As an illegal, I'm not even fit to slave away at the plant like everyone else in the village. And if Cha Seol called me back one day because Serin falters, I'd be returning to Snowglobe for another crack at stealing someone else's life. Is that what I really want?

"And what if Serin delivers?" I press on as Hyang stares at me, speechless. "Then I'd be stuck here until the day I die. I'd never see my family again, or even hear their *voices* again. And what kind of life is that, deprived of freedom, kept from loved ones? It's no life at all, is what it is. Returning to Snowglobe to kill off Haeri and reclaim Chobahm is not an act of murder, but an affirmation of life.

"It goes against my grain to give in without a fight," I say in conclusion. "I inherited that tendency from my dad."

Hyang is quiet for a long while. Then, finally, she lets out a sigh and says, "It's my fault. I've been too strict in the name of protection. I see how it's backfiring now. What you're feeling is—"

"No, Ajumma." I cut her off, shaking my head. "There's

an actor in my town who moved back home when her Snow-globe career ended. Her name's Jo Miryu. Have you heard of her?"

Hyang's face goes slack with shock and recognition. Of course she has. Miryu was the star of the show that led Hyang's grandfather to his esteemed award.

"She's treated like some kind of ghost or . . . plague," I continue. "Some people try to ignore her, and other people hound her every time she steps out of her house. All because of what she did in Snowglobe." I sigh. "I wonder how she's doing now since the accident—"

"No!" Hyang wails, startling me. "What are you talking about? Is she okay?" she demands, her eyes wild and her voice frayed. She, who wouldn't even accidentally stumble within arm's reach of me, is suddenly on me, wringing my arm, desperation in her face.

"Wait," I say, things clicking into place. "Was Jo Miryu your retired actor friend?" I ask incredulously.

"I asked you if she's okay!" she shrieks, hysterical. "Is she hurt?"

"She should be better since she's had medical care," I begin; then, as Hyang's face twists with grief and pain, I recount the night I was taken by Cha Seol: Miryu at the bus stop, our harrowing trek to the clinic, Cooper's visit and Director Cha's proposal, and my second stop at the clinic. I haven't even gotten to the part where Miryu was choking with terror at the mention of a black limousine when Hyang erupts from the couch, nearly knocking over the coffee table with her knees.

"That bitch!" she cries, shaking with rage. "Clearly, Seol's limousine ran her over! That murderous, sociopathic psychopath! *I hate her! I hate her! I hate her!*"

I try to calm Hyang down without affirming or denying her accusation. But Hyang is in a state, and she goes on for a good twenty minutes, stamping her feet, punching the couch cushions, cursing Seol and everyone else: Ghost? Plague? How could people treat Jo Miryu like that?

Eventually, Hyang heaves herself onto the recliner and dissolves into no-holds-barred sobbing.

Shackled as I am, I can't offer her a hug or even fetch her a pacifying bottle of soju. So I stretch my free arm to its limit and grab a box of tissues from the coffee table.

"Here," I say, flicking the box to her as she erupts in another flurry of anger and outrage.

"Cha Guibahng. That son of a—"

The box of tissues hits her square on the temple. We both freeze.

"I . . . I—I'm actually really sorry, Ajumma," I stammer. "I thought you'd want the tissues. I swear I was listening. Please go on."

She turns her tear- and snot-streaked face to me.

"Wait," she says. "How come *she* is Miryu but I am Ajumma? I'm only two years older than her. Do you realize that?"

Then her face crumples again, and she goes back to sobbing.

"I don't know," I say, feeling absurd. "I guess I felt like we shouldn't be too chummy with each other? Given our context?"

When she finally runs out of tears, she throws her head

back, closes her eyes, and takes a few deep breaths. Then, dropping her face to me, she looks me in the eyes and says, "Thank you, Chobahm, for saving my friend."

I find myself smiling at her—smiling for the first time since waking up in this house, to this nightmare.

Can you please stop by the post office and see if there's any mail for me? The name is Jo Miryu.

Miryu's correspondent smiles back at me, her face puffy and red from all the crying she's done for her best friend.

Forty-eight hours out of handcuffs, and the joy of moving my body as I wish hasn't diminished. As I'm standing over the sink with soapsuds on my face, it suddenly dawns on me.

"Why didn't you send her a Christmas card or something?" I ask.

Hyang is leaning against the doorway, sucking on the straw of a soju bottle.

"There's no post office here," she says flatly. "No telephone, either. We're completely isolated."

She goes on to explain that their only connection to the outside world is a truck that delivers the essentials from Snowglobe every few weeks. Sometimes things that aren't essential as well, I suppose, since I, too, was smuggled here inside an oversized package from Seol.

Hogwash about being completely isolated, though. Hyang and Seol continue their twice-to-thrice-monthly communications without a hitch, with Seol updating Hyang on my performance as Haeri, and Hyang lying to Seol about keeping Serin in her care. When I call her out, she replies, "I know somebody who knows somebody. I have my connection, and Seol has hers."

"Connections?" I repeat.

She tosses me a towel and plops down on the couch.

"Yes, connections," she repeats, grinning. "You'll find out eventually."

I take this opportunity to casually resurrect the subject that she crushed and buried the other day.

"Can connections sneak me *into* Snowglobe, too?" I say. "The shipping box is still sitting around the back."

Her grin gone now, she sighs and looks at me, exasperated. "And what are you going to do in a place with a camera for every square foot?"

"The cameras aren't for surveillance."

Rolling her eyes, she says, "Seol has access to any footage with your face in it."

"But she has to wait a week," I point out, and it's true. Even directors have to wait a week before they can view the recordings. Hyang's a former director herself—she can't have forgotten this.

"Just lend me a decent outfit from your Snowglobe days," I tell her. "I know I can sneak into the station as Haeri."

"You're going to sneak into where?" she says, her eyes bulging.

"The *station*," I repeat. "Imagine me walking onto the stage during a live weathercast to stand side by side with Serin. What better way to show the world that there's more than one Haeri? That neither of us is real, and that the real Haeri is dead?"

"That's the stupidest thing I've ever heard," she says,

putting her bottle of soju down on the coffee table. "Do you think Serin will just sit back and let you do that? She'll call you a liar and a fraud. And who do you think people will believe? You'll just be exposing yourself to Seol, who will have you killed."

"What if you back me up, Ajumma? Testify for me? You've kept all her letters and—"

"And you think people will believe a failed director prematurely exiled from Snowglobe over almighty Director Cha Seol? I can already see the headline: *Director's jealous little sister hatches an absurd ruse!*"

I knew getting Hyang's support wouldn't be easy, but I can't help feeling disappointed by how fast she dismisses my plan. Still, I'm like my father—nothing if not persistent.

"So you expect me to hide out here for the rest of my life and be content to hate Seol from a safe distance—as if *that* does anything?"

She makes a face. After a moment, she says, "That was a dig at me, wasn't it?"

"It wasn't, but maybe it should have been one!" I yell.

She lets out a laugh. "If you're finished, can I tell you what *I've* been thinking long and hard about?"

"Suit yourself," I say, turning my gaze out the window, to the gray, sagging belly of the sky on the other side of the dome.

Hyang quietly rises from the couch and disappears into the locked room. When she reemerges, her shoulders are slung with a mountaineering pack, and she's holding a second one in her arms.

I scoff. "What? You're kicking me out now?"

"No actor has ever dared to expose a director's abuse on camera," she begins. "It's a losing game, calling out the person who edits your footage. And those in front of live cameras—news anchors and weathercasters—they are royals who have no desire to rock the boat, you know what I mean?"

"Will you please get to the point?"

Hyang tosses a pack to me and I catch it, staggering at its weight.

"The point is," she continues, "if you're going to cause unprecedented trouble, you'd better do it right."

I stare at her in disbelief. Is she offering to help?

"What?" she says. "You disagree?"

"Ajumma . . . You're taking me to Snowglobe?"

"Yes, ma'am," she says, heading back into the room. "But first, we need to make a couple of stops."

It's a long moment before I recover the power of speech. "Thank you!" I yell. And then I erupt into laughter.

"Yes, laugh. Laugh while you still can," she says, and closes the door behind her.

I stand there, not sure what to do with myself, and a few minutes later, the door opens again and a heavy parka flies out and lands at my feet. A musty smell rises in the air.

"Where are the stops?" I ask.

Hyang produces a small notepad from her vest pocket and begins flipping through the pages.

"Our first stop is"—she pauses on a page—"Ja-B-6."

Ja-B-6?

"In the open world?" I repeat, uncomprehending.

She ignores me and disappears back into the room. I hear drawers opening and closing and bags rustling. A minute later, she calls out, "Just so you know. This will be my first time in the open world. So if you have any survival tips for subzero climates, share them now."

"I thought we were heading for Snowglobe," I say. "Why are we going to the open world?"

Hyang appears in the doorway again, and she flings out more winter gear: fur hats, expedition-weight mittens, and boots.

"*Why?*" she echoes. "Because we'll need reinforcements."

THE SURVIVOR

Predawn, the retirees' village is all but deserted. Empty roads crisscross the ruins of ancient high-rises that cast shadows on squat log cabins where the residents live. "What are all those high-rises about?" I ask Hyang.

"They've been here since before the beginning," she replies, breathless. "Since the Warring Age."

The woman has been waddling like a penguin under the weight of her pack, which would be lighter without the two jumbo bottles of soju she refused to leave behind. I offer to carry a bottle for her, but she turns me down with a solemn shake of her head.

"Let's keep moving," she grunts, and picks up the pace. "My god, it's cold!"

I look at her with some concern. It's not any warmer in the open world.

It takes us a few more hours to finally make it to the border crossing.

"That's it. I'm dead," Hyang declares when we finally arrive, and throws herself on the frozen ground, backpack and all.

I look for the gate, but the view is no different from Hyang's backyard. Where is it? I keep looking, and after a while, my frustration begins turning to anger. Then, finally, some lines coalesce in the gloom ahead. At first, it seems like another log cabin, but then I see the wheels. Soon a hulking truck is revealed, the biggest one I've ever seen, taller than the double-decker that takes us to the plant back home, with a giant snowplow mounted on its front. Then a face pokes out of a cab that's perched at least six feet off the ground.

"You're here!" says a bright voice.

In the next instant, the driver's-side door swings open and the owner of the face and voice jumps out, landing on the frozen ground with catlike agility.

She heads for us, and I immediately look down to hide my face, heart clenching. Hyang, still on the ground, lazily taps me on my calf.

"Say hi to my friend, aka connections," she says.

Hyang's friend reaches out to shake my hand. "Pleased to meet you. I'm Hwang Sannah," she says, and pulls down the scarf covering the bottom two-thirds of her face, exposing a scar running across her right cheek.

My jaw goes slack. *Hwang Sannah.* The only death row inmate who survived the biathlon championship in the history of the game. I clasp her hand awkwardly.

"H-hello," I stammer.

She squeezes my hand, hard, her eyes assessing me.

"I wondered why Seol would go out of her way to send Hyang a crap-ton of apples in an oversized box," she says with a rueful grin. "I figured she had no idea what her sister liked. But I guess I underestimated her depravity."

She lets out a throaty laugh, and I'm mesmerized by the scar that dents her cheek like a long dimple.

"The scar on your cheek," I blurt, too stunned to contain my thought, "—is it from the championship?"

"Why, yes," she confirms, clearly pleased to be recognized. "Did you watch it?"

All I can do is nod, overwhelmed by this infamous figure who's right in front of me.

At the championship three years ago, Sannah took a total of five bullets, beginning with the one that grazed her right cheek. But she was still breathing when the last of eighteen competitors disqualified herself by exhausting her time limit. Hence no champion in the women's division that year.

"How did you end up here?" I ask her. "I thought the retirees' village was just for former directors."

"Right?" she says, pulling Hyang to her feet. "Get in the truck. I'll tell you on the way."

We climb up to the cab and Hyang urges me in first. Sandwiched between her and Sannah on the long bench seat, I peer out the windshield at the thick glass dome around us. Sannah grasps the steering wheel and depresses the clutch with her foot. The engine roars to life, headlights flooding the dark.

"Biometrics. Only my fingerprints can commandeer this baby," she explains proudly. Then she lets go of the steering wheel to cut the engine and snuff out the lights. With a tip of her head, she invites me to put my own hands on the steering wheel. When I do, a pulsing alarm explodes in the cab.

"Pretty awesome, right?" she says, returning her hands to

the wheel. Instantly, the alarm is disabled and the truck roars back to life, shining its powerful headlights on the glass ahead. In fact, the brilliance is so intense that the glass begins to look silverized, like a mirror.

"Whoa!" Hyang cries, turning to Sannah and clapping her hands like an excited child. "So this is what you were talking about!"

Sannah moves the gearshift back and forth like a magician's staff, and the truck rockets toward the glass. I don't even have time to panic. The truck meets the wall head-on, and the next thing I know, we're through the glass just like the mirrors in Snowglobe and out in the open world. Hyang and I turn to each other, eyes wide and mouths agape.

Sannah's truck hurtles across the frozen plain. Hyang pulls me to her and points a finger at the sideview mirror outside her window. The mirror dome of the retirees' village recedes into the distance, gleaming intensely under the rays of the rising sun.

"Snowglobe sits at the end of this mountain range," Sannah informs us. "So we'll be driving along it for the next two hundred and fifty miles or so."

Only then do I notice that the chain of ice-capped mountains runs right through the dome we just moved through.

In the sideview mirror, Hyang's eyes have gone remote. "Did you know that the dome is the original Snowglobe?" she says.

I make a noise of surprise, trying to recall the bits of knowledge I learned in history class.

One year, Snowglobe relocated. Shortly after the resettlement, the Yibonn group held its inaugural actor audition, and a year after that, the first shows began to air on TV.

"They had built the original dome—the current retirees' village—with two-way glass that allowed you to look out but not in, because, back then, defense was everything, and the glass acted as a sort of camouflage," Hyang begins, and continues with a quick review of world history.

When the ice age first came about two hundred years ago, the world order of individual nation-states had already been eroding, with governments and economies falling like dominoes around the globe. At the beginning of the shift—both in climate and in the way of the world—temperate climes remained in certain areas of the earth, but those disappeared as climate change intensified. Thankfully, widespread ownership of personal vehicles kept ordinary folks mobile, most of them adopting a nomadic lifestyle in which they moved around, searching for a habitable environment. Few accepted the climate catastrophe as their new reality, with the majority of humanity refusing to hunker down in one place as the grip of the chill kept tightening around them. Meanwhile, the patches of habitable environment were limited and continuously dwindling, so it wasn't long before the lucky inhabitants of these territories started erecting unscalable borders and taking up arms against the never-ending trickle of climate migrants.

A young woman named Yi Bonn lived in a place where the natives built a mirror dome over their whole territory. She came from a powerful family who had owned a media empire during the Warring Age. In fact, it was her family that had funded the mirror dome to protect her and her community from the invading hordes outside.

"Military power alone cannot sustain peace, and the geothermal energy that remains is limited. Beginning here and now, we need to create a new order for our society. No more guns. No more tears. No more blood. We will achieve peace, stability, and progress, the Snowglobe way." Hyang recites from memory the famous Snowglobe speech made by Yi Bonn, the eponymous founder of the Yi Bonn Media Group.

"Hah! That's what I was supposed to learn all those years ago!" Sannah says, her eyes darting to the dashboard navigation display. "I get it now! So the new dome was built with clear glass, because they were done fighting off invaders."

Her eyes lit with the joy of belated learning, she goes on, "Couldn't they just swap out the panels and stay put, though? Why did they have to relocate?"

"Simple. The original dome had gone up where it had because it was the founder's homeland, not because it sat on abundant geothermal resources like Snowglobe does. You know what a bona fide igloo the retirees' village is." Hyang says.

She smacks her lips as if all the talking has made her thirsty for her choice beverage. Twisting around in her seat, she reaches for her backpack, and as she does, a beep comes from somewhere inside the cab. Hyang whips around and turns to Sannah.

"Is that it?" she gasps, her eyes wide with alarm.

"That's it," Sannah replies unenthusiastically.

I look back and forth between the two. "What is *it*?" I ask.

Sannah just grins. Hyang is quiet, gazing off into the distance, her expression troubled.

"You asked me how I'd ended up in the retirees' village?" Sannah begins. "Let me tell you how an expelled Snowglobe actor got to drive the shipping truck."

"She's kryptonite among directors—working or retired. That's how," Hyang says, coming back to herself.

Sannah lets out her hearty laugh and resumes. "A surprising number of retirees blow their money on stupid things, and by the time they move into the village, they're broke and have to work at the plant like the rest of us. Unused to doing without, though, some decide to steal. Food, cigarettes, alcohol, and whatever else this truck carries. But the cargo doors only operate on the driver's fingerprints. So they scheme—*If only we could overtake the driver . . .*"

She trails off, looking to Hyang, who picks it up, *"But how would we take out the bitch who couldn't be killed with bullets? With kitchen knives and clubs?"*

What had put Sannah on death row and made her a human target in the arena was her infamous murder of her director. With a kitchen knife, no less. A brutal and coldhearted murder, news media wouldn't stop reporting at the time.

"When they announced Sannah as the year's target," Hyang goes on, "the whole village came out to celebrate. Murder a director? A wretch like that deserves to be perforated like a honeycomb, people said. Everyone gathered in bars to watch the championship." Grinning, she continues on to the inevitable ending we all know. "But then, holy shrimp! Five shots later, the wretch still refuses to die. And though she's barely breathing, she raises her fist in the air like she's the victor. What a savage. What a monster. Stay away from that kind of abomination, they say. Then one day, she shows up in the village as the new trucker. Shocked and outraged—and scared—all everyone wants is to get rid of her, but no one dares, and not just because they don't want to violate the peacekeeping agreement, not again.

"You see, every outgoing director is required to sign a peacekeeping agreement prior to admission to the retirees' village. They broke it with the truck driver who preceded me—a retired director himself," Sannah says, glancing at me. "He was slain by a drunk mob wanting to take the truck one night, and as punishment, Snowglobe held off replacing the driver for the six long months that followed, cutting off supplies to the village for the duration.

"But don't think no one learned a lesson," she adds, lifting up the hem of her jacket to reveal a pair of handguns tucked into the holster at her waist. "You may have already guessed it. These babies are the only firearms in town, and they also use biometrics."

As Sannah has been speaking, the beeping has gotten louder and faster, and I'm starting to feel uneasy about it.

"What's the beeping?" I ask again, looking back and forth between my companions.

Hyang's smile vanishes and Sannah replies, "Oh, that? It's a bomb."

I look at her, stunned. Is she joking?

"The truck's location is monitored and tracked by the Snowglobe radar system. The moment it strays from a predetermined route, the alarm goes off. The sound ratchets up the farther and longer you go off course. When it reaches a single, continuous *beeeeeeeeeep*—then it's *poof!*" she explains with the cheeriness of someone describing a party balloon popping.

"Are you serious? A bomb?" I say, panic surging.

"Relax," she says with a laugh. "I'm unloading you guys and resuming the route before it can happen."

I know that Sannah is dropping us off at a train station halfway between the retirees' village and Snowglobe, but I have to ask, "Do we have enough time for all that before the alarm flatlines?" I'd love a firm answer, but I suppose I'm expecting reassurance more than anything.

"Oh, I hope so," she replies with maddening nonchalance. "This is my first time straying. I guess we'll find out."

I swallow my terror with an audible gulp.

THE RESEARCHERS

We drove for another four hours, until the beeping was almost a constant single tone, before we decided that, for everyone's safety, Hyang and I would ski the rest of the way to the train station.

We activate hot packs and tuck them under our layers of gear, and as we pull down our goggles, Sannah brings the truck to a stop. Even Sannah can't hide her concern, though hers is more for Hyang, who has never been out in the open world before.

"Hyang," she says to her. "Please tell me you're going to be all right." Then she turns to me and smiles—her scar dimple making her strangely more fetching—and says, "Best of luck."

As I thank her, the beeping kicks into a new, frightening intensity, and Hyang and I rush out of the truck. From inside the cab of her roaring metal beast, Sannah waves goodbye, and we step into our skis. The light of the train station glows faintly in the far distance.

Side by side on our skis, Hyang and I glide toward the light.

"Crap! This wind!" Hyang curses for what feels like the hundredth time.

I raise a mittened hand and tap it against my ski mask. It's frozen stiff with my breath against the lung-piercing cold, and the inside of my nose feels raw and tight every time I draw a breath. Ironically, it's comforting. It's like coming home.

"Aaaaargh! Shit!" Hyang screeches again. "Why does it have to be so cold!"

She told me earlier that she'd always loved a good skiing workout while living in Snowglobe, and true to her word, the woman matches me stride for stride, making me wonder how she could be the same person who spends her days on the couch with a soju bottle stuck to her face. We're making steady progress, but the train station is still a long way ahead.

"That bomb!" I shout to be heard over the hiss of the wind and snow. "Do you know where in the truck it's planted?"

A violent gust throws pellets of hard snow at our faces, and Hyang shouts back something I don't quite understand. Something about the sixth lumbar vertebra.

"What?" I shout, and she turns her face up to the sky and issues a series of swear words.

Then, turning back to me, she shouts, "The bomb! It's planted inside her body!"

As I process her words, she continues shouting, "It's not the kind of bomb you imagine! It doesn't go off and obliterate everything around it!" She pauses briefly for more howling and cursing, and explains, "The bomb's the size of your thumbnail, and it stops the host's heart!" She lets out a curdled laugh. "Did you think they'd blow up the truck? With everything in it?"

So the only person in that truck risking her life was Sannah? As though she can read my thoughts, Hyang says, "Aren't my connections pretty awesome?"

I can see her beaming with pride behind her ski mask and goggles.

"But why?" I ask, because I want to know. "Why did she risk her life to help us? To help *me*?"

"Don't feel like you owe her anything," Hyang answers. "Sannah has her own towering hatred of Snowglobe."

I want to probe further, to learn more about what caused Sannah to commit what is generally considered to be the most hideous murder of all time, but the distant whistle of the train cuts me off.

"Oh, crap! We're going to miss the train!" Hyang cries, and picks up the pace of her gliding strides, cursing mightily again. "Push yourself, Bambi! Push!" she urges. "You block that train with your whole body, if you have to!"

I press myself to move faster, yelling at her back, "You're far better suited for that task than me, Ajumma!"

The reinforcement we seek is in the Ja-B-6 settlement, which means we need to catch the Ja-line train; and because train engineers are chosen from settlements at the terminus of the lines, the engineer of the Ja-line train has to be from Ja-P-22, my home settlement. Racing for the station with everything I have, I pray that the engineer is Jo Woong, a brooding man of few words who rarely shows interest in other people.

Safe and gradually defrosting inside the train, I lean back in my seat. We boarded only minutes before the doors slid closed, and the engineer seems to appear immediately, making his rounds.

"What's the purpose of your visit?" he says, and through the mirrored lens of my oversized goggles, I see Hyang plaster on a fake smile. "We're scientists measuring geothermal energy," she says. He seems happy with her answer, and after a few more perfunctory questions, the engineer takes his leave.

Hyang pulls off her fox-skin hat and coat, giddy with the warmth of the passenger car. I take the moment to remove my layers, too, then realize that the black suits and ties we put on when we left her house make us look more like private security guards than climate scientists. When I express this concern to Hyang, she assures me that it's more important for our clothes to say that we're from Snowglobe than to say precisely what we do there.

What feels like only minutes later, the engineer reappears, this time with hot tea on a tray. Hyang reaches for a cup, stretching her arm extra far so the diamond-studded wristwatch peeks out from under her suit cuff. Its extravagance screams Snowglobe and reminds me of when Cooper first showed up at the clinic looking for me. One glance at those buffed leather wingtips, and I knew he was from Snowglobe.

Hyang sits up straighter in her seat and sticks her chest out proudly. She takes an elegant sip of her red tea, then explains to the engineer, "Recent studies have probed the possibility of geothermal energy outside Snowglobe. The Yibonn Corporation is full of pioneers; they took an interest in the studies and hired us to take samples along the rail routes."

The small-town engineer regards us with naked awe and admiration.

"Wow," he sighs. "You're doing such meaningful work."

Still hiding behind my goggles, I snatch another look at his earnest smile. "Is there anything I can do to make you feel more at home?" he asks.

His eyes are on my goggles; no doubt he's wondering why I'm wearing them on the train. Once again, I let Hyang respond for me.

"Oh, my research partner just had an eye procedure done. You know, to correct her vision?" Hyang tells him. "It makes her extremely photosensitive, so she has to wear the goggles over the next few days. For protection."

I nod in affirmation and press the teacup to my lips, the steam clearing the frozen crust of ice on the outside of my goggles. I can't let him hear my voice. Not *this* engineer.

This bright-eyed and bushy-tailed, overly earnest engineer of the Ja-line is none other than my own twin brother, Ongi. Apparently, his persistence at the plant paid off.

But what about the kid's faintheartedness and high need for socializing?

"A vision-correcting procedure!" he cries in amazement. "Wow!"

In fairness, he looks good—better than good, in fact, almost as if he were born for the role, and it makes me smile. Privately.

A few quick raps sound against the metal body of the train then, and someone calls from outside, "We're all set. You guys are good to go." It's the supervisor of the Ja-A-1 plant letting him know that they're through unloading cargo.

"Got it! Thanks!" Ongi calls. Then, turning back to us with that open smile, he wishes us a pleasant trip before crossing the narrow door into the engineer's cab. The muffled sound of his voice communicating with traffic control flows out briefly. A few moments later, there's a mighty hiss from the tracks, and with a jerk forward, the train is finally in motion.

Hyang and I are the only passengers in the passenger car, and I finally breathe out as the train begins to accelerate. Though, like the cargo cars, the passenger car is windowless, I picture us cutting through the white plains that make up the outside world as I take in the space my twin brother now calls home.

The passenger car might be that in name only, as it seems to function more or less as Ongi's living quarters. Aside from the handful of passenger seats, there's a wall-mounted table with two wall-mounted chairs, across from which are a wall-mounted cot and a camper-style bathroom.

Before long, the train's rhythmic chugging begins to lull my heart, which took a beating when I first saw Ongi emerge from the engineer's cab.

"Put these on instead," Hyang suggests in a low voice, and hands me a pair of dark sunglasses. "You look pretty ridiculous."

But I turn them down. Ongi may be too naïve to suspect anything, but I can't underestimate the power of our history. Being twins means we go *all* the way back.

Instead, I get up and go to the bathroom, and with the door shut and locked behind me, I check my face in the palm-sized wall mirror. The ski goggles hide the upper half of my face, and their bubble lens refracts the light in a rainbow of colors, creating a mild distraction in itself. For a single item of disguise, it's not doing a bad job. The train sways gently from side to side, and with it, my reflection sways in the mirror. I try for a smile, pushing away the gloom gathering inside me as I picture what lies ahead, what I have done. Me in a ridiculous black suit, impersonating a climate scientist, with a drunk, on our way to meet with a reinforcement shrouded in mystery.

Six hours later.

"Only two more hours to Ja-B-6," Ongi informs us, crossing into the passenger car. "Are you hungry? I'm famished," he adds.

And he should be. At each stop, he jumps out of the train and chats up the plant's supervisor as if he's known them all his life. Every few stops, Hyang and I have stepped off as well, making a show of collecting geothermal data. Whenever we do, Ongi takes it upon himself to educate the curious dock-hands about our endeavor, his face lighting up with pride as if he is somehow responsible.

Ongi produces his meal and sits down at the table. Seeing him perched over his supper of a single row of vegetable kim-bap, I feel guilty about having gobbled the thick ham sandwiches Hyang packed for us. Ongi has turned on the train's autopilot so he can eat, and the train lumbers along steadily, but he can't stop stretching his neck to glance at the tracks ahead or the dashboard inside the engineer's cab.

"You have six more days on the tracks?" Hyang asks Ongi.

"That's right," Ongi replies brightly, and pauses to swallow his food. "Six more days till I'm home, at the end of the line."

"Doesn't it get kind of lonely out here, or stressful? Away from home for weeks at a time?" Hyang probes.

"I don't consider it to be an *ideal* career choice," Ongi answers honestly.

"How does your family feel about you working such a dangerous job?" Hyang asks, moving on to the next question I've given her to ask.

"Sure, they have concerns," he says, his tone darkening a shade. "I was more worried about leaving them behind for weeks on end, though, what with my grandmother not doing too well. Honestly, I wouldn't have been able to pursue this path if it weren't for my twin sister." Here his bashful smile returns. "Because her acceptance into the directors' program came with financial support, my mom was able to quit working at the plant to stay home and take care of Grandma."

Something hot rises in my throat, and tears burn in my eyes. The sight of Ongi wolfing down his meager supper, even as he talks of our family's improved circumstances, hurts, knowing the excess I've had in Snowglobe.

"That's wonderful," Hyang continues. "That you were finally free to pursue your dream."

Ongi considers this a moment before he responds. "I don't know. I might have to blame my sister for that dream," he says with a laugh. "Since she could speak, she was telling people she'd become a film director one day, and that meant I needed a dream of my own to parade around. I wasn't interested in becoming a director—or an actor, for that matter—and no one really dreams of working at the plant. And then it came to me one day. How about being a train engineer? It's every kid's dream to ride the train, right?"

He reaches for the kettle and pours more red tea into our cups.

Hyang gives me a sidelong glance and leans in. "*Aww,*" she resumes in a syrupy voice, "a twin sister . . . you two must have a special bond."

I shoot her a furious look behind my goggles.

"Absolutely," Ongi agrees. "It's getting close to half a year since I saw her last, but her school year is over in June. Film school students can't come home for the summer, but she can invite family to campus. She's going to freak out when she finds out what I do now. I've been keeping it a secret so I can surprise her."

He gives another humble smile, and my heart aches with the memory of the days when we used to thump through the knee-deep snow together, chucking snowballs at each other, or just lazing in front of the TV, watching our favorite shows.

Tears finally brim over when, thankfully, Ongi gathers his stuff and returns to the engineer's cab. I wait for the next round of clacking from the rails to loudly suck back in the tearful snot making a mess of my face.

I turn to Hyang. "Would you be disappointed if I wanted to ride all the way home with Ongi?"

THE DOPPELGANGER

Hyang looks at me in surprise, her hand holding the teacup suspended in the air.

"Are you serious?" she says, leaning closer and squinting in search of my eyes behind the goggles.

"Why not?" I say in a small voice. "This train is bound for home. Your sister doesn't have to find out if you don't want her to."

She heaves a heavy sigh. "Do you remember the souvenir she gave your family—the camera-shaped golden trophy thingy?"

I nod and she continues, "Well, that 'gift' is a video camera hiding in plain sight. It runs for years on a tiny built-in battery, *and* Cha Seol has real-time access to its recording."

My stomach falls and my ears buzz. This is a joke. It has to be. I refuse to believe it, even as Hyang continues talking. "The video quality isn't the best in the world," she's saying, "but the tiny microphone can capture even whispers."

If this is true, going home and turning it off or shoving it deep in a closet would alert Seol on its own.

"What are you saying?" I'm shouting in spite of myself, my disbelief turning to rage. "She's been spying on my family this whole time?"

Is there a depth to which the evil woman won't sink?

The door to the engineer's cab pulls open and Ongi peeks out, brows raised in concern. Hyang smiles serenely and says a few words of reassurance, and he ducks back into his cab. I'm racked with guilt for him, for my family.

"It's not like I haven't thought of sending you off to another settlement," Hyang says. "But the idea seems worthless now that I know how Miryu has been doing in yours. Smuggling you to a third location so you can evade Seol's radar? And then what? Live as a ghost all your life?"

A deep sadness comes over her eyes, and she adds, "It's Seol who needs to pay, not you."

She falls silent and I nod solemnly, gazing into the dark engineer's cab, where Ongi stands all alone at the controls.

"Thank you for bringing us safely to our last site," Hyang tells Ongi, dipping her head in a shallow bow. I follow suit and dip my head in his direction, too, though I might have squirmed a little bit.

Ongi dips his head in kind. "Are you sure you're getting on a different train for the return trip?" he asks.

"Yes," Hyang chirps. "The Ma-line happens to go through this town, which works great for us."

Ongi is leaning against the cab window, a soft smile on his face, and I etch the image into my mind, not sure when I will see him next.

"I wonder what the chances are of running into you in Snowglobe when I visit my sister in June," he says with an earnest chuckle. "Regardless, I hope our paths will cross again someday. Who knows, right?"

"Right!" Hyang replies, attempting a chuckle herself. "We'll be hoping for the same."

"In that case, until we meet again, Dr. Kim Seolwon and Dr. Yi Woon," Ongi says with another dip of his head, and we finally part ways.

I follow Hyang, holding that final image of my brother in my head, as we trudge through the snow toward the plant, shivering in the cold once more. As we near, a middle-aged woman appears from the rear and calls out to us, "Over here, please!"

We soon learn that the woman is the plant supervisor of Ja-B-6, and Hyang introduces us as the occupational safety and health auditors sent from Snowglobe. The woman looks as surprised as I am by who we are and gives us a strained smile. Hyang simply turns up her charm and asks to be led to the plant's break room.

Inside, I begin to thaw in the relative warmth. The break room is a tiny space crammed with three bare cots. Hyang and I sit side by side on one, waiting for the supervisor to return with a plant worker named Myung Somyung, at Hyang's request.

The supervisor was reluctant, asking why we wanted to speak to a worker when she could just field our questions herself.

"If, by any chance," she said nervously, "this is still about the past incident, I can tell you right now that we've put up all kinds of reinforcement since. I promise you that the plant will still be standing here in a hundred years."

From what I could gather from her anxious rambling, several years ago, the ceiling in the central motor room had come down on the workers below, killing and maiming a dozen people. Needless to say, the tragic incident disrupted the plant's energy production for a while thereafter, during which the whole of the settlement suffered mightily and the Yibonn was none too happy.

Hyang, affecting a shrewd, professional, and yet sympathetic tone, assured the fretting woman that the purpose of our visit had everything to do with improving workplace safety culture and morale, and nothing to do with punitive measures. It took a minute, but the supervisor finally relaxed and went to get Myung Somyung.

Hyang's veneer of calm authority drops the moment the supervisor leaves us, her agitation surfacing as she gnaws at her fingernails like a rodent.

"So how do you know this 'reinforcement'?" I ask, more to distract her than anything else.

"I don't," she says blankly, and spits out a sliver of fingernail. "Not yet."

I'm looking at her, bewildered, when the door creaks open and a girl steps in, silhouetted by the hallway light. She swivels to latch the door behind her, and it's almost as if she wants us to get a good look at the pistol on her hip. Turning back around, she crosses the room to us, and the sight of her face is like a punch to the gut.

"You're looking for me?" she says.

Behind my goggles, I stare at her, breathless.

Her coarse hair is cropped short for efficiency, just like mine was before Snowglobe. And the dirty, sweat-streaked face below it . . . it's mine. Or Haeri's. Or Serin's. My pulse is beating so loudly in my ears, I barely hear Hyang say, "Yes. But first things first. Did your supervisor say you can head home straight after the interview?"

"Sure," the girl named Somyung replies in the familiar register. "She also threatened to dock this week's pay if I said anything stupid."

Hyang pounces on this. "So how about we move the interview to your house so she can't monitor you?"

Somyung sneers, raking her fingers through her sweaty hair.

"This interview," she says, her tone one of mild disgust. "It's a ruse, isn't it? Let's just cut the crap and get to the point."

I blink, speechless, and glance at Hyang, who I can tell wasn't prepared for this, either. She fumbles for a response, and Somyung presses on, "Cha Seol sent you, didn't she?"

Looking at us with contempt, she continues, "Four years ago, that lunatic came out here and pitched me her insane idea."

Then the three of us are riding in a school bus full of little kids returning home from school. Our fellow riders, their tender cheeks flushed with cold and eyelashes blooming with frost, haven't stopped staring at me and Hyang since Somyung introduced us as scientists from Snowglobe. Perhaps the sunglasses and goggles are attracting more attention than we would have received without them. A girl of ten or so swivels in her seat and waves her hand inches from my goggles, grinning curiously.

"Can you really see through those?" she asks.

"Yes, sweetie," I reply, pitching my voice low in an attempt to infuse it with some authority.

These kids have never met a real-life Snowglobe resident before, and their questions bombard us throughout the ride: *How come we've never seen you on TV? Do you have to be a genius to become a Snowglobe scientist? Can I try on your goggles? Do scientists have to protect their eyes all the time?*

Thankfully, Somyung's stop isn't far from the plant, and we get off before their inquisitiveness and keen observation blow our covers.

In her tiny kitchen, Somyung fills two glasses with tap water.

"You're no scientists, that's for sure," she says, setting the glasses down roughly on the three-legged table before us. "So what do you want?"

Narrowing her eyes, she leans close and peers into my goggles. I swallow and turn my gaze to a large wall cabinet displaying an impressive collection of firearms, from a tiny pistol to the largest-caliber rifle I've ever seen. Dread sizzles through me, not for the first time since we arrived. The skull collection lining the front of her house outside wasn't the most welcoming display. Were any of them human?

Hyang takes off her sunglasses. Reaching for the glass of water, she drains it in a few large gulps.

"That's pretty impressive," she says, gesturing toward the cabinet with her empty glass.

"Family heirlooms," Somyung supplies proudly, and sits down. "We were in the gun business before the world turned to frozen shit."

Forcing a smile, Hyang ventures, "What goes in that empty spot?"

Somyung crosses her arms in front of her chest and leans back in her chair. Grinning like Haeri when she's feeling mischievous, she says, "The pistol I pack. Loaded."

Hyang's smile falters. "Can you tell us more about Cha Seol's visit four years ago?" she says, changing the subject.

"She told me that Haeri was dying of some terrible illness, but that she didn't want to die—or more accurately, that she didn't want the *show* to die," Somyung says, rolling her eyes. "She told me she came out here to uphold the dying girl's wish, to find her replacement."

As her words sink in, my hands curl into fists. That means that Director Cha had already tried to swap Haeri out four years ago. Fists clenched in my lap, I feel hate boiling up inside me all over again.

"Somehow, she knew that both my parents had died at the plant when the ceiling collapsed," Somyung continues. "She tried to talk me into following her to Snowglobe, for a new life as Haeri."

Hyang hesitates a moment, glancing at me, before pressing on. "Why didn't you go?" she asks.

Somyung gives her a blank look, as if gauging the seriousness of her question. Then, with a sharp laugh, she throws the question right back at her.

"Why would I want to live as Haeri when I was born Somyung?"

The absolute self-assuredness of her answer stuns me.

"And then the girl keeps living her fabulous life, right?" Somyung continues. "A terrible illness, my god. She looks better than before, if anything. Every time I catch her on TV, she's so bursting with life that the pixels making her up could spontaneously cross the screen and reassemble her in my living room.

"And while we're on the topic, let me ask you: What possessed Haeri? A *replacement*? Does she think other people's lives are so empty and meaningless that there's no point in even seeing them to their ends? Gosh, these celebrities are so lost, and detached, and full of themselves." She snorts. "Since then, I haven't been able to look at her without wanting to puke."

She punctuates her disgust with a sour shake of the head. Hyang reaches for her backpack and unzips it. Drawing in a big breath through her nose, she lifts her face to contemplate me for a long moment. Then she suggests that I take off my goggles. I hesitate, but eventually pull them off and reveal my face to Somyung.

Somyung draws herself up, eyes wide with shock.

"Goh Haeri?" she whispers, perhaps regretting all the harsh things she's just said about the girl who seems to be sitting in front of her. I'm about to explain when Hyang slaps a metal file folder she's dug out of her backpack onto the table.

"All right," she sighs. "I'm doing this even if it kills me." Then, drawing in another long breath, she looks up at Somyung. "Please don't shoot. Or at least wait until I'm done."

"You don't have to be so dramatic," I quip nervously.

What is she up to?

Hyang goes on, "I've thought a lot about it, but there just isn't a gentle way to break this news. So here goes—"

My heart begins a slow pounding. Whatever she's about to throw at us is going to be huge. Somyung, too, regards her warily. Then, drawing her pistol from the holster, she sets it down on the table with a thud.

"I might have to shoot you if this is about me becoming her replacement," she warns.

Hyang pulls two documents from the folder and holds a page out to each of us. I snatch up the paper and begin skimming. It's the school enrollment paper created when I reached school age, with my first-ever ID photo attached to it. *Name, Jeon Chobahm, DOB, Dec. 25, Height, 3 ft, 1 in, Weight, 48 pounds, Settlement, Ja-P-22, Grade, 1st, Family, Grandmother Jeon Wol, Mother Jeon Heewoo, Father Yim Hahnyung (deceased), Brother Jeon Ongi,* etc.

"What's this about?" I'm murmuring vacantly, when my eyes jump to the letters under my ID photo.

Goh Sanghui (egg donor), Yi Ohyun (sperm donor).

"Egg donor, Goh Sanghui?" Somyung echoes me, her voice tight. "Sperm donor?"

"Mine says the same things!" I say, looking up at her, then to Hyang.

Hyang bites her lip and squeezes her hands together so hard that the knuckles turn white. Her eyes are two reddening pools. "Seol wasn't looking for Haeri's doppelgangers. You'd all been *conceived* so you could be Goh Haeri one day."

Somyung and I turn to each other, our eyes mirroring the chaos churning within.

THE SHOW GOES ON

Mom and Dad tied the knot in the year of the Yibonn Media Group's hundredth anniversary. A ton of people from the open world had been invited to Snowglobe to join the corporate ceremony.

Cha Seol, a recent film school graduate, had been working as the subdirector of Maeryung's family show under her famous grandfather, Cha Guibahng, who was the director. Though the show was a perennial success, Cha Guibahng wasn't taking much pleasure in Maeryung's firstborn, Goh Sanghui, who couldn't seem to pull her weight. But one day, Goh Sanghui began dating her longtime crush, Yi Ohyun, which boosted the show's already high viewership. The freeloader was finally earning her keep.

A few months later, however, Ohyun broke up with Sanghui, and they went back to being friends. Not long after, Guibahng summoned Maeryung and threatened to fire her daughter, *the dreadfully dull and unlikable girl without an ounce of talent,* from the show. Maeryung, desperate to keep her daughter in Snowglobe, came up with an idea: to have Sanghui carry Ohyun's unborn child. And *that* is how the idol named Goh Haeri was conceived.

Immediately, Guibahng hired a team of world-class geneticists and began designing the baby, who would inherit all the right physical traits from her beautiful father, Ohyun. Then Guibahng put his ambitious granddaughter Cha Seol in charge of the spin-off show after he singled out Miryu to star in the new crime show he'd been developing.

"This is when Seol comes up with an idea that should never have seen the light of day," Hyang says, sighing miserably.

Cha Seol and Cha Guibahng scoured the profiles of the open-world couples invited to the ceremony, for men who resembled Ohyun in age and physical appearance. And you guessed it. Among the elect were the young couples who would become the parents of Jeon Chobahm, Myung Somyung, and Bae Serin.

Guibahng invited the couples to his estate for a private party. The jaw-dropping excess of the party included a spa treatment and total-body massage for the women, during which all of them conked out without exception. Not long after they returned home, the women found out they were pregnant. My mom had already been carrying Ongi. What she didn't know was that I had joined him during her trip to Snowglobe.

The baby girls—clones of one another who were completely identical in appearance and genetic makeup—mostly arrived on schedule, including Sanghui's Snowglobe baby, Haeri.

"There were more," Hyang says, her strained voice hardly

raised above a whisper. "I heard that some of the babies had congenital defects and didn't survive the first few days."

I picture the frail old woman who kept vigil by her granddaughter who arrived with a defective heart. How is she not my real grandmother? And the only mother I ever knew . . . How is it possible that I'm not hers? What about Ongi? Are we not twins?

"What Guibahng and Seol wanted was to hatch a character who the entire viewership found irresistible," Hyang continues. "They started with the looks. Every inch of you is the result of scrupulous planning. From the lines of your eyes, nose, and mouth, right down to the length of your fingers, everything was designed to satisfy certain aesthetic demands, kind of like a concept car."

The rest is what Cha Seol suggested to me, including the part about leveraging Bonwhe to infiltrate the Yibonn mansion for a show that would end all shows.

"Why did they need so many Haeris?" Somyung speaks up at last.

Hyang sets her jaw. "To disperse risk," she explains. "Having a spare Haeri, multiple spares, in fact, is insurance against an unpredictable future."

"What do you mean?" Somyung demands, her eyes flaring.

"Genetic engineering can trigger certain health risks. In Haeri's case, those included neonatal death due to heart defects. And even though she survived those odds, life's still full of nasty surprises that could derail everything—car accidents, choking, drowning, teenage delinquency, you name it. Your parents weren't mere surrogates, either. Having provided the natural piece of the puzzle, Guibahng and Seol sat back and waited for your parents to provide the nurture piece; to see which Haeri had the right temperament to deliver their vision for the show. No one planned for Sanghui's baby to be the forever Haeri just because she'd been carried by her famous mother."

"What the *hell*," I hear myself say, and the next thing I know, I've snatched Somyung's pistol from the table and I'm leveling it at Hyang with a quaking hand. My vision closes in. I feel my pulse jumping in my right index finger.

"What?" I say, my voice shot through with rage. "Genetically engineered clones? Cha Seol picks the winner?" I'm screaming now. "What is wrong with you people?"

The tip of Somyung's pistol dances wildly before Hyang's face, but she isn't fazed.

"I have no answer for you," she says miserably. "I only wish I didn't know what depraved stock I come from."

"What stock?" Somyung says now, looking from me to Hyang, her voice caught low in her throat. "Who the hell are you?"

"I am Cha Seol's sister. Cha Guibahng's granddaughter," Hyang says sadly. "I only learned what they'd done a few years ago. That's when I decided to leave Snowglobe for good. My sister wouldn't accept my decision, though. She insisted that she needed me as a directing partner and as a best friend. Then our grandfather had the stroke that's kept him in the hospital to this day.

"I found out all the details then," Hyang explains, tears coming to her eyes again. She confesses to her complicity, and the fear that allowed her to distance herself from her family instead of doing something to help us.

"You make me sick," Somyung spits. "My mom almost *died* giving birth to someone else's child."

"Hell," Somyung breathes, pressing her palms against her inflamed eyes. "Some of us just have all the luck."

Then she turns to me and smirks. "And look at you with the pistol in your hand. Do you even know how to use it?" She laughs. "So what's your story?"

I say nothing, all the strength leaving me. I drop the hand holding the pistol, and Somyung moves in to gently pry it away as Hyang volunteers a brief summary of my backstory, pausing occasionally to compose herself.

"You're kidding," Somyung mutters under her breath as she inspects the pistol. "She didn't even undo the safety."

Then, turning to Hyang, who's drying her eyes with the backs of her hands, she says, "Can I call you Ajumma, too?"

Hyang nods.

"Ajumma," Somyung says, "you've done *nothing* with what you knew about the Goh Haeri project. I'm not here to condemn you for your pathetic weakness, though. Heck, I can almost appreciate how conflicted you must have felt about standing up to your sister and grandfather." She pauses for a moment before she continues, "What I want to know is, why now? Why do you stir the pot now, going through all the hassle of tracking me down and disturbing the peace?"

Her eyes red and puffy, Hyang wets her parched lips. "This is embarrassing," she says, "but I'll tell you why.

"My friend Miryu loathed her role as a serial killer. It was something she was conned into long before she was thrown out of Snowglobe when the show ran out of fresh murder ideas.

"The assassination of my friend's soul. That was the first murder I ever witnessed," Hyang says, her voice faltering again.

"Growing up in a family of directors, I'd been blind to the wrongs that were being committed in the name of ratings. I truly believed that editorial or directorial decisions, however incomprehensible, were consented to by the actors whose sole priority was to remain in Snowglobe. It was only after I saw what happened to Miryu that I understood what was really going on.

"Alas. Never having stood up for anyone or anything my whole life, the only thing I knew how to do was run away.

"Then Seol ratcheted up her effort to draw me back into the project. She did everything she could to trigger a sense of sibling loyalty. Each passing day was hell. I never said yes, but I also couldn't say no. She was my big sister—she'd always been my hero."

Hyang sucks in a deep breath. "So I turned to alcohol," she continues. "It was the only thing that could dull the edge of my agony. The moment I could feel my senses sharpening, I'd dull them again with more alcohol.

"Eventually, I managed to flee to the retirees' village, and I realized that I couldn't stand the residents—they are all former directors. That's when hopelessness took over completely and I closed myself off from the world. Time passed, and eventually Seol sent a letter informing me of Haeri's suicide.

"I was devastated, and furious, so I began going through

the documents I'd smuggled out of Snowglobe when I left. I was finally ready to use the evidence I had to bury my family for what they'd done, but I had no idea where to start."

Hyang pauses for a moment and looks at me. "That's when Jeon Chobahm was shipped to me in an oversized package of apples. Chobahm told me about Miryu's cursed existence back home, and of the girl who would rather fight to the death than surrender to injustice. This girl, who had come from nothing, had more attitude than she had any right to, and it gave me pause—made me reflect on my own attitude. I knew I couldn't change the fact that I'd been a coward, but I hated the thought of continuing to live my life in shame."

The room falls into silence. Through my tears, I'm finally beginning to see this woman for what she is, another casualty with all the tragic scars her heart bears.

Somyung gives a somber nod. "So what's our plan?" she says.

Hyang is quiet for a long moment. Then, glancing at me, she finally says, "This was inspired by an idea Chobahm had. We'll round up all the Haeris out there and march into the studio during the livecast. What better proof of the Goh Haeri project than all of you together in one place?"

"Wait," I say. "How many more of us are there?"

"I wish I knew," Hyang sighs. "Seol has the files scattered across several storage units. What I stole came from just one of them."

"Do you happen to have"—I fumble for the right word— "*her* file, too?"

I can't bring myself to single out the dead girl by referring to her as Haeri. Not anymore. Every one of us had been given a name, after all.

Hyang understands. "No," she says, choking on her voice again. "I don't have Yeosu's. Her name was Jo Yeosu."

Jo Yeosu.

It's the name Bonwhe tried on me in the woods.

"Yeosu never suspected any of this, of course," Hyang adds. "Why would she have, right? She must have thought killing herself would end it all."

"Couldn't she have chosen a different way?" Somyung asks, sounding both angry and frustrated.

Hyang shakes her head. "Yeosu wanted *revenge*," she says. "Not long after she moved to Snowglobe, her parents went missing in their settlement. It was Seol's doing, of course— making sure Yeosu would have no one to run to."

Bonwhe's voice echoes in my ears again: *Your last letter read a lot like a farewell, and I was pretty worried.*

My heart wrenches at the thought of Yeosu's pain, and the depthless loneliness and despair that must have consumed her when she wrote that letter to Bonwhe.

Then it hits me like a bolt from the blue.

"Was Yeosu even Sanghui's girl? The girl born Haeri?" I say. "And where is she?"

The pain in Hyang's face deepens.

"Dead, most likely," she says, barely getting out the words. "I confronted Seol with the same question. She told me she'd already taken care of everything. End of discussion."

My stomach heaves. As if everything that came before weren't terrible enough.

The girl we'd all been in love with was an illusion. Yeosu

killed herself to end that illusion, but it's still not over. I'm trembling with rage. For her, for me, for all of us.

"I'll start packing." Somyung's voice brings me back. "We'll probably need a firearm or two?" she says, moving toward the cabinet.

ONE MORE COPY

The break room at the Ra-H-11 plant is surprisingly spacious. I count ten cots and about two dozen sleeping bags on the floor. It's a good thing we arrived in the afternoon, otherwise the room would have been packed to the gills with exhausted workers.

"It's nice to know there's a plant out there where break room use is egalitarian," I quip.

Somyung nods. "The supervisor here must have a modicum of integrity."

Prior to boarding the Ra-line train out of Ja-B-6, Hyang informed Somyung's plant supervisor that Somyung would be traveling to Snowglobe with us for in-depth study. To our surprise, the supervisor took the news with barely suppressed glee, saying Somyung would be a shoo-in as a hunter or maybe border patrol. In a low voice, she let us know that, though she could appreciate the orphaned girl's hypervigilance, her attitude and open carrying of guns intimidated people at the plant, including herself. Hyang just responded with an impatient grunt, and I glared at her behind my goggles.

Shin Shinae is the name of the clone living in Ra-H-11 settlement. She balked at the idea of being interviewed at her home, claiming that it was the worst-possible place on earth for such a thing, since all four of her retired grandparents live with her family, along with a gaggle of cousins who are still too young for school. This alone isn't so out of the ordinary by open world standards, though Hyang couldn't hide her astonishment that a dozen people could share a three-bedroom home. Soon, Shinae revealed that the bigger problem was the fact that her mom, who'd been recently fired from her bus-driving post for drunk driving, is at home now also, which is why we ultimately stayed in the break room for the interview, with Somyung standing guard at the door.

Shinae is trying to puzzle out the implication of the document Hyang handed her. I sit down at the table and take the moment to finally remove my goggles as Hyang tells Shinae the true reason for our visit, her explanation more coherent than the last two times she's explained.

"So that's all of it," Hyang concludes. What had begun as complete confusion on Shinae's face has faded over the course of Hyang's explanation, and she appears oddly at peace now, a mystifying smile on her lips. Was she even listening?

Hyang shoots me a look, clearly confused by her reaction as well, then tries again: "I understand if you're feeling overwhelmed by—"

"You're damn right I'm overwhelmed." Shinae cuts her off, snapping back to the here and now. Only, what she appears to be is more than overwhelmed. She appears *thrilled*.

"So what does it mean for us?" she asks, her eyes twinkling

with excitement. "When all is said and done, we're victims, correct? Can we expect some kind of compensation?"

Call it a failure of imagination, but neither Hyang nor I foresaw that kind of response.

"I've always dreamed of escaping this family," Shinae says in a swift breath before letting out a triumphant laugh, as if gratified to have finally gotten the truth off her chest. "I've just about had it with them. I do care a lot about my mom, though."

Hyang and I blink at each other as Shinae resumes, her voice growing more animated, "My dad never stopped believing that my mom cheated on him; they'd been distant for a while before she got pregnant with me, you know what I mean? So him and the rest of the family labeled her a whore, and me a bastard." Pausing here a moment, she looks down at the tattered gray headband in her hand. A bitter smile. "Even this stupid thing, too. It used to be red—my father gave it to my mother on their wedding day. I had to steal it back from my cousin because my grandmother had given it to the little shit.

"I used to put myself to sleep imagining that my real parents would come bursting through the front door to reclaim me one day," Shinae adds, her voice turning sad. "They'd be so rich that they could buy me headbands in every color of the rainbow."

Silence falls, and I think of Guibahng and Seol. Their brutal ambition has ruined so many lives over the past seventeen years.

"My mother should be compensated for her suffering, too,"

Shinae says, her voice upbeat again. "She'd been driven crazy enough to want to run my father over, if you ask me."

Hyang and I exchange a look.

"Is—" Hyang begins cautiously. "Is that how she lost her bus-driving job?"

Shinae nods. "She wasn't drunk at the time," she says with a smirk. "She was stone-cold sober, and I don't blame her. She'd had enough."

Hyang and I are silent again, processing the shock.

"Don't worry," Shinae says, rolling her eyes. "The oaf is fine. She hit the brakes at the last minute. That poor woman doesn't have it in her to kill anyone, or anything, for all the good that's done her." She pauses to contemplate the headband. "I'm not my mother's daughter, though." Focusing her eyes back on us, she chirps, "So thanks for coming to my rescue. I'd have preferred not to have been born at all, but it's too late for that."

Hyang opens her mouth to say something but fumbles her words as Shinae comes around the table and examines my face more closely.

"Amazing," she breathes in wonder. "It's like looking in the mirror." Then she breaks out giggling like a little girl.

I glance at Hyang. "The compensation you're imagining— you're talking about cash, right?" I say. "We can't guarantee that. I mean, we haven't thought that far, at least not yet—"

"Are you serious?" Shinae responds, her voice rising, upset.

I nod apologetically. We've just been focused on bringing Cha Seol and Cha Guibahng to justice—setting legal precedent for all the other directors out there. I had not thought about money.

"How have you not crunched any numbers yet?" Shinae demands. "What's your plan for after the live exposé? Do you know what you want to do when the dust settles?"

I look to Hyang again, and neither of us has a response. Sighing, Shinae jerks a thumb at Somyung at the door. "What about her? Does she have a plan? Please tell me *someone* has a plan."

"A plan?" I finally repeat, just to say something.

Shinae holds her eyes shut for a moment, then opens them again. "Were you really going to go home with nothing to show for your sacrifice? For all the unwanted exposure? And what about your family? They may no longer consider you a relative, you know."

I open my mouth to object to this last point, but nothing comes out. Will I lose my family by revealing the truth? My mind goes numb.

"Money *protects* you," Shinae continues. "It opens up doors that were closed before."

Finally, Hyang finds her voice, erupting in a nervous laugh. "You're something else, aren't you?" she says.

"Tell me about it," Shinae returns. "It's exhausting, to always be the only one thinking." Then, jumping to her feet, she says, "When's the train coming? I want out of this town. The sooner, the better."

"So you're in?" I say, unsure but hopeful.

"Hell, yeah," she says.

"Even though there's no guarantee of compensation?" I add.

"I'll have to wrangle it out of someone myself, by the looks of it. But don't worry. I will."

"Do you need to go home and pack?" I ask, and she ponders the headband in her hand again, then looks up.

"Nope," she says. "I already have all I own."

I let out the breath I'd been holding anxiously. The last Haeri we could trace has joined us.

"It's only an exposé if we succeed," Hyang says as we join Somyung at the door. "Otherwise, it's a crime. Well, more of an insurrection. A violent attempt at taking over the network," she adds, looking at each of us.

I give her a somber nod, well aware of the consequences should we fail.

"Even Seol doesn't think she's doing anything wrong," Hyang says, her eyes downcast. "I'd hate to end up being another deluded adult who misleads you."

Hyang's apprehension in pulling us into a crime only solidifies my faith in her, but when she launches into some kind of disclaimer, telling us how anyone with misgivings is free to break away, Somyung cuts her off.

"Can you please stop?" she says, clearly fed up. Flicking her chin in Shinae's direction, she continues, "Do you think I came along just to smell her sour headband?"

Shinae looks Somyung up and down. When her eyes fall on Somyung's pistol, she allows a smirk to spread across her face. "This thug's with us?"

Hyang bites down on her lip, suppressing a smile. "I guess this proves everyone's on board," she says. "We'll work on harmony and cohesion as we go. For now, let's get something to eat."

In the cafeteria, our ski goggles and dark sunglasses attract strange looks. There's little to do but pretend everything's fine—that all Snowglobe residents wear sunglasses and goggles to dinner. Behind her owlish sunglasses, Hyang grimly assesses the dessert on her tray: a single segment of mandarin. In a whisper to Shinae, she asks if she could pay for a few more. This earns her a lecture from Somyung, who reminds her that a Snowglobe resident would never be hungry enough to fret over mandarins. Shinae then delights herself, sharing her vision of a future where she'll be able to have a whole box of mandarins to herself while she watches TV. Listening to them, I find myself smiling for the first time in a long while. And laughing, too, albeit furtively.

We are making fast work of our supper when, all of a sudden, the cafeteria stirs and someone turns up the TV to its full volume.

"Breaking news this evening about President Yi Bonyung," Anchor Chung says in a serious voice.

"According to Hong Hwa, the media group's spokesperson, the president was transported to the ER upon collapsing in her office this morning."

The screen cuts to the VIP wing of the hospital in Snow-Tower.

"The president hasn't yet recovered consciousness. It is said that her grandson, Mr. Yi Bonwhe, is at her bedside."

I glance reflexively at this week's issue of *TV Guide,* which is lying face-up on the neighboring bench. Below the text about upcoming shows is a catchy headline in a bold font and large typeface: IS THE VP HIDING OUT WITH HER NEW BEAU?

"Two summers ago, President Yi had an emergency heart procedure following a similar collapse. During a board meeting this morning, a temporary replacement . . ."

I look to Hyang. Her eyes are fastened on the screen, assessing this curveball hurtling our way.

THE LOVELY GIRLS NEXT DOOR

We wait for the arrival of the Ma-line train in the make-shift foyer inside the plant's rear entrance. Hyang rummages through her backpack and fishes out a tiny glass case, which she hands to Shinae.

"Try these," she says.

Shinae opens the case to reveal a pair of blue contacts and examines them curiously as Hyang runs her eyes over the rest of us. It's a full week's ride to Ja-A-1, our destination and the nearest settlement to Snowglobe, and we'll be riding in a passenger cab that doubles as the engineer's spartan living quarters, like we did with Ongi. It's useless to deny the fact that it would be torture to cling to the goggles, sunglasses, and silence throughout the journey—we need disguises.

Hyang tips back Somyung's head and inspects her bite, opening and closing her jaws. Frowning in concentration, she says, "We have to make sure that the false teeth fit correctly, or they'll come loose while you eat."

Somyung adjusts the set of teeth and closes her garish red lips around the overbite. Her eyes are covered by the thick, straight bangs of her pink wig. There's no danger of anyone confusing her for Haeri.

"Ugh, I just can't do it," Shinae complains, frowning at the blue contact lens perched on the tip of her finger. The skin around her eyes is smudged black—she went full panda with the eye makeup.

"Let me help you," I say, first making sure my false nose hasn't slipped out of place. Breathing is a bit tricky, with its comically high bridge glued to my face, but it's fine. Worlds better than the giant goggles. I hold my breath and carefully guide Shinae's finger to her eye.

Across from us, Somyung is reapplying lipstick, her lips growing in size with each fresh sweep. Thankfully, the shriek of the approaching train stops her before she can turn herself into a circus clown.

Then we're stepping out into the -50°F temperature. Under the natural light, we forget the cold and erupt in laughter at everyone's absurd new looks.

"The ski mask really brings out your smoky eyes, Shinae," Somyung observes dryly, and we all howl with laughter. I get the feeling that our journey to Snowglobe won't be all grave and solemn after all.

"Who would have thought I'd be transporting a real-life Snowglobe resident in this train!" The Ma-line engineer cries out her excitement, pouring warm boi tea into the paper cup in my hand.

She's been bursting with joy since we, a team of occupational culture and safety researchers returning to Snowglobe, boarded her train three hours ago. Poking her head into our car every chance she gets, she wants to know how we're doing, if we want more tea, or if there's anything else she can get for us. Really, she's just looking for the tiniest excuse to engage with us.

The soft murmur of her TV reaches us each time she swings the door open, and I can hear that it's *Goh Around* keeping her company in her solitary cab.

This time, the engineer laments how she never gets to interact with people from Snowglobe despite all her trips to the warehouse that's joined to the city. Then, with a shy smile, she reveals that she's never skipped the actor audition—not even once.

"Do you know what the best part of my job is?" she says. Without waiting for an answer, she plunges back into her monologue. "Having the time to dream up all kinds of scenes, with the privacy to act them out to my heart's content. I get to train on my train." She briefly flushes at her own joke. "You saw Kim Jenho asking Haeri out at the championship last Christmas? I've imagined myself in her place, and I don't know if I would have been able to say anything coherent in front of all those people. Haeri is one amazing girl."

Out of the corners of her panda eyes, Shinae glances my way, her face red with the effort of subduing her laugh. Somyung's eyes, too, shout at me.

I stare back in a silent warning, and the engineer jabbers on, "Family, money, friends, looks . . . put her in a burlap sack, Haeri would still look perfectly put together. If I could choose to be anyone, it would be her, for sure. She's the whole package." She sighs dreamily, then lets her rhapsody trail off. "Almost too good to be true."

The four of us squirm in our seats at this last bit.

All I want to say is "Bull's-eye, ma'am. Bull's-eye."

In that way, we continue toward Snowglobe, the engineer's fandom flaring up while she remains clueless about the fact that she's delivering her idol's assassins. The irony is too rich.

Sannah opens the truck's cargo hold, calling to Hyang in the pas-senger seat up front. "Panda and Rhino made it!"—referring to me and Shinae.

As we left straight from the plant, Shinae had no skis, not that she would have taken one of the only two sets her family of twelve shares. So I, the strongest skier among us, volunteered to pull her behind me on a sled, from the train station to our next stop, back to Sannah's truck.

Catching our breath, Shinae and I climb up into the cargo hold to join Somyung, who's already settled in.

"Good job, Bambi," Somyung says.

A moment later, the woman responsible for the catchy moniker comes around the back. It's been close to two weeks since we left the retirees' village, and Hyang has yet to acclimate to the elements of the open world. Her teeth chattering, she apologizes, "Sorry, it should have been me bringing up the rear."

Sannah chuckles. "We're all just glad you aren't weighing us down," she says. Then, swinging around, she points to the large box sitting in the far corner of the dark cargo hold.

"There's a box of supplies for you," she says. "If you need anything, give the wall a few kicks, okay?"

I open up the box and check out the contents. There are a portable stove and some blankets, handwarmers, and thermoses. But it's the packets of hot cocoa powder that jump out at me.

"I think we should be all set," I declare, holding up a packet, which triggers whoops of excitement from Somyung and Shinae.

We thank Sannah again.

She smiles. "I'll see you all in Snowglobe, then."

"Yes, ma'am!" the three of us shout in unison.

"There wo-won't be a sec-second to lose once we get there," Hyang adds, her teeth chattering violently. "We'll si-signal you five minutes before our arrival, so stay alert."

We nod, our mood turning somber again. Then the door shuts, taking all the light with it. A minute later, we hear the roar of the engine, and then we're motoring through a frozen plain that's indistinguishable from a thousand other frozen plains, not that we can see anything from inside the cargo hold. In four hours, we'll arrive at the Snowglobe airport to be processed through customs and immigration. Somehow.

Firing up the portable stove and relying on what little heat and light it creates, we begin removing our makeup and other means of disguise. Then I pull out the big flashlight from my backpack and place it upright in the middle of our little circle. The low light casts ghoulish shadows on our identical faces, and soon we're all laughing again.

"I have an idea," I say. "Let's start a man-on-the-street

kind of show someday. The three of us can walk around and quiz people: Guess who's who?"

I'm mostly joking, of course, to lighten the mood, but it just reminds us of the one question we're trying to ignore: What will become of us after tonight?

"Tell me we're doing the right thing," Shinae says, worry creeping into her voice. "How did you guys sleep on the train? I didn't. At all. I couldn't stop wondering if wanting money is finally going to drive my life into the ground." A self-deprecating laugh. "Be honest, aren't you guys scared? We could end up in prison. Violation of media and broadcasting law? That's serious stuff—"

"Stop it," Somyung says. "Why would we end up in prison? *We're* the victims here. Did you forget?"

But the look on her face communicates more uncertainty than conviction.

Shinae persists, "What if we're arrested before we even get to the studio? Sneaking into Snowglobe is a serious felony."

"Do you want to go back home, then?" Somyung asks sharply.

Shinae shakes her head. "No," she says. "That, I don't want to do."

We're all quiet for a while, absorbed in our thoughts.

"Hey, to be fair," Shinae says, "I was born to be a lovely girl next door, not a border jumper or terrorist. It's totally natural to cycle through some fear and doubt right now, don't you think?" she adds, glancing around at us. When we don't speak up, she mutters, "You guys are the psychos, then."

A few moments of heavy silence tick by. But then someone

stifles a snort and it's all over. The three of us dissolve into laughter that won't stop until there are tears in my eyes and my abs hurt. I can't even say what's so funny.

When our laughing fit subsides, I declare it hot cocoa time, and a few minutes later, we're clutching at our cups, chatting like we never could on the train.

Shinae asks Somyung, "Have you ever shot a person?"

Somyung nods.

"Dang! I'm jealous," cries Shinae. "If I'd had a gun, I wouldn't have had to suffer through my dad all this time. No. Not my dad. The buffoon of a man who I *thought* was my dad."

Whether she's serious or not, this opens the floodgate for more candid talk. When we finally exhaust the list of haters, the topic naturally veers to the people we love.

"Hey, Bambi. Do you really not have feelings for Jehno?" Shinae asks.

"We're friends," I say. "But that'll be over soon."

"Friends? Come on!" Somyung yells.

And in that way of poking and teasing, we keep up a mostly happy chatter, though the mood turns appropriately somber when Somyung recounts her parents' fatal accident or I talk about my dad's sacrifice.

I find myself missing these girls already. When all this is over, occasional letters across the frozen wasteland will have to do, if we even get to do that.

Tap, tap— Tap, tap, tap—

Hyang's signal silences us, and the muffled sound of her voice drifts in through the heavy wall.

"Five minutes!" she says.

And we all know what to do. With a look and a nod, we swing into action, peeling off our arctic outerwear and changing into outfits borrowed from Hyang's wardrobe. Then, turning off the stove and the flashlight, we wait for our next signal in the dark silence of the cargo hold, squeezing each other's hands. Soon, Sannah's truck comes to a complete stop. We've arrived.

FRIDAY NIGHT FEVER

The door rolls up with a metallic screech, flooding the cargo hold with daylight. The agent, silhouetted against the blinding backdrop, murmurs a stupefied "What the—" Then *bam!* Somyung's tranquilizer hits him in the neck. In the next instant, his eyes roll back in their sockets and he crumples to the ground like a rag doll. Somyung jumps out of the truck and squats next to him to appraise her shot.

"Just a few hours' nap, buddy," she says, a pleased smile on her face.

I jump out and fish the car key from the agent's pants pocket. He plays a bit part in a low-performing show that's been hobbling along for three seasons on the strength of its director—Cha Joonhyuk, Cha Seol's father.

I have my connections, and Seol has hers.

Is this man Seol's connection? Or is it the other way around, with him maintaining his residency in Snowglobe in exchange for doing Seol's bidding?

"Wait a minute. Isn't this Liam Solulu?" Shinae says,

also recognizing the slumbering agent's face. She clucks her tongue. "Too bad. He's going to miss all the action."

Somyung gives a low snort of acknowledgment, her eyes steely. Then the three of us are ducking down behind the truck, watching as Hyang pushes and jerks Sannah toward the gleaming customs office, pressing a pistol against her head. Sannah, her hands tied behind her back, pleads in terror, "Please don't shoot!"

Inside the office, an agent looks up from his fingernails. His eyes jump at the scene out the window. Scrambling from his chair, he races out the door with his handgun.

"Freeze!" he shouts, aiming his gun at the duo. "Put down your weapon!"

The fuzzy office slippers on his feet undermine the authority of this command. And despite the urgency of the moment, the phrase I've once heard on TV pops into my mind: *Clothes make the man.*

"No!" Sannah screams. "Don't shoot! She'll shoot me, too!"

At a loss, the agent hesitates. Meanwhile, Somyung sneaks around to the front of the truck and fires her dart gun for the second time.

Pshwing—

In the next instant, the agent falls down in a heap. The three of us then charge at Sannah, who puts on a great show of fighting back: kicking, spitting, and screaming as we tie her up to the agent, who is now literally sleeping on the job. Then we race to Liam's car as she screams and curses at us.

"You think you can take on a director?" she yells as we pile into the car. "Ha! Take it from me—you *will* fail!"

Somyung and Shinae pile into the backseat, and I jump in next to Hyang, who's behind the wheel. The three of us slip on our dark glasses as we roll out of the grounds. Every one of us is itching to talk about Sannah's award-worthy performance, but it'll have to wait. We're in Snowglobe now, where cameras surround us, even inside this vehicle that's delivering us to our destiny. So we maintain our act, cursing and mocking Sannah, though we sidestep her last line: *Take it from me—you will fail!*

Yes, it was all a part of her act, but the scripted line hammers darkly at my heart.

"Gah! This damned traffic!" Hyang curses, bringing her palm down hard on the steering wheel. The clock on the dash reads 9:37 p.m. Thirteen minutes to the live weather segment, which means twenty-three more minutes of live air left on *News at 9.* We have to take over the Control Room within that time frame, or it's all over.

During the hour of *News at 9,* the Control Room assumes complete command of Channel 9's output. That is, whether or not our exposé reaches viewers' screens depends on its censoring of the live feed. At ten o'clock sharp, when the weather segment ends, Producer Yi Dahm, as the chief of the Control Room, will switch off the red LIVE button, transferring the command back to the Master Control Room.

The first step in our mission is to storm the Control Room and secure the LIVE button so the command stays with us after the news hour, until we're through telling the world the truth about Haeri.

"For crying out loud," Hyang mutters, drumming her fingers on the steering wheel. The rest of us alternate between nail-biting, praying, and rocking restlessly in our seats.

It's Friday night, the best time of the week for most Snowglobe residents. The sidewalks flanking the main street are bustling with people cutting loose for the evening. I switch on the radio, and the news crackles from the speakers. Anchor Park's voice reports:

On the one hundred eleventh floor of SnowTower, the banquet for the sixty biathletes invited to this year's championship is in full swing. Let's hear from the reigning champion, Kim Jehno, and the previous year's champion, Priya Maravan.

Shinae halts her droning prayers at the sound of Jehno's name. "Bambi, it's your boyfriend!" she cries, her mood momentarily lifting. "Turn up the volume."

As for my own mood, it sinks deeper.

"Hi, I'm Kim Jehno," his smiling voice says. He cannot imagine that the girl he's crushing on is about to be extinguished.

"Yes, I've pasted the championship logo on my rifle. For good luck! Hopefully, it'll deliver for me."

The merry voices of Anchor Park and the champions soon fade into the background as we turn our focus back to managing our breath and sending up prayers to whoever.

"What's the other Control Room? The Master Control Room?" Shinae says, and I switch off the radio. "Why can't we go there right away?" she asks. "Didn't you say it's the Master Control Room that has command of the entire system? Why can't we just take over the whole network so more people can see us?"

"Wouldn't that be nice," Hyang replies sourly. "The problem is that no one knows where the heck it is."

As the name implies, the Master Control Room sits atop the hierarchy of Snowglobe's broadcasting system to oversee and regulate the whole of its operation. According to Hyang, even directors with thirty years of experience don't know its physical location. Its daily temporary transfer of authority to the Control Room during *News at 9* is a symbolic act upholding the twin principles of freedom of the press and media independence guaranteed by the Snowglobe order.

"In short, if we don't take over the Control Room within the next twenty-three minutes, our plan will go up in smoke," Somyung clarifies for Shinae. "And if that happens, we'll be in police custody by this time tomorrow."

"Then why are we just sitting here? Isn't that SnowTower right there?" Shinae says, looking out at the tower in the distance.

I confirm it with a nod.

"Should we run?" Somyung says, her hand already yanking at the door handle.

"No!" I yelp before she can do anything rash. "It only looks close because it's so big, and—"

Too late. The door flies open and Somyung and Shinae spring out of the car.

"No!" Hyang shrieks. "Come back!"

But it's no use. The girls won't stop. Hyang turns to me, eyes wild, but all I can offer is a shrug. She lets out a curse and undoes her seat belt. Pulling at her door handle, she warns me, "Brace yourself. You're about to experience a lifetime's worth of Snowglobe road rage."

Then we're out of the car and running. Horns blare and angry voices erupt from every direction as we weave through the stalled traffic toward SnowTower.

Night has finally swept the city, intensifying the kaleidoscope of lights twinkling from the shops and restaurants lining the busy sidewalks. We're racing through the crowd, their chatter and laughter careening and ricocheting around us. Despite our sunglasses, which are conspicuous at this time of day, no one pays us more than a curious glance. We are in Snowglobe.

From behind the show window of an electronics store, a giant flat-screen TV streams *News at 9*. The usual white caption scrolling on the lower right corner displays a temperature of 70°F, trailed by a crescent moon icon that signals a clear night sky.

I turn my focus back to Somyung and Shinae, who are running a few feet in front of us, their backpacks doing a wild dance.

Suddenly, Somyung swings around. "I don't believe it!" she cries to me and Hyang, her face red and glazed with sweat.

"Don't believe what?" I say.

"I'm hot and sweaty," she replies, her face arranged in a sort of wonder. "Outside!"

"What?"

"I'm roasting! How do people live here?" she says, grinning ear to ear.

I burst out laughing. The next thing I know, all of us are laughing. Again.

"Stop it! I'm starting to feel weak," Shinae protests, unable to stop laughing herself.

"But seriously. Is this temperature for real?"

Seventy degrees Fahrenheit. We bounce through the pleasant air toward the tower, shrieking with laughter none of us can explain.

Drenched in sweat and panting, we finally tumble into the lobby of SnowTower. The security guard murmurs his shock at the sight of my disheveled hair and bare, inflamed face glistening with sweat just moments before the weather segment. I quickly explain that the special guests and I need to head up to the studio at once, and he rushes us up without another word, bypassing visitor registration and all the rest of the security protocols.

Then we're in the elevator, shooting up to the 204th floor. Exactly twenty-nine seconds later, there is a ding and the doors slide open. We file out and head straight for the studio with Somyung—armed with two handguns—in the lead.

THE TAKEOVER

nside the studio, I lock the soundproof door. Getting in was a breeze, with security temporarily deactivated for the convenience of staff who are constantly running in and out of the space. *News at 9* is in full swing.

"According to Spokesman Hong, Vice-President Yi Bon-shim will attend the anniversary event scheduled to be held in a week . . ."

Anchors Chung and Park, standing on either side of the massive touchscreen, take turns delivering a summary of the day's trending news. From the floor manager to the run crew, everyone's attention is focused on the anchors.

Shinae keeps watch at the door. Somyung and I follow Hyang up the stairs and sneak into the Control Room. Inside, producer Yi Dahm and her team are stationed at the blinking console overlooking the news set below, absorbed in monitoring and conducting the live production. Off to one side, a wall of production monitors flashes images and captions being broadcast; and in the center of this wall, the LIVE button glows red.

"Get ready, Haeri," Producer Yi says into the microphone of her headset. "Sixty to rolling."

That's my cue, too. I pull the trigger.

Pshwing—

The feathered dart grazes Producer Yi's upper arm and hits the console before sliding off to the floor like a children's toy. Producer Yi wheels around, her mouth turned down at the corners.

Crap!

The slowest half second ticks by as she lets her eyes sweep over each of us standing there against the door, her scowl morphing into a blank look and then into an expression of utter confusion. When, at last, her eyes rove to the pistols in Somyung's hands, her mouth goes slack and terror settles in her face.

Blood thunders through my temples. My fingertip pressed against the trigger, I'm about to fire another dart when Producer Yi releases a heart-stopping scream. The crew jolts around from the console and everything falls to pieces around us.

And what do I do? I freeze, watching numbly as if all this is a nightmare unfolding before me. Finally, Hyang snatches the dart gun out of my hand and nails Producer Yi in the forehead, sending her pitching to the floor with a sharp cry. The sound editor goes down next, a feathered dart in her neck, clutching at the emergency phone.

"Evacuate the room. Then no one has to get hurt." Somyung's even voice reaches me as if from a deep well. I swivel my head to see her holding the rest of the crew at gunpoint—until the technical director suddenly breaks off and lunges for Somyung.

"Run!" he cries to the rest of the crew.

Gripping her arms and pushing her against the wall, he tries mightily to wrench the guns out of her hands.

"What the hell, man? Do you have a *death wish*?" Somyung cries, struggling against him. Clearly, she wants to avoid hurting him if she can help it. "Goddamn it, Bambi!" she yells. "Where's the dart gun?"

Slowly coming out of my stupor, I look around for Hyang and the dart gun, only to realize that she's whirling in a mad waltz with the two remaining crew members, heaving and banging against the walls as one solid unit.

My stomach clenches and my heart pounds against my rib cage. I need to do something, anything. But what? The next thing I know, I've flung myself on the technical director's back and have him in a choke hold. Soon a pained, gurgling noise escapes his throat and he lets go of Somyung. But in the next instant, his hands are around my wrists, wringing the life out of them as he tries to shake me off.

"Shit! My wrists!" I cry in agony.

Somyung looks to me and Hyang, torn as to who to rescue first. She cries, "Hey, Hyang! What about now? This qualifies as a dire circumstance, doesn't it?"

Hyang made us swear that deadly force would only be used under dire circumstances, for self-defense.

"No! It doesn't—" Hyang manages to get out before one of her adversaries jerks her head back by a fistful of hair. This clears my line of sight to the monitor behind her, which currently displays Anchor Chung's face frozen in disbelief. A moment later, her voice tumbles out of the speakers with urgency.

"Breaking news, ladies and gentlemen! It—it appears that the studio is under attack."

She lifts her face from the live camera and peers into the Control Room. Her stunned eyes lock on mine as I tighten my hold around the technical director's meaty neck. It takes a moment for her to accept what she sees.

"Haeri?" she murmurs. A consummate professional, she quickly recovers and continues delivering a sort of blow-by-blow of the news.

"Ladies and gentlemen, the weather presenter Goh Haeri appears to be in the Control Room . . ."

Then something explodes to my left, and my vision goes black for a few moments. Through the roaring in my ears, I can make out distant, muffled voices crying out for me.

"No! Bambi—!"

"Chobahm! Chobahm!"

Something warm and wet slides down the left side of my face, blurring my vision. I try blinking my eyes back to focus, but they refuse. Someone shouts, "What are you waiting for! Shoot him! Shoot that bastard!"

A blast obliterates the air, and the technical director under me pitches sideways to the floor, where he writhes and screams in pain. The two besieging Hyang scramble up to their feet and flee the Control Room. A moment later, there's a shriek, followed by the sound of someone tumbling down the stairs, and then a keening cry.

"Ladies and gentlemen, Haeri and the assailants have just fired a gun in the Control Room!"

Anchor Chung's voice tears out of the speakers again, but that will be her last line tonight, as she joins the rest of the terrified crew being herded out of the studio by Shinae.

After a minute, Shinae calls up from the bottom of the stairs, "Everyone's out! But where's Bae Serin?"

Up in the Control Room, Hyang, Somyung, and I are all reeling. When no response comes, Shinae hollers again, an edge of terror rising in her voice.

"Hey! Hello! Are you guys okay up there?"

I manage a whimper for her.

The left side of my face pulses with pain. Shattered glass is strewn across the floor, where the technical director is clutching at his blood-soaked pant leg, moaning in agony. Hyang raises the dart gun to his left cheek.

"You crazy bastard—what if you've blinded her?" she says, her voice turbulent with anger.

Then the technical director lets out a cry and crumples sideways to the floor, the peacock feather of the dart planted in his cheek.

Hyang crawls over to Producer Yi and pulls the headset off her sleeping head. Tossing it to me, she says, "No time to waste. Go now!"

I glance at the wall of monitors still dutifully displaying the vacated studio from all angles. The LIVE button in the center remains on.

Somyung and I hobble down the stairs to the studio and join Shinae. Shutting the door behind us, Shinae fires up the torch and begins applying its flame to the doorframe. The white, silicon-like material lining the door's casing turns as hard as concrete under the heat, sealing the door to its frame. After this, nothing short of dynamite could open the door, or at least, that's what Hyang told us.

"Done! Let's go!" Shinae says as sirens wail in the distance.

The three of us rush toward the news desk. We don't have much time. At all.

"What the hell are you doing?" a voice says, stopping us in our tracks. Turning to the voice, we see Haeri—no, Bae Serin—staggering out to us in the harsh studio light, dressed in a white short-sleeved sweater and a matching knee-length skirt. The shock in her face is almost too painful to behold.

"I see." Shinae speaks up first. "She's been hiding there." She jerks her chin to the set.

Serin, who'd been waiting for her cue on the other side of the rotating platform as if it were any other night, is glowing and camera-ready, looking every inch like the Haeri we know.

"I said, what the *hell* are you doing?" Serin repeats in a wild, trembling voice, her eyes jumping to each of us.

"Someone jabbed me in the neck without explanation or warning," I say, taking a step toward her. "Now it's your turn for some disorientation. We don't have time to explain."

Astonishment turning to terror, Serin's eyes sink back in her head.

Through the teeny speakers of my headset, Hyang urges us on, "We're running out of time! Get on with it, now!"

The side of my face starts to throb again and I raise my hand to it. I can't see myself, but my fingers tell me what a mess it is. My left eye is swelling shut, and an oozing crust runs from my brow to my temple.

"Sorry, but we have to hustle," I tell Serin, wiping my hand on the hem of my shirt. "Stay out of our way. And pay attention. Things will begin to make sense."

Then the three of us head for the news set.

"No, you can't! I won't allow it!" Serin shrieks, stepping in front of us with outstretched arms. Her eyes flash in the glare of the overhead lights, a kind of understanding already dawning in them. She seems to have sorted out what we're about—and what her connection to us might be.

"I'm Goh Haeri!" she shouts, curling her lips and showing her teeth. "And for the third time, what the hell are you doing here and why are you headed for the set?"

The three of us exchange a look. After all, Serin is one of us, and she hasn't agreed to our plan. Her objection has more stopping power than any weapon. This is clear from the look on the face of Somyung, the only one of us who's actually armed.

"What are you doing! Wake up!" Hyang's urgent cry comes through the headset.

"Let's go," I say, and charge for the news desk, brushing past Serin, who flings herself at me.

"No!" she screams, digging her nails into my arm. "No! You can't!"

I pull off the headset and toss it to Somyung.

"Why don't you two get started," I suggest as Serin begins flailing at me, stomping her feet like a child having a tantrum.

"I'm Goh Haeri!" she shouts, her voice breaking with fear, rage, and desperation. "Don't you understand? I *am* Haeri!"

Somyung and Shinae are still standing there, hesitating to go on without me.

"What are you doing? Go!" I shout as Serin pulls me down to the floor. We proceed to roll in a mad scramble, the pain in my face searing. But it turns out that she's no athlete. I quickly come up on top, pinning her down.

"Go!" I plead to Somyung and Shinae, who are still rooted to the spot. "Please!"

Finally, Somyung sets her jaw and starts toward the news desk, nudging Shinae forward. In a few steps, though, Shinae glances back at me, and her brows bunch in confusion.

"What's that on your forehead?" she asks.

What's on *my* face? What's on *her* face, is what I want to know. A tiny red dot has appeared on her forehead. Wait. There's another. Followed by a third, a fourth, and then a fifth. When Somyung turns around, there's a whole galaxy of red dots across her face.

That's when a voice intones, "Drop your weapons and put your hands over your head. You're surrounded."

Serin stops thrashing and looks up. As she does, a clutch of red dots descend on her face, too. I look up to the newsroom above. Blood is pooling in my swollen eye, blurring my vision even more, but I can still make out the dark forms poised at the windows. There's a whole SWAT team aiming their rifles at us.

AN OLD PROMISE

SnowTower, as the home of the rich and the famous, as well as the most vital facility in the whole of Snow-globe, is heavily guarded. And though I'm not so naïve as to think that all security staff should be as mild and friendly as the lobby officers on the first floor, I didn't imagine that they'd be a paramilitary squad. Today, the squad appears to have been reinforced with the biathletes attending the banquet on the 111th floor.

I start searching the faces behind the rifles for Jehno's. When our eyes meet, he draws back from his scope to stare numbly at me. Plucked from the event, he's still wearing his fine silk suit; so is Chun Sahyun, crouched over her rifle a few feet off to his left, though it's a fancy cocktail gown in her case. I shift my gaze back to Jehno. His eyes have gone remote with shock, shock at seeing his Haeri in my blood-crusted face.

A dozen or so SnowTower security officers hang back nervously in the shadow behind the snipers. No matter how intimidating their black uniforms, bulletproof vests, and firearms are, these officers don't look equal to the crisis at hand. And who can blame them? This is probably the first real-life situation they've ever had to respond to in their career, or in the history of Snowglobe, for that matter.

The voice descends again. "Drop your weapons. I repeat, drop your weapons, then put your hands up and get down on the floor."

I wonder if they know how much the soundproof windows cut down the amplification and authority of the megaphone-aided voice.

"Surrender, or we'll fire," it rumbles, or tries to.

The three of us exchange a long look. And in the next moment, we're charging defiantly for the news desk. If we, the three of us side by side, make it into the live camera's field of view even for a second, half of our mission will have been accomplished.

Sounds of explosions and shattering glass follow. Warning shots have been fired. We manage to duck behind some studio equipment, shaking. Serin is curled up on the floor, her hands pressed against her ears, screaming in pure terror.

"Drop your weapons and freeze," the voice comes at us again. "We will not hesitate to fire again."

Inside the Control Room, Hyang is hysterical. She is screaming at the top of her lungs, "Stay put! Don't move!"

The shots have etched a sizzling pattern on the tempered windows of the newsroom, but they haven't blown holes. Not yet. The next round of shots, though, will; and it will likely prove fatal.

"Your resistance is futile. Surrender," the voice demands.

Serin, her snow-white outfit rumpled and stained with

my blood and her hair wildly disarranged, cries out from the floor, "I'm not with them! You know me! I'm Haeri! Goh Haeri!"

"You have committed an act of terrorism by attacking the broadcasting station," the voice returns. "Do not be reckless with your words or behaviors now."

I keep seeing Anchor Chung's bewildered face staring up at me from the news desk floor.

Ladies and gentlemen, the weather presenter, Goh Haeri, seems to be in the Control Room . . .

All of a sudden, Serin gives out a deranged laugh. "No!" she cries back. "Anchor Chung's report was wrong! Look! Just look! Don't you see how much those imposters look like me? She thought I was one of them!"

I'm not sure how much anyone in the newsroom can hear through the soundproof glass. Even using a megaphone, the voice sounds anything but mega. Whether it heard her or not, it ignores her.

"Drop your weapons and surrender," the tin-can voice intones again.

"What do we do?" Somyung says, turning to me.

Holding her with a look, I raise my hands above my head and push up to my feet, turning slowly in place to face the newsroom above. The man behind the megaphone turns out to be Tyrr Schwarkel, a former cop who had achieved fame with a crime show until he was dishonorably discharged for abuse of power.

Clad in the same all-black SWAT team regalia, he is apparently leading the operation. But the designer sunglasses perched over his nose? In this circumstance? The vanity of it makes me laugh—the expression *fashion over function* making a quick entry into my mind. And then I remember. Even now, dozens of cameras are rolling all around us. Everyone here is playing a role in one show or another; and footage revolving around the current situation is bound to kick up drama for any show that needs it.

For Schwarkel, this could be a golden opportunity to return a hero from the rubble of his disgrace, which explains the dark glasses, pious expression, and over-the-top posturing.

Raising the megaphone to his mouth, he begins rumbling into it again, his voice charged with the righteousness and authority of a man tasked with saving the world.

"We will not negotiate with terrorists who threaten Snowglobe's peace and security. In order to protect the citizens and to serve the public, we will . . . ," he warbles on. And on.

Considering that we're surrounded by Snowglobe's top snipers while the one armed person among us has only two tiny pistols, Schwarkel's speech is hysterically outsized. It wouldn't surprise me at all if the self-promoting opportunist was the one who pushed for the involvement of biathlons in the first place.

"Shit," Shinae says, looking as if she is about to combust with rage. "Tell me!" she lashes out in tears. "How else do you expect us to go up against Cha Seol! It's her who you should be going after! Not us! Don't you get it?"

"Shut up, you terrorist!" Serin shrieks, coming out of her silence. She wants to make it clear whose side she's on.

"To reiterate—" Schwarkel, ignoring all this, resumes.

Shinae glares up at the thundering man, shaking. But then

her eyes bug out. I follow her gaze and see a figure behind Schwarkel moving into the window.

It's Bonwhe.

Snatching the megaphone from Schwarkel, he turns to the staff surrounding him. A rogue word here and there manages to reach us down below, such as *right now* and *phone.*

Serin springs to her feet.

"Young Master Bonwhe!" she cries out, gazing up at him rapturously through eyes bleeding black with mascara, as if witnessing the arrival of her savior. "It's me, Young Master! It's Haeri!"

She doesn't get that the title she's offering also gives her away. She holds her arms up in his direction like a child wanting to be picked up. Somyung looks on, disgusted.

It's 10:06 by the large digital clock on the studio wall. Unlike on any ordinary day, the LIVE button on the camera facing the news set still glows red, and command of the network remains with the Control Room, where Hyang holds fast.

I peer up at the newsroom. Bonwhe's eyes rove from me to Serin and back, his face a mask I can't read. Schwarkel, who disappeared briefly, reappears by his side, holding up a desk phone. Fixing me with his eyes, Bonwhe picks up the receiver and presses a button. The next moment, the glass phone booth in the corner begins pulsing white at regular intervals, like the ringing of a phone.

Bonwhe, somewhat impatiently, motions with his head for me to pick up. But Serin beats me to it.

"Yes! Hello!" she bleats into the receiver. Leaving the booth wide open, she begins talking hysterically. "Young Master!

This is Haeri! There's been a terrible mistake! I swear I have nothing to do with whatever this is. Please—I'm scared." She swivels her head to radiate her hate for me. "They keep talking nonsense about getting rid of me, killing me." A choked sob. "Please, Young Master, please help—"

I feel a stab of sadness for this girl who is so desperate to hold on to her life as Haeri that she continues to perform for the cameras rolling around her even now. This might just be the performance of lifetime. Come to think of it, was she holding back while wrestling with me on the floor just a few minutes ago? Haeri would never punch, kick, or choke like a savage. The girl who sank the syringe into my neck has to remain hidden.

"Yes, of course. But . . . ," Serin protests, her voice trailing off to a pitiable whimper. "Yes. Okay."

She sets the receiver back in the cradle, biting her lip and shaking, her eyes on the floor. Finally, stepping out of the booth, she draws in a ragged breath and lifts her face to let her eyes burn me.

"Take the next call," she says, so upset she can barely speak.

I look back up to Bonwhe, who is standing in the newsroom window. Slowly, I reach for Producer Yi's headset, which I'd flung on the floor. Picking it up, I look back up at him. After a moment, he gives a nod. Schwarkel leaps in with some kind of objection, but Bonwhe doesn't even acknowledge that the man spoke. Holding Bonwhe with my eyes, I put on the headset and connect to Hyang in the Control Room.

"The station's power supply," I say in a hushed voice. "Are you sure it's fed only by the Central Power Plant?"

"Yes, I'm sure. Why?" Hyang says, a sliver of hope rising in her voice. "What does it have to do with anything?"

"You said the station will black out if the Central Power Plant pauses; and there's no backup, correct?"

"Correct."

"Good. That's all I need to know."

"What are you—"

Hyang's voice sizzles from the tiny speakers, but I pull off the headset and set it back down on the floor. Then I step into the phone booth and shut the door before picking up the receiver.

"Let's proceed," I say, packing all my will into my voice. And what choice do I have but to speak for Yeosu, who can't be here in the flesh? Looking up at Bonwhe, I continue, "You once promised to make her pay." Something seems to stir behind Bonwhe's stony face. I press on, "You don't have to do anything. Just get out of our way. Please."

My heart clenches at the thought of Yeosu, who trusted Bonwhe to free her from Cha Seol's cruel game. Bonwhe is silent. Then I see his shoulders sag.

"I'm sorry," he says at last, his voice caught low in his throat. And the words that follow couldn't be more underwhelming.

"The Yibonn Media Group is not at liberty to permit your request at this time."

THE EXPOSÉ

Canned words from the big boss. Straining to stifle any emotions, he drops his voice even lower as he continues, "What's kept Snowglobe peaceful and thriving all these years is its fairness and equity. We cannot reward those who threaten our system with violence and intimidation, no matter what the excuse or justification."

"Fairness and *equity*?" I scoff. Glancing out of the booth, I see Somyung and Shinae huddled by the live-feed camera, watching me for any signs of hope—or despair. Even as they do, their eyes flick anxiously at the red light of the camera, as if their lives depend on it, which they do.

"What are you talking about?" I shoot back, anger rising in me again at this betrayal. "You know what goes on behind the cameras! You know what kind of scum Cha Seol is! She must be exposed, if only to prevent others from—"

"I am speaking as a representative of the corporation." He cuts me off, sounding almost petulant.

So what? Was that supposed to be a roundabout apology? For any inconveniences he may be causing? His plea for me to understand his difficult position? Did he just slip out of the role he claims to inhabit?

Why do you care about me?

Because you're you.

Yeosu's Bonwhe, the only person in Snowglobe who has intimate knowledge of her heart, has been overwritten by Bonwhe, the deputy CEO of the Yibonn Media Group. I am going to overthrow the latter, then.

"Fine. Then prove that you're not just hiding behind the virtues of fairness and peace. Stop us without using force," I say, glaring up at him now. "Turn off the Central Power Plant."

I watch him draw back a little, looking shocked.

"I can't pause the entire network just to stop you," he replies after a moment.

"Why not? Wouldn't that be more peaceful than stopping us with bullets?"

He says nothing and I continue, "Just what I thought. Uninterrupted service supersedes any virtues, after all, doesn't it? Of course you'd never shut down the Central Power Plant. Or *any* other plant." He cocks his head at this, narrowing an eye. "Because Snowglobe would literally freeze up the moment there's trouble with the power supply."

The mirror I ran into at the Christmas party dropped me off at what my fevered brain concluded was the yet-to-be-revealed prison. And that's where I saw the man with the pink heart tattoo under his eye, sweating inside his gearwheel alongside hundreds of fellow inmates.

Then, on my first visit to the studio, I learned that my inmate had been executed on December twenty-third. So how was he laboring in the bowels of the estate on the night of the party, on Christmas Eve?

Who were these people and what were they doing? Over the endless hours on the road with Hyang, I had puzzled over this question—and hit upon a theory.

Snowglobe is the only place in the world that escaped the murderous freeze, owing to—supposedly—its abundant natural geothermal energy. But if that's true, then how did I come so close to freezing to death that night? Why was the air as frigid as the open world right in the middle of Snowglobe? Could it be that Snowglobe's supposed geothermal jackpot is a lie? That the energy needed to control the temperature is from the secret power plant running on the slave labor of prisoners we all think have been executed?

"You lied to me," Bonwhe's voice accuses from the other end of the line.

Tell me what you've learned. From the moment of the mirror till now. Be concise.

When he confronted me in the woods, I didn't bring up the new prison, or the secret power plant; not that I was aware of the place's vital importance to Snowglobe at that time.

"You lied to me, too." I toss it back to him. As he murmurs his incomprehension, I press on. "You had no real intention of helping Yeosu. How could you have? You're a Yibonn, after all."

He stiffens at the sound of Yeosu's name coming out of my mouth in the third person, confirming what he suspected: I'm not her. Then terror settles around his eyes: *Where is she?*

Then I serve up the clincher. "You tortured her with hope when you knew in your heart you couldn't deliver."

"Is she . . . ," he tries, fighting his worst fear for her, but he can't go on.

"I'd like to believe that your heart was in the right place," I say.

I have to give him that. In the woods that night, his eyes, liquid with emotion while gazing at me, at Yeosu, almost made me fall for him, too.

"This is your chance to honor your promise to her. Let us take down Cha Seol, and I'll keep my promise to stay quiet about the mirrors."

His face locks up again.

"Understood," he says, at long last.

I watch as he turns around and dismisses the tactical force surrounding us. Then he presses the receiver back to his face.

"I guess I'll learn in time," he says. "What's your name?"

I hesitate a moment, fingering the crust on my face. "Jeon Chobahm."

"Jeon Chobahm," he repeats. "So those were your shoes."

Serin remains flopped on the floor, her head thrown back, gaz-ing blankly up at the newsroom. I walk over to her and tear out the earbud and the bloodied microphone clipped to her shirt. She doesn't resist, but doesn't react, either. Her eyes are fixed vacantly on the newsroom above, even as I slip the earbud into my left ear and clip the microphone onto my shirt front. Glancing up, I see Jehno's stunned face looking from me to Serin and back, trying to comprehend the incomprehensible.

Switching on the microphone, I hold out my hands to

Somyung and Shinae in invitation. The three of us then head for the news desk in lockstep. We line up before the live camera, Somyung and Shinae flanking me.

I briefly lift my eyes to the newsroom. Bonwhe, still standing at the windows like a statue, peers down at us. Schwarkel, too, his arms crossed in front of his chest, is motionless in anticipation of what we have to say.

"The monitor's all set. You girls are looking good." Hyang's voice sounds in my ear. "Whenever you're ready."

A deep breath, and I begin, "Hi, everyone. It's the girl next door who you've loved and supported for a long time. But did you know that she never truly existed?

"I was brought out into the world to inhabit the illusion of Goh Haeri one day. And I did. My name is Jeon Chobahm, and I was Haeri for a while."

Somyung and Shinae follow me in a similar vein. And then, squeezing each other's hands for strength, we expose the Goh Haeri project. Hyang's voice in the earbud informs us that she has the supporting footage queued up, and we watch what the viewers are seeing at home on the monitor above the camera display.

Before I know it, the video has ended and I'm saying, "We demand punishment for everyone who took part in this crime organized by Cha Guibahng and Cha Seol."

Just as I begin to relax—we got to reveal the truth, finally—Hyang's voice comes on through the earbud again. "There's more," she says.

I don't know what to say—we're going off script now. I plug my other ear with a finger to concentrate on her voice. "This isn't over, Chobahm," she tells me. "Now tell them,

Those who turned a blind eye to their abhorrent act should also be held accountable for their complicity."

I drop my eyes to the floor and keep them there to hide my shock from the viewers at home. Is she serious? This was never part of our plan.

"No dead air, please," Hyang says in my ear.

I stand there speechless. Is she turning herself in? Thankfully, before she can urge me to speak again, Somyung comes to my rescue.

"What are directors, after all?" she says. "Who gave them the privilege to play with people's lives? Actually, let me ask you, the almighty directors"—she pauses a moment to peer into the camera, her lips pressed together in a tight line—"do you think other people are merely here to play minor roles in your major lives? If it's okay to step into other people's lives and rearrange things in the name of entertainment or education, where do you draw the line?"

Her voice swells with anger, and I see that her resentment stretches beyond those who she is directly addressing. Orphaned at thirteen, Somyung was left to face the harshness of the world on her own; and for all I know, Cha Seol might have been just one of many people who approached her with a false promise of rescue.

As for me, yes, the woman sweet-talked me into believing that I'd be correcting the course of Haeri's life for everyone's sake. But that was just gravy. In my heart, I'd already accepted the deal Somyung had categorically rejected.

Somyung's hand trembles in mine. Squeezing it tight, I repeat the line Hyang fed me. "Those who turned a blind eye to their abhorrent act should also be held accountable for their complicity—" I pause to compose myself. A big breath, and I add, "I take responsibility for having been a willing participant in the cover-up while masquerading as Haeri, who I knew was dead."

Serin groans her disgust from the floor, and Somyung and Shinae turn to me with wild eyes.

"What are you talking about?" Somyung protests.

Shinae sighs, "Come on, Chobahm!"

Hyang barks through the earbud. "That's nonsense and you know it! You never had a real choice!"

Maybe. The big things, like my conception and birth, may have been predetermined, but I wasn't without free will. Did I have to devalue my own life to the point where I pounced on the chance to live as someone else?

I remember what Somyung said. *Why would I want to live as Haeri, when I was born Somyung.*

Peering into the camera, I continue, "I can't pretend to be an innocent victim. In the end, I let Cha Seol take advantage of my discontent . . . and my ambition."

I wanted so badly to be someone someday; and if that was a successful director, all the better. But why not expedite the dream by simply stepping into the empty shoes of one of the world's most beloved actors? The only price I had to pay was writing off my one and only self.

Shinae lets out a deep breath. Then, turning back to the camera, she begins, "Well. I suppose I should also confess . . ."

Hyang's yelp of displeasure stabs me in the ear.

"I'm only here for the money," Shinae continues. "For the compensation. Which should be staggering, if the justice system works."

"Fine. Go ahead and tell everyone," Hyang groans.

"I'm not as noble as Somyung or as cool as Chobahm," Shinae says. "I'm just . . . angry. I grew up watching my dad abuse my mom for having me, and my mom? She's never been able to push back, because of the bastard girl she had to protect." Shinae's lips quiver, and she takes a moment to catch herself. She glances at me and Somyung, and when she speaks again, the words that follow are more deliberate, composed. "We don't know how many of us there are. Some might even be watching this right now, watching themselves on the screen. If you are, let's unite. All of us. Let's unite and take our lives back. Cha Guibahng and Cha Seol owe us an apology. And compensation. Apology and compensation."

Then the three of us exchange a look and a nod. Turning our faces back to the camera, we say together, "That's all from us. Thank you for tuning in."

In my ear, Hyang says, "We're wrapping in three. Two. One. Cut!"

Then the red light of the camera turns off, at last.

Silence descends over the studio. Everything is still. Serin sits motionless on the floor, gazing listlessly at nothing. Up above, Bonwhe peers down at us like a stone statue, his face as unreadable as ever.

Then comes the racket of the police breaking down the studio door. I glance up to see Bonwhe disappearing into the newsroom, a line of staff trailing behind him. We remain rooted in front of the camera, squeezing each other's hands in case one of us falls.

The promise of a grand and brilliant life has been scrapped along with the Goh Haeri project, and all that waits for me now is the howling unknown. The odd thing is, I finally feel peaceful. I'm free again—free to dream my own dream, free to make my own mistakes, and most of all, free to express my love to those I hold dear. I could do all of that and more— today, tomorrow, and every day.

GOODBYE, CHANEL 60

Dressed in a blue inmate uniform, Cha Seol sits across from me behind the glass partition. Her fiery red hair has faded to a dull brown, but the color brings out the crackling intensity of her amber eyes. She holds me steady with those eyes, a rueful smile pressed to her lips. It takes a while before she finally picks up the phone.

"Look who's here," she purrs into the receiver.

"Do you even know which one I am?" I say, fighting to maintain composure.

She scoffs.

I repeat myself slowly, loading each word with hate. *"Do you even know which one I am?"*

This time, she considers the question a moment, or pretends to. Then, leaning forward languidly, she props her elbows on the counter. "Serin was okay at pretending to be Haeri, but awful at impersonating *you*." A laugh. "Just. Awful."

"You left my family alone. Why?"

She cocks her head to one side, affecting confusion.

"Yeosu's family," I hiss, feeling my lip curl. "You made them disappear so she had no one to go back to."

She gives me a long look. Then, letting out a snort, she says, "I helped them relocate to another settlement. To an upgraded house." A pause. "Is that so bad?"

Oh, how I loathe this woman. Suddenly, I'm on my feet and pounding my fist on the glass, shouting, "Yeosu was devastated—she thought they'd been killed because of her!"

Yeosu had said that in her diary, which was found during a police search and seizure of Maeryung's home after our exposé. Handwriting analysis proved the diary admissible evidence in court, and the news media made parts of it public.

"I never told her I'd killed her family. It's unfortunate that she jumped to that conclusion," Cha Seol says breezily, infuriating me further.

Goring her with my eyes, I slap the front page of today's paper on the glass partition and hold it up for her review. She takes in the bold, oversized headline, DEATH PENALTY FOR THE CHA DUO? before letting her eyes zip across the page. The article, which focuses on the baby carried by Sanghui, details how the devious pair's sentence will hinge on the status of the missing girl.

Cha Seol leans back placidly in her chair. "She simply vanished one day. In fact, I'd like to know what happened to her myself."

I clench my teeth. Lies. Lies. And more lies.

"You're unbelievable," I mutter.

If the investigation fails to prove it's more than a simple missing persons case, the duo will likely escape the death penalty.

Cooper's murder didn't even make it to trial, due to some

obscure clause in the law that prevented nonresidents and nonactors from testifying in court; me, in this case. The same useless law dismissed my involvement in the whole enterprise. As noncitizens, Hyang and I couldn't even be charged or tried. We simply didn't exist in the eyes of Snowglobe's justice system, not beyond the matter of improper entry.

Meanwhile, Cha Seol was maintaining her innocence, laying all the blame on her incapacitated grandfather.

Bursting with rage, I shout, "You told your sister you took care of Haeri yourself!"

But the police have yet to discover proof of death. No remains, no evidence of foul play, either. No nothing. Only suspicion.

Cha Seol's eyes flick away, then return to me. "I didn't have the guts to tell Grandpa that I'd lost her. I lied to Hyang about it, too."

"Liar!" I snarl. "You took her out of Snowglobe and killed her, didn't you? Where is she?"

"If that's true, there should be footage. Right?" she says innocently. "Of me taking her on the plane or something?"

I slam my hands against the glass. I want to shred her to pieces.

"I'm asking you because Snowglobe camera footage can't be used as evidence, and you know it!" I say.

Yes, the Goh Haeri project was a crime of rare egregiousness, more far-reaching and devastating than any fraud, theft— even some murder cases Snowglobe had seen in the past. Still, it wasn't an exception worth compromising one of Snowglobe's founding principles for: *No footage taken for the purpose of entertainment is to be used to incriminate actors. The Yibonn Corporation is not in the business of surveillance.* The ideology has been dutifully kept all these years, and it isn't about to be broken now.

Plus, Haeri no longer existed in Snowglobe. We had killed her off on live TV. This meant that no director was attached to the name, which, in turn, meant that no one could legally access her footage anymore. Simply put, her recordings wouldn't be viewed by anyone for any purposes, investigative or not.

"It's not like ending her useless existence had never crossed my mind," Cha Seol allows, glancing away again. "I just couldn't put it into action." She sighs and adds, "For her to run away like that . . . She may have sensed what I'd only been contemplating."

"You're lying again!" I shout, seething with anger, with hate.

"There's footage of her disappearing into the woods," she says, lifting her eyes to me again. "That's the last I saw of her."

"The woods? You mean the restricted zone?"

She nods. I spring to my feet, knocking back the chair. I need to tell the police. Maybe it could lead to her, or at least to her remains.

As I leave the visiting room, I stop and swing around one last time.

"You're a *murderer*," I rumble. "How do you live with yourself, destroying lives like they're nothing?"

Her amber gaze seems to waver for a second, though I may be projecting. "All I wanted was to change the world. With you. With all of you."

I snort. "On whose authority?" I'm shouting again. "Who elected you to change the world? And did you ask if we wanted any part in it?"

She gives me a long, bemused look. Then she laughs sardonically. "You can't stand being told what to do, can you? You're all so similar, though I should have known."

"What are you talking about?"

"Figure it out yourself," she says, grinning. "Hope you do sooner rather than later."

"What the hell are you talking about?" I repeat, but she doesn't answer. There's nothing more to say. I turn around and slam out of the visiting room, burning with hate.

Before I left the jail, I shared what Seol told me, and the re-sponses from the police and the Yibonn Corporation were swift. In a matter of hours, drone cameras were deployed all over the woods where Haeri had supposedly fled. Sadly, all came back empty-handed. More nothing.

Channel 60, home of *Goh Around,* was deleted from the network altogether. People could turn on the TV and select the channel, but all that greeted them now was a silent black screen. They could try scrolling up from Channel 59 with a press of the up arrow on the remote, and the screen would just skip to Channel 61.

With prompt excision of Channel 60 from the network, the Yibonn Corporation sought to bury its appalling failure of ethical oversight, and as soon as possible. It was probably in this spirit that our live exposé only received brief coverage on *News at 9* the next day, and then never again. The dozens of actors, including Jehno and Schwarkel, who had been pulled into the scene on that fateful day would normally have provided pure gold for productions, but all recordings involving the incident had to be scrapped because they were "tainted," meaning illegal for use, by the presence of us nonactors.

Production of *Goh For It* was suspended by the network indefinitely, following a rushed conclusion of its tenth season. If renewed in the near future, the show would most likely track the matriarch's journey through the justice system alongside the Cha duo.

As for me, Somyung, and Shinae, we were put up at one of the guesthouses inside the Yibonn estate along with Hyang and Serin.

The press, in their eagerness to deliver, has been indulging in all kinds of speculative journalism, one of the leading suppositions being that the court would convict the defendants and confiscate their property to pay restitution to the victims.

As for the live weather, Fran, whose cancer is finally in remission, has temporarily stepped in to fill the vacancy.

Tomorrow's high will be eighty.

I turn to the TV and see Fran smiling his megawatt smile, Botox and inch-thick foundation concealing the cancer scars.

"As for tomorrow's low, we're looking at a comfortable seventy."

"Seventy!" Somyung exclaims. "Seventy above zero?"

Out in the open world, such a temperature is too abstract an idea for us to form any opinions around, no matter how many times it's repeated on TV. Now that we're able to experience it in the flesh, we're finally alive to it. *Whoa, only sixty-five today, but it's warming up again tomorrow.*

Shinae is bent over the fan letters and postcards that pile up on the table every day. They come from all walks of life across Snowglobe and the open world. Expensive postage doesn't seem to discourage the people who write to us, as their letters regularly outnumber those originating from Snowglobe.

Ever keen on matters of money, Shinae tallies up the total postage fees for today's haul.

"All this support," she sighs. "How will we thank these people?"

Not having a penny among us, we're living purely on the Yibonns' largesse; they even pay for the stationery and stamps we need to communicate with our families back home, at least for those of us who have any.

It wasn't so much that we wanted to stay in Snowglobe. In fact, we were prohibited from leaving until the court could decide how to handle our contradictory and inconvenient status of victim-offenders. And that's when the Yibonn stepped in to volunteer its patronage, perhaps as a public gesture of penance for all that happened under its watch.

Clutching a stack of postcards, Shinae begins going through them one by one. "It's like people want to know more about us each day."

Thanks to the Yibonn Corporation, which advocated for us to view the proceedings in person, we've been able to attend each hearing of the Goh Haeri project case. Predictably, our outings generate abundant press coverage; so various photos of the three of us appear on the front pages of newspapers after we've gone to court.

More often than not, Yujin is there occupying a seat in the back row, waiting for me, just so we can exchange a secret look and a smile. A few times, I've also spotted Uncle Wooyo's face among the spectators, but the crowds of reporters rushing him outside the courthouse seem to have driven him away.

Looking up from a postcard, Shinae reports, "This person wants to know how we're being treated here."

"And *this* person wants to know," Somyung chimes in, a postcard in her hand as well, "how we're all getting along with each other."

I laugh and glance to the stairs—Serin must be brooding on the next floor.

"Well—one of us is ghosting the rest of us," I joke.

The five of us have been cooped up here for a month already, and Serin has yet to utter a word. Judging by her death glare, her animosity is most incandescent toward me and Hyang; and since Hyang is frequently out these days while helping with the investigation, it's mostly me who bears the brunt of Serin's silent fury.

Shinae sighs, gathering up the mail in neat stacks.

"Still nothing from Haeri," she says in a deflated tone.

Every day, she sifts through the mail looking for something from Haeri, be it from the Haeri who disappeared into the woods, or any of the unknown Haeris out there.

"It may be a case of no news is good news, you know?" I say, and I do hope it's true; that all the Haeris who may be out there are content with their lives and reluctant to disrupt them by reaching out to us.

As soon as Fran's weather segment wraps up, Somyung switches off the TV. "When will the Yibonns let us know?" she says. "It's been a good week."

We've requested a talk with the Yibonn family, but they've only responded with a generic, though graciously worded, message delivered to us via the butler that it can wait. With the president still out of the office, the official second-in-command, her daughter, Bonshim, must be too busy to tend to these trivial matters. Anyway, what we wish to discuss with the Yibonns is our response to all the fan mail.

From a far corner of the living room, the security guard clears his throat. Our heads snap up, suddenly remembering his silent, shadow-like presence, which we've grown numb to over the month.

"Young Master Bonwhe has arrived," he announces. Pressing a finger against his earpiece, he listens for further instructions, then looks to me and says, "Young Master would like to see you, Ms. Chobahm."

The girls and I exchange a glance. The time has come for us to give back to the fans who have given us so much.

A NEW BEGINNING

The Yibonn estate is the largest private park in Snowglobe, so vast that traveling from one point to another in a motorized vehicle is not necessarily an act of extravagance—or laziness. This evening, however, Bonwhe and I stroll through the garden. The sunset has cued the activation of hundreds of landscape lights, and off in the middle distance by an outbuilding, Assistant Yu stands by.

"So how are you all doing in there?" Bonwhe says.

"Fine," I answer, "I saw in the news that the president's recovering. I'm glad." I wonder whether I should start calling him Young Master, considering that I'm no longer his Yeosu.

"Thanks," he says. "Yes, Grandma is feeling better now. But it'll be a while before she can resume her full duties, attending official events and such."

The corporate ceremony this year was noticeably pared down, and talking heads speculated that the low-key celebration had more to do with repairing its public image than protecting the president's precarious health.

"And how have you been?" I say. And I don't know why, but I feel a sudden tug of mischief and add a "Young Master."

Bonwhe stops walking and turns to me with a smirk.

"Young Master?" he repeats. "Why now?"

I ride the momentum and blurt, "Because only Yeosu gets away with breaking that rule. No?"

"I think you and I are past that now," he says after a long beat, which makes me feel sheepish all of a sudden. I let out a little laugh to fight off the recollection of threatening him from inside the phone booth that day. Kindly, Bonwhe resumes his steps without another word.

We walk in silence for a while. Birds and insects chirp from their hiding places. The evening air is fragrant with the scents of flowers and shrubs of all shades imaginable.

After some hesitation, I venture, "Yeosu's diary . . . is it real?"

Her diary was epistolary in form, as in, each entry was a letter she had written to a confidant, imaginary or real.

"No," he replies without ceremony. "I put together the letters she'd sent to me and fudged a journal. Then I snuck it into her grandmother's house."

I'm still working through my surprise when he adds in a darker tone, "I couldn't let my promise turn into an outright lie."

You tortured her with hope when you knew in your heart you couldn't deliver.

Had I been too harsh? I want to pursue the topic of her diary further, but something like guilt and regret holds me back.

We continue strolling side by side, maintaining a few feet of distance. The moon is radiant in the deepening sky.

After a while, Bonwhe speaks up. "We're inundated with letters from viewers, wanting to know how you're all doing and whether there's a plan for a show starring all the Haeris, and so on—"

"We get the same kind of mail every day." I jump in, eager to take the opportunity to broach the subject. "And as much as we appreciate the support and attention, we also realize that it's pressure."

"What do you mean?"

I glance at him. "Don't you know?" I ask.

He says nothing, and with a weary sigh, I continue, "Viewers want to be let in on all the details. Our origin, our complicated bonds beyond just being clones, identical twins, triplets, quadruplets, or whatever. They want to know everything."

He lifts his face up to the sky and gazes at the faint stars that have begun to appear.

"Do you know there are also voices complaining of preferential treatment?" he says, dropping his gaze to me. "Those people aren't happy that you're allowed to stay in Snowglobe without working as actors like everyone else, and at the estate, no less. They say the corporation's support for you is excessive. Unfair."

He pulls a small stack of letters from his suit jacket and holds it out to me. "These are just a few of them."

I pluck a letter from the stack and skim it. The author, who identifies herself as the engineer of the Ma-line train, writes that the terrorists, who hitched a ride in her train for a whole week, were vapid little things obsessed by hair and makeup. That is, when they weren't foaming at the mouth with talk of money. She emphasizes how none of them appeared traumatized by the truth of the origin they'd supposedly just learned, or mourned any losses, like they pretended to do on TV.

Tasting something bitter coming up in my throat, I fold the letter roughly and hand it back to Bonwhe.

"She may be spreading these rumors while she travels. *The girls are only after the money. Their intentions are suspicious. The Yibonns shouldn't be so accommodating.* The complaints are coming from all different settlements now," Bonwhe reiterates, quite unnecessarily.

It isn't that these opinions catch me by surprise. We watch the news, read the papers, and tune in to radio shows. And then there are the angry protestors outside the courthouse.

"The Haeris are a threat to Snowglobe!"

"Prosecute the Haeris for illegal entry and terrorism!"

"Prosecute Cha Hyang, the puppet master!"

Their shouts ringing in my ears, I take a calming breath. "Give us a chance to respond to these people. We want to."

"Respond?" he echoes in surprise.

"Yes. Let us explain ourselves on TV, so people can see us for who we really are, beyond being victims or villains."

"I thought you all couldn't wait to leave Snowglobe."

"We couldn't. Initially."

Mom's letter told me that she and Grandma had caught the exposé at home. Apparently, Grandma rose from her chair and shuffled to the TV, and without a moment's hesitation, singled me out from Somyung and Shinae with a trembling finger, shocked and confused at seeing me in the shape I was in. Her tearstained letter brimmed with love, and I was over-whelmed by grief and gratitude. And in that moment, there was nothing in the world I'd rather do than return to my fam-ily. But I know I can't go back yet.

"If we went home now, we'd always be remembered as ca-sualties to be pitied, or hideous bloodsuckers, neither of which we're okay with," I tell Bonwhe. Then, pausing to look him fully in the face, I let the words pour out of me. "Please let us see what our exposé has started. Give us a show. Let us invite witnesses. People who truly know us from our lives outside."

He stares at me, speechless. "A show?" he says after a mo-ment. "So you have it all planned out already? Including the part about inviting witnesses into Snowglobe?" He chuckles.

I smile but stand my ground, crossing my arms.

"Oh, come on. You must have had an idea," I say. "Un-less the security guard *and* butler have both been sleeping on the job."

"A show featuring nonactors? It's never been done," he says flatly.

"There's a first time for everything," I counter. "It'd be different from all existing formats," and even to my own ears, I sound like an experienced director pitching her idea to a board of executives.

"Yeah? How?" he demands.

"To start with, it would be the first show ever made acces-sible to Snowglobe residents, too."

We want to answer to everyone, not just to the viewers out in the open world, but to actors in Snowglobe, who include the protestors on the steps of the courthouse.

"Let us decide who to invite," I say. "Hyang could direct. And before you go on and ask—no, we'd like to politely decline any corporate intervention beyond the level of scheduling and programming."

He just stares at me, a grin flickering across his lips, looking generally amazed at my brazenness.

"To have closure on the scandal, you know?" I continue. "It'll help people rebuild their trust in Snowglobe, too."

Then I feel a huge weight lifting off my chest. I smile. I can't help it. But the look on Bonwhe's face darkens.

"The moment you leave the estate to stand in front of the cameras, all the protections are gone," he says.

"We expect nothing less."

Exhaling a long breath, he gazes off into the distance. "I'll let you know what the board says. We'll have to check the regulations."

We start back to the guesthouse, my spirit soaring. Bonwhe quietly matches my stride. There's one question still burning a hole in my throat, but I swallow it for another day.

In all the time I've spent snooping around behind the security guard's back, I have yet to find a single magic mirror in the guesthouse. I'm not sure if they've been switched off, or if they just aren't there. I can't stop thinking of the Haeri who seems to have fallen off the face of the earth. Could she be at that place where the undead are still breathing, working the wheels?

We come up on the steps of the guesthouse.

"I'll keep you posted," Bonwhe says.

Assistant Yu appears from the shadows and escorts him to

wherever he's headed next. Watching them leave, I vow to remain in Snowglobe for as long as it takes to find Haeri, or to get to the bottom of her disappearance. That's how I'll redeem myself to her.

I pray that she lives.

Epilogue
I PRAY THAT SHE LIVES

Ten days later, Yibonn Media released an official programming announcement for our new show, a strategic move demonstrating their commitment to making things right. The news gave Serin real hope that she might be able to rebrand herself. Somyung and Shinae, despite their initial trepidation, soon warmed to the idea, since it meant prolonging our time together. Hyang, our leader extraordinaire in all things illegal, was named both the show's director and a member of the cast.

Meeting the guest-witness quota, three for each of us, turned out to be more challenging than I'd imagined. Somyung, unable to think of anyone, asked the network for more time. Serin invited her parents, but they ended up declining the invitation. Thankfully, Shinae's two guests, her mom and a childhood friend, arrived two days ago and are acclimating to the new environment.

As for me, I invited two. For now. One is Ongi, who embarrasses me the moment he steps out of the president's private jet, booming, "Here I come, little sister!"

I fall right into my role and give him my conditioned response of disapproval, but in the next moment, we're jumping up and down in each other's arms.

Then I see my second guest in the distance. Her eyes dart over the faces gathered to greet her—before pausing on Hyang, who's standing next to me. She heads over to us with even steps, her gaze holding Hyang's all the while. Then she's finally in front of us, her mouth clamped tight.

"It's been a while, Miryu," Hyang says. "Tell me you were bored to death without me."

Miryu's stony face breaks into a beautiful smile, and then the two are in a tearful embrace. When they finally break apart, Miryu turns to me and says, "Thank you for the invitation. From the bottom of my heart."

I take her hands and squeeze them. There is new strength, new life shining behind her eyes. Or maybe it's warmth. Yes, warmth, too. And I can't keep from smiling for the two of them.

Ongi, on the other hand, is still unsure of Miryu. I feel his elbow in my ribs. He shoots a quick glance at Miryu. "Did you invite anyone else?" he whispers.

"Not yet," I tell him. "I still have to get the invitation out. But I will."

This summer is projected to be a hot one in Snowglobe. I'm already looking forward to it, to spending it with these people of mine.

THE AWAKENING

I open my eyes. The act feels strange, foreign somehow. My body is as heavy as soaked cotton, but my head feels clearer. On the nightstand are a bottle of water and a drinking glass. Pushing myself up on an elbow, I'm reaching for the bottle when I notice a VHS tape with a little note attached to it. *Be prepared for what you're about to see,* the note advises.

Moving to the tape deck, I slide in the VHS and push the play button on the remote. The screen opens to an empty news set. In a few moments, three girls walk in, hand in hand. Blood covers half of the face of one girl; and with her eye swollen shut, I can barely see what she looks like. The other two are in better shape, though their wild hair testifies to some serious struggle—or derangement.

"Hi, everyone." The girl with the blood-crusted face speaks up. "I was brought out into the world to inhabit the illusion of Goh Haeri one day. And I did. My name is Jeon Chobahm, and I was Haeri for a while."

What?

All my senses sharpen and I focus on the three girls. The

familiarity of their identical faces makes me go hollow inside. Then unidentifiable terror sweeps into the void. I draw in a big gulp of air and let it out slowly, just to make sure I still can.

The girl wearing a grimy headband is saying, "We don't know how many of us there are. Some might even be tuned in right now, watching themselves on the screen in total confusion. If you are, let's unite. All of us. Let's unite and take our lives back. Cha Guibahng and Cha Seol owe us an apology. And compensation. Apology and compensation."

They gaze into the camera, serene and triumphant. Then the girl with the bloody face thanks the viewers, and they sign off. The screen goes blank.

My pulse thunders in my ears. All around me, the air is held in suspension. I may not know what day it is, or where I am. But I'm sure of one thing. It's that *I* am Haeri. This exposé didn't wake me up to the fact. I have known it all my life. Absolutely and without question.

Knock, knock—

Someone's at the door.

A KILLER'S WISH

"**M**i, Miryu?" Chiyub sputters his disbelief.

I try not to let his fear bother me. In fact, I press the barrel harder against his neck, and his hands shoot up into the air, where they tremble like dead leaves in a breeze. The terror in his eyes is stark.

"I'm sorry?" he croaks.

The necklace he wanted to put around my throat slips through his fingers and falls to the table with a metallic *clank*. Outside, a passing car blares Christmas carols.

Chiyub chokes out how he wants to honor my wish for us to remain friends. I peer into the candleholder, into the camera it conceals. "Cha Guibahng expects you to express your undying love for me here, too, you know."

"What?" Chiyub murmurs, losing his focus at my absurd statement. Actors can't slip out of character or hint at directorial input on air. It's Theater 101.

I rise to my feet, dragging the barrel of my pistol up against Chiyub's head. For the sheer fun of it. I say, "My job is to dispatch the men who walk into my trap, one by one. And yours? To love me anyway."

Chiyub came to Snowglobe three years ago. Settling in the house next door, he began edging his way into my life. When the slate went off one day—he was helping me move some furniture—I asked if he'd ever watched my show while living in the open world.

With a sly grin, he said, "You bet I did. But shows are just shows," before going on to tell me that his great-aunt had been an actor. But now, my pistol leveled against his skull, Chiyub pleads for his life. A bitter taste fills my mouth. If he considered me his friend and not a monster, he'd try to talk me out of this, but instead, he's begging for his life like all the other fools I've had to put down. It turns out he, too, was only in it for the male lead role, blindly taking Cha Guibahng's directions.

"You flinched every time my fingertips so much as *brushed* against you."

Clever editing may be deceive the viewers, but not the self.

"No! You—you're wrong!" he squeals. "I—I was just—"

"Last week, Guibahng told me that I can stop killing. Do you have any idea how happy it made me?"

For Guibahng's years of exploitation, I have only myself to blame. Now he wants to shake things up before fans turn away from a show whose bloodshed has become repetitive. He even dropped hints about shifting the genre. How about a romantic drama? A homicidal maniac transformed by the power of love? Please. What a load of crap.

I slide my gun down to Chiyub's shoulder.

"Go," I tell him with a quick shove of the barrel. "And not a word to Guibahng."

It'll be a week before the director has access to the footage. Not a ton of time, but it should be enough for me to tie up the loose ends of my life in Snowglobe.

"Th-thanks!" Chiyub murmurs, and scrambles off. He doesn't seem to realize that I've never killed anyone without Guibahng's directive.

"Are you sure it's okay for you to come to my house like this?" Hyang says, though the look on her face is one of pure delight.

I take the glass of red wine she thrusts at me and settle on the sofa. Hyang pours herself some sparkling wine. On the coffee table is a tray of hors d'oeuvres, some cheeses and other finger foods she knows I like. Outside the bay window of her eighty-eighth-floor apartment, the sky is rippling with northern lights. Again. She would have called me over had I not volunteered, insisting that the view is too amazing not to share.

I shift my gaze to her across the room. "So you're going to keep playing the fool?"

She lifts her face from the vinyl collection she's sifting through.

"What? What are you talking about?" she says, playing the fool.

"I know you asked your grandfather not to make an issue of my breakaway."

Any footage with a director in it gets edited out; and an

actor caught on film hanging out with another director for purposes that don't serve the show is in violation of breakaways. If the who and where of my transgression hadn't been Hyang or her apartment, her grandfather would have tried to leverage the offending footage against me when he first caught wind of it. His granddaughter's involvement is the only reason he hasn't.

"Oh, that?" Hyang allows, grinning.

She and I first met at a birthday party of a remote acquaintance. Striking an instant friendship over how bored we both were, we made an early escape to a nearby pizza joint even before the birthday candles were blown out.

"Why don't we forget about the actor-director stuff for now?" Hyang said. "We'll hang out here like regular people—just you and me. What do you think?"

I thought it was fantastic, of course, and the pizza alliance survives to this day. With her, I can be myself, instead of the Jo Miryu who can't stop killing.

I watch her as she places a carefully selected record on the turntable and lowers the tonearm.

"Thank you," I hear myself say then. "For everything."

Soft music begins flowing from the speakers. Hyang searches my face a long moment.

"What's up?" she says, concern creeping in her eyes.

I take a big breath, unsure how to begin. But soon, I'm saying, "I think I'm done."

She gives me a blank look, processing this declaration. "So that's why you've been living like there's no tomorrow over the past few weeks?"

She's not wrong. I saw her five times in as many days. Once

we strolled the streets together. Another time, we cooked ourselves a very nice dinner. On other days, we watched TV, read, or just enjoyed each other's company, all within the one hour a day I allowed for myself to break away from the cameras without raising concern or suspicion. It was the best week of my life.

"I'd have left a long time ago if I hadn't met you," I tell her.

"I hate to sound like a director," she says, working mock authority into her voice, "but coming and going is not up to you."

As if I didn't know that already. The power to make that decision lies with the viewers. As long as the ratings indicate their wish for me to go on, I can't quit. But the show seems to have peaked. I don't need a crystal ball to see that it's just a matter of time before I get the boot, so what's wrong with staying ahead of the curve?

"Tell me what's bugging you. Let big sis take care of it," Hyang says, drumming her fists on her chest like a gorilla. Her clowning makes me laugh, but sorrow soon swells back up in me. I push away from the sofa and move to the window.

"Hey, Miryu," Hyang calls, a sharp edge rising in her voice. "If you leave like this, we may never see each other again. Are you okay with that?"

Her words plunge a knife into my back. I don't say anything. I can't.

"Please," she begins. The next thing I know, she's standing behind me, turning me around to face her.

"You know you can tell me any—"

She stiffens at the tears streaming down my face.

"What's wrong, baby?" she asks, her own face twisting

with grief. "Is it your show? Is something happening that you can't handle?"

Hyang has no idea what havoc I go around wreaking in my life, in my show. The only person in Snowglobe who has access to an actor's internal life is the director, and since no actor would dare violate the anti-spoiler rule for Hyang, a working director herself, she is completely in the dark. Occasionally, people who recognize us from one place or another might murmur what they will behind our backs, but they clam up when Hyang wheels around to confront them. Might as well. I'd rather that she doesn't know who I really am.

"How about this?" Hyang says, clutching at my arms. An edge of desperation rises in her voice. "I'll be your director. Transfer to my show. You can just be a licorice. A sweet essential."

If only. Slowly, I shake my head. "I can't." What I don't tell her is that I won't allow myself to enjoy such a life, a life of ordinary joy, even warmth, which I've denied so many. I can fill the rest of my life with guilt and bitter regrets, and still, it wouldn't be enough.

"Why? Why not?" she demands, tightening her grip around my arms.

Off in the corner, the Christmas tree we decorated together twinkles with lights.

"Promise that you'll send me a Christmas card every year," I say, my voice thickening again. "So I know you're doing well."

Perhaps once a year, I can allow myself a day of joy. Or am I being selfish?

"As long as you feel like it, that is," I add, fighting back the tears that want to surge again. "So I'll know that you're over us when the card doesn't come one year."

"Come on," she pleads, burying her face in my shoulder. She is silent a long moment. Then she says, "You know I hate writing."

Classic Hyang. I let out a snort of laugh, welcoming the comic relief. But that's when Hyang breaks down, raking my heart with her sobs.

"I'm sorry," she chokes out. "For wanting you to hang on here forever. I have no idea what kind of pain you're in, or how much you're struggling."

"I've hung on because I wanted to," I tell her, which is true. But there was no hope in my hanging on. An actor and a director can never be together. Once a week, and no longer than thirty minutes, is the limit of an acceptable breakaway, beyond which she and I are guilty of breaking the law.

Over the course of this doomed relationship, I committed five more murders. For two of them, I was detained by the authorities as a strong suspect, which in itself was a departure from the routine. I never leave evidence or witnesses, ever, and anyone who has followed the show knows that. This time, again, I was eventually released for lack of evidence. Surprise, surprise. Needless to say, all was just a cheesy editorial sleight of hand designed to provoke some tension and drama for the show, which had begun its decline.

We hold each other in silence by the window. After a while, I hear myself say, "How many Christmas lights do you think are on right this moment?"

Hyang responds by growing rigid, holding in her breath. Out in the open world right now, someone is sweating on the wheel that powers that tree.

"This godforsaken world! To hell with it!" Hyang erupts all of a sudden. I press her tighter against me. "Right?" A small laugh. "To hell with it all. Snowglobe, the Yibonns, and everything else."

I look numbly out the window at the dazzling city skyline. Would someone please straighten out this crooked world? I'd be too happy to lend them a hand, should one stained with blood be acceptable.

THE SAGA CONTINUES!

Look for the second book in the Snowglobe duology, available in spring 2025.

ABOUT THE AUTHOR

Soyoung Park majored in communication and media at university. She is a winner of the Original Story Award and the Changbi X Kakaopage Young Adult Novel Award. She is the author of the Snowglobe duology.

ABOUT THE TRANSLATOR

Joungmin Lee Comfort is a Korean-English translator. Her translations have appeared in *Clarkesworld* magazine and *Best of World SF*. Her recent co-translation of Kim Bo-Young's *On the Origin of Species and Other Stories* was longlisted for the National Book Award for Translated Literature.